I Cheerfully Refuse

Also by Leif Enger

Peace Like a River

So Brave, Young, and Handsome

Virgil Wander

I Cheerfully Refuse

A Novel

Leif Enger

Grove Press
New York

FIRST EDITION

Printed in the United States of America

First Grove Atlantic hardcover edition: April 2024

This book was set in 12.5-point Granjon
by Alpha Design & Composition of Pittsfield, NH.

Library of Congress Cataloging-in-Publication data is available for this title.

ISBN 978-0-8021-6293-9
eISBN 978-0-8021-6295-3

Grove Press
an imprint of Grove Atlantic
154 West 14th Street
New York, NY 10011

Distributed by Publishers Group West

groveatlantic.com

24 25 26 27 10 9 8 7 6 5 4 3 2 1

for Robin

first do no harm

HERE AT THE BEGINNING it must be said the End was on everyone's mind.

For example look at my friend Labrino who showed up one gusty spring night. It was moonless and cold, wind droning in the eaves, waves on Superior standing up high and ramming into the seawall. Lark and I lived two blocks off the water and you could feel those waves in the floorboards. Labrino had to bang on the door like a lunatic just to get my attention.

Still, it was good he knocked at all. There were times Labrino was so melancholy he couldn't bring himself to raise his knuckles, and then he might stand motionless on the back step until one of us noticed he was there. It was unnerving enough in the daytime, but once it happened when I couldn't sleep and was prowling the kitchen for leftovers. Three in the morning—just when you want to see a slumping hairy silhouette right outside your house. When the shock wore off I opened the door and told him not to do that anymore.

But this time he knocked, then came in shaking off his coat and settled murmuring into the breakfast nook. I knew Labrino because he owned a tavern on the edge of town, the Lantern, where the band I was in played most weekends. He was lonely and kind and occasionally rude by accident, but above all things he was a worried man. He said, "Now tell me what you make of this comet business."

He meant the Tashi Comet, named for the Tibetan astronomer who spotted an anomaly in the deep-space software. From its path so far, Mr. Tashi believed it would sweep past Earth in thirteen months. He predicted dazzling beauty visible for weeks. A *sungrazer* he called it, in an article headlined *The Celestial Event of Our Time.*

I admitted to Labrino that I was awfully excited. In fact I'd driven down to the Greenstone Fair and picked up a heavy old set of German binoculars with a tripod mount. Didn't even haggle but paid the asking price. I wanted to be ready.

Labrino said, "These comets never bring luck to a living soul, that's all I know."

"How could you know that? Besides, they don't have to bring luck. They just have to show up once in a while. Think where these comets have been! I've waited my whole life to see one."

He said, "You know what happened the last time Halley's went past?"

"Before my day."

"Oh, I've read about this," said Labrino. Whenever things seemed especially fearsome to him, his great bushy head came forward and his eyes acquired a prophetic glint. "Nineteen eighty-six, a terrible year. Right out of the gate that space shuttle blew up. *Challenger*. Took off from Florida, big crowd, a huge success for a minute or so—then *pow*, that rocket turns to a trail of white smoke. Everybody in the world watching on TV."

I told Labrino I was fairly sure Halley's Comet was not involved in the *Challenger* explosion.

He said, "You know what else happened? Russian nuclear meltdown. One day it's, 'Look, there's the comet!' Next day Chernobyl turns to poison soup. Kills the workers sent to clean it up. Kills everything for a thousand miles. Rivers, wolves, house cats, earthworms to a depth of nineteen inches. Swedish reindeer setting off the Geigers. I wouldn't be so anxious for this if I were you."

I couldn't really blame Labrino. The world was so old and exhausted that many now saw it as a dying great-grand on a surgical table, body decaying from use and neglect, mind fading down to a glow. If Lark were here she would prop him right up and he wouldn't even know it was happening. But she was late getting home from the shop, and I, like a moron, felt annoyed and impatient, also weirdly protective of a traveling space rock, so I said, "It still wasn't the comet's fault."

"I'm not claiming causation," said Labrino, his skin pinking. "I'm saying there are signs and wonders. The minute these comets appear in the heavens, all kinds of calamities start chugging away on Earth."

I opened my mouth, then remembered a few things about my friend. He had a grown son living in a tent on top of a landfill in Seattle. A daughter he'd not heard from in two years. His wife had enough of him long ago, and he was blind in one eye from when he tried to help a man crouched by the road and got beaten unconscious for his trouble. That Labrino was even operative—that he ran a decent tavern and hired live music and employed two bartenders and a cook who made good soup—testified to his grit.

I said, "Is there anything you'd like to hear, Jack?"

He lifted his head. "Yes, that would be nice—I'm sorry, I don't mean to be such awful company. It's just the times. The times are so unfriendly. Play me something, would you, Rainy?"

My name is Rainier, after the western mountain, but most people shorten it to the dominant local weather.

I fetched my bass, a five-string Fender Jazz, and my tiny cube of a practice amp. Labrino was calmed by deep tones. They helped him settle. Sometimes he seemed like a man just barely at the surface with nothing to keep him afloat, but I'd learned across many evenings that he was buoyed by simple progressions. Nothing jittery or complicated, which I wasn't skilled enough to play in any case. My teacher was a venerable redbeard named Diego who explained the ancient principle "first do no harm" from early bassist Hippocrates: lock into the beat, play the root, don't put the groove at risk. Diego said a clean bass line is barely heard yet gives to each according to their need. If I played well then Labrino saw hillsides, moving water, his wife Eva before she got sick of him. There in the kitchen he relaxed into himself, eyes closed, mouth slightly open, until I feared he might crumple and fall to the floor.

Thankfully Lark arrived before that could happen, gusting into the kitchen like a microburst. Laughing and breathless, her hair shaken loose, she had a paper bag in hand and a secret in her eyes.

"Why, Jack Labrino," she said. "I thought you had forgotten all about us," which pleased him and changed the temperature in there. Right away he dropped his apprehensions and started talking like a regular person, even as she went straight through the kitchen and set her things in the other room. Out of Labrino's sight but not mine, she shed her jacket and sent a sly smile over her shoulder.

I picked up the tempo, increased the volume and landed on a quick straight-eight rhythm, which turned into the beginning of an old pop-chart anthem I knew Labrino liked. He grinned—a wide grin, at which Lark danced back into the kitchen and held out her hand. Labrino took it and got up and followed her lead. She whisked him about, I kept playing, and Labrino kept losing the steps and then finding them again—it was good to see him prance around like a man revived. By the time I brought the tune to a close Labrino was out of breath and scarcely noticed as Lark snagged his coat and lay it over his shoulders. With genuine warmth she thanked him for coming and suggested dinner next week, then he was out the door and turning back to smile as he went.

"Thanks for getting home when you did," I said in her ear. We'd stepped outside to see him off, his coat whickering in the hard wind.

"You were doing just fine. But you're welcome all the same."

Labrino made it to his car, eased himself into it. It seemed to take a long time for the car to start, the lights to come on. Pulling out he waved, then drove slowly down the street.

I felt my lungs relax. I liked Labrino, wanted him to be all right. But I also really wanted him to go home, and be all right at home.

Lark said, "Sometimes your friends choose you."

She took my hand. Her eyes flared wide then got stealthy, and at the bridge of her nose appeared two upward indents like dashes made by a pencil. It was irresistible, my favorite expression—of all her looks it built the most suspense, and it was just for me.

~ *quixotes*

BACK INSIDE Lark picked up the paper bag she'd carried in earlier, holding it close to her chest as though what it contained were embarrassingly lavish. Clearly drawing out the pleasure of reveal she said, "We have a boarder coming tonight. We'll have to get the room ready."

We had a third-floor attic that was sometimes for rent. It wasn't much—a bed in a gable with a half bath. Mostly it lay vacant. Not for lack of travelers—pitted and hazardous as the highway had become, a lot of people were on it. Nearly all were heading north and keeping quiet. So we were careful about our attic. Yet we were also, as Lark liked to whisper in the dark, quixotes, by which she meant not always sensible. Open to the wondrous. Curious in the manner of those lucky so far.

I said, "You seem pleased about this boarder. Somebody we know?"

"It's not who he is. It's what he brought." And she reached in the bag and pulled out—slowly, with glittering eyes—a book, or rather a bound galley, an advance copy produced for reviewers. It was beat-up and wavy with ancient humidity, blue cardstock cover flaking badly. Printed in fading black was its title: *I Cheerfully Refuse*.

"You can't be serious."

Lark laughed. It was her habit when delighted to rise lightly on tiptoe as if forgotten by gravity. *I Cheerfully Refuse* was the personal grail of my bookseller wife, the nearly but never published final offering of the poet, farmer, and some said eremite Molly Thorn, a woman of the middle twentieth. Molly lived many lives. Essayist, throwback deviser of rhyming verse, chronicler of vanished songbirds, author of a single incendiary novel in which the outlaw protagonist speaks in couplets and occasional quatrains. Lark said she was a cult author before they became the only kind.

"He had this galley copy with him," she said now. "Kellan, I mean, the new boarder. He came in the store with a little stack of titles. What are the chances?"

"How long have you looked for that book?"

"Since I was twelve." By then Lark had read everything else of Molly Thorn's thanks to her mother, a profligate reader and purveyor of impertinent ideas.

"Have you already finished it?"

"Haven't started even." She was up on her toes again. "Rainy?"

"Yes?"

"You want to read it first?"

I hesitated. I wasn't sure I wanted to read it at all.

"I know, me too," she said. "I'm almost afraid to open it."

We went to the attic and put sheets on the bed and two heavy quilts against the draft. Swept the room though it was neat. While we worked Lark told me Kellan was young and scrawny, with concave limbs and a red rooster comb for hair. She said, "You're going to notice his hand."

"His hand."

She described a mottled claw burnt to ruin. Glossy and immobile, it got your attention.

"This Kellan, is he a squelette?"

The term, French for skeleton, was popularized a decade earlier when a dozen Michigan laborers seemed to vanish. It happened at a factory like many others, manufacturing drone rotors and home-security mines on the west Huron shore—night shift, dirty weather, they stepped out for a smoke and never came back. Ordinary American citizens, filling six-year terms for bread and a bunk under the Employers Are Heroes Act. No one imagined a dozen gaunt ingrates fleeing by water that violent night, bolting an outboard to a patched pontoon and piloting through fifty miles of mountainous waves to the obscurity of Manitoulin, then mainland Ontario where they were discovered by a grandfather with a beret and a crooked walking stick like a wizard's. Their haunted forms rising out of the grass so startled the old Québécois that he hobbled into the fog shouting, "Squelettes! Squelettes!" Since then thousands of such laborers had made similar desperate breaks.

"I didn't ask."

There was a reading lamp up there and we left it on for Kellan. I went downstairs, filled a pitcher with water, and brought it up with a glass to set on a stand beside the bed. Out the gable window the light of a boat shone on the violent sea. Nobody should be out there. Most of the time nobody was. I couldn't see the boat at all, only its light, which pitched queasily and dimmed and vanished and reappeared among the endless swells.

Kellan arrived soon thereafter. It was early still, about nine. We heard his car making sounds of distress long before it pulled in. Big old square precentury Ford. He opened the back and pulled out a child's cardboard suitcase of fading plaid and carried it blinking into our kitchen.

Lark was right about the rooster comb and bony limbs. She had not mentioned his protruding eyes or nervous demeanor. She was also right about the claw. I offered to carry his suitcase upstairs, but he held it to his chest as though I might rob him. He was dinky and frail with a sheen on his brow. He moved as if encountering resistance.

"Have you eaten?" Lark said.

"I'm all right." He was clearly starving but seemed to weigh the meal against the obligation of eating in our company. The road makes introverts. Lark told him: Take these stairs all the way up, they creak like a houseful of spooks but they're safe, the light's on in your room.

And up he went, suitcase in hand, dragging his shadow like chains.

~

I woke in the night. It took me a minute to remember we had a stranger upstairs. A bedspring spoke, a floorboard. The half bath tap went on and off. I heard Kellan paw through his suitcase, then what sounded like the very faintest white noise. Distant static or airflow. This was so quiet and went on so long I stopped hearing it.

"You're awake," Lark whispered.

"Sure. Are you?"

The question was sincere. Lark was a lucid sleeptalker and could listen and respond as though fully alert. Sometimes we had whole conversations while she slept.

She said, "I think so."

We whispered back and forth. There's a pleasant whirr you get when your favorite person wants to stay awake with you but can't. It was three in the morning and we both knew she would go to the shop at seven. She loved the shop. She also loved seven. What she had was built-in.

I said, "Did he tell you where he got that book? Or was he too shy?"

"Not shy," she said. "Enigmatic. Obscure. In subsequent days he'll win renown, but he won't really like it."

I smiled in the dark—Lark had the habit, when very tired, of predicting upshots in the lives of people just met. She never let them hear these yet-to-comes, these subsequents, which were purely for herself and sometimes me.

"But where is he going in the meantime?"

I could see her fading and only asked this to hear her voice again.

"To his uncle's in Thunder Bay. Oh, Rainy."

"Yes?"

"Will you help him fix his car? I think he needs a part."

"Probably more than one."

I rolled to my side and after a moment felt the warmth of her palm against my back. That's how she preferred to slip away. I liked it too.

From upstairs came the sound of hollow metal hitting the floor and rolling, coming to rest against the wall. Like a thermos bottle or a bit of plumbing. Then quiet, and we slept.

the Greenstone Fair

LARK WAS GONE when I woke. Clean sunlight shifted on the ceiling, ravens murmured in the eaves. For the first time in weeks I couldn't hear waves hitting shore.

Like always I stepped outside first to see what the lake was thinking.

It's called a lake because it is not salt, but this corpus is a fearsome sea and if you live in its reach you should know at all times what it's up to.

For now a calm day beckoned, the sky washed clean.

You enjoy these days when they come. They are not what the lake is known for. The year after we moved in a cloud gathered on the surface and rose in a column twenty thousand feet high. It was opaque and grainy and stayed there all summer like a pillar of smoke. That season two freighters went down in separate storms—a domestic carrying taconite and a Russian loaded with coal. People blamed the dark cloud because in both cases it shredded before an arriving storm only to reconstitute after, like a sated monster at rest. It was also true that by this time many satellites had been taken out by rival nations or obsolescence, so ships using GPS often found themselves blind in a gale, but the scowling cloud was hard to ignore. A belief took hold that the lake was sentient and easily annoyed.

But not today. I took a quick stroll to the shore where a bit of homebuilt seawall slumped over the water. An otter poked up its round head, flashed sharp teeth, and rolled under. The lake was dark and flat. It was a blackboard to the end of sight, and any story might be written on its surface.

Back at the house I scouted the fridge. Breakfast for the boarder was up to me. We had a dozen fresh eggs—a luxury—also bread, jam, a bag of greenish oranges. I poured beans in the grinder and stood turning the handle. There's no way to do this quietly. When I glanced up Kellan was standing by the table giving me dubious looks.

My impulse was to laugh. Those startled eyes! He looked like a bagged fowl released into daylight.

He said, "Is Lark here, or just you?"

I told him she'd gone to the shop. He looked like he wanted to go there too. "People your size make me nervous."

It wasn't an unusual response. I tapped grounds into a filter and nodded at a chair. Something about Kellan felt familiar, not his face but his frame and bearing. Scrawny-aggressive. Pants held up by knotted twine. I said, "I'm not dangerous, most days."

He sat, swallowed, still looked anxious. This was never to change. He was terribly narrow front to back, by which I mean he was a ribbon. The neck of his T-shirt was a stretched mouth and his gingery hair grew thickest on the bony ridge of his skull. I had a great-grandmother who gauged the health of her poultry by their spiky red combs and he was robust by this measure. His other bird feature was the claw hand that looked pulled from a forge and rubbed to a waxy shine.

I set about frying eggs. "You're a welcome arrival," I said, to put him at ease. "That book you brought, twenty years she's looked for it."

He nodded but said nothing, transfixed by the sight of breakfast taking shape before him. Mouth open, eyes narrow, he tilted stoveward. It didn't seem unlikely his good hand would dart out and seize the spattering pan. Given this rapt audience I tilted up the cast-iron and basted and peppered with all the flair I could manage. I was a little proud of my sunny-side eggs and slid them with slices of fried toast onto a stoneware plate.

Kellan ate like a man falling forward, a pileup of elbows and tendons. Even his wrists were concave. My throat lumped a little, watching him. Most of us knew how it was to be hungry. Frequently we'd been *close enough to care*, as the song says, though the only person I knew who'd actually starved to death was my great-uncle Norman who did it on purpose, another story. This young man wrapped his claw around the oval plate and leaned down as though it might pop out some legs and zigzag away. I broke more eggs. Eventually he leaned back and rubbed his face and squinted out at the sun.

"Where to from here?" I asked. What was it I recognized about this Kellan? I couldn't have told you—not yet.

He didn't answer at first, then murmured "farm" and "Ontario" with gaze averted. I must have seemed nosy and in fact I was. I mentioned the Molly Thorn book again—how hard Lark had looked for it, how happy it made her to have got a copy at last.

"Um," he replied.

"Where did you find it, if I may ask?"

"Mm."

His reserve didn't surprise me, nor the fact he'd been more forthcoming with Lark the previous day. Knots untied themselves at her approach. Then I happened to glance out the kitchen window. Kellan's massive auto leaned into the grass like the lethargic rhinos of old.

"Haven't seen wheels like that in a while," I remarked.

At which Kellan's head bobbed up. You could see he was proud of his daft huge car.

"Ford Ranchero."

"What a survivor. Lark says you need repairs."

And this was the thing that got him talking—not easily, he still looked away from my eyes as though I'd struck him recently, but he did narrate in chirpy bursts how he'd found the antique Ford in a salvage yard only a week ago. It had a new head gasket and did not leak oil, though acceleration left behind inky blue clouds that took a long time to disperse. After two days the front end began to knock. Intermittently at first. Now it banged all the time like something trying to get out. An old man in Wisconsin diagnosed a corrupt ball joint. Maybe more than one. Kellan wondered was there a mechanic in Icebridge.

"Everyone in town's a mechanic. Your problem is going to be parts."

"Lark said you might know where to find them." How easily he said her name, Lark, like he'd trusted her for years.

I told him Greenstone was the place. No guarantees of course but generally you find what you need in Greenstone. If you don't find it, someone will make it or try to make it. How I love that town. I could tell you stories but not right now.

Kellan fell quiet, asked for more coffee, went to the window and drank it watching the street. He peered back and forth, leaned close to the glass and gazed into the sky. An early spring day with watery sun. I fried one more egg and laid it across a slice of bread, ate it while wiping down the counter. Kellan suggested we take the Ranchero for a drive so I could hear the noises it made.

"I'm no mechanic," I said.

"You said everyone is."

"Everyone else."

The car started after a series of complaints. It was a handsome tumbledown brute. It had rough ocean-colored paint through which smooth continents rose up and peninsulas and islands of hardened putty. Once it had been nicely kept. These old cars remember smoother roads than I do.

We took a short ride to demonstrate the issue. To say the Ranchero knocked is polite. It pummeled. It dragged a nightstick across the bars. Kellan shouted over the racket while I craned around to see what we were leaving on the blacktop. There was no chance of him driving on to Canada. It also had a broken window, so a bunch of loose papers in the back took flight and flapped all around like somebody's wits. I grabbed at the air until my fingers got hold of one. A tattered sheet covered with drawings of faces. They were not caricatures or cartoons but fast portraits. All the faces were different, but their expressions shared a certain exasperation. Nonplussed. When we pulled back in behind the house the papers settled to rest. Kellan eased into the yard and shut off the engine. I helped him gather the drawings.

"These are good," I said—I'm no judge but anyone could see their humor, stubbornness, life. They held your eye. They seemed to lean out from the page as if meeting you partway.

Kellan allowed he made the drawings to put him at ease. Plainly they also embarrassed him, and he shuffled them up in a pile and tied them with a twist of string from the glovebox. Then he asked could I drive him down to Greenstone in my less-derelict car to look for parts.

I didn't really want to at first. It was Saturday, and my band Red Dog had a gig later. On playing days, I liked doing things for Lark or working on the sailboat in the shed a block up the street. More later about the boat, which actually needed some hardware—chain plates, turnbuckles, a good marine-grade compass. All of which might be found on a lucky day in Greenstone. Besides, it was nearly planting season—I could visit the seed merchant. Also the Fair can be hard to navigate your first time or two. Also I liked Kellan. His plucky doomed optimism, his drawing habit and rooster hair.

"Let's go then," I said.

~

We drove southwest on the expressway. The term is residual—a level road once, now it's seamed and holed, with shoulders of pavement sagging into the ditch. There's a spot where two flash floods in a month blew out a culvert, then a third came down and tore away sixty feet of blacktop plus the rubbly subgrade beneath it. Though technically it's a state highway, the state first ignored our complaints, then told us they were "seeking to allocate funds," then promised to repair the break but never did. That's what you get for living up here. None of the major families reside on the shore. Some still vacation nearby, but these are not people who travel by car. You might see their helos whacking past on long weekends. Sometimes they fly low for an intimate glimpse of citizens on the ground. I used to wave but they never waved back. After more than a year a pair of loggers, a basement contractor, and a retired mining engineer showed up with their skidders and chainsaws and a cement truck with rotating drum and rebuilt the missing section with pine logs and concrete. They also arranged for forty linear yards of black-market culvert, which arrived in the dead of night and was lying in the ditch at sunrise. These adults set the world right again in thirty-six hours asking nothing in return. I will say you don't want to hit that stretch doing more than twenty-five.

Kellan relaxed, underway. From being loathe to mention family he began describing them in bright vignettes. His restless uncle Vern who designed a plan to fabricate roofing shingles from urban sewage, arid climates recommended. The cousin who disappeared for two weeks and returned hairless and speaking in holy tongues. A mutinous six-year-old niece who filled her stomach with classroom air and burped the Pledge of Allegiance. I kept laughing while he talked. Not everything he said was funny but he was funny saying it.

I began to understand what was familiar about Kellan. He had a kid-brother quality. You wanted to take care of him. He didn't talk about his hand but wasn't self-conscious about it either. It wasn't really a hand anymore. He couldn't hold a fork with it or a pen, though later I would see him successfully clamp a large paintbrush in it, swiping back and forth. Sometimes while talking he'd reach up with the claw and scratch the side of his head. It looked great for that. I tried not to ask questions that would pin him down. Given his gaunt frame and the way he looked around as if for ghosts or grim authorities, I assumed he was a squelette or fled menial who'd signed for the usual six-year term and found conditions unbearable. But then he suddenly volunteered that he was trained in microbiology, specializing in food science.

"A teacher singled me out. An aptitude for chemistry is what she said. Wanted me to design dietary supplements. For the astronauts, that's what got me. Astronauts! That's where I thought synthetic proteins might take me."

At this, my breath caught. As far as I knew, there hadn't been a space program since it had failed—decades ago—to return a profit for investors. But I was wrong! The final frontier still beckoned! I asked him about it.

"Ha, no." Seeing my excitement, he gently informed me *astronaut* was the prevailing idiom for the sixteen or so families who ran coastal economies and owned mineral rights and satellite clusters and news factories and prisons and most clean water and such shipping as remained.

I tried not to show my disappointment, but what a letdown! *Bummer city* as great-uncle Norman moaned in his long twilight. And sure, of course Lark and I had media once—internet, TV, the vivid suspect world delivered secondhand, ready always to predict our moods and sell us better ones—but we were early abandoners. A great many idioms got past us.

Obviously, Kellan went on, the way to prosper was to work for the astronauts. You wanted to be needed. You shot for indispensable—indispensable was the goal—but then for all his aptitude Kellan never met an astronaut, never achieved this fabled career path. He did get a position on the line manufacturing freeze-dried entrées for their bull terriers but breathed some bad fumes in an industrial fire and got real sick, so they let him go. The topic shut him down, and we traveled the last few miles in silence.

I was confident Greenstone would pick him up. Icebridge can be dull, but Greenstone on a Saturday flies all the colors. It's medieval in the best way. You roll in on 61 to a huge cloud of steam tumbling off cauldrons of fish and root vegetables boiling at Lou's—alluring, but there's even better fare out on the pier, the ancient ore dock where train cars once dumped taconite into the holds of ships. That was decades ago, but the dock's still there on its bony pilings to host whatever is needed.

We parked a few blocks up the shore and walked past old cars and trucks, thin horses eyeing each other's rumps, a pair of oxen with runny noses and bags strapped under their tails to catch the exhaust. Weary hounds rested under a tree in which a gray parrot muttered cavalier indecencies. Pennants snapped in a rising breeze. I was real happy, but Kellan looked doubtful about the whole enterprise. Admittedly Greenstone looks like a place where you might find trumpets, goats, jesters, and pies baked with four and twenty blackbirds but maybe not a specific vintage auto part. Still it was Kellan's best chance without a risky haul south or waiting weeks for uncertain delivery.

The pier reared up over us as we approached. I never tired of this canopied street on tarry black stilts rising out of the water. Tents and signage in all hues from shore to terminus twelve hundred feet out, a stretched circus of brilliant conniving hawkers and traders and painted insignias and hens in small cages saying *Aw? Aw?* A buttressed ramp rose in a gentle curve to the high dock—the ramp lined as usual with musicians, many of whom I knew and nodded to as we wound up through them: my friend Manny Panko with battery amp and reverse-body Gibson playing a credible Mozart/Tom Petty fusion, the slap-bass maestro Darby Slake riffing in ways I could only envy. Face painters were decorating old people for free, so the pier was peppered with ancients guised as penguins and armadillos and oddly sorrowful tigers. We continued plying up through the merchants, stepping under their tents and out onto cantilevered platforms perched over the forty-foot drop to the water—flowers, baked rolls and pizzas, leathered oddments of cameras and ocular gear, drifting clouds of spun sugar, old clothes and kitchen knives and reclaimed paraffin and tabletop radios including a wood-paneled Sony playing news of the world from the BBC, none of which had much bearing on invisibles like ourselves but maybe pertained to astronauts. I bought a sausage made by Narlis Newcomb, whose permanent shop was a few blocks inland and whose gigantic pigs were riveting to watch, snorting and humping and rooting around their murky acre.

Watching me closely, Kellan bought a sausage too. He seemed unequipped to be out on his own. Besides his youth, his burnt talon and chicken hair made him look terribly vulnerable. I never had a kid brother and always felt the loss. The kid brothers in books and movies and obsolete comedies were forever screwing up, getting bullied, stealing candy, wiping boogers on the wall, telling obvious lies with dire cost to neighbors and crochety relatives. I always liked those kid brothers, noxious yet somehow innocent. They often seemed lucky at first, until the lies or the boogers caught up with them. In all cases they were worth protecting, often needing the occasional dose of guardrail wisdom. I resolved to keep an eye on Kellan as he wended his way toward the automotive booths set up halfway down the pier, just before the brewers and distillers and hemplings in their knitted hats and the low-stakes cheaty games of chance.

As always there were half a dozen auto-parts vendors whose inventory changed constantly: piles of tires and rims, sparkplugs in grubby small boxes, sleek bruised all-or-nothing lithium batteries. Kellan pulled a slip of paper from his pocket with "ball joint" written on it and a series of numbers, and here's what I mean about kid-brother luck: the very first vendor, a woman called Grabo whose knowledge was vast and whose long hair was plaited into flat kelpy strands, took Kellan's note and nodded him toward a waist-high crate of miscellaneous bits. Kellan leaned over the crate and raked around with his claw.

I was about to say hi to Grabo when another customer surged ahead. A bruiser by any measure, holding a set of disc brakes and demanding a discount. There's a blunt tone people take who are used to deference. Grabo was eighteen inches shorter than the oaf in question and gazed at him unmoved.

Stepping aside I recognized the man. An officer of the law. Apeknuckle we called him. My God he was massive. Even off duty he made me uneasy. I glanced over at Kellan. You never want the law near a kid brother, but then Apeknuckle was busy trying to bully Grabo. She was normally a ready bargainer, but her pride was up and she stuck to her price as Apeknuckle swelled and purpled. Only now did I notice that Grabo held in her hand a sort of modified crankshaft. It was strangely graceful with most of its flanges sheared away and she used it to gesture and reinforce her argument. What a clear low voice she had. What a sinewy forearm. I don't know what Apeknuckle said to Grabo then, but he did lay hands on her. To that I will attest. Quick as eyesight Grabo whipped that crankshaft around and down went Apeknuckle with his knee the wrong way. He didn't yell at first but when he tried getting up there came a bright snap after which it was shrieks to raise your hair. Even knowing what he was you had to feel for him, bucking and roaring and trying to make the knee regular again, while several nearby vendors lined up next to Grabo in solidarity—one offered to give Apeknuckle another tap, if that was what she wished. You'd think the scene might drive customers off but not really. If anything more came crowding. Only Kellan was spooked enough to scurry away, and I was glad he did, a kid like that with no reserves. In fact the two of us backed off, watching the crowd make room for an electric cart carrying two medics who knelt down looking gravely into Apeknuckle's face. One administered a tiny injection and the great brute went silent and rolled up his eyes while they lifted him to a gurney. As it trundled past a boy of ten reached out and gave Apeknuckle's nose a hard twist for later.

After this excitement we repaired to the stall of a local brewer who'd won awards in former days and still made a malty stout you could eat for breakfast. I asked Kellan if he had found the right parts for his Ford. No, but on the way back to Grabo's we got sidetracked by a little darts game in which I lost a few dollars, and that made Kellan buoyant enough to lobby for a second pint. Then we got hungry and worked our way back toward the food stalls. Market day gets away from you if you let it. In my carelessness I nearly stumbled over a stack of tabloids tied loosely with twine.

It was the latest *Mosquito*.

I didn't much credit the *Mosquito*, a humid little twelve-pager of raggy pulp and irregular publication. It styled itself a rebel paper, making much of the danger it posed to what Kellan would call the astronaut class. Most of its articles appeared under wiseass pseudonyms like Paulette Pinecone and Freddie P. Squirt. The *Mosquito* wanted to antagonize power, but that's a tall order when you won't name sources and also can't spell. Reading was on the ropes anyhow—who pays attention to a newspaper that doesn't proofread its own masthead?

the **MOSQUITO**
distrubing the sleep of kings

This edition however had a story about a group suicide in Green Bay. I knew people in Green Bay. I picked up the paper. The suicides were high school age. Five girls, three boys. They did it at one of their homes when the mom was out of town. They played some music, had a nice meal, and ingested the pharmaceutical known as Willow, a rising star in the market of despair. Willow was named for the sensation it was said to evoke of climbing through alpine tundra toward whatever comes after. The story included a quote from a heartbroken friend of the dead. The boy was twelve. He felt betrayed they had gone without him. It wasn't suicide he said. It was exploration. He said Earth was all but done and they wanted to see if another world existed as some claimed. They'd been working up to this. Like all explorers they had a credo. *Go in search of better.*

My eyes blurred. I threw the paper in a bin. I'd heard of this Willow toxin before—Labrino had talked about it. He wanted to get some, put it in a drawer. Hoard it for when things got untenable. The day was turning dark until I became aware of a sturdy presence speaking in a friendly way. Narlis Newcomb had joined us. He was carrying a jug of water and heading back to his booth. Narlis, farmer and pork virtuoso, was describing to Kellan his own arrival in Greenstone, his harrowing flight from the sectarian South, his joy at snow. He was easy to be around, reassuring, a man with the dignified brow and reasoned speech of a Roman citizen. It always picked me up to listen to Narlis. He was protective of his friends and thought all kids were his own.

Narlis wanted to plan a dinner. It was his cure for everything, and he might not be wrong. Narlis threw dinners that started small and spread like news. While we talked Kellan drifted back up the pier, a veteran already of the Greenstone Fair and easy on his feet. He soon reappeared looking delighted. Cradled in his claw was a slight bronze disc whose lid opened to reveal a working compass, its red needle pointing roughly north.

"Is this what you were looking for?"

Kellan was so pleased with himself I couldn't say no, even though what the boat really wanted was a liquid marine compass that would mount securely in the cockpit. This one was more suited to a kid's pocket on a day hike. But how thoughtful! He laid it in my hand. I held out some money he wouldn't take. He said he owed me for the time and trouble. I asked whether we shouldn't go back and have another go at Grabo's box of miscellany, but Kellan claimed a stomachache and asked that we head out.

While we were driving back to Icebridge Kellan's fretfulness returned. He fell quiet and I let him. I was thinking about the innocents in Green Bay. I couldn't stop imagining their voices, their pale hands and bluing fingernails.

Then Kellan stirred and looked over at me. "I like your butcher friend."

"Me too."

He said, "This would be a good place to stay if I could."

"Maybe you can," I said, my mood lifting.

"I can't, though," Kellan said, looking out the window. A bird was flying low beside the car, keeping up with our speed over that rugged stretch of road. "No I can't. I'm what you think I am."

"All right."

"Squelette," he said as if insisting that I understand.

"All right."

"Rainy," Kellan said, "you going to give me up?"

"No."

"There was no staying in that place," he said. "Not one more day."

"Best to leave out details."

"I made it to a friend's house. She threw a coffee cup at me. Said I had a six-year contract and what kind of person gives that up?"

"What kind does?"

"The kind that won't die in captivity." Gazing out the window he added, "Why do people think we look this way?"

His reflected face and collapsing posture looked so bleak I fell into the old quixote habit of resolving to do whatever I could for this poor kid, whether he stayed or left and at whatever cost to me, which gave me a pious glow all the way home. Then Kellan tripped walking into the house and three heavy automotive chunks dropped out of his jacket and hit the wood floor like cannonballs.

He feigned astonishment, clawed at his scalp, claimed he'd only tucked the parts into his coat for convenience. "I was about to pay for those ball joints," he said. "Then that big fight! Guess I got scared and forgot."

"You didn't forget—those weigh more than your head," I pointed out.

"Sometimes I disremember," he said, "ever since my injury." He held his ruined hand up in the light to glint.

I didn't buy it, but once you begin excusing someone it's easy to continue. He said he was sorry and took out a billfold and set cash on the table. Said he'd be grateful if I would go back next week and pay Grabo on his behalf. Next moment he wondered if I might assist him tomorrow installing any of these ball joints. To help him, as he said, "tame the Ranchero." Then he would be on his way.

I thought about this during the evening, while Red Dog played the Lantern. It was a good night for Labrino, the house pretty full, no fights that I saw, our drummer Harry Lopes happy at the moment and therefore playing a nice tight set.

And yet I was unsettled. Much as I liked Kellan, I had to wonder if Lark and I were falling into something here. Some hole deeper than would be easily got out of. I found myself playing only familiar bass lines, staying in the pocket, doing the reassuring walk-ups and resolves, seeing in my head a series of endings in which cloud banks dispersed and I stood with Lark in the slanting sun. In one sequence, during a three-song set where the blues evolve to balladry then exuberant rock and roll, I had the briefest glimpse of us launching the old sailboat on a day when the sea had put away her crown of lightning, and I startled the band by laughing into a live mic, a sudden soft bark. I laugh when I'm happy, and getting home that night I laughed again, for Lark was waiting up to show me a series of sketches Kellan had done that evening—of people he'd seen on the pier, of thistly Grabo and looming Apeknuckle, which Lark giggled over even though she felt bad about his knee, and finally one of Lark herself, a fine-lined sketch in variegated ink, light sepia at the edges darkening to coffee. He'd captured her joy and untamable hair and even the scarlet grandeur of her cheekbone birthmark—it had a gentle S-curve like a river glyph. Some saw the mark as a flaw or deformity but Kellan obviously loved it as I did. That spoke well of him, wouldn't you agree? Like the others, Lark leaned out from the page. She shone and sparked. She seemed about to speak.

⁓ *when a flame is lit, move toward it*

WHEN I MET LARK there were two things I had to do, two ideas to embrace or lose my chance. Reading was the first. I could read but rarely did. My parents, ahead of their time, had little use for books, so I grew up a knockabout. It's fair to say in my case size preceded sense. I wasn't a bully—well, probably sometimes. I'm not without regrets. Call me a genial fighter, a boy of six words, a lummox grinning over pancakes. Adults mentioned my appetite and big hands, my aptitude for labor. In a grade-school Robin Hood play I was Little John. What a good role. I took to it naturally and suppose I never really stopped.

By age twenty-eight I was working as a house painter and sitting in with two or three tavern bands in Duluth. At noon one winter day I left my job detailing a stucco high-ender with hardwood moldings and a crenulated roof like a battlement. Embarrassed to eat near the meticulous homeowners I strolled a few blocks to the library for a covert lunch in a study carrel. The carrel was around the corner from the help desk where a woman with a quiet radiant voice explained technology to ancients. There didn't seem to be any nonancients in the library that day—only her at the desk and me, who just wanted a warm place to eat a cheese sandwich. Crane as I might I couldn't catch sight of her, which only made her voice more arresting. The library had recently scaled back its services, and there was a long shuffling queue waiting for assistance. What happened to their online therapeutics? Why had their credits been refused? Their inquiries were nervous, angry, imperious, frightened. Her voice in reply was low and melodious. It settled them, reminded them they were in the right place. I hadn't felt anxious at all, sitting at my carrel, yet I too felt soothed by her delivery and shut my eyes to listen. Almost right away it became impossible not to imagine hearing that voice morning and night. A voice that was the opposite of panic. On my way out I tried again to glimpse its owner, but she was obscured behind a mammoth gesturing clergyman filing a subversive-materials complaint.

Same carrel next day, another cheese sandwich. I went back hoping to hear again that easy low music, and sure enough there it was, addressing the agitation and pain of the tearful. This time I sensed a trace of humor or affection down inside her voice. Again I was stirred by a nameless melancholy, by envy for those who lived within that frequency. I didn't think of it in those words. Picture a voice like a river's edge where the water turns back on itself, orbits quietly, proceeds downstream in laughter. This time when I left she had gone on break. Again I was denied the sight of she who had beguiled me.

In later visits, I paid attention not just to tone but to content. Pulling books as camouflage I took a carrel nearer her desk though still out of view. She did far more than direct people to charts and information. She had a way of answering unasked questions, finessing and adjusting her recommendations. History for the ambitious, novels for the lonely, poetry for the heartbroken. All of it a lettered world alien to me. I began to take notes—"Dickens," she replied in a near whisper to one request, and *dikens* I wrote in stub pencil. Why, you ask. How would I know? When a flame is lit move toward it. Titles, authors, barely floated notions—whatever she said that's what I scribbled. I didn't yet know the word *oracle* but she had that smoky appeal. There seemed no person she couldn't understand, no question too dead to resurrect. She told a bored girl about a sixteenth-century poet whose goal was to read *everything ever written.* Think about that. The girl did not believe her but I did. Apparently this poet went blind in the attempt. *Luminous* is another word I didn't know.

I finished the affluent stucco but kept eating in the library. By now I'd affected a nonchalant stroll past the information desk and found to my increasing turmoil that even beyond her bewitching voice I wished to look at her forever. Her twisty dark hair fleeing its restraints. Her wine-dark river's kiss of a birthmark. Chancing a single casual glance at her green eyes, I got an impression of curiosity and wit and maybe a little mockery zipping around back there like fireflies.

In desperation I acquired a notepad and ballpoint and expanded my use of the library to actual books. Dickens turned out a hard go (*Twist*, no, the beatings go on and on) but I stuck with it. Next writer on my scrappy list was this woman Connor whose people were confused and malformed and placed in the world as if by the god of cruelty. I could hardly bear those stories, yet linked together they became a rope ladder you climbed with knees and elbows out of whatever dragged you down.

After this I seemed to enter a zone of madness. It's a blur now and was then. I couldn't afford not to work, so to sustain the madness I worked badly, falling into books while latex congealed on my brushes and rollers. Not everything caught but some did. I loved the crazy fight where Beowulf goes hammer and tongs with Grendel in the longhouse, gripping the monster's arm like the world's first clamp and finally tearing it off, hairy shoulder included, and hanging it in the rafters to drip. Holy smokes! I was taken in too by the long boat ride of Odysseus with its thousand interruptions, Circe with her ominous pig yard, what had to be an invigorating layover with Calypso, and the startling wit of the cyclops announcing a nice surprise for Odysseus but then guess what it was: *You shall be eaten last!* Well, come on—painting jobs thinned into the distance as these stories swallowed whole afternoons, a dazed reader rapt in stormy light cast by Lake Superior that raging autumn when the sun got lost for seven weeks straight in a rack of permanent clouds. I banged and barged through dozens and hundreds of books discovered in my eavesdropping sessions, not just adventures but also poetry, sweet Jesus, by Greeks and Brits and Japanese whose silky names I never can remember. Did I understand it? Not by half, but when it thunders you know your chest is shaking. These thieves and lovers and wandering poets—what big lives they had! I began watching everyone I met for secret greatness. I read about vanished glaciers in books of scorned science, then a monograph by the raging climatologist Holloway who predicted Lake Superior would shortly warm enough to yield bodies that had lain on the seafloor for centuries—"the navigators, cooks and ancient braves, the unlucky swimmers of antiquity." And sure enough Holloway hadn't been gone a decade before these dead began coming ashore, washing up in the shallows, waxy and gaping in their period clothes, frightening children on the beaches and once tripping up a fleet of racing yachts as they foiled to an upwind mark. After Odin traded an eye for knowledge I had eight days of sympathetic response where my own left eye went dark. Recalling the poet gone blind in his zeal I considered taking a breather, but by then was deep in the tale of a minotaur who falls for an American waitress. I couldn't bear the suspense. Would they find happiness together? I bent down to the pages with my solo eyeball blinking constantly to keep from drying out. Reaching the end, I discovered I still had both eyes after all—they both worked fine, and in fact were full of tears.

It was in this time of compulsive immersion I read the work of Molly Thorn, whose name popped up more than any other in my scattershot notes. It wasn't even her real name, Lark later confided, but rather the alias by which she safeguarded her prized and peculiar family. In any case her work was hard to track down. The library had some Molly Thorn poetry, an essay collection, and the single versified novel Lark described to one reader as "tangy," but all were loaned out. After asking a few local musicians I learned a drummer named Sunderson had the novel. Fairly sure he never read it. Accepting a few dollars he passed it to me in a crinkled brown bag, looking at my eyes with suspicion. By this time of course reading itself was slipping into shadow. There was a sinuous mistrust of text and its defenders. The country had recently elected its first proudly illiterate president, *A MAN UNSPOILT* as he constantly bellowed, and this chimp was wildly popular everywhere he went. Once during my days in the carrel a belligerent crewcut approached Lark's desk barking that reading was "a dark art," and she lowered her voice, saying it was the darkest of all and wouldn't he love to try it? I don't remember his reply, only his shaggy hoarse tone shaking with ignorance and desire. I wondered did I sound that way and if so how to stop.

Since those days, Lark had managed to locate everything of Molly's except this rumored volume, *I Cheerfully Refuse*, which was on the docket when its publisher sank like the last of a shocked armada. Maybe a few hundred of these advance copies survived. Some said it was a memoir, some said a parable in response to the short period in which so many things counted on went away. A onetime book scout of Lark's acquaintance described it as a covenant with the forthcoming. A vow to creatures not yet conceived. I was glad for Lark to have got hold of it at last, but apprehensive too. The perfect book remains unread.

~ *when you see him standing in your kitchen*

NEXT DAY Kellan and I tried taming the Ranchero, setting out first on a low-key hunt for talent. Roy Ess two blocks inland was a clever mechanic but wouldn't answer the door on Sunday which he called a day of rest though Roy had done nothing besides rest for twenty years. We tried Maudie Antoinette, who had more tools and know-how than anyone but had given the weekend to her austere grown children who kept coming back to eat sumptuous meals and object to their upbringing. When she opened the door a floury warmth emerged along with voices raised in complaint. We tried a few others but eventually gave up and went home, where I knocked dirt out of a jack and found my piecemeal sockets. We stood outside awkwardly looking at the car atilt in the grass until there was no choice but to make the doomed stab. We ratcheted up the front end and got a wheel off but neither of us could discern the ball joint from the filth and rust comprising its approximate location. We then traded off crawling under and peering upward into the mystery until Kellan forgot and leaned on the car with me underneath, and down came the whole sad rhinoceros. Pour one out for antique clearance ratios. Kellan shrieked and I skidded out to find him sweating and transparent with guilt.

This is how I discovered his gas habit. His medicine if you will. He was so fraught at nearly crushing me that he vanished into the attic. I was fraught too and my back full of gravel—I growled forbiddingly at him, but once cleaned up I climbed the stairs to let him know all was forgiven. A rumbly hiss was audible behind his door. When I went in Kellan lay on the bed with a befogged mask over his nose. A tube ran from the mask to a squat steel canister on the floor. His forehead was dank and his eyes swam with innocence.

"I have a scrip," he murmured, showing his claw like proof.

Maybe he did but probably not. I figured it was just common nitrous. I knew at least two enterprising farmers who'd learned to process the gas and sold it to dentists and private clinicians and anyone else needing an hour's respite from the dark & lonelies. I'd sampled it occasionally myself, back in my knockabout days. I sat on a stool by the bed and Kellan was aware enough to reach down and ease the regulator toward oxygen. I asked how he was. He blinked gravely above the mask.

When he began to talk it was gibberish. I let him roll. His stack of sketches lay on the floor under a sharpened pencil and I picked them up. There was a pretty girl with hair pulled back and eyes downcast, smudges on her cheeks. An old man laughing. A woman in a checked shirt displeased at being drawn. I spent a minute or two with each while Kellan looked mildly on. Some characters recurred. The smudged girl Kellan had rendered four times on a single page, eyes down or away until you flipped the paper and she looked directly at you, to startling effect. A young man also appeared several times, face at an angle, eyeing the viewer cornerwise. Smart-looking kid. He knew something we didn't—that's how it looked to me.

"My friend Marcel," said hazy Kellan. "He was on the ship."

"What ship was that?"

"The medicine ship."

This phrase lit up an old hallway for me, and I tried to follow it with another question or two, aware the nitrous had loosened Kellan's tongue, but then he interrupted himself saying, "No, I got to leave." He sat up suddenly. "I got to go before he gets here."

"Before who gets here?"

"Werryck," he said.

It's a strange name and not phonetic. I learned the spelling later. It rhymes with cleric, or barbaric.

"Werryck? Is he from the ship too?" I held up the sheaf of drawings. "Is he one of these?"

Kellan shook his head. His language became earnest florid nonsense. His description of this Werryck was so contradictory I thought he never saw him. He was an old man of drooping neck cords yet also an inescapable force. He had a skin condition called *scala repugnia* yet was irresistible and smelled lemony. He'd outgrown the need for rest and had not slept in seventeen years. In tones both fearful and fawning Kellan spoke of a chiseled specimen, eyes of icy blue and so forth, who'd been some sort of military specialist until an astronaut bought his bloodhound talents. His toadies loved him with monastic devotion though he brutalized them regularly for reasons no one pressed him to explain.

Almost to myself I said, "I wouldn't turn you in, you know."

"To who?" he said from far away.

"To this godlike Werryck of yours. Or to the police, for that matter."

"The po*lice*," he said, as though they were kittens. "I am not worried about the police. In fact," he continued darkly, "let the police worry about me. Mm, let them come. Let them find me if they can." He gave a slow dismissive wave as though mystifying pursuers.

I had to hide a smile at this turn toward the stagey. Clearly he thought of himself in operatic or luchador terms, but then these inhalants work on people differently. I get unbearably maudlin on nitrous; the lovelorn drummer Harry Lopes becomes a Zen sphinx of dignity. Evidently Kellan entered a region of verbose grandiosity where enemies waited in every shadow. Luckily they were easily flummoxed—all but Werryck, relentless hellhound and necrotic Adonis.

"He never comes in the door you expect. There is no preparing for Werryck," Kellan said. "There's no spotting him early. You think he won't come but he will. You're strong and big? Doesn't matter. Listen to me. When you see him standing in your kitchen, you slip out the back. Be quiet, be quick. Don't hunt for your wallet. Don't grab a coat. Go out the window if you have to." His voice rose thin and pale, then he felt for the regulator and boosted the gas. Moments later he lapsed into a vowely slipstream past my comprehension.

Here's why Kellan's "medicine ship" stuck in my head: I have an early memory of the bronchial pandemic that swept through when I was seven or eight. My mother got a mild case and recovered, but people all over were coughing their lives out, packing hospital wards, dying at home in their beds or on their bathroom floors. It got so bad for so long that a shipping trillionaire converted a portion of his fleet into traveling hospitals, one of which spent half a year in the harbor at Duluth. A heroic spectacle, that ship—topsides gleaming, pennants flying like mercy for us all—Dad drove me down to the waterfront to see the endless line of people and gurneys and ambulances and long cars moving along the pier. The ships saved a million lives, but when the tycoon died his heirs reconsidered this legacy. They formed a partnership with a shrewd pharmaceutical astronaut and began developing therapies they identified as "crucial to an orderly future." I didn't know what those therapies were, but if Kellan was there he had an inkling. And also a talon hand.

Later I told Lark about all this. She didn't really listen. It was evening and her assistant Sylvie had just stopped over, breathless from cold, with a note about a cache of books soon to come available at a Seventh Street pile in Duluth whose owner had lately succumbed. The note described a mix of paperback Westerns, romances, and mysteries, including a collection Lark excitedly called the complete McGee. There was a shelf of botanical texts and a crate of seldom-seen reference bricks: a few *Merriam-Webster*s, a *Concise Oxford*, a short stack of Ruskins, a copy of *Henley's Formulas for Home and Workshop*. Lark wanted to buy the lot and was heading to the shop to call the estate and begin working up an estimate. While she rubber-banded notes and wrapped herself in wool, I related our sad attempt to tame the Ranchero. At the news of my near crushing she seized me fiercely and upbraided me for carelessness in a way I always liked; when I mentioned spook demigod Werryck she murmured only, "Mm, how awful," abruptly distracted by lateness, the darkening windows. Above all she was absorbed by the job to be done. By the thing in front of her. Lark catching scent of a book cache was something to behold. She opened toward the sky, light gathered around. Out the door she went with an eddy of late-season snow catching in her hair.

~ *a bear in human form*

MONDAY MORNINGS I spent with a parlor full of children in a large house where the wind blew through and everyone wore coats. Ostensibly I was there to "impart music fundamentals," but their supervisor Cora warned me early these were demanding children. They all rated at least five on the Feral Comportment Continuum. Some were sevens or eights. Most had received in utero chemical violations that rendered them impervious to reality, so my true assignment was to distract them an hour a week with songs and stories. That was all I could do in any case since theory and notation are mysterious to me. As for the students, they were energetic, impulsive. We hit it off. My size was in my favor; sometimes I held my arms out straight and let four or five of them dangle and swing until they wore down enough to listen. Several believed I was a bear in human form, and I was careful not to screw up this impression. Until I was ten I believed my own grandfather was a Kodiak bear. His shaggy head, his rolling shoulders. His discomfort with houses and language. It still seems true. I liked those kids from the start and this never changed even when things flew apart around me as you are soon to witness.

I remember this particular Monday because one of the boys, Tonio, whom Cora warned me was a "high eight" on the Feral Comportment scale, seemed unusually detached. Normally when Tonio saw me he leapt up and came at a sprint, dodging chairs and classmates, putting his head down and ramming it in my stomach as hard as he could. He was big for his age and the first time it happened Cora tried to stop him and got flattened. Now she let him run. My impulse was to sweep him up and twirl him round my shoulders, but this frightened him beyond control. What he needed was for me to take the hit then hang onto him until quiet arrived. I didn't mind. Tonio had a broad pale forehead with a small heart-shaped cleft at the peak. In class he never spoke but responded to music by leaning slightly to one side while his eyes defocused as if looking inward. Maybe he saw people in there or herons or moving rivers. Maybe he was a secret Billy Pilgrim about to come unstuck. The songs I played in Cora's chilly parlor were chosen largely by what Tonio might like.

I walked in that day with bass and battery amp and a handful of recordings. The kids saw me and started bellowing favorites. Octopus Garden! Don't Worry Be Happy! I expected Tonio to leap up and bust my ribs, but he sat isolated on a plastic ottoman with bits of yellow foam poking out the seams. I called hello to the kids one by one—got a few names wrong and they corrected me with aggressive shouts. When I said Tonio he gave a stilted smile and drifted back to his fugue.

No doubt there were times I went through the motions, but something was off with all the kids that day. They were addled and pent-up. To get them back I went full-on with the zingiest stories I had, about Django Reinhardt becoming King of Jazz despite his ruined fingers, Robert Johnson's cigarette with smooth old Satan at the crossroads, early maestro Orpheus playing dates in hell to free his girl. Valiant stuff you'll agree, with major stakes and undertones of ceaseless torment. It should've brought nosebleeds of joy and terror, but no. The kids sizzled with impending violence. They'd had snacks before I arrived and now flung bits of cookie and dried fruit. Chiefly, they flung them at Tonio, an easy target. He covered his face with his arms, which somehow made them meaner. As if they'd all awakened to some threat he represented. I gave up talk for music—played upbeat melodies, invited them forward to lay their fingers on the fretboard, let them twist the tuning knobs to hear the rise and fall. I spoke quietly while hitting sonorous notes on the fat strings, an attempt at stupefaction that didn't work except on Cora who dropped off immediately with her hands dangling and her narrow mouth open like something come untied.

At the end of this long hour I was loading the car when Tonio slipped out the door. I didn't notice until he was halfway to me—Hello my friend, I said, but then a small pack of classmates poured out after him. Their flat eyes, their wet teeth—Tonio fled awkwardly toward me, was shoved from behind and landed on his face near my feet. What surprised me wasn't their spite. Kids can't always help it. Their souls are new and feeling their way. The surprise was Cora who stood behind them in the doorway. She mirrored their cruelty—no, she steered it, a beaky meanness of lips and chin, looking down at Tonio as he crawled between my shoes for safety. Well, anger rose in me. If they wanted a bear, then all right. My chest grew broad, my neck thickened, a growl formed in the earth and came up through my lungs. Instantly the kids fell back. They slumped and paled, remembered their small selves. Cora remained looking my direction with overt disgust. When she went inside at last I told the shaking Tonio all was well. Count on me, I told him. Tonio listen, I said—because I was naive and large with fury—you tell the others you are under my protection. Look at my face, my shoulders. Do you see these hands? He nodded but was miserable and still afraid. I said,

You tell her too. Your teacher. Tell her you and me are friends. Say it back to me. *Friends* he said. It didn't change his terrified expression. It's taken all my life to learn protection is the promise you can't make. It sounds absolute, and you mean it and believe it, but that vow is provisional and makeshift and no god ever lived who could keep it half the time.

~ *an affable ghost anchored nearby*

IT DISTURBED MY MIND, what happened with Tonio. When I was his age a little swarm of kids appeared when I was walking home through alleyways—I was probably humming to myself, which is like having company in a way—and I was suddenly beset from all directions and tripped and ended up in the gravel shielding my face from their kicks. The great surprise to me was how simple it was to get up again—how insubstantial these kids seemed, their flimsy blows—how all I had to do was swing my arms like clubs and this posse I had dreaded for months bounced off me and fell away and wiped their cheeks in defeat. Nobody got hurt bad, and that night I could hardly sleep for the buzzing realization that I was large among my classmates. I might not be the most alert or have a dazzling future, and sometimes it took ideas a long time to get from my brain to my hands, but still I had been jumped by four kids and got back up and scattered them like mice. Things got even better when the same four found me at school. To my wonder I was no longer an object of hatred. In fact it seemed I was now topmost among them. For a few days I was happy and big chested and with my new friends patrolled the halls and the playground and certain alleys and hidden places. They didn't fear trouble and almost every day seemed to find somebody new for me to knock down. I didn't mind. It made them laugh and made me feel important when yet another boy came at me sneering and ended up in the dirt. But a day came when they got the attention of an older kid. He was from another school, wasn't any bigger than me but looked way tougher. He had an almost mustache and a ponytail and I thought his eyes looked mean, though it was probably just the effect of his brows meeting in the middle like they did. Right away this kid plants one on my chin, which really stung. My eyes got hot, and I was suddenly so mad I got hold of him around the waist and lifted him off the ground and threw him down as hard as I could. To this day it's a painful memory because of the way he didn't get up but instead laid there curled and stricken with his mouth opening wider and wider and no air going in. I dropped to my knees trying to help somehow, but my friends took this as a signal to get down there and pound on him some more, and I had to lay about and throw them off and finally chase them away while this older kid got his wind back and sat up and looked around. We didn't talk or anything. When he finally got up and walked stiffly away, I went home. Next day my friends all hated me again and made little darts out of straight pins and threw them at me during class to see where they would stick.

When a day turned hard it was good to hang in Lark's orbit, but she was at the shop and didn't need me looming around. I spent the afternoon in the pole shed we rented at zero expense from a neighbor who just wanted it occupied as a vandal deterrent. A few years previous a small cruising sailboat had landed in my possession. A project boat you'd call it. A relic from our neighbor Erik Haflinger, who got it in trade for seven cords of slabwood back when people still imagined things would even out. I used to check in on his ongoing restoration, though it seemed to me as lost as causes get. Would it ever sail again? I doubted it but Erik didn't. He named the boat *Flower* which I thought sort of lame until Lark informed me she loved it. I'd stop over and there Erik would be on the ladder, unscrewing stanchions or sanding the coamings that rimmed the tidy cockpit, rethreading lifelines, sometimes just leaning around on deck smoking something he called *airplane* which was shipped to him at high personal risk by a renegade nephew. Erik's old man was a sailor in the US Navy who later delivered private yachts across the deadly seas, not just the Atlantic and Pacific but also the Black Sea with its resurgent piracy and the anoxic Indian and the post-ice Arctic where rogue waves swallowed dozens of freighters a year. Did I already tell you I feared the lake? Erik liked to repeat his dad's contention that Superior was on par with any water on Earth for flat-out menace. A three-hundred-mile fetch of malevolent spirit. I was silently glad the boat was his not mine. "You a sailor then?" he asked early on. He was showing me *Flower*'s tiny interior, its curved coach roof and crazed portlights.

"Not yet," I told him.

We sat on low stools under time-darkened timbers, and the steam from our cups rose curling into a sunbeam. I had sailed once with Lark years ago. It sealed us forever, that trip, and also made the sea a thing I loved best at a distance. But safe ashore, who is immune to the warmth of rubbed teak, a gimbled bronze lantern, coffee steam rising in sunlight? I admired Erik. I liked his stories. It felt nice to imagine that I, too, wanted a sailboat. I didn't really. I wanted the twisting steam.

By now I'd read enough to know what *irony* meant but not what a devious bastard it is.

Inevitably Erik enlisted me in perpetual reno. We repaired the teak-and-holly sole, removed an obsolete transponder from the hull and patched it with Greenstone epoxy. He was a versatile craftsman and easy talker. He meant to take *Flower* down the Soo, through the Greats and clear to the salt. He had a spooky old sister living in a hut among the Thousand Islands en route to Montreal. It was medicine, listening to him dreaming his way through that daft archipelago, many isles no larger than the shacks or wayward chalets perched atop them, home to haints and wights among whom his mischievous sister felt at ease.

When Erik got sick he didn't know what it was. He only felt himself contracting, his lithe strength evaporating. The ladder steeper daily. One morning I found him in a muttering heap at its foot. His dream of taking a resurrected heirloom to the far side of everything—that dream dissipated like the vapor it was. I kept up the daily visits because what Erik suddenly needed was someone to lift him bodily and dangle him to allow his spine to stretch out for ten to twelve minutes, morning and night. There are pulley arrangements for this sort of traction but Erik said they were uncomfortable and dangerous and didn't work. As the months passed he got lighter. A time came when he didn't want traction anymore but still wanted company. To the end he asked to be carried out and set down in a chair by the hull to smoke and talk about his dad and his sister. It is not easy to make a friend let alone lose one. When I told Lark he'd offered us the boat she said Yes, by all means accept, let him thank you in this way. So Erik wrote a one-page will. There was my name in handscript artless as a boy's. I had to turn away.

I miss Erik. I used to wish I'd told him about my lone sailing trip, the one with Lark. I don't know why I didn't.

Sailing was the other thing I had to learn for Lark. She grew up in a patchwork family of sailors—her dad, whom she adored whenever he was around, had pulled an old hull out of somebody's field and added a scrapyard mast and rigging. He told Lark the sea would kill you fast unless you knew its language and a little physics, and she learned these easily and stored them away. Lark's mother trusted neither the boat nor her husband, who was not above an impromptu voyage if arguments or creditors drew near.

This trip was her idea.

We'd got past our early days together and no common warnings had flashed. Not that I'd have noticed—I was lost already and wanted to spend it all on her, the days and nights, the whole foreseeable. So when she suggested renting a boat and sailing to the Slate Islands, remote and Canadian, I was all in. The Slates—can you feel the pull that name exerts? It might refer to anything—their geologic structure, their hue on the dusk horizon. I feel it even now. Sure I had no sailing experience; sure I understood the lake was impulsive and its weather notorious. This was after the corruption and failure of most GPS—recently, Superior had sunk two loaded ferries and the coast guard cruiser sent to rescue the passengers. These tragedies did not sway me. If anything they drew me more. Lark wanted adventure on a small boat full of sails and ropes and bottles of wine. She wanted me along.

The boat was a little fin keel cruiser peeling at the waterline. We rented it from a rangy kid who got it from his uncle who died too young of something. This is how you get boats I guess. He ran us through the minimal systems, the marine diesel and battery lamps, the insulated built-in box where we stacked groceries over thirty pounds of ice. The boat leaned slightly when Lark stepped aboard and fairly reeled when I followed. The boy wanted a written plan of our two-week sail. He forbade us to stray beyond the safe Apostle Islands. Lark signed and handed him the contract she had no intent to honor. To everything I silently assented. She knew what she was about. She had the knots and language. Her favorite aunt had married then divorced a beautiful attorney who lost his nerve on water. When I met this aunt she still called him *that landsman* with affectionate contempt.

We headed north on a rippling sea. The wind crossed our bow and the sails bellied thrillingly, pulling us toward the nearby green Apostles. Lark tied lengths of yarn to the shrouds and taught me to trim sails by tightening or loosening until they stopped flapping and our speed stabilized. An afternoon of this and I believed myself expert. I was a sailor! I had trimmed a jib! We reached through blue twilight and anchored in a sand bay. Lark said we'd been lucky with the wind. She smelled the air, said we had another good day or two before it went northeast. By then we needed to be tucked in somewhere. I remember my idiot confidence that we could catch whatever the sea could throw. Lark smiled and didn't set me straight. We had oranges and cheese from the icebox by lantern light.

In fact we got more than two days. They run together now. We crossed from the Apostles to the North Shore meandering toward Canada. I remember bluestone cliffs that shifted and bedazzled in the sunrise. The Greenstone harbor with its ore dock's boxy shadow. Nights the wind died and we anchored in crannies while coyotes and barred owls and herons spoke from the shoreline. All this affirmed what I believed: I was a natural sailor. Even the jump out to Royal Island across open water in a sturdy northerly did not shake me. Lark reefed the mainsail to a manageable size and though we bucked in the steep waves there was not a moment's panic. Nor did we see any of the fast low smuggling craft rumored to haunt that island. There were buildings onshore once staffed by park rangers but we saw no lights and smelled no smoke. While we rested in an empty bay surrounded on three sides by leaning pines Lark said, "You didn't get seasick today, that's good," and I took her compliment as my due.

"Seasickness is for landsmen," I said.

"I'm glad you feel that way. Tomorrow the Slates."

We rose in the dark. Lark hummed easily around the deck, coiling ropes and lashing them to cleats. It was calm and we started the diesel to give ourselves advantage. A long day coming. We motored east along the jagged shoreline and by sunup were poised at the edge of forty open miles. The wind woke in the south. Lark said, Are you ready? I was. I thought I was. She unrolled a chart and squinted at the liquid compass on its post and wrote a number. We raised the sails and were off toward land we couldn't see.

For a half a day it was as before. Then it changed. I saw it first in the set of Lark's face. She had the tiller and sometimes had me steer while she checked chart against compass and horizon and the distant hills of Ontario in the haze. The haze started getting to me. It was waiting for something, or something was in it, waiting. When the wind shifted it was almost a relief—took my mind off the haze. It wasn't a relief to Lark. The wind had been southerly, coming from our right. A comfortable point of sail. Now it was moving around behind us. It was circling. The sails slatted nervously and I had to trim them constantly. It kept changing its mind, that wind. It was confusing. The waves too were confused and moblike, mashing into each other. Lark said we better shorten sail and as we did the wind made its decision. Out of the north it came, stronger and colder. I said, "It smells different, the wind, what's that smell?"

"Trouble," she replied.

By her reckoning we had sixteen miles still to cross. She unrolled the chart and pointed our course, but the chart rattled and lifted away from her snatching fingers and took off like a gull over the waves. Moments later the gale arrived with an audible *thump* and sideways rain. The boat leaned hard and lightning forked beside us. The sky got low and sickly yellow. "Rainy? You okay?" Lark asked. I could hardly reply. A natural sailor, me! A born salt! Up came my stomach to remind me what I was, a small animal quivering in a bathtub. How did I sign up for this? Didn't I grow up in Duluth? Didn't I listen every November to the sea tearing up rocks a mile away? Lark was grim too and tore through lockers until she found what she called jack lines and tied us in. Without those straps we'd both have been lost and more than once. The boat reared up and something crashed below. Between pukes I crawled down and found the tabletop off its hinges sliding through ankle-deep water over the floor. The walls were streaming, it was coming in someplace. I climbed back up where she shouted *Bilge pump* and set me cranking at a handle in the cockpit. All I had to do was crank it up and down. It was good to have a job and I laid into it so hard Lark grinned in the storm. God knows how long we held that troubled course but eventually she pointed at a low hump off the bow and as night descended we eased into the lee of the Slates and through a narrow gap into water quiet as the bottom of a well.

In the morning the storm had moved off. A hazy sun seemed to draw its light from the water. We'd anchored in exhaustion and stayed awake no longer than it took to pump the floor dry. Lark had packed extra blankets in a sealed bag. I woke to a laugh which is the best way. She was getting out bread and eggs. Instantly I was brave again and almost mad with hunger.

Poking our heads out we saw a crescent of rock beach flanked by hills of cracked stone and pine. A hundred yards from us lay a boat—a pocket cruiser with high transom and curved sheer line leading to a short bowsprit. Its lines all neatly coiled. I didn't see anyone aboard, but Lark did and was delighted. It was an old woman, probably sailing solo. Ducking below Lark retrieved the binoculars that came with the boat and peered through them. The woman had kinky white hair to her shoulders.

"Let's row over and say hello," Lark said.

"Let her eat breakfast in peace. Let's have some more breakfast ourselves."

But Lark kept watching. I couldn't imagine what interested her so in this lone sailor. I went below for coffee and brought up hard rolls true to the name. Lark accepted the coffee but dismissed the rolls and threw one to a gull who had landed near us for just that chance. She picked up the binoculars again. Eventually nothing would do but bailing out the tender and bobbing with oars toward the shippy little cruiser with the trim lady in the stern, who heard us bumping around and watched us approach, her bemused expression clear even at a distance. I will say she looked familiar. Expectant eyes crinkling. Hair falling repeatedly across her face like a white flag that wouldn't surrender. As we got closer I noticed the boat's tiny round portholes were filled with bright flowers and tendrils twisting out to catch the sun.

"You children are far afield," she said.

She wore fingerless gloves and held a steaming mug at her chin.

"So are you," said Lark gamely.

"No, I'm quite at home," replied the lady, who stood carefully in the cockpit and cleated a line tossed to her by Lark, who asked when she'd arrived.

"After dark."

"That channel isn't easy to see," said Lark.

"It's all right if you know the way." The lady sipped from the mug. Now that we were there she looked less bemused and more, if I may, affectionate. "How do you do, and where have you come from?" she inquired, just as if she were a Narnian or a whimsical rabbit drawn in pencil.

While Lark talked I leaned back with my elbows on the gunwales and enjoyed her voice and the weak sun and the wavelets tapping at the underside of the tender. In the ease of morning we both felt confident, pleased with ourselves having come so far and got to shelter despite the storm showing its claws. Lark gave an account of our route from the Apostles and asked the lady in turn where she was from. Soon they were like lost relatives. Lark never pried but got in around the edges. You could see the old woman liked her. She talked about growing up where the plains began, about car trips into North Dakota with meadowlarks chirring up out of the ditches. I got sleepy listening and closed my eyes while they traded laughter. The old woman had an affection for badlands and murky sloughs and veins of coal burning in the earth. I remember the word *undersung*. She was talking about the bandits and vagrant Vikings and skeptical Indigenous omitted from heroic texts.

When I opened my eyes Lark had acquired a glow. She was leaning physically toward this new friend who sat slightly above us in the cockpit of her vessel. Eventually there was a lull.

"But where did you sail from, to get to the Slates?" I asked. "What was your port of departure?"

The old lady smiled at my undercooked formality. I don't remember her answer. She waggled her fingers generally toward the northeast though no ports lay that direction. As the morning passed the sun got less watery and more direct. The lady undid the scarf from her neck. I was restless and wanted to row ashore and look around, but Lark was reluctant to leave. Her voice took on a serene tenacity as though it were a thread or slim connection apt to break if quiet fell. By the time the lady leaned over and uncleated the tender and waved us off it was nearly midday. I remember five caribou came down from the treed heights of the nearest island to drink. Their hooves made delicate slipping and catching noises on the wet stones sloping into the sea.

The encounter intensified the rest of the day. We rowed to the largest Slate to climb its peak. Lark said how a family of huge meteors came burning in from deep space toward the Precambrian Midwest, one landing in Iowa, another in Wisconsin, a third here at our feet blasting a crater fifteen miles across and forcing up at steep angles these shattercone islands protecting sailors from windstorms a billion years later. She pointed out a petroglyph carved on a stone crag. A horned creature of some kind coming out of the water. Its armored back and tilted inquisitive head made me nervous but only animated Lark. She knew about the first people and their gods and beasts. Every word she spoke drew me to her. This was no doubt infatuation plus simple biological agony but it was also something I recognized as genuine trouble for me, aware that if after this trip she decided against me, then despair would come into my center and begin spreading slowly like the sickness that won't be ignored.

Back onboard that evening Lark nodded toward the lady's boat, still anchored less than a furlong from us. "Do you know that woman?"

"No, although you seemed to. You seemed like old friends."

"I think we are. All of us. Including you," she said.

I was pretty sure we weren't.

Lark looked playful and grave.

"Go on then," I said.

"I think she's Molly Thorn."

That's right—Lark's poet guide and personal champion.

Now it seemed to me I had to be careful.

"You honestly didn't see it? Not at all?" Lark looked, not aghast exactly, but surprised.

Hours ago I had caught a pair of small trout in the shallows and now was laying them on the wobbly charcoal brazier off the stern rail.

"The only thing," I ventured, quietly since sound travels over water, "is I am fairly sure Molly Thorn is departed."

It was clear from the way Lark watched my face she had not forgotten this most forward of facts. She watched me tend the sizzling fish. Now *she* was bemused. "Right, twenty years ago at least. On the other hand, Rainy, listen to me, these are the Slate Islands. Formed by a meteor and barely touched since. That petroglyph was made by a restless teenager a thousand years before Jesus. If you can bear it, I am suggesting that nothing feels impossible."

"Are you saying she isn't dead."

"No. I'm asking, what if she is also alive?"

In my defense, nothing I had read so far had floated this sort of idea except a deeply confusing essay about a house cat in a box. This pet apparently alive and also deceased. I read the essay three or four times. Maybe I missed something.

"She looks a lot like Molly," I said, to be a good sport.

"That's nothing. Many people look alike. Looks are the least of it." And Lark went on to recount certain Mollyish trace elements from their conversation—allusions to epic cloudscapes and the buffalo plains, to desolate balladry, to an exiled loved one, to a brief stint in prison followed by a late-in-life Ontario farm. No specifics declared but many implied. Her very ambiguity seemed to Lark incontestable proof.

I lifted off the fish, which were flaky and slightly overdone, and slid them onto our plates. We crumbled some bread and split a hard apple. The wine we had brought was almost vinegar and made us both blink. As the sun went behind the westernmost island we kept glancing across at the lady in question. She sat with her back against the mast, scarf at her neck, her hair a patch of snow. In the dying light it may have been possible to believe anything. For my part I believed she was mortal and had arrived by normal methods of sail and wind and not by conjuring or astral contrivance.

"Just like you and me," I said.

Lark let it ride. We finished supper while the light drained. Across the water the lady lit a paraffin lantern, fastened it with a clasp, and hoisted it up before she went below. The lantern swung gently in the upper rigging.

I said, "In the morning we'll row over and ask."

"We'll do nothing like."

"You're a romantic," I observed. It sounds like an accusation but it was my favorite thing about her.

She said, "Of course. *I'm* the romantic. How many weeks did you eavesdrop on me to give yourself the best possible shot?"

It was disquieting to be caught out this way—and magnificent. She wasn't disappointed or mad. Her voice was pensive with a cautious undernote as though someone might be listening. "You read *Beowulf* for me. Did you think I didn't know? You read *Moby* and *Quixote* for me," adding, as if landing on something, "You are Quixote himself."

The way she said it, I felt flattered at the comparison to the resolute madman whose eyes saw noble steeds not nags and glory not manure. There's something in romance if it puts you on a boat with the one you adore, in a harbor no storm can penetrate, with an affable ghost anchored nearby. Hope flared—warmly it blazed, it stayed for at least half the night. But I woke later and crept barefoot onto the foredeck. Across the bay the tiny sloop lay like a painting in its paraffin glow. In the morning we would leave this timeless harbor and sail back over a volatile sea whose business with me was unfinished. I didn't want to go back out.

A romantic fears romance is not enough. It wasn't enough for Quixote—did you know that? I wish I'd never finished that book.

Romance was a trapdoor for him and finally gave way, for the old knight lost his bold lunacy and belief in giants—without which who would've read his thousand pages?—and used his last moments to denounce all tales and frivolity, and died like any fretful pensioner, his concluding mission in this world ensuring his stupid will got notarized. In the end it was all churchmen and attorneys, even for Quixote. That's what made my mouth go dry. That's what kept me up till dawn, and I'm sorry to lay it off on you, if you didn't know, or had managed to forget.

trouble me no more

APRIL CAME and Kellan was still around. Increasingly cautious of being seen, he wore in public the paper mask of those prone to infection, also the knitted hat Lark gave him from the lost and found. It had a pattern of waves around the brim topped by a knitted octopus. He pulled the hat over his ears and the mask over nose and mouth. When his eyes flattened you knew he was grinning. He began visiting the shed regularly to help with the boat or run errands or ask what he could do around the house. He replaced rusted flashing in our roof valleys, repaired our chicken coop. It was empty of chickens because two years earlier someone came in the yard and stole all seven hens plus the rooster and most of the eggs in the coop at the time. Two eggs, that's what this person left. Heartsick, Lark gave me hers and I ate them both for breakfast feeling angry and humiliated. Lark missed those chickens. She loved their pirate looks and urgent voices as well as their unsettling meanness—there was a very attentive fox one summer who finally just gave up and moved on. It was the eggs I missed. The coop was in disrepair since I'd scavenged a few of its boards for stair risers and the wire to discourage a porcupine gnawing our porch. Kellan put that coop in shape in an afternoon.

He was good at seeing how things were and how they ought to be. This time of year there'd be peeping chicks available in Greenstone. I was ready to tolerate chickens again if we could eat more omelets.

Kellan still had episodes of fear. One night I woke to him shouting in the attic—howls, shrieks, yips like six dogs fighting. I swarmed up the stairs in my shorts to find he'd fallen asleep with the gas running and was out of his head. When I burst in he thought I was come to kill him, then I had to hold him down which didn't dispel the impression. All I could do was avert my face and restrain his limbs repeating *Deep breath Kellan* until his panic subsided.

It took several minutes for the gas to clear his system. When he could speak he remained unsure of reality. He demanded I identify myself and was tearfully reassured until suspicion took hold and he found it necessary to demand again. I went downstairs and warmed milk in a pan with brown sugar. When I returned he was still not himself. His words did not connect. He said he was a lab rat. He thought I might be the terrible Werryck in disguise and held his ruined hand away from me. He uttered a series of syllables in a whisper, repeating them over and over as though casting a spell that wouldn't take: *compliance therapeutics*. Eventually he quieted and lay on his back but his eyes stayed open and the fingers of his burnt hand made pencilly sounds against the wall. I spoke to him softly. I said we were friends. Whatever he was up against, Lark and I would help him through. He relaxed, his eyes fluttered. Then I said, "You know we want what's best for you," at which he came off that mattress electrified and struck me twice across the face, east and west, then twice more. I won't say it didn't sting, but he was terrified and not himself. I caught his flimsy flailing wrist as gently as I could.

~

Next morning Lark left Sylvie in charge at the shop and came down to the shed where I was rebedding portlights on the boat. The ladder made a certain delicate creak when she climbed it. I was glad when her oval face popped up over the gunwale.

"That cache is open for viewing," she said. "Let's hit the city tonight."

"How many books?"

"More than a thousand, less than two."

Big hauls like this were getting less frequent. Of course there were still lots of big homes in the port city, piles built in the early twentieth, with varnished woodwork and antique porcelain and leaded prismatic windowpanes throwing color around. The private libraries of the dead were the chief means by which Lark kept her shop in inventory.

"What time should we . . . Oh, no, we're playing tonight." Red Dog had a gig at the Bruiser, a bar no one liked, not its customers or even its owner. Still a paycheck, however. "Do you have to go tonight?"

"Yes. Another buyer's driving up from Saint Paul in the morning."

I felt an undertow take hold. Part of it was just hating to miss what might be a merry outing. You don't know what's waiting in an old house. Once in the cloakroom behind a marbled hall we found not just the promised crates of books but also a gigantic mask made of duck feathers, a suit of armor for a small dog, and the upper half of a human skeleton in a cardboard box. There were wooden candlepins and a Lupinesque monocle and a dumbwaiter packed with syrupy booze.

"Can Sylvie go with you?" I said.

"No, she has the kids. But she offered me the van. It'll be fine."

"Maudie?"

"No."

"What about Kellan?"

"I'll just go alone," she said. She meant it would be easier. By evening Kellan himself might be a risk to have along. After the previous night I couldn't disagree, but it worried me that she sometimes—no, often—put the shop ahead of her own well-being. She acted as if her faith in words and sentences would always be enough to keep her safe.

"It'll be fine," she repeated, but I wasn't happy. Fearless as she was, these roads were haunted at night. Back in December a friend of ours got robbed driving to Duluth. Jablonski. He slowed down on a rough stretch and saw two naked little kids sprinting along in the ditch. They were pale and frostbit and even their feet were bare. It had snowed the night before yet there they were zipping and dodging through cloud-lit hollows like some kind of abomination. Jablonski stopped and got out and called to the kids whom he now saw were attached at the wrists by a length of cable. They stopped and came toward Jablonski shaking with their hands out. He started toward them only to hear something chattering up in his truck cab which turned out to be an old ragemonkey of a senior citizen rooting through the glove box. Jablonski had left the engine running and now the old man, jaw snapping open and shut, put it in gear and surged slowly forward, swinging the passenger door open. The two naked kids clambered into it and there stood Jablonski in the ditch, watching his taillights shrink to nightfall. It was only one incident months ago yet these pale specters had not receded. I asked Jablonski who they could be and he said Ignorance and Want.

"You're nervous about this," Lark said.

"I am."

"Because I am feeble and delicate and easily upset?"

"Jablonski is not feeble but now goes armed at night. What if I get hold of Spoder? If he'll cover for me, I can go along."

Spoder was a former music teacher who sat in with Red Dog if one of us got sick. He knew our sets but was given to tantrums over the mix. Once in a wordless rage he held his breath until he tipped over and struck the large cymbal with his head, making a handsome sound.

"Oh for God's sake," Lark said.

Then it turned out she went ahead and asked Kellan who insisted on going. He donned his paper mask and octopus hat and even suggested they take the Ranchero, which had a good front end now and room in the back for the cache. Lark thanked him for the offer but in the end they borrowed Sylvie's van. A cold light rain was falling when they left.

Minutes later I left too, for the Bruiser. The rain came steadily. A few miles up the shore I passed Jack Labrino's place. He was rarely there, living mostly at the Lantern, but his house was lit. I was driving slow in the rain and saw him standing at the screen door, hands in his pockets. He looked dressed up, for Labrino. Recognizing my car he held up a hand. I didn't really want to stop but did.

"It sure is Rainy!" he said, opening the screen door.

I never knew what to do with that joke, so smiled and said I couldn't stay, I was heading up to the Bruiser.

"That place is objectively terrible," Labrino said pleasantly.

"It's downscale," I agreed. "If you would hire us every night, we'd never have to play there again."

Labrino smiled. His hair was washed, his face smooth. He wore woven huarache sandals and a loose cream linen shirt like an old man remembering women. In this context his black eye patch was no reminder of tragedy. It was dashing. It was bold regalia. With

Labrino I had learned to expect despair—I was so relieved to find him relaxed and comfortable I laughed aloud. He laughed with me. "Come sit down a minute."

"Looks like you have plans," I said.

"No, this is fine. It's just right, in fact," he said, waving me in. The place was clean. He'd lifted all the shades and a nice smell came from the kitchen, like a berry pie nearing completion. Berry pie was not the default scent at Labrino's. He nodded me toward the living room and disappeared into the kitchen where I heard him shutting off the oven and lighting a burner and filling a kettle to boil.

"Well then, fill me in," I said when he joined me.

"On what?"

"On whatever good news you got today." I nodded around at his orderly house. Framed photographs and swept fireplace and the shelf of model tractors. Everything seemed close and scrubbed as if a filter had been removed.

He looked me over with restraint. He said *well* a couple times and then stopped. At length he sat on the couch and talked about his son Edmund who worked at a landfill in the Pacific Northwest and who was shaving down the debt he owed his employer by living year-round in a tent. Usually, I only heard about Edmund when Labrino was feeling low. Now he seemed at peace. Unbothered. He spoke about his son in a kind of proud blush, in which even the fact of Edmund's tent seemed more elegiac than difficult.

"I asked him to come today, but he wasn't able. It's a long haul. He's a good man though, Edmund is."

I asked Labrino about his daughter. Lacey. She'd disappeared going on two years ago from her home in western Michigan. A good number of our conversations had been about her. He feared she'd been trafficked or was ill or dead. But even on this topic Labrino now seemed, if not rosy, at least pragmatic. He said no person arrived in this world waving a guarantee.

"Labrino, are you all right?" He seemed serene. Also, not the case every day, quite lucid.

"Maybe you would do something for me."

"It's in the car," I said, meaning my bass. I made to rise.

"No, not that. You're a good friend, Rainy! No, just go in the kitchen and see if that pie is cool enough to cut. You know where the dishes are. Bring each of us a big slice. There's cream on the counter. Don't skimp."

The kitchen too was tidy. Reassuring. It was too bad Edmund had been unable to make the trip.

The pie had a shiny latticed crust atop scarlet filling. I cut two pieces and set them on small plates. They were nicely set. I spooned up the cream. When I carried them in Labrino was beaming.

"I'm glad you're here, Rainy. I am," he said, then described in exuberant detail picking the berries himself the previous summer, how he visited the overgrown orchard that used to welcome tourists before the owner defaulted and was escorted off the property. The bank chained the front gate but it was easy to make your way through verdant nettles and foxtail to pick currants and big dewy blueberries, even raspberries occasionally, though most of the canes had died away and the small remaining patch was reliably guarded by a colony of paper wasps it didn't pay to challenge.

Labrino talked and gestured. He was quite unlike the brooding person I had come to know. He requested more pie and cream. When I asked with friendly caution whether his gout would punish him for this he replied he was not worried. Listing on four fingers his gout, his swollen joints, his declining vision, and his forgetful mind, he declared, "These earthly matters trouble me no more."

This pronouncement, delivered with a kind of sideways piety, made me set down my plate.

"Labrino," I said.

Of course there'd been clues, but he was so up-tempo, so elevated. So clean.

Seeing my hesitation he said, "I took it, Rainy. The Willow. I did."

"Wait. Jack. When exactly?" I leapt up. Labrino remained where he was, relaxed on the couch, looking up at me with a bite of pie still on his fork.

"Are you thinking of sticking that nasty old finger down my throat?"

I was.

"Well, you can spare us that awful scenario. It's not a pill. It's like a slip of paper, it just dissolves. I took it forty minutes ago." He craned at a wall clock shaped like the sun. "Forty-seven minutes."

"Labrino—"

"No, listen. Listen. I had a good day. Cleaned up a little, can you tell?"

"It looks nice."

"I used to hate cleaning, but not today. Some of these windows are so old the glass is wavy. Everything you see through them is prettier. If I were going to hang around, I'd wash them more often. And paint these walls. I didn't realize how dowdy they were. And refinish these floors!" He smiled. "You know what, just washing the dishes was so pleasant I almost changed my mind."

"Why didn't you?"

"You know why."

Of course I did. We had talked many nights, or rather early mornings. He felt confusion coming. The world was confused. It was running out of everything, especially future. Labrino had read about those Green Bay kids. Maybe it was time to go in search of better.

I said, "Does Edmund know about this decision?"

"We had a conversation. More than one. I invited him to come and see me out." Labrino nodded as if to himself. "What is said to my boy does not always land. Sometimes it has to circle a while. I hope he'll show up, in the next few weeks. He very well might. I'd be grateful if you kept an eye out. The house is paid for. It will be his in less than an hour."

"What about the Lantern?"

"Edmund would never be able to cope. It would ruin him. I'm leaving it to Harry."

"Does Harry know?"

"No. You think it'll cheer him up?"

"It's his favorite place," I said. "He prefers it to his house."

That pleased Labrino. He seemed only increasingly at ease with the situation, while for me the opposite was in full swing. Look at me, a lucky man—lucky in love, in work, in health. I hadn't much experience with anguish, though I'd watched Labrino endure it for years. Now it felt like part of his anguish was being passed on to me. God knows he had extra.

I said, "Do you want anyone else here, right now? What about Harry? You've known him forever, you're leaving him the bar. Francie's always been crazy about you."

But he waved all this off. The clock sped forward. It was just going to be me. I didn't want to fall apart at such a time but felt something behind my eyes like the curling edge of paper catching fire. Labrino may have sensed it. He leaned forward and told about arriving in Icebridge decades earlier. He'd gone to school in

Minneapolis on a literature scholarship that had to be among the last of its kind. This was after library defunding but before the hard-shell patriots got in. All but broke, clutching his futile degree, Labrino drove north and east heading vaguely for Canada on Highway 61. At the Icebridge stoplight he was halted by a slightly built black bear spinning like a top in the intersection. The bear was lanky and mangy and voluble. It had found a child's sled somewhere, a concave plastic disc. It sat on its rump in the disc and with front paws turned itself in circles while Labrino laughed helplessly in his car. He told me that's what made him decide to stay. As omens go, an exultant bear is hard to ignore.

"How did I not know that story?" If I had seen a bear spinning in an intersection, that's the first thing I would tell everybody I met.

He said grief had cost him heavily. Sadness banished heartening memories. Now some were returning. He treated me to five or six more as they arrived. Labrino was more than generous with his final hour. Abruptly, he interrupted the story he was telling.

"Oh, hey," he said.

"What is it?"

It seemed to me Labrino was paler than before. And perspiring slightly. A faint astringent smell came off him, like a chemical spill at a distance you hope is safe.

He said, "Now I wonder if you'd play something. Maybe step out and get your bass."

"Maybe I shouldn't leave."

"Get your instrument. There's time. You know what I want to hear."

I went out. If anything it was raining harder and in retrieving the bass I dropped a coil of cable and lost a minute trying to pick it up. When I got back he was sitting with his pie plate in his lap. Head tipped back, eyes half-open, knobby hand lying palm up beside his thigh.

No pulse could I find. Labrino was gone.

It didn't feel that way, exactly. It felt like he was still nearby somewhere. Like when a person goes in the next room and you just have to talk a little louder. I set up the amp and plugged in. He used to request a certain song at the end of all our Lantern gigs when he was feeling melancholy. A tender rock standard, a hymn for the weathered suitor. I turned up the amp and struck a note and then got up and opened the door, in case his spirit was lingering within, say, thirty yards of the house. It didn't seem unlikely. I shut my eyes.

Thought that I was through with loving
Cast aside and castaway
Now there's color, now there's music
Ever since you looked my way—

The music conjured a picture in my head of Labrino as he must've been, once. A man of avid hopes and abundant plans. You don't love a song like that unless there's a bit of it inside you still, even after you've got old and accepted the growing disorientations in your life. Somehow I hadn't recognized that youthful Labrino inside the aging one, hadn't seen what it meant that to his last day he tried to keep certain pathways open, pathways to beauty and color. I played the song straight through. It's one of those tunes the writer didn't know how to end, resorting instead to the old fadeout chorus, which I stretched out as long as I could, touching the strings softer and softer until the rain on the roof was all I heard.

~

The book cache turned out to be among Lark's greatest triumphs since opening the shop. She and Kellan followed directions to a Seventh Street redstone pile with a pair of concrete lions in front. The owner—whose owlish portrait Lark said appeared to possess hilarious knowledge—had finally died, having persevered through droughts, hungers, university shutdowns, the surge of lunatic creeds and the purchase of cops by astronauts. The grandson planned to turn the place into rentboxes and sooner was better. No reader himself, he assumed Lark was a fool and met her on the front steps with a price that made her laugh and turn around. No, wait, said the grandson. In the end she and Kellan went upstairs and perused. In fact it was a splendid cache. It contained more than two hundred hardcover volumes purchased as part of a bookseller's first-edition club, so there were signed novels by pop titans of the late twentieth, Clavell, Benchley, H. Robbins, along with Tin Drum and Chatterley and Potter and other rakish volumes that escaped the fundie bonfires. There were books on restoring genetic seed lines, on earthen houses and gravity plumbing. The things that catch on in the backwinds of history. Half a dozen untouched books of *New York Times* crosswords, their clues obscured under decades. And as promised, the complete McGee, a shelf of vivid pocket-size pulpers about a freelance quixote in Florida. With Lark present the grandson took a phone call in which the Saint Paul bookseller canceled her next-day appointment due to hijacking chatter. It gave Lark leverage. The deal was struck.

I got home before they did and wasn't sure what to do with myself. Labrino seemed with me still. My hands were lumpen and I shivered violently and dropped the house key and fell over my own gear in the kitchen. I showered hot and finally quit shaking. The sadness wouldn't come off.

After playing the farewell he wanted, I used Labrino's antique landline. The regional dispatcher instructed me to wait for the ambulance. Did they think I'd leave him alone like that? It took almost an hour getting there. The medic, with sympathetic eyes and a badly formed spine, needed help moving the body. Between us we got Labrino zipped up and strapped in. The medic had many questions for me—about Labrino's family, his state of mind, my relationship to him. It was shocking how much about my friend I did not know. I kept having to dry my face.

When Lark and Kellan got back from Duluth they were so buoyant I mentioned none of it and was relieved to help them schlep a thousand-plus books from Sylvie's van to the back of the shop through the alley entrance. A narrow hall snaked between restrooms and what once had been bank offices, and we lined that hall with volumes packed in old liquor and citrus cases. Lark was exhausted but full of light and pleasure. Kellan seemed illuminated too, murmuring softly behind his paper mask. We got home in the small hours.

In bed Lark put a hand on my shoulder. "Rainy, what's the matter?"

"I'm tired, it's two in the morning."

"That's not it. You're all shut down. What happened?"

She wept when I told her. I didn't *want* to tell her. I wanted the sadness to wait until tomorrow, but then she asked, and it couldn't. She'd spent far less time with Labrino than I had but in some ways knew him better. She was aware he ate badly; she used to bring home bread from the shop and send it with me to the Lantern. He loved the sourdough though its chewy crust challenged his wobbly molars. When I got home she always asked about him, and once, I recalled, issued one of her spontaneous subsequents about him. "One day Labrino will catch the largest fish anyone can remember," she said. "People will buy him drinks, and a woman he doesn't know will kiss him on the mouth in front of everybody. She'll be rich! His life will improve though he won't always think so while it's happening."

"I said that?" she wondered now when I reminded her.

"You did."

"It's so good. If only it had happened." We lay watching the vague square of the window, the swooning fir tree shadow outside it. From overhead came the muted hum of Kellan's medicine pump. Sleepily Lark said, "Rainy, are you planning something for me?"

"Like what?"

"Like a revelry. For my birthday. Come on."

"What if I was?"

"If you were, maybe you should call it off."

"Because of Labrino."

"Yes, it's too hard. At this moment, I mean."

Minutes passed. I said, "If I was, I would call it off, if that's what you truly wanted."

She didn't reply.

I said, "It's also possible that an event   what did you call it?"

"A revelry."

"That a revelry is exactly what we need. At this moment, as you say."

Sometimes at night I could hear her smiling. To encourage it I went on, "In dark times, few things lift spirits like a revelry. It's common knowledge. But I'd call it off, absolutely, if you wanted me to. If I was planning one."

She said, "Don't make me laugh, Rainy. I'm still so sorry about Labrino."

"Me too."

"I think I want to sleep now."

"You're sleeping already."

"I don't think I am."

She was.

a church you could bear

LARK WOKE ME early. We spoke in low voices and were out of the house before daylight, leaving Kellan upstairs. Lark cut an armful of damp lilacs and a bough from our crimson maple; in the car she tied these into a lush spray while I drove. When we reached Labrino's the world still rested in shade. His place looked soaked and clean. We parked and stood at the closed gate of his listing waist-high iron fence.

"It's good you were here," Lark said quietly.

"It didn't feel very good."

"I know. It's still there, in your face and shoulders."

I didn't know how not to feel I had failed my friend Labrino.

Lark said, "Rainy, you could've driven past but didn't. He needed somebody, and you stopped and listened." She made me look at her, pulled my face to hers. "You're a man who stops and listens. If that's not the definition of friendship, it's close enough for now."

The lilacs and maple leaves came into color as the sky lightened. She hung them on the fence. We stood there until the sun pulled free of the horizon. Then it felt strange to remain any longer.

Lark said, "If we're going to get those books on the shelves, we'd better hit the shop."

~

It was called Bread—the shop—because it started as a bakery. It was the best place in Icebridge even before Lark got there.

The owner was Maudie Antoinette, who made one variety of bread, domed peasant loaves that rose all night to be baked in the morning. Creamy inside with a dark crust that looked split by lightning, it made a meal by itself or with whatever else you had. The story is that Maudie fell in love decades earlier with a Spanish baker and surfer who imparted this recipe then vanished. The note he left said, *I am returning to Europe before it closes*. Maudie made forty or fifty loaves a day. Hers was the only place in town people lined up outside. She had a blunt benevolent face and the most defined forearms I ever saw.

This is how Lark got involved. We'd been in town less than a year. One morning she bought the last loaf and Maudie, musing at her own hard work and tiny profits, referred to herself as Gimpel the Fool. Of course Lark knew the bread-baking hero of the old story, and from then on the two of them were friends.

There followed evenings in which they compiled lists of cherished books. Some I'd heard of, most not. Maudie also had a barter arrangement with a local distiller named Dodge, so these evenings got mawkish and boisterous. One night I dragged in late from an upshore gig and Maudie was still there, pink and giddy with the news that Lark had agreed to sell used books at the bakery. One small shelf to start with. It felt exciting, precarious. They really just wanted an excuse to hang out mornings with the smell of fresh bread, but I knew firsthand the sway of Lark. Properly wound up, her voice rippled, her eyes threw signs and portents. I remember a phrase, *agent provocateur*. One shelf became two. Then a wall. Then eight-foot rolling racks from a shut library in Hayward, Wisconsin. Maudie suggested changing the shop name to reflect its inventory. Bread and Books. Loaves and Lit. Pulp and Provender. Lark laughed off the idea. She said all of it was bread.

Loaves were coming out of Maudie's ovens when we started unpacking the books. We took a case at a time, Lark scanning titles and authors, me shelving the books appropriately—fiction, history, biography, philosophy—customers appearing under the silvery bell announcing their arrival. Most were there for the bread, which departed quickly, or for Maudie's pastries—triangular cinnamon cookies, fruit turnovers, barely sweet scones with a few currants and a licorice essence.

I was still shelving when the door opened and an old man came leaning in on a cane. He had thinning yellow-white hair and a nodding smile that appeared habitual. He wore a wool cardigan with oval horn buttons and resembled any number of collectors and freethinkers and frowsy amateurs and birdwatchers. His eyes were bright and he looked around the bookshop as if he'd heard of it for years and finally come to see it for himself.

Lark behind the counter asked was there something in particular.

"Oh no, I'll just look around. So much to see," he replied pleasantly.

Lark caught my eye. She was proud of that bookshop, we both were. It didn't draw crowds but rather individuals, some of whom came a long way to see what Lark had found.

The old fellow moved easily and cruised up and down the teeming stacks murmuring with delight, the chance sigh suggesting a pleasant surprise or perhaps a gap in inventory. He took one of Lark's wire baskets and made a little pile. I remember he liked pastoral titles, field guides, the obsolete sciences.

"I wonder," said the old man to Lark as she rang up his purchase, "what you might have under the counter?"

Not a question she got every day. I listened closely while continuing to unbox McGees, the racy Dell originals flaking back to ragstock.

"As it happens," she told him, "you've come at a good time."

His brows went up. Reaching under the counter Lark pulled out the Molly Thorn.

"Well then," he all but whispered.

"Exactly," she agreed.

"May I handle it? Thank you." He didn't riffle the pages but instead turned them tenderly. "I was never sure such a thing existed."

"I wasn't either," Lark said.

They went on in this way for a while. I finished shelving the pulp McGees and a half box of South American libertines and they were still talking. In a tone of restrained yearning the old man wondered was the Molly Thorn for sale.

"Not right now, I'm afraid," said Lark.

"Before you have heard my offer?"

"Don't offer."

"May I come in tomorrow and ask you again?"

"Of course. Maybe you'll find something else."

He said in any case the shop was worth the trip and he would surely return. He paid for his stack, reached in his pocket for a pair of knit gloves. If he wore a hat he'd have doffed it. Then he left, a jaunty oldster and authentic book sprite. I was glad he'd showed up. Lark would smile all day now.

"Molly's your current Strad," I observed. Long ago she had explained to me an apex pleasure of shopkeeping: sometimes you had one item, a gem you kept under the counter and did not mention. A rare edition or signed opus. She called them Strads after the Italian luthier each of whose fiddles remain worth a city or two. If someone was savvy enough to ask what was *under the counter* they earned a chance to examine the Strad. Delight was the expected result.

Lark was so gratified she fairly blazed up. I felt the grief of earlier begin to move aside, to make way for something happy. Lark's birthday was in two days. Even as we worked Kellan was rounding up chairs and paraffin lanterns and strings of electric lights. I'd already spoken to Dodge about libations and to Narlis Newcomb about a soup he made with sausage and potatoes and slightly bitter greens. Maudie had given me a knowing look that very morning. She was handling the pastries. Lark would not be surprised, but she would be glad and radiant, and I would bask in the shine.

I was about to leave when there was a muted bump at the alley door. I got there in time to see a manky old hybrid coasting away with the aspect of a hat pulled low. At my feet lay a small bale of newspapers crisscrossed in twine. The *Mosquito*. I looked both ways and bent over and snagged the bale. I wasn't happy to see the fungoid tabloid that showed up erratically without explanation. If you don't know who delivers, how can you tell them not to?

"Who was that?" said Lark.

I held up the bale. Lark and I had argued before over accommodating the papers. I voted for immediate composting. She put no credence in the *Mosquito* but "aligned with the principle."

"What principle?"

"More words are better," she said.

"They can't spell 'disturb.'" In matters of language I was a zealous convert.

"They might still learn. Language is armor."

I agreed, but as armor goes the *Mosquito* was flimsy. Lark ended up keeping the papers but put them behind the counter. When she wasn't looking I took one. There was a badly sourced story about the so-called medicine ships. They were said to operate in international waters to avoid legal scrutiny and to specialize in "C&C therapies," which meant Compliance and Conclusion. The rest of the issue was given to Willow stories. Five people had concluded in a Michigan backwater. Two more in northern Wisconsin. At a housing block in Chicago nineteen of all ages went in search of better. They turned on the radio, rented a bouncy castle for the kids. It was a veritable shindig. I did not want the paper in the shop.

That night Lark turned thirty-six. A warm spring evening. Rain purpled the streets then cleared off. Before she got home Kellan and I set up tables in the yard, hung lanterns from the leaning fir, strung a web of dim solar bulbs and fueled the generator. The grid was reliable except when needed. By the time she arrived around seven the whole of Red Dog was there, "tuned up and primed to howl" as Harry loved saying, as if we were boisterous rogues. It's true Harry could howl if love was upon him, and lead singer Francie had a pleasing shriek too rarely employed, but Pierre (keyboards and rhythm) was reliably sullen and needed constant praise. We started with a low-key set, mostly twelve bar, key of E. Harry led our spare arrangements and I locked right in. We sounded as good to my ears as we ever had. The music lifted like steam, it rose off the yard in invitation. Sure enough people began to appear, some with food to share, others not, it didn't matter. Soon the yard was crowded. Maudie arrived and was first to dance in her long skirt on the grass. Old friends, neighbors seldom seen, whole strangers. We stayed with the blues and Francie sensing a vein of covenant sang in her scratchiest aching voice, the reason we cajoled her into the band to start with, and it began to resemble what I once imagined church might be like, a church you could bear, where people laughed and enjoyed each other and did not care if they were right all the time or if other people were wrong. As the light fell I was startled and pleased to see the old gentleman from the bookshop sitting in a folding chair against the trunk of our big fir. How did he find out? But it didn't matter—anyone at all might show up for Lark. His face was so restful and satisfied I thought he was sleeping, until a glimmer escaped his half-shut eyes. We played well into darkness, then someone remembered there was food and warmth inside.

The house smelled like Narlis Newcomb's alluring soup. Narlis adored Lark like everyone else. In fact Narlis tried to instigate a sort of movie moment, where people would stand and deliver funny earnest speeches about her, but his timing was off. The house still full of small conversations. Besides the soup it smelled like tea, table wine, Dodge's caustic spirits, flowers, tree bark, and damp dog—several dogs arrived with people and several on their own to foster an edgy détente. As for Lark she seemed to incandesce, to move over the floor not touching the boards. The old man had brought whiskey that turned out to be legitimate retail, though I didn't know the label which boasted a haughty gallant with mustache and epaulets. Setting this bottle on the counter the pensioner eased off to a corner to smile and maintain a mannerly distance. He wore a charcoal wool jacket with narrow lapels, a knotted black scarf, long thin black leather shoes. I never met one in person but from old movies I'd have guessed he was an impractical professor and advancer of theories. He would understand how a cat or a poet could be alive and dead at once. Easy with everyone he also looked through them as if into the next room.

He was like a man waiting who enjoys the wait. It took a little time to work around to him and ask where he was from. "Take a guess," he replied, as though it were a game. He did have a slight accent, but I was untraveled and didn't want to play.

"Northern Europe," I said.

"Close enough."

I asked if he were a teacher and he said long ago. He did regard me more closely than I liked. As if I were oddly shaped or otherwise anomalous. He asked what I thought it was "all coming to."

"What is what coming to?"

"Your very decent life here." He gestured round. "Your unconcern, your community, your paper currency. Your 'freedom,'" he said, as though the word itself were whimsical.

What a strange question you will say. It didn't seem so then. We understood the margins where we lived. Some still enjoyed resenting the far-flung coasts for their gleam and influence, but I think we all accepted the grace of the overlooked. Again I asked where was home for him. He allowed he traveled a good deal. That alone meant he knew people in high circles. For the first time I wondered was it a bad thing this papery gentleman had wandered up to Icebridge and was here in our house talking with people, also listening. I said We make no trouble here.

"Of course not," he said. "But trouble comes through sometimes, as you know. Arrives on its way to somewhere else. Maybe decides to stay."

It might have sounded threatening but didn't. We kept our home a temperature where the rhetorical was allowed. Around this time toasts were called for. The old man was hailed as the bringer of quality spirits. Nodding he put his hands up, said, "Very well but I am a newcomer." Of course by now he'd spoken with most and made a good impression. He reached for the bottle and cracked the seal, at which Lark got on a stool and reached for a high shelf. She brought down a carton with rows of tiny glasses—communion cups from a deacon's estate where she had once bought books. She wanted everyone to sample the good bottle, though we'd all be ruined for Dodge's after that. Then the stooped academic poured daintily into those dozens of cups. I remember how he dipped and nodded, handing them round as if he'd known us for years, before raising his voice in a modest and eloquent toast. He described Lark as a treasure, a boon on which the town relied. He praised her taste and restraint and what he called her lavish reach. He said concerts and restaurants were well enough but a bookstore was civilization. Among ourselves he seemed a genteel remnant—once he started none wanted him to stop. He ended with a quote from Molly Thorn about the soul that knows itself "and knowing, spends it freely." Then he raised his communion cup, we all of us drank, and it was a moment of love.

And this is when I noticed—because I looked for him, to include him—that Kellan wasn't there.

I wandered into the kitchen, the porch, the pantry—no Kellan. I stepped out to the alley. It was crowded with cars and bikes. A cold fog had climbed off the lake and the chill felt lonely and fresh. The Ranchero was in its usual spot. I stood outside a few minutes enjoying the quiet, then noticed a glowing orange spot. A man sat in the shade of a neighbor's garage. He pulled on the cigarette that had got my attention. I stepped over to join him. He was sitting on a stack of old bricks, had a drink beside him in the grass and two of Maudie's rolls on a paper napkin.

"Evening," I said. "We haven't met."

He watched me but said nothing. When he drew on the cigarette his face was narrow and red in the glow. I asked was he here with friends.

"Passing through," he said. A common enough phrase in Icebridge, a mostly polite reply indicating a wish to be left alone.

Fair enough. A swell of laughter came from the house. I started for it, then turned to ask, "Did you see a kid come out? Twenty or so, on the slight side?"

"No."

"All right. Safe travels."

He smiled privately in the way of people putting up with something.

I went back to the party. A small dog had urgent business outside and I opened the door for him, then was distracted by a knot of kids pawing through band instruments we'd pushed into a corner. A minor troll had got into Harry's drum set, and Maudie's miniature dark-haired granddaughter was screwing up the dials on the bass amp. She twinkled and sparked; she was clearly limitless. I shooed them back to their people. Lark drifted through the house, admiring guests, touching their arms, getting the latest about their kids and their exes, the beloved and despised and those who'd gone ahead.

Still looking for Kellan I went upstairs. He wasn't in his room, though his clothes and gear lay scattered about, his hosed mask and canisters. I heard water running in the adjacent bathroom. There was a cough, the water stopped. The door opened and there stood the old gentleman. He appeared preoccupied and slightly embarrassed and smiled at me distantly.

"My apologies," he said. "There was a line downstairs. Even five years ago I could've waited."

"It's all right. Have you seen anyone else up here?"

"I have not," he said, and I followed him down the steps, an awkward, tentative descent. He smelled like medicine or a vitamin cream. The top of his scalp was a dappled moon, and on his neck, just above the scarf was a troubling growth like the pad of a thumb.

~

In the quiet afterward, Lark tucked her head under my chin and hung on. The guests were gone. The food and drink had been enough. No one got too elevated or too honest. The house was rumpled and creaky, ours again. From the faraway attic came the oddly reassuring hum of Kellan's gas machinery. We doused all but two small paraffins and sat up a while, letting everything dissolve.

"Did you see what that kid was up to with Harry's drum kit?" I said.

"I did."

"We wouldn't let our kid do that at somebody's house."

"Not for very long."

"You see him steal one of those communion shots?"

"Made me like him," she said.

"Everything makes you like them."

People say happiness is overrated, but Lark and I were happy and I don't think it is.

"What will that kid be, one day?" I asked.

"Stoic philosopher," she replied.

"Maudie's grandkid?"

"Immune to the gallantries of astronaut suitors," Lark said. "Benevolent mayor of someplace big."

We went to bed at last. The night stilled, Lark laid her palm against my back. As time began to swim away she seemed to realize there was a set of subsequents she'd never issued. Never thought to imagine. Our own.

"We sailed back to the Slates," she said. She used the past tense, I don't know why. She may have been asleep. "We took our own boat. We anchored a month. Now I think we never left." Her voice was soft and she made a poem of short declaratives, things not precisely true but so generous to me I cannot write them down. If I say I forget, is that okay? She talked about our children, the girl and boy we never had. How they grew up adventurous, watching the stars like familiar books they longed to read again. They were afraid sometimes and complained or wept but kept on growing and became those sturdy adults getting on the ride. She gave them names, our kids. The names fit exactly the attributes described. I don't remember what they were.

~ *sea like a shroud*

I'M GOING TO LOOK AWAY, soon.

I'll have to look away and trust you'll understand.

There's a manner of telling what happened but description is not it. The act of describing is supposed to heal and we are exhorted to "talk it through," but sometimes that won't hold. Friends encouraged me to try it and I did. I tried with these friends and with a solemn lay pastor and a lay therapist which was the only kind nearby. How well they all meant. I valued them and tried to talk it through. When the moment comes I'm going to look away.

I can tell you Lark woke early and went to the shop as usual. That I rose somewhat later and moved through the house in the shadowy ease a person wants after revelry: gathering plates, glasses, bowls, flatware, running the sink full, resting my hands in warm water. At some point I thought grumpily about Kellan, who'd helped set up only to bail on Lark's evening, then came back late and got stoned, his machine humming in the floorboards. It made me kind of mad. At noon I put together a toasted cheese and ate it in the stillness and only then clomped up the stairs to wake him.

I wanted him to help spade up the garden. The weather would soon moderate. Lark had sprouted tomatoes from seed weeks earlier. Our plot was large and spading it was a big job, usually one I did alone.

But Kellan was gone and this time really.

The blankets were heaped and his canisters gone and his child's cardboard suitcase missing from under the bed. No sign no note no indication. I went to the window. No Ranchero. I admit sharp disappointment. Bitterness no doubt. Against judgment I went and got attached. You'd like a note at least. I shouldn't have been surprised but was. Kellan just seemed like that paranoid kid brother I thought would stay despite his dread of pursuit.

Of course he was gone.

Stepping out on the small balcony that hung off the attic, I looked upstreet and down and out to sea. A dog whimpered somewhere. A pair of ravens muttered in the leaning fir. Someone had a chainsaw running not close enough to annoy.

Icebridge moved at normal low velocity.

"Maybe he just discerned your gardening plans," Lark said. She was making light, trying to cheer me up. She and Maudie were the only ones in the shop. "I'd leave, too, if you sprung that spade business on me the morning after a big soiree."

"He skipped the soiree. It was after noon. Also, I didn't spring it on him. I didn't think of it myself until halfway up the stairs."

Lark put a hand on my arm. "Your feelings are bruised. I'm sorry, but didn't he talk about leaving all the time?"

"He did," I agreed.

"Did we drive him away?"

"No."

"He was paid up till the end of the month," she said. Lark kept all the ledgers.

I was quiet. Gently she said, "On the plus side, I will like having the house to ourselves."

"I did come to think of him as a kid brother," I admitted.

"Which he has completely lived up to," said Maudie, joining us. "A young man lives in your house, eats your food, does a few chores to keep you sunny, then vanishes without a word. That's the definition of the term."

"Is it?"

Maudie was winding up to expand on kid brothers when the atmosphere perceptibly darkened. Outside and in—the bulbs in a pair of sconce fixtures beside the door browned and flickered.

"Oh my," Lark said.

"Hang on," said Maudie.

I opened my mouth but the wind cut me off. Normally wind gives audible notice, you hear it coming. Not these lunatic microbursts. They hit like a slap. When they do you always think the world might not recover. Overhead something bounced on the roof and took flight. There was the sustained high note of a vibrating guy wire. We peered at the yellowing sky. Happily, the bursts don't last long. People emerge afterward to estimate wind speeds. A hundred ten, a hundred thirty. There used to be a wind gauge bolted to the fire station, but it blew off into the lake.

We stepped back from the window. The burst shrieked in the crannies. A Wellington boot cartwheeled by, then a peeled-back quarter panel from somebody's car. A potted pine tree scraped upright down the sidewalk at a fast pace. A flock of shingles tore through. Then a red dog resembling a fox went skidding down the street baring her teeth at the wind and Maudie shouted, "There goes Vixen!"

Vixen barked soundlessly as she slid out of view.

A minute later the storm was past. We made a cursory check of the shop, but its old bank walls shrugged off all weathers. Maudie said, "Poor Vixen. A real fox would find a hole to crawl into. I better go find her."

I caught Lark's glance and offered to help.

Icebridge looked swept. The pavement was clear of sand and debris. Everything loose had flown or tumbled or slithered east. While we called Vixen and investigated backyards and alleys where she might've found shelter, I wondered about damage to our house. It had stood up to many a burst, but you never know.

We looked for the dog for almost two hours. She was an older creature and Maudie's constant companion. We started where she'd slid past the window and followed the street until it ended a block shy of the water. The shallows were thick with bobbing papers, tree limbs, items of laundry. No dogs. Some kids were out scavenging after the blow and we enlisted them, then worked back to Maudie's on cross streets. I finally left her in her kitchen stirring up brownies, hoping to feed them to the kids if they returned with Vixen.

It's hard to describe now, the walk home.

This part I'll talk out.

There was no sense of dark approaching, except for a set of spreading clouds and the smell of incipient rain. I saw a tall man slurping peaches from a tin can at the former bus stop. He was long shinned and gaunt and bent double over the fruit. It was easy to imagine him suddenly unfolding to a great winged height.

Reaching our yard, I was briefly glad. All was right. Nothing had blown off. The spade stuck out of the ground where I had left it. All siding and shingles remained.

Inside the house, nothing was right.

I entered the kitchen to drawers pulled free, to emptied

cupboards and chaos underfoot. Confusion struck. At first I blamed the storm. Had I left windows open? Water dripped somewhere. I moved through on numb feet. The sofa lay on its back. It sank in that people had done this. Lark's overstuffed chair was slashed. I called her name but no answer. Maybe still at the shop.

The stairs were scattered with pieces of clothing and up I went at a run.

More wreckage—dressers turned, closets gutted, our mattress an obscenity. Even the plumbing was sacked. Water pooled, looking for an exit.

I found myself in the attic hall.

The bedroom door half-open.

I saw her foot, twisted and wrong—Lark's bare ankle, not itself.

A spray of glass, the corner of a tipped chair.

I saw the handle of a tool I would soon hear described as a "lump hammer." It is what it sounds like.

I entered and knelt. Gathered her up, stood wavering, sank back to the floor.

Look out the window, will you? At the clouds, ripped at the edges and moving fast. The sea like a shroud. The eaves bare of ravens, every bird flown.

~ *promises I made and meant and broke*

THE AMBULANCE DRIVER was the same compassionate scoliotic who'd come for Labrino. We recognized each other at once. He had time to say, "It's you, I'm so sorry," before he was joined by the law. I will not waste your time with these policemen. I do not remember them. When the songs are written they will not appear. They walked noisily speaking in rude voices like men performing. The oldest of them not thirty and a "lead detective." He pointed his short blunt finger at whomever he was talking to.

At first they thought I did it. Maybe this is standard. They told me to sit in the kitchen and left a man with me while the others went upstairs. I could hear their muffled speech and floorboards shifting under their shoes. No doubt they took photos and picked things up and set them down again and poked here and there with a pen. The man with me was nervous and narrow-faced and wouldn't meet my eyes. I said Do you have questions for me? Apparently not. He paced the kitchen crunching over the littered floor. Bean seeds and glass and bits of dry pasta. Outside a few neighbors gathered in the alley near the vehicles. Lark's assistant Sylvie was out there holding her little girl. Maudie beside them. All had been in this house twenty-four hours earlier laughing and singing and toasting Lark. They stood in cold postures in the spattery twilight. Eventually came decisive movement upstairs then the repeated bump of a gurney being guided none too easy down the steps. I heard the ambulance driver say *Hey, gentle* but down they clumped these goddamned brutes pushing poor Lark zipped in black paper through the kitchen out the back door to the ambulance.

There she went, and a moan came up from people gathered.

Here is what the policeman wanted to know: Where was I when this happened? Would I describe our marriage as happy? Who was the primary wage earner? What things did the two of us quarrel about? These and similar he shot at me from behind his bellicose finger. His cell phone burped and he looked at it, reporting as if it were news to me that I had "no history of violence." Instead of starting one there and then I answered quietly. Lark and I were happy. We did not fight about money or much else. I told about leaving her at the shop to look for Maudie's dog. Maudie was standing in the alley—right there. Go ask Maudie.

When finally it penetrated that I was not my wife's murderer, he asked did anyone mean her harm.

"It might not have been Lark they came for." I told them about Kellan whose greatest fear was pursuit. Kellan whose last name we never learned. I said Kellan maintained what had seemed outlandish ideas about his size in the fugitive landscape. So much for my adult judgment. I described his arrival and habitual suspicion. His reluctance to divulge his past or plans, his avoidance of crowds, including last night's revelry.

At this I recalled the bookish old guest. His remarks about trouble now stood forth—how it arrives en route to somewhere else. Maybe decides to stay. While I didn't know Kellan's last name, I knew the name he feared most.

"He dreaded a man called Werryck," I said.

A little color left this policeman's face. His finger slumped and rejoined its hand. He looked away, seeming to hover over his next question. "Was he here? Did you see Werryck yourself?"

"How would I know?" I explained the open-door nature of Lark's parties. "An old man came. We didn't know him."

Even as I described him, the possibility seemed to diminish—so frail, the old collector, feeling his way down the steps. His shortness of breath, the pitted moon of his scalp. "I doubt he is the man. He didn't look well. Lump on his neck like somebody's thumb."

Abruptly the lead detective stood up.

"We are through for tonight."

The other men roused themselves and were out the door without a word, though I endured one more dose of the pointing finger.

"I will come back tomorrow and you will be here. There is still the matter of your harboring a fugitive. You did so knowingly. Are you listening to me?" he added, because I was looking out the window instead of at him. I nodded. I could look at him or listen but not both at once.

Before the vehicles were out of the alley Maudie was in the kitchen. She grabbed me around the chest—she was very short and also quite strong. She took me to her home and set me up in a guest room off the kitchen. She put out towels and showed me the light switches. If I woke in the night I was welcome to the fridge and cupboards.

I didn't sleep—at first didn't want to and later couldn't. I'd have welcomed whatever extralegal assistance but none was available. You don't want to hear about my buzzing limbs or gummy lungs, my head roving in the borderlands. A little before dawn something scraped and made a plaintive sound. I stumbled through Maudie's kitchen to the door, opened it. Vixen came in. She was a prancing sort of dog but not then. Her vulpine ears were matted with blood and she limped on her pretty black paws. I picked her up and set her in the sink and warmed some water to rinse her wounds and sores, then heated us both some milk. She followed me to the guest room and climbed on the bed at my feet. Instantly she slept, and I soon followed.

I lost track a while, then. No way else to say it. Maudie and Francie and Harry were at the house a lot at first. There was cleaning to be done, and those three did most of it while Pierre propped me up with coffee or meals over which he said things I don't remember about God and mercy and long-suffering and the cloud of unknowing. Pierre was kind in his way by which I mean tone-deaf. He said I was welcome to stay at his house if I was uncomfortable at home, then reminded me his house was small with a territorial cat puking where least expected. Maudie also invited me to stay. So did Harry, who'd just inherited the Lantern and was cleaning the space upstairs. To none could I say yes. Lovely as they were the offers felt too near my face. Fourteen years I'd lived in Lark's orbit. I couldn't right away inhabit someone else's. Among these friends Maudie was most plain-spoken. She said after Labrino she feared I too would believe I was finished and take what she called steps. Admittedly the idea had pull. I was too tired then to think about finishing, but had I encountered a greenish Willow beside a glass of water it might've seemed wise or proper or even ordained. A quick dissolve, a slice of pie. Ninety minutes of warmth and clarity and then whatever's next—an alpine meadow, a sunlit coast. Maybe nothing at all.

~

There was the question of a service. Maudie helped arrange it—no, she did everything.

Near Icebridge is a place where the land rises straight out of the sea three hundred feet. We gathered on a day of cold sun, Lark's favorite kind. Climbed the looping trail up the backside of the hill—my friends from the band, our neighbors, some dozens who knew Lark from the bookshop. As with her birthday there were people I didn't recognize. An old woman with a white bob, a trio of unaccompanied small sisters, a dark-eyed man I'd never seen but who wept silently and carried in his hand *A Tale of Two Cities*. In fact nearly everyone carried a book, some two. A few were classics, but there were also crime-solving widows, memoirs of war and armistice, scarlet confessionals and tales of love gone wrong. Among these others I saw Molly Thorn's short treatise against despair entitled *The Optimist at Midnight*, which I never read though Lark called it Molly's "funniest book if you can bear the pain." Francie hummed the ancient melody known as the Tennessee Waltz which was known before that by many other names stretching back to its beginnings in the Pictish fog—a tune to catch, and it did, and wound itself around us until I loved everyone there with all I had. Arriving on the summit of blue-green stones etched with ocher lichens we were met by a north breeze, but when I offered it Lark's ashes it turned abruptly southwest and carried them out over the long shining waters. I loved the wind for that. It carried her in the direction of the Slates.

Then I got home and could not bear the house.

Couldn't sit still or fall asleep but instead walked through rooms in purgatory. I've heard many griefstruck keep expecting the loved one to appear. There's an urge to phone the lost member, to write a note about the sunrise or good coffee or the flurry of waxwings among the berries. The person's presence remains default. The loss is less remembered than received fresh each time.

To my desolation Lark's absence was complete.

There hung her prints on the walls. There stood the end table lovingly salvaged. All around were her books and garden seeds, her skillets dangling in the pantry. Every surface in the house bore her signature as did my past and future, yet she was so thoroughly gone I struggled to recall how it was before she left.

I only wanted to remember her in full, do you see? I didn't imagine getting her back—no, not yet I didn't. I only wanted to summon the size and shape and color of the joy we offhandedly accepted. What could be simpler than that?

One afternoon I found myself in the attic. I'd stayed out of there, fearing its power, but in my purgatory I did drift up finally and was surprised to see one of Kellan's silver canisters lying on its side in the closet. Cool and smooth. Heavy in the hand. A mask and regulator hung on a hook behind the door. I sat on the bed and adjusted the mask over my nose. Faint plastic hint of disinfectant and disease. I turned the dial, heard the hiss and hum. Inhaled to the very bottom of my lungs.

Why do this to yourself you say, and I reply Why not?

As enemies go, despair has every ounce of my respect.

In this way the broken summer passed. It seems I left the band—didn't so much quit as stop remembering to show. There was an emergency or two over this, my poor friends sitting in my kitchen wringing from me promises I made and meant and broke. There were debts and bills, expressions of concern, statements of dire finance. All hieroglyphs. The policeman with the finger visited as promised. He showed me an old photograph of Werryck. It took a moment to run the eloquent Molly Thorn admirer backward through time until he became the blond stern commander in the photo. What sealed it was the humor in his eyes.

"That's him," was my declaration, "He didn't do it," the swift retort. Apparently the man could not be touched. This cop was now bent on believing Kellan murdered Lark. "An absconded menial, a thief, a person moving through." I reminded him Kellan had left before it happened but no response. His eyes were empty. Lawmen will invoke the law but the only law they really know is gravity. Force flows downward and Werryck was far above these local badges. Well, all right. I no longer need despise this dank policeman. Let us release him nameless from our story.

We reach a night at summer's end. Late August I suppose. I couldn't sleep in the house so for weeks had gone to a northeast woodlot people called the Cedars. The Cedars had bottomless shadows, a lush overstory, trunks of twisting bark. A standing lullaby that place. In the evenings, I'd walk out with a pillow and wool blanket. Sprawled on mossy ground or propped against a tree I slept and sometimes seemed to feel the deep-down bass line of the world. Maybe you know it. The song you don't hear holds you up. Deer got used to me as did raccoons and wolves and fearsome weasels until I might have been the wild bear some kids believed I was. More often than not I woke with Maudie's dog Vixen asleep across my ankles.

The night I'm talking about was cold. August as I said but October on the ground. I had two blankets and wanted a third. My back was against the wide cedar that had come to be my favorite. Vixen twitched in dreams. What arrived that night was a forceful memory of Lark. So vivid I was right inside it. Her last night in this life, asleep after the revelry. "We sailed back to the Slates," she said in that rarest of all subsequents. "In our own boat. We stayed a month. Now I think we never left."

I'd forgotten the boat. In my solitude and lunacy it stopped existing.

But Lark had remembered it, on our last night together.

Next thing I was lurching through the Cedars—in the dark, taking branches to the face, Vixen trotting alongside pleased and confused. Out of the woods into starshine, onto the road past the Icebridge sign, the firehouse, the co-op. Half a block from the boat shed Vixen peeled off and headed for Maudie's.

I unlocked the shed. Not much light but none was needed. I climbed the ladder like a man reaching home.

Lark wasn't there, but I could imagine her there.

In fact I couldn't imagine her not there.

The boat creaked in its cradle. I opened the hatch and eased below and settled onto the bunk.

~ *the windmill is a giant*

I SURFACED to a pile of sandpaper, to soft light blading through hatches. My throat was dry but my bones didn't ache as they had after sleeping in the Cedars. Sitting up I took stock of the cabin—the half-complete projects scattered about—then stood and smacked my head. *Careful there Gulliver* is what Lark would've said. I rubbed my face, which felt strange to my fingers. It felt strange because of the smile.

Maybe you're tempted to feel relief: he's turned the corner!

No.

What corner?

There are no corners—you know that.

What did happen is I spotted a length of teak trim lying on the opposite bunk. I'd removed it months ago and now picked it up, sighted down its length. It was knobby with old varnish, had a few inches of soft dry rot on its backside. Without thinking I opened a galley drawer, found the folding knife Erik used for everything from oak to cheese. The rot scooped out easily. A bit of sandpaper came to hand and began moving over the teak. A warm clingy smell sifted up. There was varnish in a can someplace. There were screws and a drill. That was all I knew for sure.

These things I repaired in the weeks that followed: the heavy mount that would hold the marine compass I still meant to buy, two ruinous turnbuckles at the base of the shrouds, the crazed plexiglass foredeck hatch, seized winches, leaky icebox, the tiny gimbled alcohol stovetop producing chilly flame. Beneath that stove I also found a long-barreled antique pistol in an oiled rag—walnut grips, a handsome sheen. I wrapped it up and tucked it away.

Erik had done a good deal of structural work but ignored certain things. The diesel engine under the cockpit—its seals and belts and hoses rotted, its fuel hard to acquire. I didn't even attempt to fix it, leaving it in place only for weight and stability. More urgently, Erik hadn't replaced the chainplates—straps of heavy steel anchoring stays that keep the mast upright. These plates were pitted and flaky with corrosion. They were a warning. I made plans to visit Greenstone, where a man I knew cut scrap steel to custom dimensions.

During these weeks I returned to the house only for its kitchen, bathroom, bookshelves. The house with its shadows and scents opened me to waves of exhaustion. My legs shook, my veins constricted. The boat hadn't any mirrors but the house had several that captured my furtive self moving as if to avoid detection. Inside that place I wasn't just alone but felt the harm it did me. On the boat I was also alone but with the persistent sense of Lark nearby. She was walking over at this moment, carrying books or sandwiches. Was that her foot upon the ladder? Or—if not nearby—Lark seemed at least somewhere, someplace real, a destination reachable by someone resolute.

On the boat I knew Lark wasn't finished.

If she wasn't finished, neither was I.

No doubt you see where this was headed. I didn't—not right away. I sanded and greased and had my meals and slept aboard and failed to see it coming.

Remember the trip we made to the Slates, the woman Lark claimed was Molly? You may recall I didn't buy it. I'm fairly sure Lark didn't either. Not really. You know how this is. We were sailors and explorers, aspiring quixotes headlong for each other. Half the things we said were whimsy, the other half permission.

But now, as the boat began to get its color back, I had to reevaluate. Maybe Lark was onto something bigger than she knew.

Maybe now and then the windmill is a giant.

If it were so—if there were even a chance the bemused old frizzy sailor in the Slates was Molly Thorn—then many streams suddenly converged. Lark's lifelong case on perilous waters. Our encounter with the white-haired sailor herself. This antique boat falling unbidden to our hands. All joined in such a way that something begun long ago now became a pattern.

If I were to see Lark anywhere, it would be in that place where the meteor struck and thinned the world, and islands rose to shelter tattered souls who made the trip.

That night in the lamplit cabin I spoke my plan aloud to test for cracks. "I will finish the boat and sail to the Slates."

It thrilled me—that name again, the *Slates*, its fateful sound, like a set of chiseled tablets yet to be discovered.

Icebridge had long since stopped maintaining its small marina. It had no employees, no insurance. Its docks and pelican poles were tombstones tilted by neglect. There was, however, an at-your-own-risk understanding that allowed aspiring boaters to tie up to the crumbling seawall. All I had to do was pay a handyman named

Cooper to back his tractor into the shed and pull *Flower* on her trailer down to the water. Cooper crept down the ramp until she drifted free, then gave me some advice about starting the outboard. I let it idle a few minutes, then eased the boat over to the seawall and tossed Cooper a line. It was a sunny day with a light breeze, the sort that makes you forget your terror of this selfsame water. I spent the rest of the afternoon raising the mast, tightening shrouds, threading the mainsail into its groove and folding it down on the boom. The boat heeled and creaked as I moved about. I wasn't scared at all.

My courage held as the week began. I liked sleeping in *Flower*'s tiny cabin and carried aboard blankets and a few clothes and my tiny practice amp. Yes I still felt shifty and alone, yes I drank the liquor Dodge delivered as his offering to my sorrow. And yes I still indulged in Kellan's canister elixir, though not as much and not for long. The regulator's cicada whirr became an admonition. It struck me Orpheus himself would not pass through that veil were he impaired and frousting about on the crooked limbs of nitrous.

The less I used it the more I remembered. For example I woke and knew it was Monday and gathered my things and drove to the vast drafty house of Cora's troubled students. Climbing to the porch I heard music and peered in at the window. A young woman, not Cora, sat at the piano. She played very well and spoke or sang while doing so. The kids were rapt. They murmured and swayed. Only now did I remember I'd not been here in months. Softly down the steps I went. Driving away I glanced back and saw a forehead lean against the window. It was Tonio. He didn't wave.

Against my will, I also began to remember the evil of the day. That day.

At first I'd been unable to think about it. A gulf opened in time and my mind would not go near it. Eventually I tried—or thought

I did—to tie the harness on and descend. But nothing appeared to me down there. I dangled in a lightless solitude.

Now the abyss began to show itself. Details of the day returned. The quick brutal storm, the scoured streets in its wake. Burst glass and bean seeds in the kitchen. For the first time I imagined the thing itself. Lark arriving home to find the house in ruins and a man inside it, bashing through the sheetrock—looking for something, it didn't matter what. She tried to get out, was blocked or prevented, fled upstairs. Here my mind's eye failed. It had nothing to go on. This is because I never saw Lark fearful. I didn't know how that would look.

These pictures now pursued me through my days. The bastard in our house always indistinct, a blurry man-shaped hole in the world.

Only on *Flower* did I find refuge, and I made that boat my home.

I began to feel I was already gone—just needed a few things to make it real. New chainplates, so the mast wouldn't topple. Sails a little less like salvaged bedsheets. All procurable in Greenstone. Cash was short, though, so it seemed just one more fated stream when Harry stepped aboard.

He said Red Dog was "off" without me. Francie had been keyboarding the bass parts but didn't like doing it and the sound lacked heft. After inheriting the Lantern from Labrino, Harry had closed it down for paint and renovations. The reopening was Friday night. With an apologetic look he produced a little stack of money.

Would I come back and play?

~

Harry had planned this event as a fresh start. Cheap drink and lively music are safe bets, and we arrived to an early hum.

It felt good to be back with my friends. It wasn't what had once been normal—that was over—but as we tuned and nodded to each other, adjusting the monitors, testing the mics, it occurred to me I might remain. The boat was nearly ready, but the weather was the sort to change your plans. The rain had started early; now came the wind with winter on its shoulders. Water froze in the gutters. Surely it was glazing the deck of the boat tied up lonesome on the seawall.

That first warm hour in the pleasant tavern would return to me in dreams.

Harry counted us off and we played a set establishing credentials. The bass felt at home in my hands again. I could've wept. Halfway through the set Harry stood up with drumsticks in hand and took a mic and said generous things about Jack Labrino. How resilient Jack was. The tougher things got for him the kinder he became. Nodding to me, Harry then paid tribute to Lark, to her generosity, to the size of the vacuum she left behind. I wasn't expecting his eloquence, and something inside began to shake. While Harry talked the electricity kept flickering, lights browning and surging, and that plus Harry's gratitude and the beat of icy rain against the windows bound us all together. Harry sat to cheers and launched us into the blues.

The power flicked off. In the dark was abrupt silence, then laughter, then clapping as Harry vamped along on the drum set, keeping us alive.

The lights came blazing back.

There stood Werryck, just inside the door.

He seemed taller than I remembered, somehow younger, though clearly the same man who'd bumbled into the shop and bought a stack of books and later lifted a stirring toast to Lark in her own house. What stands out to me now is the clear enjoyment in his face as he leaned against the tavern wall. He smiled. His head bobbed along to the rhythm. The dance floor filled. The door swung open and two men entered. They nodded to Werryck who nodded back then looked at me directly.

In that look I understood he'd killed her. No, he didn't swing the hammer. But her death was down inside his eyes.

I understood too that he was here for me. Kellan had said *Don't pack, don't grab a coat, go out the window if you have to* and now my enemy had come and nothing lay between us but the dance floor. Here is my confession. I hadn't one brave or gallant thought as he hung in the back and watched us play. Neither plan nor strategy, no, but the instant he leaned ahead and began shouldering toward the stage I set the bass line crosswise. Cut a new path for the song, so it became a story of mayhem, ruin, a boy severed from all he loved. The room turned fearful. Dancers whirled and collided. I urged the band on, I felt Harry's panicked look but pushed us into a dream of war. In the surge and crush Werryck stalled. I unplugged with a blast of static and went out the back.

I drove home half sideways over ice. The house was lit to the attic.

Neighbors in raincoats—Maudie among them—stood watching from the street. Men were visible moving about behind the panes. I saw a painting tumble off the wall. I slowed, lowering my window.

A man with a brazen face glared from my own doorway. I had seen the face before, in the alleyway, behind a lit cigarette. Instantly the blur in my mind—the man-shaped hole—acquired detail and dimension. He lifted a hand to point at me. The hand was swathed in a thick white bandage.

Maudie saw me, too, and shook her head. We didn't exchange a word. With her eyes she eased me past.

The harbor was dark except for one sodium-vapor lamp near the water. I parked where the seawall ran out from the beach. It strikes me odd now but didn't then that I carried the bass with me, unprotected in the sleety rain, as though it might be of use. The wind lifted spray off the water and flung it ashore.

The boat when I reached it heeled away from the seawall, straining at its lines in the gale. I stood wondering how and whether to climb aboard. What decided me was a freezing gray wave that soughed over the breakwater and drenched me to the shins. Headlight beams scissored through town. I leapt to the decking, slipped and somehow stayed upright. Went below, wrapped the bass in a blanket, emerged to see a black angular car pull up under the light pole. I knelt at the outboard and primed the gas line. Lightning shuddered at my back. The motor started in five pulls. Werryck stood by his car watching through binoculars. His two men headed up the seawall while I threw off the dock lines. Ice fell out of the sky churning the lake to fury. The tiller bucked in my bloodless fingers. Werryck in his long gaunt coat stood in the glow of the sodium lamp and watched me out the channel.

⁓ *white-maned horses*

I DON'T KNOW how long he stood watching since who had time to look? The channel was narrow, stuffed with waves. Some burst over the seawall with spumes shearing off in the wind. I couldn't even hear the puny outboard in the gale. Rain sheeted over my face and down inside my jacket. Ice coated the deck and lifelines and shrouds. I twisted the throttle full as the boat left the protection of the breakwater. A cresting wave thrust the bow in the air and I lost my feet, landed on my back beneath the tiller. God how the motor begged and stalled and coughed and then kept running. Next wave heaved the boat aside. The danger was less in sinking than being driven onto the rocks. Steering at an angle into the waves I made no headway but at least stayed parallel to shore maybe fifty yards off. Down in the cabin everything crashed around. Every plunge brought more water aboard. The boat got hard to steer. Lights darted and bobbed ashore—men clambering along the rocks. A flashlight's beam struck my face. I heard their shouts. We would run aground unless we turned, but the waves made that impossible.

What I needed was a way to stop. An emergency brake. And *Flower* had one.

Lashing the tiller in place, I went forward hand over hand to the prow where the anchor was clamped down. I pitched it overboard and hung on while the rope went hissing over the side. The rope was bolted to the boat's very frame and when we reached its length the whole vessel shook and reared around into the wind. Onshore the lights gathered. The men were waiting for either the rope to break or the anchor to come free, and they would have me. But now, pointing straight into the waves, the outboard urged *Flower* slowly ahead. I went forward collecting the anchor rope in my hands as it slacked. When we passed over the anchor I braced and hove and felt it leave the bottom. By the time it slid up over the side my limbs were jelly. I reset the anchor in its clamp. We still pitched godawfully but the lights behind got discernibly smaller. When the sleety rain turned to sudden thick snow I felt decently obscured and left the helm tied to go below.

Pitch-black and ankle-deep. I found a gas match and held it up. Bins and blankets and bits of paper washed forward and back over the floor. The hull groaned while water streamed off the chainplates. I checked there were no open ports then left that heaving scenario and climbed back out to the weather.

How did that night pass? With my wet bones shaking in my parka. Aware of a stinging pain I reached up and found a long diagonal cut across my chin. I had no idea of the shore, how far I'd got or whether there might be rocks or shoals ahead, but the gale eventually began to tire. I opened the locker and lifted the red tank—it rang nearly empty in my hand. Below I found the sails stacked in a cubby, dragged them out and found the smallest, a triangular scrap of heavy cloth. This little storm sail I carried forward, clipped to the forestay by its four brass shackles, and hauled up snapping. The moment I trimmed the sail it turned serious and quiet as the boat sped down into a trough then up the facing wave.

A hopeful moment! I'd got a sail up, my first since Lark and I set out for the Slates fifteen years before. *Flower* put her shoulder down and forged across the wind. The waves were white-maned horses. As the light grew I had the reassuring sight of the shoreline less than a mile off. I killed the engine. Erik said the greatness of this boat was its long lead keel encased in iron. Not speedy but it tracked straight and would steer itself true for weeks on end if you let it. I took my hands off the tiller and shut my eyes.

In stories the sailor wakes after the storm and behold the sun is up and the world is yellow and azure after black gales. The water running alongside is clear, suggestive of health and adventure and above all freedom which were his reasons for going to sea in the first place. Up he rises, neat as you please, and goes prospecting for breakfast.

But I can tell you I woke with a neck too stiff to raise my head, and there was no yellow sun. The sea had not become benign, though the wind howled less. Through it all the storm sail had pulled us along like a champion. Gradually we neared the shore. I picked out rooftops, individual trees, a raven on a bare limb. I slapped life into my legs and went below.

Where it was full of filthy water. Half a foot at least. It slid to and fro over the floor of the boat. There was a pump, I now recalled—a manual pump. How did it work? Erik had showed me once. Wracking my memory, I located the pump handle loose in storage and fitted it into a socket built into the cockpit wall. I cranked it up and down. There was a moment's resistance, then something gave and the handle moved about loosely. I cranked for twenty useless seconds.

I was lightheaded with hunger.

Guess what, I didn't want to be on a boat anymore. I wanted to be on land. In fact I wanted nothing *except* to be on land. The land was close, too. A hundred yards off! A good grassy smell came from it that made me weepy and profane. Some voyager me. Much as I'd worked on *Flower* I was ready right then to leave her forever, to swim ashore and walk to whatever town and buy a cup of coffee and sit in the sun. Lark and I once took life a year at a time. As the world shifted we went to a month at a time, later a week. At this point an hour would do. I'd take twenty minutes in the sun. I was cold and hungry and getting the headache that comes of no coffee. In that instant I made what Lark used to call an Executive D. I'd swim ashore and see what offered.

Flower eased into a calm bay. The wind had faded entirely. I went forward, put the anchor down and watched it settle on the clear sand bottom.

I straightened up, and that is when I saw the woman.

Short and sharp and old—that's how she looked to me. She wore a stiff green jacket and was walking along the shore watching me instead of her feet. At first I was glad to see her. A living person on land! I felt as if I hadn't seen one in months, though it had been only hours since I played music in a tavern full of them. My impulse was to wave and I did, but the way she came up short and didn't wave back killed the greeting in my throat. While I watched she took a small set of binoculars from her pocket and held them to her eyes. She didn't smile but instead stood there like a crisp dowager scouting for reprobates. I watched her back. I actually went below and fetched my own binoculars. The German ones I'd bought to watch the comet. They brought her close and flattened her into the rocks and dunes behind her. She wore rubber boots with olive tops and yellow soles. A leather strap was slung at an angle across her chest. With crisp movements she put the glasses in a coat pocket from which she produced a notebook and pen and made notes. She got out the binocs again and looked at me. She wrote some more.

"Hello," I called. It was ridiculous, this watching. We were close enough to talk.

But she wouldn't talk. Wouldn't answer me at all. She made some final notations then walked back up the beach. The leather strap I'd noticed was not connected to a handbag or rucksack but rather a holster. It held a pistol of some kind. I didn't call out to her again. A hundred yards down the beach she turned onto a path that took her into trees and out of sight.

There I stood in doubt. I had called out in a friendly voice and her reply was to examine me like a distasteful specimen and write things down. In my mind the notes took on the tenor of prosecution. Just like that my plans changed. The shore was not my friend. I hung the binoculars on their strap by the companionway so they'd be handy, then got busy with the bilge pump.

It was a simple one—a pump with rubber bellows meant to draw water through a plumbed hose from below and send it out astern. Of course it hadn't seen use in decades, so the bellows had shredded when I worked the handle.

Erik's tools were in a long narrow box of blue steel. It was full of oily water I dumped carefully over the side. At the bottom was a scrum of washers and screws, a bottle of machine oil, wrenches of the box and open and crescent variety, a hand drill and bits, a drum of rubber cement and three wooden cones six inches long, waterlogged and turning fuzzy. In a hanging locker was a man's raincoat and I laid the ruined bellows on it and cut a new one from its rubbery fabric. There was just enough cement to fit this makeshift bellows to the frame. I secured it with the existing clamp and a plea for luck.

The canister said the cement would dry in an hour and I used that time to haul soaked things up from the cabin. Socks and long-sleeve shirts and a pair of French military pants. A leather belt, sodden sail bags, the handheld compass from Kellan. While cleaning up, I discovered a can of baked beans, two tins of sardines, and a sealed sleeve of crackers—I was preparing to open the fish when the woman arrived back onshore. A man was with her. Tall, big gut, a man in boots. He shared the woman's sense of purpose and her binoculars and also, when I shouted a greeting, her reticence. He didn't pull out a notebook but instead a cell phone that he poked with a finger and put to his ear.

I didn't like this. The hour wasn't up but I fitted the pump handle in its socket. Gave the handle a stroke. There was resistance. Two more strokes and the pump took hold, five more and water surged up the pipe and poured out astern. Business. The man spoke into the phone with urgency while I settled into a rhythm, alternating arms at every forty. In twenty minutes my back and shoulders ached but the boat rode higher in the water. Onshore the man paced about. The woman was up on a rise of land, binoculars trained on the distance. I thought she was watching the road.

Ten more minutes and the pump sucked air. And then little *Flower* woke up. Oh God I felt it happen, I saw it in her lines and her bearing on the surface. The wind began to rise—not a hard blow but light out of the west. The weather had something in mind. The air looked yellow as in pictures of harvest and a haze rose off the water. Columns of fog forming up like spontaneous shades of people long past. They rose twisting in the light breeze. The man watched and I sped up my housekeeping. When everything necessary was either below or secure on deck I untied the mainsail where it lay folded on the boom and shackled its head to the halyard.

The moment I rattled that big sail up the mast, the man onshore responded. He'd taken a seat on a driftwood log but now leapt to his feet shouting something at the woman. I couldn't tell what. She shouted back. The fog thickened. The man got out his cell and made a series of staccato pronouncements. As the freshet caught at the sail *Flower* swung round to her anchor. The woman came running down the beach. Small rocks bounded away at her crunching footfalls. I hauled at the anchor, its rope piling up on the foredeck. The woman knelt awkwardly at the water's edge. She reached back for the pistol. I dropped the anchor on its nest of rope as her shot sliced the fog above my head. I slipped, landed hard on my shoulder, crawled to the tiller. Out we moved steadily. As the sail filled, a perfect small hole appeared in it, the flat pop of gunfire arriving a moment later. For some reason I imagined the sound bouncing off the sail while the bullet, free of encumbrance, sped on forever. I turned and could no longer see the beach or the people on it. All was fog. Even the sail was hard to see. I was flying, a slow and fearful flight in the belly of a cloud.

~ *so young to be in jail*

FLOWER bore away north. I hate to think where we'd have been if not for that opaque mist rising all round. Minus the fog, that woman could've reloaded and kept trying until she ran out of bullets. She could've driven to town and bought more, haggled over the price and come back and shot at me until her finger tired. As it was the fog swallowed me like a whale and I was released to ponder the new world.

What I had was a toy compass, an incomplete chart book of Superior, and no idea where I was. Somewhere south of Icebridge. I went below and opened the ports and storage lockers so air could move through. Cleaned the floor with a rank towel. Lark said a boat knew when you cared. When the fog broke up, the shore lay far behind.

I had a ruinous headache from no coffee. During supply-chain interruptions coffee was the one thing Lark and I agreed to hoard so we never went without. We might not have fruit or tomato sauce or decent flour but we held fast on the sacred bean. Which made the headache nearly unbearable but so what? You bear what you have to. Red Dog used to do a lighthearted hymn *Obla-di Obla-da* and I sang it now in a feeble headache voice. It didn't help at all, but I did remember the sardines. Got them out, opened both tins—miraculous shiny small fish—piled them on crackers, and ate with preposterous satisfaction. When the sardines were gone I crumbled more crackers into the tins, let the crumbs soak up the last of the oil, and scooped them up with my fingers.

The food lifted my spirits, and even the dreadful headache began to disperse. The wind was slight and *Flower* gathered speed though there was scarcely a wave. Mists parted before us and closed behind, and all was silent except the water slipping alongside and the occasional cry from a gull. In this way we cruised northeast which seemed a safe course and eventually I let her steer herself and went below to count up what was good and what was ruined.

Here are the books that survived.

Folsum's Anchorages, by V. V. Folsum
Instant Weather Forecasting, by Alan Watts
Handbook of Knots, by Des Pawson
How to Sail Around the World, by Hal Roth
A Field Guide to Animal Tracks, by Olaus Murie
Mammals of the Great Lakes Region, by Allen Kurta
I Cheerfully Refuse, by Molly Thorn

Seven is not many books with which to go to sea. Most had been left aboard by Erik. I arranged them on the fiddled shelf on the starboard side of the cabin, in this order because it seemed their natural maritime hierarchy, with books on anchoring and weather and knots of utmost importance, and Molly Thorn as a last resort. Much as I loved Molly when Lark was alive, that is how much I dreaded her now. I'd stopped over at the bereft shop one afternoon to see if the galley was still under the counter. It was. Eventually of course she'd lost out to her curiosity and read *I Cheerfully Refuse* in a single long evening, sometimes exclaiming or reaching out to touch my knee or whispering some fond profanity, and I remember she insisted on reading aloud a longish poem about loving a person who wasn't there and hadn't been there in a long time and wasn't likely to be there ever again. Believe it or not the passage was riddled with humor, one of those pieces that makes you laugh when you want to cry—in other words, Lark's favorite sort of writing. That was the last thing she ever read to me, so the book was both dread totem and sacred relic. It lived at the bottom of the shelf.

You understand I didn't truly know my voyage had begun. Maybe I still thought there was a choice. Maybe because I'd imagined the kind of departure described in salty memoirs where the sailor stocks the galley with tinned meats, and four dozen eggs properly cushioned, and triple-wrapped bricks of cheese, and as much fresh produce as they can get through in a week (after which they rely on canned), and as many bottles of wine as will fit in the cool dark bilge of a pocket cruiser. Nor did I get to make a brave soft speech of goodbye or hand my house keys to whomever might agree to stay there and keep it warm and safe. I'd told no one about my plan because I knew how it would sound and was afraid that voiced aloud I wouldn't believe in it myself. Would I have gone through with all this if not forced out? Even now I held in reserve the chance of going home.

It made no sense that Lark was gone, or that Werryck had turned his gaze to me. What did I have that he had not already taken?

Standing below with *Instant Weather Forecasting* in hand the boat abruptly heeled a few degrees. The rigging moaned. I climbed up into a renewed and darkening fog. Thunder murmured over the water; the clouds stirred into a familiar crown. Going forward I took the half-dried blankets from the lifelines and stowed them below, readied the anchor on its clasp, and steered for shallow water.

Flower neared a forested shoreline with two large houses, abandoned. The chimney of one had crumbled; the windows of the other were burned and broken out. I didn't love the idea of anchoring in front of these bereft witnesses but the bay had a sand bottom and protection from wind any direction but east. Down went the anchor in twelve feet. I dropped the mainsail in a light rain pocking the lake's smooth surface.

Below in the darkening cabin I began to shake. It started in my legs and moved up my spine and worked down my arms and into my fingers which quivered in a way I couldn't stop. How could I not shake given the fear and rage in my veins and the hatred for those who murdered Lark and hounded me and shot their idiot guns in my direction?

I said aloud, "Lark," and repeated it a few times. It's not that I expected an answer, yet she had a way of being I never understood. Her instincts ran counter to my own. Now without them I felt lost.

This is what I mean. Her bookshop, Bread, was a success, but dealing in adventurous verse and unapproved literature got it targeted as the merry purveyor of rebellion it unquestionably was. A few years after it opened a young patriot with fallen arches drove four hundred miles to throw a bomb through the window and speed out of town. This dour savage had changed his name legally to Large Beef. I forget why. The bomb was a threaded pipe stuffed with red-dot gunpowder. It had no detonating mechanism and didn't explode but instead laid on the tile floor looking mildly embarrassed. Twenty minutes out of Icebridge a wheel came off Mr. Beef's mini truck and spun down the road ahead of him. He had a long walk back to town on his painful feet, knees collapsing inward. I was new to ironies and watched them pile up. If Large Beef could read he might've made a working bomb, but would a reading Beef want to? Lark didn't think so. She followed his arraignment and trial, brought him up in conversation. Hope that boy's all right. So young to be in jail. She learned his name was William before he got it changed. Imagining a stirring narrative, she wrote William a kind letter. Maybe someone would read it to him. He sent back an infantile drawing of a raised middle finger. She wrote to the court requesting leniency. When Beef got eight years I was relieved, but Lark was only sorrowful. For weeks her face looked soft and bruised.

"He did try to blow up your shop," I reminded her one night as we sat in the garden. "He made the stupid bomb in his stupid garage, then drove all that way to toss it through the window. I bet he'd like to take another crack at it, if he could."

"I know," Lark admitted. "He probably would."

"So what do you think should happen to this Beef? This William? If not jail then what?"

"I don't know. Long life, I guess. How about a clear mind? Work he enjoys, someone to laugh with, couple of happy kids. That would do, don't you think?"

It was the same list she wanted for herself. For me. I was irritated. For all I cared, Wild Billy Beef could rot forever and so could everybody like him.

I felt the same way now about these current enemies and had no wish to wish them well, but I was also shaking as though my organs were trying to get out, and I knew if Lark were here she'd have some way to think of this that might restore serenity. Again I said her name aloud, and though it didn't conjure her, the thought ingressed that a little music might calm my skittish fingers. I unwrapped the bass from its blanket. The practice amp was aboard, its battery still fresh. I plugged in and tuned by ear and found a slow progression.

A strange thing happened that evening as I played: the boat commenced an odd thumping sound, like something soft hitting the deck, not in any rhythmic way but like someone tossing rolled socks to the floor. I didn't pay it much mind at first, because the boat was rocking ever so gently and I imagined it was simply something in a locker or cabinet rolling to and fro against the side of the hull. But when I finished and tucked the bass away, I went up to check the anchor and, sliding open the hatch, startled a sleek seagull who raised his wings as if for balance and hopped to another perch. Why hello, I said quietly, then saw the whole foredeck populated with gulls who had landed and tucked into their fluffy down and were comfortably at rest. The side decks were also embellished with gulls, so too with the tiller and aft rail. So soothing was their company that I tried to retreat below without noise or disruption, but the gull I'd first startled—who must've been sitting on the hatch as I opened it—said a small phrase, *murk murk*, and quietly lifted himself in the air. At this the others took notice and, still without panic, decided en masse to go rest someplace else, someplace without a greasy emerging behemoth. They got up in a small cloud of twenty or thirty birds and flew off with faint questioning cries. How easy and unworried they looked, rising and reforming. How lyrical the piping of their wing feathers. How I hated to see them go.

~ *Tonio to the letter*

I WOKE UP having dreamed a song, a song about the comet. It had about a million verses that faded fast, but we were all of us in it—Lark and me, Maudie, Werryck and Kellan, Harry the drummer, the seabirds from last night. It was foolish and alluring. The comet was threaded throughout, circling back as comets do, along with the man who saw it coming, Mr. Tashi, who appeared as a fastidious notetaker and recorder of nocturnal blips, a slight man who did stretches and practiced deep breathing. It soothed me to think of him. It slowed my pulse to believe in a quiet far-off scientist staying with his work. I pictured Mr. Tashi at his telescope. Outside his door were heads of state, astronauts, costumed generals, frothing zealots waving witless flags. Mr. Tashi ignored them all. He remained composed, gazing at the heavens with his notebook on his lap. I think it was a good song. I wish I could remember it.

Then I heard church bells, the last thing I expected and welcome news indeed. A town was near. Breakfast. The red gas tank still held a tiny sip, enough to motor out of the cove. Scattered gulls dotted the quiet water. Some rose up when I passed but most were undisturbed. Soon a water tower appeared over the trees. The name on it was Lightner.

I knew Lightner, southwest of Icebridge toward Duluth. It used to have a small grocery store and public dock. Rounding a parklike headland I saw the municipal waterfront—the shut-down fly shop, fishing pier, shut bakery, tavern with seasonal chairs tipped up on a deck overlooking the water, and a bike rental place, also shut. I lowered a bucket and poured lake water over my head, pushed my hair back, straightened my shirt, located dock lines and hung three rubber fenders off the side. It was my first solo docking and I bumped the pier hard. A few things tumbled below but I managed to scramble onto the pier and cleat us fast.

No one was on or near the dock. Even in better days Lightner was a town of less than a thousand. With a little money and a drawstring bag I walked into town. The bells rang again, drawing my attention to a peeling structure with a tilted steeple and a yard sign suggesting we rejoice. The door was ajar with a handful inside and two kids restless on the sidewalk. As I approached, they were talking about three people who died that week in Lightner, a couple in their thirties and their visitor, apparently a cousin.

"They took the Willow," volunteered a boy of maybe twelve, bright eyes and dark circles.

"I'm sorry to hear it," I said.

"The TV was on," the boy said. "They were on the couch. They were just watching TV."

"Did you know them?"

"Not the cousin. I bet it was his idea, the damn suicide."

"Don't say that," said a girl who might've been his older sister.

"Don't say what?"

"Suicide. It isn't suicide when you do it like that." She paused. "It's stepping through the door. That's all it is. They went in search of better."

"Did their lives stop?" said the boy.

"It's not the same."

"Did they take the stuff?" said the boy. Every time I looked at him he seemed in tougher shape. Dirty cotton shirt and puffy eyes and blotchy places on his cheeks.

"Knock it off, Garrett," his sister told him.

"And were they all dead an hour later?"

"Quit it," she said.

"Suicide," said Garrett.

"You shut up, or I'll tell Dad," said his sister. "He'll sign you up for compliance meds. He wants to anyway. He says you're a seven on the Feral Compartment."

"Comportment," Garrett replied.

There was silence in which the kids noticed me easing away.

"Hey, who are you?" said Garrett.

No doubt I looked rough. It occurred to me to be careful. I'd been shot at no more than twenty miles down the coast. "Is there still a grocery store?"

Garrett's sister said, "Three blocks down. Across from the gas station."

"All right. Thanks." I left them still debating the disturbing event while somber music issued from the church.

I was anxious to buy food but first wanted fuel for the outboard. The gas station sold three-gallon plastic jerricans, and I carried two of these to the counter. The woman there said to go ahead and fill them at the pump then come in and pay so I did that, on impulse adding a tin harmonica from a spinning display and the topmost brick of cheese from a discount pyramid. When I paid with cash she said, "You run out of gas? How far up the road?"

A pair of glasses lay on the counter and she put them on, looked me over, and peered through the plate glass as if trying to find my car.

"Not far," I said.

"You need a ride, I can call somebody."

The church bell rang three times. I said, "I was sorry to hear about the suicides."

"They weren't suicides," she said.

"All right."

"They were stepping through the door," she informed me. "One day you wake up and know there is no future. I got two older brothers and they've both got the Willow for when that day arrives. If I had the money I'd buy that medicine tomorrow, put it in the drawer. You never know. There's not a soul I'd ever blame who went in search of better."

I stuck the cheese under an arm, lifted the gas cans and headed for the dock, noting low clouds in the east. Going back out there was unappealing but I'd worry about that later. More immediately I planned to drop the gas at the boat, then hit the grocery. Glimmering fantasies beckoned—fresh eggs, a good loaf of bread, a bag of oranges if they had some. You know how hunger will plant in your mind some very specific item? In this case I landed on canned ravioli, so salty and slick, O captain my captain, and knew right then that would be my breakfast. I'd heat it up and enjoy the whole slippery business right there at the Lightner dock. I hefted the gas cans, picked up my pace. Was nearly trotting when round the corner of the shut cafe hove a big-barreled form I didn't wish to see and whose name I'd never actually learned. He had sunglasses on his face and a painful hitch in his stride. Officer Apeknuckle upright in uniform. I didn't expect him to know me let alone say my name, which he did with a worrying scowl.

"Good morning, Officer. You're back on your feet," I said, alluding, like an idiot, to his humiliation at the Greenstone Fair.

When he removed his sunglasses I was surprised at the age and sorrow in his eyes. He said, "That's your boat, isn't it, down the dock."

"It is."

"Then listen to me, Rainy. You get back on it and don't dick around. You head straight out. Get far from land. Nobody wants to go out there, maybe they'll let you be." At my blank expression he continued, "These out-of-staters are not to be confronted. They belong to astronauts. Whatever you did, they noticed."

This turn of events was nearly as alarming as the sight of Apeknuckle himself. It was as if he'd mistaken me for a friend.

"Officer," I said. "Can you tell me what I did? They—" My face stung. I couldn't say Lark's name. "They tore up my house. This morning people shot at me. If you know what's going on, I wish you'd say."

"You stole a thing from someone large."

"I swear to you I didn't. They knocked holes in my walls. I don't have one idea what they want. Maybe I should wait for them and ask."

Apeknuckle shook his head. "I believe you, but they won't. What they'll do is hurt you. Whatever you don't give them they'll take out of your bones."

"I did nothing. It's a mistake."

At my authentic confusion Apeknuckle shook his head and pinched the bridge of his nose. "You got to leave. At least two of them saw you from shore—"

"Right, they shot at me, they put a hole in my sail—"

"And they're on their way here, with others. You get on that boat. You cast off and you head straight out."

I nodded but didn't move.

"You're still standing here," he said.

"Why are you helping me this way?"

"Well, come on now," said Apeknuckle. "Tonio thinks you spin the world."

It took me a second to place the familiar name. "Tonio?" Saying it brought it clear: Tonio's large head, his heavy lower lip, the sense of life stomping hope day after day after day. Run Apeknuckle back in time you'd get Tonio to the letter.

I said, "Tonio's a great kid."

Apeknuckle looked down. His voice shied away. "You head down to your boat now and disappear. That outboard isn't going to move you very fast. I don't know how much time I can get you."

I set down the gas cans and reached in my pocket, found the little blues harp in the key of E. "You give this to Tonio. I'm not going to see him for a while. He'll like it. Tell him to practice and Mr. Rainy will give him a lesson next time I see him."

Apeknuckle turned his face and held out his hand. I placed the harmonica in his palm, then picked up the cans and fairly sprinted down to what was now my home on Earth. I started the motor and let it idle while undoing the dock lines, coiling and stowing them once *Flower* was pushing through calm water toward the gloom offshore. Only then did I look back at the dock. I did not see the frightening small woman or the tall beaky man with his military sweater, but the thought arrived that all anyone had to do to find me was drive along the coast glancing casually lakeward. My getaway vehicle had a maximum speed of seven miles per hour and could be seen eight miles away.

I missed the eggs and the bread and the oranges and coffee I didn't have, but it was the ravioli that hurt. Its briny flavor with notes of beef and tin.

The light slumped, the breeze freshened. In the east was a distant anvil cloud that would probably come for me later. What I wanted more than ravioli was for someone else to take the lead. Somebody with solo chops, like Lark or Robin Hood. With no such thoroughbred on hand it was only me, and a shaky protagonist I made—scared and starving, pushed by a whining insect outboard onto the blackening deep.

~ *the garment was occupied*

A CHOICE was now presented.

In the night I had thought of a rational plan. It rested on sensible people. I could sail southwest to Duluth, arrive in a day or two. Lark and I maintained relationships there—the painter who employed me had come to see us in Icebridge, a man of compassion who'd worked for attorneys and judges. Lark knew people from her library days, friends who knew the pulse of neighborhoods and often met her when she drove down to scout a cache. Among these I was certain to find counsel, advice, some kind of help—at worst, a ride in somebody's car with a hat pulled over my eyes.

No—at worst, I would contact a friend and by doing so put them in immediate jeopardy.

I tried to reason it through. My headache was gone, the morning was calm, the sun two fingers high. Hazy green hills lit up to the north.

Light scattered itself on the wavelets. The breeze was cool and easy from the west.

In that moment I seemed to know what would happen.

Maybe I tricked myself, with help from the weather. Probably I thought—like the lucky ones do—that the lake was on my side. Hadn't it bailed me out already? Saved me with storm and fog?

I seemed to know I would reach the Slates, if that were the way I chose. Once there I would throw down the anchor and wait for Lark to find her way. Whether she did was not up to me—still, if the dead and redoubtable Molly Thorn could do it, it followed Lark could too. The electrifying idea took hold that she might be there already—waiting, in the same still harbor we'd entered as two and emerged from days later as one.

That was my shimmering state of mind. Call it foolish or snakebit, call me unwound by hunger and grief. Up came the breeze at a pleasant ten knots. I raised the main and hanked on the jib. I blame or credit the sun for this, and its friend the temperate breeze.

And a decent going I had of it. In all my time on that violent sea these were the easiest hours, with smoky light and winds moderate past belief. The compass was imprecise so I sailed by best guess, with an eye on the western hills tracing the sun's trajectory and lashing the helm to sleep. After nearly two days a tree line separated itself from gray horizon. Binoculars suggested an island. I trimmed for its southernmost tip and reached it as the sun dropped behind the mainland. The wind declining I coasted along, nearing the shore, lowering a weight to find the depth. All those years ago Lark and I passed an ancient great island known as Royal and once protected as a park. The rocks at its southern tip rose up like horns in the mist.

For the first time in days I knew where I was.

I threw down the anchor and dined on cheese.

~

Next day slid past like the island itself.

A flock of small birds rose out of the trees moving together like smoke, while a heron or egret stood in the shallows intoning dark notes. At first light, *Flower* catching a breeze, I saw the back of a mighty fish breach the surface alongside.

I got out the chart book and *Folsum's Anchorages*. I was now formally in Canadian waters. There was an X on the chart and the word *Fremling*, identified by Folsum as the name of a ship that wrecked here in the 1920s. A small freighter converted like many of the day from sail to steam. It came from Belgium with a load of tinned fish and comestibles and six Icelandic horses stabled belowdecks. The horses were small and mean from the crossing—they'd been purchased by a trader in Thunder Bay whose daughter had "fallen under the spell of the breed's large eyes and wanton manes." Folsum is worth reading for the footnotes alone. The *Fremling* discharged sardines in Duluth and took on hard winter wheat from the Dakotas, then refueled and headed for Thunder Bay only to meet a northeasterly gale that arrived with pockets full and made the horses buckle in their stalls. Reaching the island behind me, the ship sought shelter in the main channel, but the gale was clever and switched directions, trying this and that point of compass, finally settling in the southwest and mashing the *Fremling* against a bedrock column until it burst open, spreading a layer of wheat over the churning water. Of twenty crew just one survived the wreck, a young Italian sailor who remembered the horses and opened their stalls as the water rose around them. He caught hold of a mare who carried him to safety on the island, where he was rescued days later by salvagers who wondered whence these irritable ponies came.

Passing the pile of rock on which the *Fremling* had foundered, I compared that ship's hard luck with my own. The lake had turned gold and romantic. The mainland was all treed Canadian hillsides, mist rising out of them like pleasing thoughts above the hard work required to live there. As the day passed I ate most of the hard salty cheese, a thirsty diet. In former days, people drank straight from the lake but no longer. Erik had left me a manual filter he said would remove all manmade pollutants plus giardia; every hour or two I'd pump a pint of potable water and drink it with a slab of cheese.

While looking at charts I checked the Slates, still long days away.

When the lake was calm and beautiful, as now, its wavelets patterned with shifting ovals, I fully expected to reach the Slates intact, and for Lark also to find her way through whatever navigation her current self could access. But when the weather turned, with early darkness and warlike clouds and confusion at the edges, then I became agnostic on the subject of Lark's spectral return and downbeat about the boat itself let alone my ability to pilot her to a clutch of islands I saw once fifteen years ago. There were times it seemed impossible.

All that day I worked up the channel. All day the sky was clear and the sun convivial and distant trees swayed in profligate beauty. I began to feel quite sentimental toward *Flower*. What a stout small craft she was. I was not much sailor nor navigator yet she'd protected me in all conditions. Look at her move, reaching along on a mild southeasterly, telltales streaming like pennants from the shrouds.

Gradually, the big island gray-greened into the past while new ones bristled up forward, bouldery steeps not shown on the chart. When a great pedestal of striated rock stood up in the north, I had to stand myself. An island of majesty like a raised fist. The sail went slack entering its wind shadow. Carried forward by momentum I saw Lark for one long moment in the island's craggy sheer. What I mean is her face took shape in the ancient stone as I drifted slowly past. Her eyes were shadows, her lips ridges softened by distance, her hair a sweep of climbing firs. I held her gaze like holy fire until a puff of wind arrived and moved us on. My position on the surface changed. I exhaled, and she was gone.

I anchored that night beneath a low headland some miles from Thunder Bay. The city was not visible but its light gathered softly in the northern sky. After checking the anchor chain I went below and turned in early intending to sleep through the hunger. Incidentally this never works. In that gentle anchorage I woke from dreams of bread breaking open in steam, of ripe pears piled on a wooden table. The last of the cheese sat in loose wax—I could reach it from my bunk—but no. I remembered now that Harry the drummer once ate only cheese for a month. Part of a ritual or propitiation condoned by a secret order he aspired to join. The price of admission was a constipation crisis in which his midnight screams startled the neighbors. All this to achieve entry into yet another brotherhood of disappointing secrets. Eventually I unblanketed the bass guitar and played there in the unlit cabin—nothing complicated, just running slow scales, the old pentatonic liturgy up and down the board. Nothing took shape in my imagination, no ideas presented themselves, but my stomach did seem to quiet. Watery moonlight glimmered through the ports, the music settled around me like rest.

I was about to set the instrument aside and try again to sleep when something thumped quietly against the hull. Up went my neck hairs, but almost immediately there was a second soft thump, then a third. Warmth surged inside me. My seagull friends were back! I wondered if they took some comfort in low tones, maybe deep tremors were a kind of avian invitation. Sure enough as I continued to play, almost like replies came a series of little knocks and brushes, along with the minute greetings of wavelets running along the hull. Taking care this time, lest I frighten them, I went to the overhead hatch and opened it slightly to peer out.

Not a gull in sight.

Yet the soft knocking persisted.

Taking a flashlight I slid back the hatch and went on deck. Nothing took flight. Out in the rapidly cooling air the muted thumps sounded more solid. I eased forward casting the beam along the hull. Driftwood, that's what I expected. A bit of shoreline rubbish dislodged by recent waves.

Then something in the water caught and held the light. A blackened coat or garment. It bobbed slightly and my insides shifted.

The garment was occupied.

A corpse lay face down on the water, one elbow slightly raised as though to ask permission.

Nudged by a wavelet its head bumped *Flower* gently at the waterline.

When the drowned began to rise twenty years earlier—as grumpy climate sage Holloway predicted—we seasiders were advised to prepare ourselves. Something like ten thousand persons were estimated to be lying on the Superior floor, sifting to and fro across the centuries. As the sea warmed, a percentage of these were bound to reappear. I'd encountered three myself—four, now. First and least horrid an old man who tumbled ashore near the town of Ishpeming on Whitefish Bay, where I was visiting a girl I already knew was not for me. All night a northeast gale had kicked shingles off her bungalow and we stayed in, making gumbo and dancing to music I should've liked but didn't. In the morning we walked along a beach, dodging milk jugs, nail-studded plywood, herring floats, a hump of twisted netting. The old man looked right at home. A fastidious side sleeper on the damp sand. His coat was buttoned with a navy collar and his shoes were sewn leather. My first returnee, and yes, I held it together—took a step back but didn't twitch or puke, didn't run away. Meantime the girl, I forget her name, was a pragmatic veteran. A northeast blow always brought a few up. Ah well. Disturbing rictus aside, this oldster was harmless. She'd had boyfriends who came home looking worse.

I never got used to them in quite that way. In fact I went the other direction. My second was a woman whose bare heels were all you saw at first. There they bobbed in the shallows. I thought grief would swallow me alive. Weeks later and still worse came the drowned girl on the Wisconsin shore. She couldn't have been ten years old, rolling up in the whitecaps near the Brule River mouth. What was I even doing there? Fishing for trout I guess. The girl's dress had kittens on it, an archaic print. She sank during Eisenhower. I wept to see her but kept my distance. Drove to town and found a deputy who got ugly fast. "Why didn't you deal with it?" he demanded. There were protocols by then: in the United States, the finder of a risen corpse was obliged to resink it, using whatever concrete or scrap steel came to hand. The law counted on citizens to do their part! "Were you *afraid*?" said the deputy. I looked away. Maybe it's silly to fear the risen drowned but look at one close. The most benign have accusation in their postures. Above all else I didn't want to touch one or, far worse, be touched. Off marched the indignant badge with his close-set eyes. I ought not've told him. I ought've known. Within days the hard-shell fundies had photos published, pamphlets raising money. The drowned girl was further proof of their convictions. *Carpe finis.* A faceless innocent in a kitten dress washes up and your cherished Armageddon must be imminent indeed.

The corpse knocked again at the hull. I took the long-handled boat hook and shoved it away. Not too hard—didn't want it to roll over and show its teeth. It drifted off ten or twelve feet and came to rest. I went below but of course the corpse was all I could think about. Not him exactly—not his life or his death, perhaps he'd gone down with the *Fremling*, who could say—no, what clutched my mind was the simple corporeal horror he contained. I was past any teenage dread that he might pop open empty sockets and come climbing awkwardly unstoppably aboard, but wasn't it terrifying enough that he was simply out there? Patient as the moon, with his bent elbow and museum clothes, a few yards from where I sat shivering under every blanket I owned?

In the end I climbed out in the cockpit to wait for dawn, waking abruptly when a pair of vocal early ravens lit on the beach. By then the corpse had drifted off thirty yards or so. A big mossy snapping turtle had climbed up between the shoulder blades and was getting a little rest.

A light breeze started from the south. I raised anchor and mainsail and was not sad to leave that fellow sleeping in my wake.

~ *our bright & zippy Kellan*

MY MONEY was no good in Thunder Bay.

The sun was straight up and the skyline looming when a tented market appeared on a green commons rising off the lake. Kids booted a ball around near the tents, which were striped and patched. Smoke drifted off braziers and barrel stoves. I'd been hungry long enough to nearly forget it but grilled chicken will remind you in a hurry. I struck the sails and motored toward a long metal dock, damning my putzy outboard. All the way in I was tormented by imagined interlopers buying my chicken and eating it all.

At last I bumped sideways into the dock and tied up to cleats fore and aft before trotting up to the market. I'd got the cashbox out of the gimbled oven and grabbed some bills. My nose led straight to the grills and braziers where locals lined up for what to them was a casual lunch. I joined the shortest line and when my turn came ordered one whole chicken with vegetables. A short man lifted the lid of a hinged barrel and smoke piled out as I handed over some bills.

"Can't take these," he said and stepped back from my expression. I was dizzy and half mad with hunger. He explained, "That's US money, friend."

I'd forgot it was Canada. I asked was there a currency exchange and he pointed at a canopy down the row.

"Save me a chicken."

He didn't answer but met my eyes with concern. He was younger than me with bristly black hair and a wide face I wanted to trust. "Next," he said.

The place he'd pointed out wasn't a currency exchange. It was a pawnshop, with the usual desperate collection of cracked screens, leather jackets, skateboards and wheel covers along with trumpets and guitars and battered amps. These gave me an idea and I galloped back to the boat ignoring leashed dogs and one braying child telling his mother I ran "like a stupid." In five minutes I was back at the pawn tent proclaiming the efficacy of my teensy amplifier, built by an actual genius named Bruce who used to sell at the Greenstone Fair. As gear goes it was comically small. The broker looked it over with a dubious expression.

"It's pretty beat up," he said.

"It delivers tonally."

"There's a ding."

"Cosmetic."

"Appearance matters," the broker primly maintained, pointing at the dented casing.

The fingertips of his left hand were calloused in a way I recognized. It was also true that every guitar in that grungy tent was clean, while his laptops and hunting-dog oil paintings were blurry with dust.

"Tell me," I said, "what's under the counter at the moment?"

His tone changed. He regarded me anew, then reached below the countertop and produced a fairly stellar Epiphone hollow-body guitar. The vaunted Les Paul copy. A gaudy blue deepening to the edge of night. The broker handled it with adoration. I didn't touch but bent over where it lay on a soft cloth next to the register.

"You can't afford it," he said.

"Probably not. But I'd like to hear it."

There was no one else at his tent just then except a greasy preteen looking at a Japanese telescope. The broker slung on the guitar while I set the tiny amp on the counter and plugged him into it.

"I see what you're up to," he said.

"Just noodle around for a minute."

He did. He was good but not as good as the amp made him sound. Unable to disguise his pleasure the broker ran off five or six riffs you would recognize, then a few of his own. He had nice clean technique. If he sounded that good to me then to himself he played like a deathless god.

"This amp is not bad," he said when his long last note decayed to silence. "What exactly is it?"

"Modified Strauss micro."

"Modified how?"

I had no idea. Bruce was a wizard whose knowledge of circuitry and reverb made and lost two or three coastal fortunes back in legitimate days.

The broker tapped the amp thoughtfully while I looked over at the food queue. It made me nervous. The queue was long. Few chickens remained. The bristle-haired man watched us with his unreadable square face. When the broker made his offer I instantly accepted. Yes, I was hungry, but I am also a sorry negotiator. Lark was the negotiator. I left the broker's tent with a short stack of Canada money.

He'd saved me a chicken—the bristly man. He handed it over in a paper carton. I carried it to a bench and ate the whole bird with my fingers, plus a baked potato with butter and salt.

Here is what I bought with my colorful dollars at the grocer's tent after I had cleaned my hands and taken a few long breaths and possibly slept sitting up on the bench for a minute or two.

Three dozen eggs in a box of crushed paper
One pale squash as hard as maple
A shingle of bacon wrapped in foil
A bag of onions and another of potatoes
A dozen cans of beans
Twenty pounds of ice

As I was picking these out the air turned cool. Midafternoon and the lake had something in mind. A black cloud island had formed on the east horizon. As I watched it rose lifting a column of rain. While the boy I'd hired pushed my stuff along in a painted handcart we passed a service station and I told him to go ahead to the dock. Like the station in Lightner this one had a display of harmonicas, and I bought another cheapie and a laminated map showing the coast of Ontario in detail. "Sailor?" said the woman at the counter. She was old and mostly blind.

"Yes."

"Where you going?"

"Slate Islands," I replied, which seemed to please her. She was from the town of Gold in Ontario and wondered had I seen it or where it used to be. I'd read about Gold in the *Mosquito* and didn't believe the story for a second—a whole small city lost when its bedrock foundation split like ice and everything slid into the sea: streets and lampposts, an abandoned cannery, mining and city offices and churches and union hall, almost two thousand citizens swallowed at once at the end of a five-day gale. I asked had she been there when it happened and she said God had arranged for her to be away, the way he'd eased Lot out of Sodom. She rang up my purchases and counted out my change with sightless accuracy. While she did so I glanced over at a bulletin board under the front window. It was full of missing persons. Daughters mostly and grown women but also some men. Everyone up-tempo in these photos yet missing all the same. What leapt at me was the rooster hair. I'd forgotten entirely that Kellan was headed for Thunder Bay, or had claimed he was until we sidetracked him. He had family nearby. It was never clear exactly who, an uncle or great-uncle or much older brother. The story changed. There on a poster was Kellan looking hopeful and funny and above all overconfident in a picture a dozen years old. My insides turned complicated at the sight of him. Below his photo was written in neat blue ink:

> *Kell, brother and son.*
> *Please call we miss you.*
> *Anyone if you've seen our bright & zippy Kellan take a moment tell us where.*

On the counter was the usual wire rack of recycled cells. I bought one. A small smooth oval like a stone at the beach. It came with fifteen minutes of talk—if you lucked into working transmission—and about that much battery life. I took the harmonica and laminated map and hustled down to the dock where the boy waited with my handcart of food and ice. Paying him took my last paper money, leaving only a few coins in my pocket. I loaded the icebox before starting the outboard and casting off. The cloud island was nearer in the east. Behind me the sun shone on the hillsides and flashed off the windows of Thunder Bay.

It took a little time to make the call.

I had to work up to it.

If it were my brother or son gone missing, I'd want to talk with those who knew him, who cared about him and wanted him to be all right. Of course I had nothing on his whereabouts. All I could offer was my witness. Kellan was likable and I liked him. He was honest when it pleased him. He had a knack for the nick of time.

I didn't want to blame him, yet if not for Kellan, Lark's life would still be happening—at home in Icebridge, hunting down caches and running her bookshop, expanding her beanfield, conversing in her sleep.

Bettering the world by being in it.

If not for Kellan her life would be ongoing and my own would still make sense.

The mainsail rattled up easily, and I turned off the engine. A breeze meandered up out of the south and we aimed east across it, outward again, toward the black cloud dragging its tail of rain.

I dialed the number from Kellan's poster. It rang four times, five, six. I imagined a man in middle age, interrupted in his garden or field, patting his pockets. His hands would be gnarled and his voice gruff and heartbroken.

"Hello—who's calling, please."

An older man and not what I expected—not bereft or bedraggled. Not sad in the least.

"Who is it then?" he asked briskly. "Come on."

"Friend of Kellan," I said, but warily. Had I heard this voice before? A grim joke was slowly dawning.

"Ah. Ah! I hoped you would call. It's Rainy, isn't it?"

It was that filth, Werryck.

I will credit him with the sentimental poster. Who knew he had the low-tech wherewithal to write "our bright & zippy Kellan" and dangle it for the credulous to find?

I pushed Cancel. Four seconds later the cell rang in my hand. It sounded like a low whistle or birdcall. No doubt it was meant to be pleasant. I refused the call and steered outward. Mist rose off the water thick as cream.

Another whistle from the cell. I ignored it. *Flower* moved steadily along in the near-silent breeze. Through a gap in the fog, lightning paced back and forth in the east.

After some time the cell beckoned again. This time I answered.

"I'm sorry to be the voice you don't wish to hear," Werryck said. "I don't blame you. I also mean you no harm and bear you no animus."

"Well, I bear you some."

"I regret what happened to Lark," he said. "I implore you to believe me. It was not by design."

It made me livid—her name in his voice. The boat heeled as I got to my feet. "*Not by design.* How can you stand yourself? I found her on the floor. I saw the hammer and saw what it did. It was not by accident."

"I understand how this must look to you," Werryck said.

"You understand nothing."

"I can tell you," he said in a tone of hard-won patience, "that the man responsible has been punished."

This contention—that something like justice had been done on Lark's behalf—made me dizzy with outrage. My sight grayed and sparked at the edges. I sat down and gripped the tiller as if it were sanity.

Werryck said, "After you slipped away from Lightner I realized you may not understand why we tried to speak with you."

"No one tried speaking that I recall."

He cleared his throat, an aggrieved sound. "I accept your resentment, but we have to reach an understanding on this man

Kellan. He stayed with you for some time, and now we need to find him."

"He rented a room. That's it."

"Let me clarify something. Give you context. I assume you've heard of the therapeutic known as Willow."

"'Therapeutic.'"

"Kellan worked on the production floor. He disinfected equipment is my understanding. Centrifuges, granulators. The assembly of pharmaceuticals is not my zone of interest. Your friend Kellan overrates his cleverness but has a talent for the easy lift. He is light-fingered but empty-headed. I expect you glimpsed this in some way."

He took my silence for affirmation.

"You wouldn't guess it, but Willow was an accident. Researchers attempting something else arrived at this instead. Lo and behold, demand is high. Had this outworker simply vanished, I'd never have heard his name. Every day they vanish. But your friend nicked ten thousand doses on his way out the door."

I sat at the tiller and looked up at the sail quietly pulling us along.

Werryck said, "You liked him, didn't you. Saw him as essentially good. You should know that the doses he stole comprise a nearly infinite bank account from which he is already drawing."

"How so?"

"Remember his car? The one you helped repair?"

I did.

"He bought it with Willow. Got cheated, from the sound of it."

Again I had nothing to say.

"Remember talking to those kids in Lightner?" he said. "The ones outside the church, perturbed about the suicides? Kellan sold those folks the stuff."

"I never took him for some blameless urchin," I said, but my voice was a forgery. Of course I'd taken him for blameless. I'd insisted on it, proud quixote that I was.

"Your old friend Labrino was another happy customer."

"You can stop, Werryck."

"You think I am cruel to say these things. No. I'm relieving you of the need to defend him."

"I'm not defending Kellan. I'm just not helping you."

"Then help yourself instead."

I waited.

"Give me something useful. A location. Any plans he talked about. His blue-sky dreams. And you will not be charged."

"Charged with what?"

"Oh, Rainy. Harboring a fugitive. Fleeing from authorities. Trading annulled currency. You'd be shocked how little of your life is legal. And yet I have the authority and will to absolve you. To vanish your indictments. Return to Icebridge, Rainy. Play music with your striving band. A small world is better than none."

As if sweetening the pot he added, "I'll see that repairs are made to your house. We believed the therapeutics were stashed there. My crew became aggressive in their search."

I hadn't thought of the house in days. Everything I loved there—its steep staircases and odd angles and the lives we had inside it for twelve years—had fled my memory. Instead what blazed to mind was the place as I drove by that last night, its windows lit and its rooms ripped up. The red-faced man standing in my doorway, pointing at me with his swaddled hand and his personal hatred.

"Take the offer, Rainy. We'll never be friends but in this we're allies. Kellan is the reason Lark is gone. The reason you're on a boat, alone, and snow coming."

"What snow," I couldn't help asking.

"The system forming over western Manitoba. I'm looking at it now. Heavy snow, cyclonic winds. It looks like a map of invasion. Are you ready for it, Rainy?"

"You don't know where I am," I said.

"It hardly matters. I've seen the lake stand up and throw a thousand-foot freighter against its chains. How long would Lark want you bumbling around on that filthy sea?"

"You clearly didn't know her."

"Get off the water and come home. She'd want you to be practical," he added, an observation so ignorant it helped to settle my mind.

"Werryck, listen. You say Kellan isn't clever. Go find him then, and leave me be."

As I spoke the breeze picked up. The boat heeled ten degrees and stayed heeled. The watery slipstream hissed alongside.

"All you can do out there is die."

"Then we won't talk again."

"You can't thwart me, Rainy."

He had something else to say but I don't know what it was. The cell with its beach-stone feel inspired me. I curled my index finger round its top and reared back. Werryck quacked spasmodically as it ricocheted over the waves.

~ *the Great Girard*

IN THE EARLY HOURS I saw what the blind clerk had asked me about—a cut in the shoreline, a perched water tower on a height of land, then what looked like a slanted bowl in the earth, as if a scoop descended to remove with stark precision some hundreds of acres. Inevitably the event was spoken of in prophetic terms, and many wondered what grave and sensual pleasures brought judgment to Gold, Ontario. But then maybe it was simply a pattern of relentless gales, the sea pounding and shoving and shouldering across the millennia until everything loosened, foundations below foundations. Even bedrock wearies at last. In the *Mosquito* account, the first witness to trouble was an ancient dog keening into the night, a white-muzzled hound leaning against a screen door, howling and howling, triggering any number of similar alarms through the community, screeching cats, a braying backyard donkey, every local citizen of the animal kingdom understanding at some level a tectonic slippage as yet undiscernible to human equilibrium. Then people began to stir, their beds tilting up as if on a sinking ship, wakeful husbands lit by open refrigerators where leftover drumsticks slid eerily away from their reaching fingers, the creak and stretch of plumbing, a final mighty electrical surge detonating transformers in glorious sequence before the world went black and floors turned to freezing mud unlike any in your memory or mine. The remaining wide basin presented itself as I sailed away from Thunder Bay on a five-knot breeze, a full moon displaying the blue-gray hollowed landscape. Once a suffering Great Lakes town, now a ghost amphitheater. I stood on the foredeck holding the port shroud. When the place faded aft I went below and fixed a can of beans in a frying pan and broke an egg into it and carried it into the cockpit.

As if to counter the despair thrown off by the lost city of Gold, the dark water then gave me two days' slow but lovely progress. I think the sea has no in-between: you get either rage and wayward lightning and schizoid frenzy or such freehanded beauty that time contracts or turns in on itself leaving you forgetful and no more civilized than a gull. In this way *Flower* and I poked and drifted in idle drafts up the coast of Ontario, past the entrance to Nipigon and up the Black Bay Peninsula. The sun flared and I got down to sleeves. The keel hummed easily over depths so clear boulders forty feet down shone like pebbles you might lean over the side to pluck. The northerly breeze smelled of spruce marshes and occasionally of damp smoke, which made me feel safe and fully forgotten. We thought we were remote in Icebridge and took some pride in that, but here along the fifty-mile volcanic stone peninsula I saw neither roads nor buildings, no emblem of human ambition or discord. That night I slipped into a primeval cleft and anchored in water still as sky. Boiled a potato and ate it with salt and a little oil, then slept in the cockpit to the booming cry of a heron. In a dream this bird surfaced as a godlike sentry guarding the entrance to the Slates. In a resonant croak it allowed me to enter. And when I sailed out again, Lark was aboard smiling and took the helm without a word. With her at the tiller I took the lines and winches. This episode was as real as the gash on my chin. The pain of waking can't be told. I sat up uttering a lament of my own that traveled over the water in a vanishing decay.

The night was translucent, the surface unrippled under fading stars. I tried to imagine the Tashi Comet, to picture where in the sky it might appear. It was comforting somehow, this clump of ice on long approach. Maybe because it was old and reliable. Just cruising through on a route it knew well, each cycle billions of miles, maybe hundreds of years. A swing past Earth wasn't even the highlight of its day! A calm came over me. My first teacher, the droll bass player Diego, said all of us were ancient beyond knowledge. By *us* he meant people and animals, rocks and seas, the stars and all the night between them. He said music woke everything up, back in the beginning, uncountable eons ago.

That day I crossed turquoise deeps under black stone cliffs. Those who imagine themselves alone on tragic planets understand the allure of desolation. A line of horsetail clouds gusted overhead in a tanbark color for which *Instant Forecasting* had no precise correlative. My best guess was an imminent blow, and within an hour a microburst came crackling over the surface. The boat was on her side before I could react. The rigging whined. The mast rang like a cracked bell and shifted in its boot. When the squall passed we returned to vertical with dripping mainsail and a strange new slackness aloft. Something had given way. Below was a scramble of books and flung pans. Sure enough one of the worrisome chainplates had cracked. I laid my palm against it—depleted steel flaking away—then took down the sails to relieve the old spar of as much load as possible.

But *Flower* was badly shaken. Even when I'd got things mostly back in place, the mast trembled as it hadn't before, and there was a new noise to worry about—a maddening clank-and-roll I couldn't track down. If I stood forward, it sounded aft; when I went aft, the clanking leapfrogged forward. I tried to ignore it, but as hours passed it got on my nerves—a stealthy lodger up to something, one I could not catch.

The chart book showed a town a dozen miles east. Jolie. The name rang because Lark and I had intended to stop there after leaving the Slates. We never did, I don't remember why. What was Jolie now? A phantom town? Another moon crater? *Folsum's Anchorages* mentioned a cafe and recommended its specialty pancakes, but Ernest Folsum was sixty years in the ground. Lashing the tiller I putted along the coast whose unseemly beauty of an hour ago now appeared forbidding. With a sound boat and sunshine, the world is yours. Now the boat clattered in residual swells and clouds jammed the northwest.

In the late shadows I limped into Jolie, easing through a slumping breakwater to the deserted dock, which had a sign on it saying: TRANSIENTS PAY AT OFFICE.

If an office existed I couldn't find it. I walked up into the streets as night fell. A closed cafe with chairs overturned. An old shake-shingled Canada Post bungalow. A redbrick cube with an ornate ICE & BAIT sign and a tufted dog curled in front of the door. The dog lifted its head as I passed but was diffident when I held out a hand. I walked into the center of the town's main intersection and stood a long time. A percussive rhythm somewhere suggested music, but I was tired and the rhythm was far away. I returned to the boat and slept.

In the morning I scrubbed my face, cautious about my chin which felt large and tender. My hair was long and looked like bad weather so I pulled it back and tried the town again. The cafe was open. It had a different name than in Folsum's day but a good pancake smell. I hadn't enough money for pancakes but found enough coins for coffee and an order of toast.

While waiting I saw a recent *Mosquito* in an empty booth and snagged it. There'd been more Willow suicides. A pair of lovelorn teenagers in Iowa. A homeless family sheltering in an abandoned Salvation Army store. A youth group aged eleven to fourteen were found by their pastor when he arrived at church in the morning. He was quoted, weeping, that he had no idea, only knew these earnest kids had a desire to go in search of better.

These stories struck harder now. I couldn't read the whole paper. Much as I wanted to think of Lark in someplace better, I knew from a thousand conversations that she never worried about that place. Maybe it was real and full of saints and poets, or maybe it was poetry itself. Her concern was *this* place. This animal world with its unfurling dread and convulsive wars and fabricated certainties, and its breathtaking storms across the water. With Willow infiltrating the landscape and its stories coming thick and fast—these explorers getting younger and more innocent—I felt desperate to reach through time. I wanted to find these kids in a moment of calm. To take their lapels gently in my hands and say, "Better is right here." I still hear it in Lark's voice. *Better is here. Stay, and make it better.*

My breakfast arrived. The girl brought it with a generous side of peanut butter and I choked up trying to thank her. She was a big, kind, dark-haired girl not afraid to approach a haggard stranger with a seeping chin wound. She asked if that were my boat at the dock and then volunteered that there was a grocery in town, a gas station, and a man who sewed canvas and could repair sails. When I asked could anyone fashion me a piece of steel and held out my hands in the desired dimensions, she described a welding shop on the north edge of town. It would be open by the time I finished my toast. Lark's theory of angels was that they are us and we mostly don't remember.

The welder was a woman named Stevie who built trailers of various sizes and repaired skidders and knuckleboom loaders for logging operations nearby. She had a pile of heavy steel from a fire tower she'd decommissioned and was willing to cut my dimensions and drill holes, even supply me with bolts. I explained about no money and she sensibly wondered what I might have to barter. Anticipating this I'd carried up in a duffel some items I had on the boat—a hundred-foot power cord in good condition, an effects pedal, two extra-long quarter-inch cords. Now that I had no amplifier these things were useless to me.

"Musician," Stevie observed.

"Electric bass."

It seemed to me her focus narrowed.

"How long are you in town?"

"Depends on the steel."

She then said, "How long since you played?"

This was Stevie's proposition: there was a man in town, Nils, a father and ex-convict dying fast of cancer. A few of Nils's friends, Stevie among them, had organized a fundraiser for his family two nights hence. Stevie had volunteered the entertainment—her daughter was the de facto leader of a local band called the Indolent Vagrants, a name so beguiling I leaned forward involuntarily. The Vagrants played whatever they liked. They had a keyboardist who'd almost toured Europe decades ago with a Scandinavian supergroup whose name I don't remember. They had a self-taught drummer with drone-core roots and a bagpipe maestro who didn't always show up but was thought to be the most proficient rock piper in Canada. Coming to the point, Stevie explained they also used to have an adequate bass player, popular at gigs for dressing like a stork or plague doctor, but this fellow had fallen in with a gloomy cult and renounced all music, preferring to cruise around collaring infidels and browbeating the merry. Stevie asked would I be willing to play the Nils benefit, and I agreed before the question cooled.

At this point a man entered the shop. He wore a clean white shirt and glasses so heavy he seemed to hold his head at an angle of discomfort to support them. Stevie excused herself, went into a back room and emerged with a tabletop radio. It was compact and substantial, encased in hardwood. She handed it over and the man hefted it admiringly and made a play for his billfold, but Stevie said no, he owed her nothing. He nodded as though used to this and began to speak, then his eyes fell on me and clouded behind his heavy glasses.

"What happened to your face there?"

"A rope and a high wind."

"May I look at it?"

Stevie said, "Doc, this fellow arrived last night by sailboat."

"I wondered whose that was," said this clean-shirted customer who did not pay for radios. He had an odd, clipped way of speaking. He came over and peered up into my face. Took off his glasses and put them on again. I bent over a little so he could get a closer look.

"How much does it bother."

"Quite a bit."

"It will get worse, left alone."

"I do clean it."

"What with?"

"Boiled water." I didn't always boil it.

"What's your name?"

"Rainy."

"Rainy, I'm Girard. The boiled water is not efficacious. Your infection is traveling. Finish here, then come down to the house."

I hesitated. I had spent the last of my change on coffee and toast.

He said, "You can see my place from your boat. There's a balcony with a stripy umbrella overlooking a garden. The garden's out of hand."

"Can't pay you," I said.

He made a gesture of impatience.

"He's a musician, Doc," said Stevie. "Maybe he'll sing you a song."

The doctor's house was high-ceilinged with worn floors and neglected plaster. His wife was not home. Forthcoming as Girard had been at the welding shop, he was that subdued and circumspect inside his painted office. He sat me down in a chair by the window, applied anesthetic to my swollen wound and got right in there with probes and tweezers. He seemed thorough and also distracted, locked away somehow, speaking quietly to himself in phrases I didn't comprehend. He asked no questions other than my age.

I said, "You are kind to see me this way."

"If you say so. How long will you be in town?"

I told him about my agreement with Stevie and the Vagrants. This seemed to lift his spirits. Dying Nils was a patient of his. He worried what would happen to the family after Nils moved on—to his wife, working half-time for Canada Post, and their two girls nine and seven, the younger with vague frailties Girard did not detail.

"Any kids of your own?" he asked.

"No."

He sat back having disinfected and bandaged my wound.

"By choice or circumstance?" He grimaced at the indelicacy of his question.

Like everyone our age, Lark and I had worn ourselves thin over the risks of introducing another life into generalized decay. She was the optimist, pointing at the bookshelf she'd already stocked with Pooh and Piglet, Sinbad, Despereaux, Charlotte, the Wild Things, Ratty and Mole. She'd also hand-painted a favorite Molly Thorn verse in graceful gold lettering running along the ceiling trim of her bookshop.

Who will ransom earth and water?
What new son or what new daughter?
Who will make of many, one?
What new daughter? What new son?

I was more cautious than Lark and less eloquent than Molly. In the end it didn't matter.

"We weren't able," I said.

The doctor nodded. Suddenly upbeat he slapped his knees and got to his feet. "All right then, come meet Evelyn."

I stayed two nights at the doctor's house. His wife was an urban farmer and I never saw her empty-handed—they were full of squash when I met her, from the tousled garden that ran up off its plot weaving vines and tendrils onto the porch and up the legs of benches and a serpentine pedestal on which she fed the birds. She harvested each day the corn or carrots or tomatoes that the doctor roasted with wine or vinegar supplied by their next-door neighbor who had a stern little vineyard of cold-weather grapes. Girard kept an eye on my cut chin, changing the dressings twice daily. He said in another week it would've turned. "Were you hoping to die?" he demanded. "You and your boiled water? Did you wish to die of septic face blight?"

"No."

"No," he agreed in an ominous tone.

That first evening I helped clean up after supper while Evelyn filled five or six paper sacks full of veg from the patch—onions, chard, beans of several varieties, also dill and basil and other herbs. These bags she stacked outside the door. While we visited and sipped from a variety of unnamed congenials, people approached, calling hello and thank you, waving to Evelyn through the screen, walking away with a sack. While this went on Girard told in compact sentences how the two of them met. He was on a cycling journey around Superior, with a sleeping bag and panniers full of rice and jerky. It was a dangerous time. There'd been drought for two years following a season of floods and biting insects. Drinking-water hostilities had led to a series of kidnappings and unresolved murders. If you saw someone on the road you kept your distance. Girard went anyway since he fancied himself athletic and fearless. Even then he was close to blind but off he went on a Raleigh fifty-pounder with a Sturmey-Archer three-speed hub. He planned to go a hundred miles a day for as long as it took, as a kind of induction or preparation for his medical practice. He told this story from behind lenses so thick you could sometimes not see his eyes at all—then he'd turn five degrees and boom, he was all pupiled iris right up in your teeth. "A noble specimen, me," he added, and Evelyn gave him a look of adoration that broke me right in two.

So the first day out he made eighty miles and expected to die in the night but drank from an orchard pump and managed to avoid crippling leg cramps. Next day he had some hills to climb and went just fifty-five. But on the third day he woke with scarlet in his veins and surged onto the highway imagining himself a French racer climbing into the Pyrenees, the Great Girard, and rode a hundred twenty miles and stretched out that night confident of a strong finish. So it went until he was eight days along, cruising through Michigan, when he passed through a region known for sand dunes on the south edge of the sea, and there among the sawgrass and trails he came upon a girl working over a fire. A cast-iron Dutch oven sat in the coals and she troweled fire onto the lid. He pulled to the side of the road and watched her. She had short thick dark hair and skin incandescent from heat. The oven smelled of roasting fruit and sugar.

"She had every advantage," Girard said. He asked her what was baking.

"Nothing you can eat on a bike," she replied.

In this way his heroic circumnavigation was thrown off course. "He made himself a problem," said Evelyn, meaning he got off his bike to flirt, then got back on and rode away when she seemed uninterested, only to change his mind ten miles along and return in confusion hoping not to be laughed at but quite prepared to endure it. And Evelyn did laugh, but she also handed him a bowl and scooped into it a helping of something she called Brown Bear in a Cherry Orchard, essentially a filling of tart Michigan cherries folded into the darkest steaming gingerbread imaginable.

"We ought to make that again," Girard said, blinking enormously behind his lenses.

"Then what happened?" I'd forgot how much I enjoy a tale of blazing love.

"Oh, we'll draw the veil I think," said Evelyn, laying her hand on Girard's. "Now, we've fed you and patched your face. You owe us your story."

She was right, and so, because it was late, and because I felt hazy with gratitude in this settling house with vines at the windows, and also because our glasses kept refilling themselves, I told them what I could of Lark. Our early days, chiefly—the part that spills out. How lovely it was to say her name again, just the alert and feathered sound of it made everything come upright for a minute. Indeed more spilled than I intended, quite a lot more, until I hit the place where

I had to look away—and even then I didn't stop but instead crossed the blurry line and confessed to these new friends my desperate and surely doomed hopes for the Slate Islands.

"She may arrive when I do," I said. "Or a little before or sometime later. She might take days to get there. The truth is I don't know how long to wait." And then—hearing this aloud, O God, my words thudding down between us like baby birds who jumped too soon—I hastily added, raising my glass, "and then there's this scenario, the likeliest one of all, which is that Lark is lost to me, and dead is dead, and I'm the most entire fool who ever came to visit."

And here's how kind these people were, Evelyn the farmer and Girard the man of science, for they neither tried to brace up my rickety construction nor pretend it wasn't there. Instead they traded a look between them, a look in which was surely a bit of sympathy for me but was mostly comprised of their own pain or secret knowledge. They let a silence fall that was somehow generous and undemanding, and Evelyn laid a hand on my arm while Girard rose somewhat unsteadily. In fact he looked undone. He said something I couldn't understand in a tone of gruff affection, and up the stairs he went.

I stood as well, but Evelyn said Wait and poured us one more glass. She explained Girard was still recovering. Five years ago he fell ill in a way that confused him and rendered his diction strange. I understood her to mean he was recovering in some larger way as well. She told me about losing their daughter to the same migrating fever Girard had caught. Their girl, Tinker, got it first and her temperature flared so violently that Girard carried her into the lake five or six times daily to bring the fever down. For a while it looked as if she would mend but no. Tinker succumbed after a month's illness. By this time Girard himself was out of his head with infection. When he resurfaced his cognition was diminished and his speech patterns interrupted. It took him many days to understand the girl was gone.

Since then he'd made valiant strides but still wearied quickly and searched for words and was bright or stormy for reasons invisible to most. "But he isn't angry," Evelyn told me. "He can be furious, but he is not angry. People call me after their checkups, worried about him. They don't even want to tell him their symptoms. He's always felt protective of them, and now it's come back the other way."

In the morning I went down to retrieve my bass. *Flower* had taken on noticeable water and a starboard list. Her unloved appearance made me feel small and fickle. I'd forgot my dauntless vessel at the first chance of comfort ashore. To make things right I spent half the morning aboard, pumping the bilge dry, reorganizing below, and polishing her winches and other bright bits so something of her might gleam in the event the sun came out. A cheese rind was gone bad in the icebox and I tossed it to a hovering gull who clamped it apprehensively then chose to let it go.

Back at Girard's I sat on a green kitchen chair in the middle of the garden and got my fingers back. It had been days since I touched the fretboard. To limber up I ran scales—major, minor, pentatonic—pulled out favorite lines and riffs from what now seemed a life of remote and curious charm. With no amplification I played only for chipmunks and bees and dangling spiders and eventually a clan of house sparrows who came squabbling and lit all over my shoulders and knees like I were a saint or a loaf of bread. I played until my hands came into trim, stopping only when Stevie entered the garden carrying a sack of tools and the newly cut chainplates, a pair of steel straps as long as my forearm. Walking down to the dock she told me how in their previous life these plates helped gird a tower installed by the Canadian government. For decades sharp-eyed fire spotters lived atop that tower. After their replacement by satellites a retired priest took a sleeping bag and spent two years up there in intercessory prayer. He had a pulley system for groceries and soap and paperback romances. There was widespread betting on how long the priest would live. Schoolchildren wrote him letters, and he sent down replies in a basket. With the world off its axis he began to be viewed as a kind of intermediary. An umbrella against the fractious deity. He was suspected of wisdom but it's a tough thing to prove. Eventually he descended with a massive beard and an awkward smile and moved to a Catholic pensioners' home to rout drowsy clerics at euchre.

The Nils event was held in the fire hall. There was a table set up with a donations box and a bulletin board with pictures of Nils and his family: in their desiccated yard, beside an icy river, laughing in front of their tinseled house. There was a memory book you could write in if you wished. I guess it was meant for his wife and daughters but many had written messages to Nils himself. *You're so brave! Safe crossing. See you there one day my friend.* There used to be talk of beating it—remember this?—of beating cancer, funding the research, finding the cure. Not any longer. Not here. Maybe the astronauts were beating it like a dirty rug but who knew? What everyone knew in Jolie was that Nils was not going to beat it. When he arrived with his pretty wife LaNona and their two girls, none of them wore the inert smiles of compulsory optimism. They were brave but what choice was there?

The place was filling. In the last moments of the sound check I noticed a tall man in dark sleeves staring in at the open door. His eyes were moist fevers and he had what are called prominent cheekbones, in his case a barely veneered skull. His arms were uncannily long and his sleeves were even longer showing only dangling fingertips. When he caught my eye I realized he must be the fanatical bass player who'd given it up for whatever basket of snakes he seemed to need. He pushed through the man keeping him out and headed for Nils, now seated with his family in the front row of chairs. I remember an old book overusing the phrase *dark personage* and I will overuse it now. Off strode this dark personage to confront the dying sinner. I began to unsling my bass—what I'd have done to head him off I still don't know, for then Girard appeared. I didn't see him coming, maybe no one saw him coming. Girard was a foot shorter than this gaunt prophet but stood between the two like the immovable object. Neither touched the other and neither said a word. What Nils made of it I'll never know, but so rapt was I at their silent staring war that I completely forgot the band, which counted off swiftly launching into a tune foreign to me. It took a few bars to find my way in, by which time the Great Girard had prevailed and the dark personage was sloping out the door, his posture incensed and his rant undelivered.

And we were playing music! Boy my hands were happy! And how fine to look across at others playing too. The drummer, whose beautiful tattoos of inner clockwork signified solid tempo and power, locked me in, and when the chorus arrived I somehow knew how it would go. Indeed nothing threw me in that first tune except the bridge which unexpectedly downshifted while I raced on ahead. But my blunder threw no one. The Vagrants had the tolerant chops of old friends who've bungled a thousand songs together. They were chunky and competent and rolled easily through swing, Dylan, new wave, ripstonk, bedlam, roots and soul. Deeper in the set I got comfortable enough to imagine the lives around me. Nils's wife LaNona, getting up and getting by with those two girls. Buttered toast in a sunlit kitchen, a stand of corn and squash out back, a coming reality where sorrow did not draw and quarter them every waking dawn.

Is it so much to ask? A three-chord song, a common life? Could we all have that, someday? Could I? As for Nils, I imagined him just as he was, only his form became difficult to follow, like a stream, or a painting that keeps moving inside its frame, shifting as you stand before it. This picture stayed until the song shifted abruptly into four-four time and I was caught flatfooted and played a terrible wrong note, honk, and the lead singer, Stevie's daughter Mina who had wondrous low range, turned around laughing beautifully at my mistake.

Two more things happened in Jolie before I went my way. The first was late that night. We'd all got back to Girard's house and meant to turn in when Evelyn came down the stairs with a tentative step and her hands full again. This time they carried a stack of folded clothes.

"I thought you might like these," she said quite breezily. They'd belonged to her brother, who passed years ago and who she said "got all the size in the family," proceeding to hold them up to my frame with feminine precision and an all-business demeanor. There was a black wool suit jacket with narrow lapels, the matching trousers, the button vest. There was a pair of soft jeans and a white cotton shirt. She had even tucked her brother's laundered underwear into a paper bag along with a pair of leather-soled shoes no sailor would wear lest he skid and be lost at sea. Standing in their lamplit kitchen I found it doubly hard to speak, first because of this peculiar generosity and also because it was plain what Evelyn was doing. Tomorrow, with the boat repaired and icebox filled, I would certainly reach the Slates. Whether or not the thing could be accomplished, she was dressing me to meet Lark. And so while Evelyn reached and squinted and satisfied herself the clothes would fit, all I could do was mutter and avoid her eyes while Girard stood by nodding with sharp small noises of endorsement.

The next morning, when I'd stowed ice and fresh water and two sacks of vegetables and three bottles of the neighbor's wine, Girard showed up on the dock. He was taciturn and looked seaward and said if the fog lifted and I held due east I would sight the Slate Islands by noon. I thanked him and shook his hand. Still not looking at me, he handed over a small photo of a girl, seven or eight.

"Tinker," he said, observing the distance. We couldn't see far just yet—half a mile out the water faded to opaque mist that rose into the dome of fog around us. In the silence I memorized that photo—the girl's expectant smile, her eyes holding back. To this day I would know Tinker if I saw her, which was surely the idea. He took the picture from my fingers and tucked it in his pocket. He asked was I ready, he cast off the lines, and I nudged out onto the sea.

⁓ *an immortal sea of influence*

IT'S A BRUTE FACT that the closer I got to the Slates the less I expected Lark to appear. My own version of romance not to say magical thinking lets me down routinely. I played briefly in a church band where the preacher's main thrust was "making things manifest," chiefly things like influence, a sturdy profit margin, sanctified carnal happiness and, for farmers, helpful weather patterns. His delivery was thrilling but then people and money and rain clouds are going to do as they please.

As for the weather at hand, the sun when it finally showed had a diluted appearance and somehow remained weak as the fog dispersed. There was wind farther out—you could see its pale wheels churning east to west—but there in the shadows of Jolie it was nothing but rumor. The falling barometer discouraged me too. Only days ago Werryck had mentioned a storm developing, a calculation *Instant Forecasting* appeared to support—yesterday's horsetail clouds had given way to a dark flannel bank in the northeast. Superior throws a nor'easter with troublesome reliability and when she does you tie things down and make no assumptions, including the notion—so appealing on sunny afternoons—that I would sail into a channel and drop anchor and be greeted by Lark in whatever vessel she'd chosen for the trip. And finally there was this: I had been honest with Girard and Evelyn. I had been slipshod and revealed my cards. That alone was probably enough to spoil whatever cosmic narrative I'd struggled to maintain.

Nothing for it, though, so I held easterly, crawling over the calm inner waters to the brawnier wind of the outer lake. The shrouds hummed, *Flower* set to the work at hand, and Jolie became a few spikes on the mainland then vanished. It was still late morning when a small familiar hump rose off the surface dead ahead. Another to its left. I went below and retrieved the chart book, reckoning by compass and sight.

The Slates.

They looked as they had fifteen years earlier. I remembered now. Low and bottle green and barely there. Deeply unimpressive but that is the way of mysterious landfalls. I have seen pictures of mighty Cape Horn whose cryptic dominion sent a thousand ships to the bottom, and in the unfailingly murky photos the great cape resembles a drumlin your grandmother climbs before breakfast. Similarly I felt a jarring disappointment at the Slates' toothless appearance. These mossy hummocks did not look like a portal to the wondrous. I'll admit to an urge to turn back. I liked Jolie, liked everyone there except one dark personage who was easy to avoid. There were worse places to make a start. I could go back to Jolie. Get work. Rent a room from Girard and Evelyn, watch the sky and water, visit the Slates another day. A day it felt right. A day when the sun was yellow fire, not a watery eye.

On the other hand, I reckoned the islands ten miles distant. Under two hours.

I lashed the tiller and went below.

It isn't easy to put on a stranger's black suit in a heeling low cabin where you can't straighten up, the sea slides burbling against the hull, and your canned goods rock to and fro in their lockers. The pants were short but the shirt and jacket fit as if tailored. There was even a paisley pocket square Evelyn had helpfully folded and tucked into place. I didn't try the shoes. Bare feet make more sense anyway, on a boat.

Back on deck the Slates were nearer and the weather darkening. We pounded along as the wind strengthened shifting to the north. No more boggy sun or tepid warmth. The horizon was dirty and the waves were back to horses. Sometimes a gust knocked one's mane clean off and scattered it abroad. The wind remembered ice.

With maybe a mile to go I recognized the channel by which Lark and I entered the Slates. It was early afternoon but dark. The black suit was wet with spray and soon to be drenched by the storm dragging its veil of rain across the channel. I started the outboard and dropped sail, tied the main to the boom and flung the bunched-up jib below. This slowed progress and I pushed along at a knot or two into rain that arrived with bewildering force. At last a clutch of tall cedars appeared on the left followed by a sloping bare rock to the right. Between the two was flat water and I steered for it, gaining the opening then killing the engine and coasting to a silent halt in the rain-hammered bay.

There, almost exactly where Lark and I had anchored years before, lay a boat.

Not one she'd have picked for this occasion.

A hulking motor cruiser with a tall gable of a flybridge.

Its lit wheelhouse illuminated a nimbus of pulverized rain. In that gray slurry it looked less vessel than unmoored building.

It was no more than a hundred yards away.

I knew whose it was. It needed no label. You never saw so grotesque a watercraft, no curves on it anywhere but flat planes only, acute angles and slash ports like a gunboat in some brutalist navy, its finish black as the void. It looked like a finder and clubber and finisher. A closed fist is good at what it does.

I stood in the cockpit entirely still. The treetops moaned and bent in the sky but on the surface was only the slightest wind. Gradually it pushed me out the way I'd come. I scarcely dared to move. The dark vessel was enshrouded then hidden in rain. I was out of the channel and back in the storm whose claws tore at that poor black suit and wrote my end in the waves.

I scarcely can describe such wind except in terms of fear. I don't even like to remember it.

Earlier I'd begun to imagine the lake on my side, a protective demigod, the queen herself, adorned with thunder, stepping between me and those who'd have my skin. So much for all that. Deceived is what I felt, and scared, and it seemed very hard that I would find the Slates, locate the precise hidey-hole Lark and I had sheltered in so long ago, only to have it occupied by enemies and have the lake turn every bit as hostile as they were. The moment I was free of the islands' wind shadow the full blast took me, and I can tell you Superior had forgot she was a lake at all—no, she was like her sister the North Atlantic and her cousins the hurricanes who pull down houses and urge barns into the sea. We imagine great storms building a wall of water, seen at a distance with its crest in the sky. But what I saw were rows of waves lining up in ranks each higher than the last and so near to one another they looked flattened as if glimpsed through a telescope. The boat began to heave as the waves lifted the stern and moved beneath the hull, which wallowed in the troughs until the next surge came. Soon we were driven along at great speed though no sails flew and I had to stay on the tiller or the boat would swing sideways to the marching swells and that would be the end. A day or two of this would sweep us against the rocks of Michigan. I remembered then Lark telling me about a captain slowing his storm-driven ship by tying a rope to the stern, then lashing to it whatever he could find—shattered spars, oars, torn sails—and flinging this mess overboard to trail behind. A sea anchor she called it. All right then. I wadded up most of my blankets, dug into the lockers and found two canvas folding chairs, a broken bronze lantern past repair, three or four inflatable fenders, and most importantly a great coil of rope along which I tied all these sacrifices at intervals like beads on a string. Cleating it astern I hove this trash parade into our churning wake. At first I despaired, because on we plunged as though jettisoning the weight had only made us faster. Then abruptly the boat seemed to recognize its extra burden. It crouched aft, slowed perceptibly and went at a slight oblique with the waves. Tying off the tiller I was able to get below and get a breath.

Heavy clouds and nearly dark, the wind northeast and building. Despite my improvised sea anchor it was plain we were sluicing along too fast. There was nothing to do but to try something I'd read about in one of Erik's books, a magic trick called heaving to in which the boat parks slant to the waves, making as it washes backward a wake or slick that creates a shelter in the gale. I still had the book and found it now, managing to light the gimbled paraffin and find the crucial passage. Fixing the process in my head I went on deck to pull up the sea anchor. It would've been easier to pull in a piano. I leaned over to cut it free, and that's when a lazy big wave crested in from the side and swept me quite gently off the boat.

I didn't flail or grab or even panic. I was simply underwater in a lathery haze and surfaced to the boat's high transom bearing away and smaller every second.

Well that was it then.

Of course it was likely to end this way. The life vest I'd always suspected was more brick than buoyant took me right under and I slid out of it and clawed back toward the sky. By now the boat was out of view except its bobbing mast, but in the last light of day I saw slicing along just yards away the rope with its cargo of lashed blankets and lawn chairs. It ripped through the water, spray leaping and spinning off it, and I lunged and caught it going past. It cut my hands to ribbons but I held on and it bore me along gasping a hundred feet behind, the rope slacking when the boat wallowed in troughs, then tightening like a scream as it surged forward. Hope is tougher than you think and at first I went ahead hand over hand, but you try doing this while being dragged fast through water forty degrees, the sea doing its best to peel you off. So it quickly became a foot or two of progress followed by fatigue and slippage. In minutes my fingers were numb as pegs but by then I'd got astride the rope and could grip with legs and elbows. In this manner I worked toward *Flower* and cannot say how long it took. Shouldn't I have thought of Lark in this moment? Called her name or imagined joining her in whatever next country might exist? But I didn't. Nothing filled my brain but the next inch of rope. Arriving at a bundle of blanket I clung to it, then crept forward again. So complete was my blinkered stupor I neared the boat without seeing it and whacked my head against the transom. Stars bloomed yet I must've held tight, must've reached up and hooked an elbow on the steel railing called a pulpit. On my life I don't recall that frozen climb but later was black from knee to shoulder after tumbling into the cockpit then the cabin below where I woke later with the paraffin lantern making yellow arcs above my head.

My second thought after the shock of survival was the awful knowledge that I still ought to heave to. If anything the gale had worsened. I'd years ago seen the glorious godawful Michigan cliffs toward which we sped in darkness. Bumping around the cabin I found the storm sail, a knife, the jack line to prevent another friendly wave from plucking me off the deck. Then it was *Deep breath Rainy* and into the icy clatter.

It's maybe no surprise that after all this commotion the heave to maneuver went ahead with foolish ease. Cutting loose the sea anchor I hanked on the storm sail, steered round into the waves and raised the tiniest scrap of main. The little jib backwinded and there we sat, the boat making no headway and drifting slowly downwind in a slick of its own making. The whole gambit took minutes and was the most startling piece of conjuring, for all around were storm and prehistoric fury, yet a zone of tranquility opened like a heavy door and we just stepped through, *Flower* and I. The noise muffled, the motion eased. I tied the helm and went below, opened a can of beans and spooned them up cold, then wrapped in a remaining blanket and slept. That is what happened. Call it the hand of god or the magnanimous queen or my own hard work abetted by luck. I don't pretend to know.

Early light and the wind did not abate.

Slowly the cabin came visible, a slaughter of pans and cans and paper trash. Such was the violence before heaving to that lockers flew open, lazarettes disgorged. Every book came off the shelf. Even the heavy icebox lid bounded away and most of Evelyn's vegetables migrated to new quarters. Moving slowly I salvaged what food I could. Onions in the bilge well, a yam crouched in shadow. Sometimes I put my head out. I never saw land, just lowering clouds and ranks of foamy spume and rain-lashed waves. Life was soaked and stiff with cold. Lighting both stove burners I held my hands and face over them, then put water on to boil while stringing things up to dry.

In this interlude of relative quiet, my stealthy lodger returned. First the dreaded quiet tap, then a skid, the sound of something rolling, all escalating into a bellicose rhythm prompted by the boat's repetitive pitch and heel. In its absence I'd forgot this irritation. Now it was back and worse. As if my filthy guest had finally gone away only to fetch a bunch of even more irksome friends with whom to play his wretched tune—*skid roll tap, skid roll tap, skid roll*—this I endured while mopping up and twice pumping the damn bilge, at which point a brassy *clang* joined the act. It had an amplifying or proliferating effect. I'm no frantic person but I hissed and crashed around like a cat in an oven until finally—stretching an arm into fetid spidery diesel-adjacent darkness—something loose and heavy rolled straight into my fingers.

A gleaming steel cylinder, so out of context it took me a moment.

It was one of Kellan's nitrous canisters.

Of course he'd helped with a project or two, so he'd spent some time on the boat. But why would he stash it here? Not that it made any difference—it was clearly his, even though all that clanking and skidding around gave it a bruised appearance.

The threaded top wobbled, came off in my hand. I peered inside. It was stuffed with what looked like tightly rolled cellophane.

I suppose at that point I knew what it was.

I pulled it out anyway—took a knife and reached down in and shoehorned that fat plastic worm from its cocoon.

It was sturdily taped. Heavy as the cylinder it came from. Held to the light, these thousands of dissolves shone green and iridescent like the willow they were named for.

And that is how, hove to in the belly of a gale in the heart of the sea in the center of the continent, I realized there'd be no simple slipping off. Werryck wasn't about to forget me as I'd wistfully hoped, for here in my hands were the thousands of deaths—or millions of dollars, depending on your angle—that were his job to recover.

So what should I have done here?

Thrown the whole thing overboard, the better to plead ignorance?

Sought out my pursuers and bargained for my life?

At the very least I might have ticked through the possibilities—weighed them carefully and made my choice—but then the boat heeled with a sluggish manner I knew too well. The bilge cover lifted slightly, a wide tongue of dark water spreading at my feet. Who can comprehend the weariness with which I jammed the death roll back inside its cylinder? I wrapped this vile object in a towel and stuffed it back beside the diesel as far as I could reach, then found the bilge pump handle and set again to work. In the end it doesn't matter what contraband you're stuck with. You put aside those questions when the seafloor wants your bones.

Two more days it took for that wind to tire and fade.

In that time the clouds blew off, the sun came up and went back down, the clouds regathered, more rain fell. Again I established the grueling routine: pump the bilge, dry the sole, eat the can of beans. The third morning I woke to calm seas. I went on deck and there lay the Michigan shore, stretching away into dawn. The sky hung slack as if from prolonged exertion. When the outboard wouldn't start I hauled it up in the cockpit and removed its sparkplug and opened it as far as possible to dry. Erik, who saw no downside to superstition, observed that all motors respond to praise. Lightheaded with hunger and weariness I spoke to it. You are a fine engine. You have seen me through a great deal. Of all engines you are the best and most reliable. Of course you're tired but listen my friend: you have more to do in this life.

Slowly we drifted toward shore. A sand bay with barren overhanging trees.

When the parts felt dry I reassembled the outboard and hung it on its mount, lowered it into the water. I primed it with fuel, yanked the rope. It cleared its throat at the first pull and coughed on the second. The third brought it roaring. I went forward, raised anchor, and motored up the coast until a water tower rose out of the trees, its paint too faded to read. Round a low headland lay the ruined hulk of a ship, smokestack angled toward shore, rust bleeding from rivets. Behind it a once-mighty ore dock slanted up from the bay like a ribcage.

In the dappled shadows of that dock a tiny wild heron of a girl stalked fish in knee-deep water. She was brown as berries and carried a long-handled trident like an ocean deity.

First thing I saw her do was ease the tip of her spear below the surface so it would not splash and frighten the fish. I thought she took a breath and held it. Her arm flashed forward, the spear darted and stuck, and her quarry must've squirmed free, because she jerked the trident out of the sand in disgust and put it over her shoulder. Its wet tines glinted in the early sun as she worked her way to shore.

O God that maple fretboard

THERE WAS A PUBLIC DOCK and I went straight for it. Hardly shrewd for someone trying to avoid notice—should've motored around a headland or two, anchored near shore and walked in on quiet streets, but I'd been three days in the storm's belly and wanted only my feet on the earth. As I tied up at the dock the sun burst out and the world began to steam: the sand beach, a rim of great stones behind it, the trees and shingled rooftops, the dock itself. The nameless water tower shimmered as if about to vanish. Evelyn's dead brother's suit smelled like an exhumation. My other clothes and most of the food were moldering aggressively. I had no belt but found a twist of rope to hold up the brother's pants. I was thinning out fast.

The boat listed slightly and I looked up to see the girl in the cockpit. The fish stalker. Her head sliding around in owlish triumph on her shoulders. That trident ready and on her face the impudent smile that comes with the upper hand.

"I saw you puttering in like some kind of a spook," she said.

"I saw you miss that fish."

"I didn't really want him. Were you out in the storm that whole time?"

"It was nasty."

"It wasn't anything. We get bigger storms every week. Your boat is what's nasty. It smells. Is that a tomato?" She pointed that grown-up spear of hers.

Indeed, one of Evelyn's tomatoes had rolled out from wherever and come to rest at the base of the mast. Somehow it was still nearly perfect, with just one flat place an inch across, a darkening bruise and badge of survival.

I asked did she want it and she held out her hand.

"Is my boat nasty?"

The girl would not say.

"Make up your mind."

"Maybe it's just full," she said.

I tossed her the tomato which she bit into, not taking her eyes from me.

"What town is this?"

"Winton."

Back in Duluth I had painted houses with a kid from Winton. He was a wiry terrier who worked faster and more precisely than me. Sundays he fished with equal competence. When he fished he did not want conversation or company. It didn't matter what water he was on—river, lake, or inland sea—he always caught something, and then he always ate it. He said he was immune to mercury. I do not know the end of the story.

I said, "Is there a pawnshop?"

She finished the tomato, wiped her chin. "Give me some money and I'll show you where to get anything you need."

If I had "some money" I wouldn't need a pawnshop, but then she said her uncle who was called King Richard had a store with a gas pump and paraffin and shelves of canned groceries, which he was happy to trade for knives or old coins or military stuff or ammunition of any kind. This reminded me of the long-barreled pistol Erik had left aboard *Flower*. It was still in its spot under the galley stove, wrapped in its oiled rag. I dug it out and held it up.

"Would Richard be interested in this?"

"King Richard. You got to call him that."

"That's his name? King?"

"No, he just likes it. It's the name of his shop, King Richard's. He has a shield with lions on it hanging on the wall. He has a sword and it's pretty sharp. Also a crown but that's just for show."

"What would he think of this pistol."

She stuck out her hand as she had for the tomato but I wasn't about to let her hold that weapon which anyway was long as her arm. I ran the rag over it and showed her one side then the other. Pulled out the clip and blew into the handle and shoved the clip back home, making all the stout clanking noises just as if I had some idea what I was doing.

"Got any bullets for it?"

"No."

"He'll want it anyway," she said.

While we walked into town I considered priorities. I carried the three-gallon jerrican for gas, an empty bottle for paraffin. Dried potatoes would be welcome, macaroni and cheese. I was low on beans and wouldn't quarrel with a few cans of corned beef. In the warm sun the drying suit scraped against my skin. I needed soap, a toothbrush. I asked the girl whether the boat would be safe at the dock or if somebody might steal it or get aboard and steal something else.

"Like what?"

"Electric bass."

"I don't know what that is."

"A low guitar."

She didn't answer immediately. In Icebridge I felt easy about leaving the boat at the dock, but then I knew everyone in Icebridge. Here I was suspicious. So far, Winton looked savage and pummeled.

"I'll need to be quick with Richard," I said.

"*King* Richard."

As the sun rose so did the wind. Skeins of sand blew down the wide street. I was aware of the heavy pistol in its oiled wrap under my arm. I never felt easy carrying a gun but soon realized it wasn't out of place here. Of the dozen people we saw on the way to Richard's, nearly all hauled around some vicious deterrent—shoulder-slung rifles, pistols jammed in waistbands, an arthritic old man crabbing along under a twelve-gauge goose gun. A woman pushed her baby in a stroller equipped with a side holster, a first for me. The girl herself looked frankly underequipped carrying only a three-pronged spear. Why all the gear, I inquired. Widespread panic? Was Winton at war with a neighboring town? I remember she looked at me sideways like she didn't understand the question or maybe it was just dull. Off she went into livelier topics. A man up the street lost three fingers to fireworks. Every so often the fingers returned to visit him in the night, two of them joined at the root and the third hopping along crying *wait for me* in a tragic small voice. Another witchy neighbor knew the future but never revealed it since the news was always bad. If she nodded knowingly you kept your head down. If she appeared at your door with a casserole you were minutes from a death in the family. The girl was good company. The sun threw our shadows in front of us, a scraggy upright bruin and a junior devil with pitchfork.

The fork suddenly pointed: we were at King Richard's. The shop had two gas pumps and a hand-painted sign of a royal crest. I tried the door, which was locked, and looked through the bars at a few shelves of beef hash and shoelaces and the grotesque faux coffee called Postum.

"Sometimes he's not here," she told me. "He'll be at home with the black dog."

"All right. Thanks anyway. I'll find someplace else."

She then convinced me to walk another few blocks along the same street to King Richard's house, saying he needed the business, that he would certainly come back and open the shop if I bought even a gallon of gas and a pack of cards. Winton didn't become more charming en route, so many steel wheels and shrines to saints obscure and front-yard stacks of gunshot liquor bottles you never imagined, but "Here we are," she sang, and if anyone has wondered what sort of person erects before his house a machine-gun cross with a crown of bandoliers, why the answer is King Richard. He sat in a lawn chair from which the webbing hung in strips, a silent shaven-headed watcher of the street. He stood up to frown hard at the girl while holding his hand out to me. I didn't want to shake it but I did—an antique custom in this germy century of ours. But Richard had an easy disregard for germs and more so those who feared them. I unwrapped the pistol and told him what I wanted. He liked the gun. He pointed out with delight where the serial number used to be. Its absence bought me credibility with Richard. He said there was no need to return to the shop—his reservoirs were empty with no deliveries all week—but he had a fuel tank out back and inventory in the basement of everything but paraffin. On the way inside, he kissed his fingertips and brushed the cross as he passed. It was made of two automatic rifles welded at right angles and mounted on a wooden post so the crossmember was eye level to average sinners. The guns looked functional and the bandoliers were full of bullets. My mood sank and I hoped the black dog was not inside that house waiting to snap and foam at my calves. The front door opened into a grubby little kitchen where Richard left me while he thundered down a set of steps and up again with surprising alacrity. He emerged with a crate of cans and bottles while giving his abbreviated memoir, wife dead of something undiagnosed, children striving in the gardens of astronauts out east, his neighbor a fearsome seer of mayhem whose spiel gained credence by the day. As he talked I became aware of something, a smell that crept out from everywhere, deep and distilled. It occurred to me that maybe the dog had died somewhere, but this was before the girl explained that *black dog* just meant sadness. I knew that creature. In any case I made my purchases and looked around, but the girl was gone and who could blame her? Richard shook my hand a second time and I got out of that stinking house. The sun was in and out of clouds. A gusty wind scooted trash along the gutters. I walked with conscious restraint, resisting the urge to go faster every step.

~

Straightaway I got under sail. Didn't even start the motor, just raised the main and swept up the anchor as *Flower* sliced past in the last minute of sun. The wind was southerly, neither too much nor too little. Supper was bread toasted on the stove and topped with a fried egg.

I was probably two hours gone when a rustling sound took my eyes off the horizon—a muffled scurry, with elbow whacks. As I watched, the lid to the portside cockpit locker opened deliberately as if by a vampire checking for daylight, and there was a set of spidery fingers followed by crazy sea-child hair and eyeballs gleaming like a plan to cut my throat.

Fairly sure I leapt back at the tiller. It's possible I roared. It seemed wicked magic, the girl being on *Flower* when I'd made good time myself and wasted not a moment getting underway.

"It's only me!" she shouted. "Come on, it's only me." She pushed the locker open and stood out in her long thin shirt like a wraith. Maybe I said something harsh. I remember how she shrank away. Maybe she thought I'd be glad to see her, on account I had been decent earlier and gave her that tomato.

"Sit down and hang on." I brought our nose into the wind and let the sails go soft and flutter and change sides.

"What are you doing?"

"Taking you home." The sails refilled, I trimmed them and we headed toward the lights of Winton, still visible on the dark horizon.

"You're not. Come on, we're miles away."

"We are, and I am."

Her fury was evident but I was furious too and scared. Already pursued by deathless bloodhound Werryck I had now, however accidentally, stolen a child whose uncle demanded to be called King and who daily kissed a machine-gun cross. In a hundred years she couldn't have chosen an unluckier sailor with whom to stow away. I tried explaining this but did she understand? She was only nine I was soon to learn—could she see how it was, or anywhere close? Can she see it now?

I said, "It's not like you're safer out here with me."

"He's not my uncle," she replied. "We're not even related."

"You called him Uncle."

"I never heard of him until my folks dropped me off, and I never saw them since."

"You're changing your story," I pointed out, but honestly who wouldn't? Who, living in King Richard's ghastly shadow, wouldn't trade it for whatever came along, including a tattered boat sailed by a talking bear?

"He smells and he's awful and he's so heavy you can't move," she added, an observation that got worse every time I thought of it.

"If he's your legal guardian—"

"I'm an animal he owns."

"Will you let me think a minute?"

"There used to be two older girls who weren't his nieces either. He'd come in our room at night and touch one of them on the head or sometimes both and they'd get up and follow him away. One day they both went someplace else. I asked King Richard where. He pretended they were never here at all. Said I made them up."

Two hours it took to reach Winton and a longer haul would be hard to invent. Yes I'd just hung on through a three-day blow, had been tossed and dragged and half drowned and frozen, the whole blue-faced parade, but try two hours captive to a fully alert child relating savage history. The storm was less painful. We often hear stories that make us desperate to help, but the person is not usually two feet away talking vividly about what will happen if we don't. There are phrases babies shouldn't know. Nearing the lights of town the breeze dropped almost entirely away, and I went down and got my bass and tuned as best I could in the open cockpit. No amplification, obviously, but on the sea gone quiet it made a nice resonant sound. The girl fell silent, her expression one of listlessness or exhaustion. My playing comforted me more than her. When I wrapped the bass back in its blanket, she said, "I like that guitar."

"Me too."

I tucked it below and took down the sails and leaned over the outboard. We neared the Winton pier.

"You don't have to be in charge of me. Just get near shore and let me swim. That way you're not kidnapping, and I'm away from that pighog, Richard."

It wasn't the last time I'd hear her call him pighog. I liked it. It was funny, and also it reminded me she was nine, quick and smart and sovereign though she was in most respects.

"Someone has to be responsible for you," I said.

"That's what Richard says, right before he's mean."

"I can't just let you run off on your own."

"People say that and then they hand me over. It isn't right. Papa Griff wouldn't do it. Papa Griff wouldn't take me back to Richard."

"Who's this now?"

"Papa Griff. He's old. He's my gramps," she said. "I used to stay with him sometimes. He's got a pantry and two griddles and a four-slice toaster. He used to be an actor, combs his hair in a pompadorg. He hid me when people came looking."

"Back up. Who came looking?"

"People Daddy knew. People in his business. Papa Griff didn't like their appearance. He has a secret door that he built himself. I stayed back there until they left."

"So where's this Griff? Where does he live? Wait, hang on. Is he your gramps like Richard's your uncle?"

"He isn't nothing like Richard. He isn't mean. He lives in Redfield."

I got out the chart book. It took her three seconds to point out Redfield on the far side of a massive peninsula like a hooked beak poking out to sea.

It was a week away at best.

We eased up to the pier, cleated her fast beneath the wide and starry. I didn't want to leave the boat there by itself. Not at night. Even from the dock we could see a shaggy crew darting in and out of shadow on the near streets. Stooping long-armed figures on the hunt.

Before we left the boat I did pull out the wrapped bass guitar, the only thing worth stealing. As for the girl I half expected her to run, to skip away and lose me and not go back to Richard. I wouldn't have blamed her. Instead she walked close to my side, a hand on the bass as though for comfort. My throat ached a little.

As we neared Richard's house many lights were burning. Some were flashlights and some torches. People were loping around—looking for the girl it became apparent. I will say that Richard's friends resembled Richard, meaning hard and humorless. Their skins like galvanized protection. Of course she knew them but for me it was all zigzag beams and hooting in the dark. Richard himself sat in his derelict lawn chair beside a smoky bonfire. He did not seem overjoyed when we came up the walk but got to his feet and stood next to the crucifix and pointed at the girl in a way that seemed a private interaction.

"Nuisance from the start," said Richard, and to me, "I thank you sir and am sorry for the bother this one put you to."

He held his hand out. This time I did not shake it, but he didn't seem to notice and only directed a dire downward glance at her whose shoulders were thrown back in mutiny.

Then Richard with groaning joints lowered to a knee and put his face to hers. "Did you see them, girl?" he said. "All the people come to search for your ungrateful ass? Look now. Look around you at the friends you don't deserve," pointing and nodding at several sharp faces with flat eyes shining in the firelight like creatures easing up to the side of a road.

He stood and stepped back. Immediately came a hard hollow concussion. The girl dropped to knees and hands. I didn't know what had happened. It took her a minute to breathe again, and then it sounded ragged.

"Get up," said Richard.

When she did I saw the rock that knocked her down.

She must've been scared. She didn't look it. I never saw her look it.

Right then all I wanted was the old anger back again. I wanted to feel a growl climb up from the earth into my legs and bust out of my mouth as a roar. That did not happen. I was the one who was scared.

"Let's step inside a minute," I said.

Richard didn't reply but led the way. Yet again he kissed his fingers, brushed that profane cross aglitter by the fire. He lifted a hand, dismissing his gathered friends who filtered away as we stepped into his kitchen. Again that smell to take the bristles off.

"I hope you aren't looking to be paid," King Richard said. He stepped behind the counter.

"Of course not."

"What then? You brought her back. I thanked you for your effort. What other transaction have you got in mind?"

My hesitation was because I hadn't thought it through and had no script in mind. There I stood dithering. Then Richard's face changed. His head sank into his shoulders. His eyes narrowed as though we had something in common. He signaled the girl to vanish and she did. How often had those piggish eyes ordered her away so that she might be discussed?

With her gone he said, "Make your offer."

I laid my bass guitar on the counter and opened its blanket.

O God that maple fretboard. That swooping mahogany body scarred and long beloved.

I looked away saying, "You take the bass. I take the girl with me."

"For how long?"

"She never comes back."

I looked down into Richard's devious crease of a smile.

"What do you think I am, you come in here and try to buy my girl?"

"She isn't yours. She arrived as payment of some debt. And I know about the others, the older ones no longer here."

"Girls who needed help. I helped."

"You're not helping this one."

"She doesn't starve in my house. No one forces her to stay. To believe one thing she says is to make a tragic error. Others have found this out."

"Are you turning down my offer?"

"No," said Richard. "No. In fact, I accept," he added in the hardening tone of one tolerating an idiot. "And I'll tell you why. This guitar will not try to burn down my house." He pointed at the ceiling, stained with greasy smoke. "Who do you think set the fire?"

I made to speak but he cut me off. "This guitar won't hide a spike under its pillow. How about that? Or put Drano in my Dinty Moore! Is that funny to you? No? I'll take your offer, but you should know what you are getting. Go on and take her. You think she'll thank you, but she won't."

At this she appeared, soundless as a genie, having thrown some kit in a drawstring sack. Out we went and the door shut hard behind us, followed by metallic snaps as deadbolts shot in place. I remember a V-shaped crack in the clouds that let the moon show its face, swollen with humidity and strangely close by.

"Call me Rainy," I told her under that moon.

"I'm Sol," she said.

And what did she think, this Sol, as we walked away from there? Reaching the sidewalk she spun and bobbed in a spontaneous boogie, but her back was sore where the stone had struck her and she turned heedful and stealthy-eyed. I too felt strangely circumspect. Distrustful of the imminent. Glad as I was for her to escape Richard's house of stink, I knew the bitter limits of my power. I'd protected exactly no one from those who meant them harm—not Lark, not Kellan, not even little Tonio of the heart-shaped head. Moreover, already it was clear Sol carried weight beyond her size. Already this ballast threw me off. I wove along unsteadily until we reached the boat, which by some shocking chance lay untouched at the dock.

Already I missed my bass guitar.

~ *probably doomed and perplexingly merry*

EAST WE BORE along the coast of Michigan, dawn hours away and just enough wind to keep the sails from slapping. When Sol fell asleep in the cockpit I couldn't wake her and finally hauled her below over my shoulder, setting her down in the forward bunk, which boasts the only privacy such a vessel affords. I had never picked up and carried a child before, and what I chiefly recall is what a furnace she was, her brow and temples a steaming bog despite the chill, and also her unlikely weight—truly I struggled to lift her, as if the whole substance and magnitude of her future were jammed into those spindly feverish limbs. I piled a blanket next to her, just in case, and went back up to squint at the chart book. We'd made about ten miles. Overwhelmed with weariness I rounded a headland and dropped anchor in calm water with pines reaching out from the shore. The place was called Misery Bay. I do not know the story. I lay down wrapped in a quilt on the cockpit bench, the long crescent of the tiller looming overhead against the stars.

White mist drenched me early. I went below to light the tiny stove and make coffee in the galley, the girl snoring up front, a reassuring sound. With steaming cup and damp charts I went out again in the first grainy light to try and see the future.

We lay at the base of a long curved horn of land reaching into the sea. Fifteen miles farther up was the opening of a waterway or canal that appeared to cut through the peninsula to the eastern half of Superior. The canal itself was thirty miles give or take using my thumb as a measure. That was the way to Redfield and the heroic Griff. I looked it up in *Folsum's Anchorages.* Redfield had two hundred residents and a breakwater shaped like an ear.

Did it make me uneasy, delivering this girl to a pompadoured keeper with two griddles and a shadowy cupboard? What do you think? And when I asked for more about gallant old gramps she was very tight with details—not her usual shortcoming in my brief experience. However, that was me standing next to her when some friend of Richard hurled the rock that put her on the ground. That was me watching Richard's eyes turn icy with approval. All respect to proverbs, sometimes they're mistaken. Sometimes the devil you know is bad enough to chance the one you don't.

We'd go find Griff and decide from there.

Another thing I liked about this plan: after leaving Sol behind, I could cruise up nearly to the center of the lake beneath the horn's protection. I could take a breath and lay in wait for a fair westerly. When it came, I'd ride it in one swift daylong reach to the doorway of the Slates. I thought, *Can you see me, Lark? Did you think I'd given up?*

And this time I'd be careful. This time I'd pay attention: circle the islands, creep up to their channels, enter their arms by a different route. It seemed to me dubious that the jagged black cruiser would still be stationed there. Now I see the cruiser had taken on the attributes of phantoms. It flickered in the rain of memory; it was there and not there. As the horizon accumulated in the east, my conviction grew that whatever might befall me I would bear. Maybe Lark would meet me there or maybe not. Either way, thinking of her made me glad again.

Sunrise streamed through shoreside pines like evidence of something. Maybe our minds decide on things before we are aware. I knew already I'd try the Slates again. How could I not? The morning Lark bought her first large cache—more than a thousand volumes, a great risk for her—I said, *How are you feeling?* Her instant reply, *Probably doomed and perplexingly merry*, was a concise report of our handmade lives.

There was movement below as Sol rousted herself from sleep. I dried my face, looked toward shore, and sighed.

Forty feet away lay another risen corpse.

I didn't want her to see it.

Oh, she'd certainly seen worse. She'd lived at Richard's. Still, it seemed best not to expose her to this horror in the opening seconds of daylight.

"Maybe stay down there a minute," I said, when she appeared scratching her head in the galley below.

At which she bounded up into the cockpit and spotted the thing straight off.

"Look at the uncle over there!" she yelped—pointing, practically waving, not startled in the least. In fact she looked a little rosy, as though she'd sighted a box of puppies and not a face-up bloated corpse with a lipless grin and strangely bright bad teeth glinting all directions.

I didn't understand *uncle* but she explained she'd lost two uncles to Superior, one before she was born and another who worked alongside her parents in what sounded like a brilliant string of unlucky schemes. One fell off a fishing boat, the other "took a swim." Neither ever surfaced. Every time she glimpsed something drifting in the shallows she assumed it was a relative.

"There's nothing we can do for him," I said. "Let's raise sail. If the breeze holds, we can reach the canal by midday."

But she was leaning over the stern, craning around for something. "You don't have a boat," she observed.

"It seems like I do."

"I mean a little boat. A rowboat you tow along behind. You know, for going ashore."

I admitted having no such thing.

Without further preamble she hopped overboard and swam in a noisy thrashing style toward the body.

"Sol," I began, but she windmilled along purposefully and couldn't hear. Reaching him quickly she circled him a few times and finally rested there supporting herself with a hand on his shoulder as though he were a piece of timber.

"Come on!" she called.

"Maybe I won't swim with corpses today."

"We got to bury him."

I said, "Is he one of yours?"

"I can't tell."

"Then he isn't. Come on back, let's go."

Her reply was to take hold of his shirt and start towing the old bruiser to shore. I was both irritated and impressed. He was a massive reddish moldering island and she looked made of twigs. Expecting she'd soon wear herself out I finished my coffee, went below and brewed another cup, climbed into the cockpit and sat down to drink it. The girl's stamina was profound. Hitting the shallows she got to her feet and started dragging him a limb at a time up the shingly beach. Of course once she got his legs and arms pointing inland there was the immovable fact of his immense torso, and that was as far as he went.

"All right, good job, let's go," I called.

She did seem to waver in her commitment, wading toward the boat up to her knees. Then a pair of circling gulls who'd been talking to each other in low tones landed near the body. That made up her mind. Back ashore she went and shooed the birds and started scooping a hollow place in the sand.

There was nothing for it. Somehow I had become responsible for a stubborn person. There was a stupid little folding shovel in a cockpit locker. I held onto it and let myself over the side.

Up close he didn't look as awful as he might've. Sure, there were the teeth and the missing eyes and nubby fingers and so forth. It was hard to tell clothes from skin over much of his surface. Still, the way Sol attended to him—as though he really were a blood relation she was glad to see, even in this condition—did allay the revulsion not to say grief and terror I'd experienced in previous encounters. We dragged him up out of reach of the waves and dug him a trench. He was incredibly heavy with rubber-tire flesh. Shoulders like hillsides the red-dirt color that blows in off the Mesabi Range. As the day warmed and we worked on the trench, I began to imagine him not just living and toiling in that primeval landscape but doing so as a kind of colossus. A towering steward of Earth whose rags could not conceal his nobility. We had to dig wide for his shoulders. We rolled him in face-up, then placed stones on him carefully. We did not hurry. At this scale all graves are bespoke. There was the sense, encouraged by Sol, that he might suffer if the mound were badly stacked. When we had a decent berm, she stood at its head and cast about for words, which in my memory were, approximately: "Wish I knew your name, I am Sol, you might be my uncle, you should rest now, me and Rainy have to leave, goodbye." Without a pause she stepped in the water and set off swimming to the boat. I never got used to that boisterous crashing stroke of hers. By the time I swung gracelessly aboard, she had on dry clothes and was selecting our breakfast from the icebox.

With the sun high we got underway and plotted a course for Redfield. There was no question but to take the canal, which would shorten the distance to the righteous Griff by several days. I trimmed the sails and then to ease our restlessness I read aloud from Folsum. Here is what he said about the canal, whose entrance we hoped to reach by nightfall:

> *Let me praise this temperate region as the Venice of the Great Lakes. The climate—cool in summer, benign in winter—is a gift of the munificent Inland Sea, and ensures that cherries, peaches, and apricots are at the center of a vibrant local agriculture. If you are lucky enough to traverse the Canal in late summer, there is a Stone Fruit Festival in the sibling communities of Blinker and Brighton, engendering pleasant rivalry between their citizens. Prizes are awarded for best pies, tarts, and canned preserves, followed by an ecumenical service on the mighty Huffin Lift Bridge that joins the two small cities . . .*

Well, it went on like this for pages, with exhaustive references to the beauty of local flora including redtop, orchard grass, and timothy. I didn't mind. So what if Folsum was wordy? Sentiment is not deadly in small doses. Anyway, I liked imagining Folsum's world, with its clean handshakes and belt-loosening suppers, its appreciation for pies, its competent mariners and tonking diesels. I remembered people who remembered those days.

But Folsum's compliments and fripperies made Sol howl. "What is he talking about? Community suppers? Who is Timothy? What does ecumenical mean? Yesteryear is a dopey word."

"Have some tuna," I said, offering the can. She got very warlike when hungry. I didn't want war. What I did want, from her evasive self, was a sense of Griff. For some reason he lurked in my imagination as an unmarked shoal off the coast of Michigan, and though she talked and talked about him, nothing caught for me. Nothing held. Everything she reported was a superlative. Papa Griff was the tallest and smartest and knew the most people, many of whom were important. Papa Griff played chess on a screen against Asian geniuses and just about always won. He caught a big fish and opened its belly in which were two gold rings and the bones of a human hand! And of course he'd built the secret closet and hid her in there with a loaf of bread and a jar of water when people came to collect her. They threatened Griff, but he was bold and stood fast. He scared them away! Nobody told Papa Griff what to do!

It didn't put my mind at ease, but it did pass the time as we scooted at surprising speed up the coastal strand. I was beginning to be impressed by my own skill as a sailor—the shoreline with its twisting cedars and streaky boulders fairly flying past—until Folsum mentioned a strong current running northeast along the coast. So it was none of me. In any case the pace was welcome. The sea was weary of its benign mood and beginning to scowl. A line of compact storms gathered themselves in the north and made to join forces. The day suddenly seemed long. I spread the chart book over my knees and worried we'd somehow missed the channel entrance. Folsum said it was marked by a green light visible for miles. I saw no lights but did see storm clouds colliding on the northern rim. Lightning sizzled around inside them. Cold dark fingers crept forward over the sea. Then Sol, standing forward by the mast, shouted, pointing at a pale winged shape high in the air catching a late stray sunbeam—and there, below it, was the channel.

The entrance was no longer lit. We could've missed it easily. It was only a gap in the shore next to a ruined jetty. Twenty minutes later I clattered the sails down and we motored slowly into the silty mouth of the canal. Even as we did the atmosphere changed: the evening stilled, a yellowish luminescence seemed to rise off hillsides right and left. When the channel broadened I eased into a kind of pocket or backwater close to shore and let go the anchor in eight feet of depth.

"What's that," said Sol, pointing again at the shape in the air—the billowing triangle or delta that had brought our attention to the channel below. It darted and rattled and soared. It looked as old as the world. She shrank back against the mast—she was shaking hard.

"Have you not seen a kite before?"

She hadn't. To put her at ease I described what it was, a bit of cloth stretched over a frame that came alive in the wind and went ranging around at the end of a long string.

"I don't see any string. It's just flying around up there, watching us."

In fact we were too far away to see the string. The big kite did look autonomous and capable, not to say fierce as it dipped and spun in the darkening sky.

Spooked as she was, that kite felt to me like hope, even a reward, maybe for delivering her from the hand of Richard, which I felt proud of at that moment, or maybe for giving an enormous corpse, that very morning, a more or less dignified burial—though it was only Sol's tenacity that kept me from leaving him to bob in Misery Bay. I knew if Lark were here she would interpret the kite as a sign of favor. An indication of the right track we were on. Lark always thought we were on the right track, even when we weren't.

In this frame of mind I heated a tin of vegetable soup that we ate in the cockpit while waiting for the storm to arrive. A storm is nothing to fear if you're snugly anchored with hot soup in a cup. But now the black clouds had separated again, like allies rethinking the arrangement, and seemed to chase one another with bursts of thunder and sheeting rain over the battered sea.

~ *bad thoughts about authority*

OUR ANCHORAGE was a few hundred yards up the canal, close enough to watch the tireless waves marauding past the entrance. Again Sol took the forward berth while I stayed up reading under the paraffin. I liked Folsum's admiration for the waterway before us—the placid miles lined by orchards, fields, and pastures, the lovely Huffin Lift Bridge *ascending to permit the passage of ships and pleasure craft*, the assemblies of children along sections of the canal, waving and holding up *signs of greeting to sailors from afar!* But the longer I read, the less helpful Folsum became. Even allowing for eighty years' disintegration, he seemed rosy to the point of credulous. Glad as I was for this inland shortcut, I also felt exposed—moving in a slow straight line, with no option for the swift escape to sea.

Before turning in I checked on Sol, and it was startling how she'd drawn in on herself, all but vanished under that blanket, knees nearly touching her chin, her whole quantity no bigger than a cat. It was confounding: the clearest thing about her had been a sense she was larger than the space she occupied. Now in her sleep she seemed barely there at all. Was she even breathing? What reassured me was simply her concentrated heat. She was a celestial phenomenon, shrinking in size while gaining density. As I stood there her eyes opened, black with panic. "It's all right," I said. It's all right. All's well. There's nothing to dread.

This reassurance was silly on its face. Nothing to dread? Far from all she knew, on a leaky boat, with a hunted fugitive?

Sol had everything to dread.

How I wished then for my bass guitar. Certainly a twelve-bar blues would calm her. Absolutely a sunlit riff would remind her she was not alone, and do the same for me. Into my head came a lullaby shuffle, the signature tune of an ephemeral brilliant band whose name I don't remember. It has a walking bass line, this song, a sleepy saunter toward a place of rest. It often came to me at night. I tried to hum it for her but couldn't hold the melody. Away it slipped like something pleasant I had dreamed.

Morning came clear and the big kite was back in the sky. Maybe it flew all night. There was a steady southerly and the wing hunted this way and that along the currents. Beneath it on sloping meadow lay a long stack of light-brown bales like a wall. Straw or marsh grass, the bales neatly piled. The barrier they made was taller than a man, longer than a freight car. Atop this architecture three kids stood elbowing each other. They were flying the kite.

"You see?" I said. "It's nothing. A kite, a toy. People fly them for fun."

We were in the cockpit drinking coffee. Sol grimaced yet claimed to love it. The coffee steamed in the cold and we watched the kids—all knees and ligaments—who had some sort of contest going, their happy yelps irresistible. Sometimes they looked at us over their shoulders. Even at that distance there was mischief in their faces.

"I thought it was something else at first," Sol said, meaning the kite.

"What else could it be?"

"A death angel," she replied.

Those early days she said many things to which I had no answer. While I sat riveted she explained this strain of angels in the sky, dour celestials stationed at intervals above the world. "They float up there seven or eight hundred feet watching us have bad thoughts about authority. They love authority. They love King Richard. They love all his friends. They aren't sure about me."

"Richard told you this?"

"He saw them every day, talked to them sometimes. I heard him do it. Every time I did something awful they wanted to take me away."

She stated this without irony, though her level of belief was hard to gauge. Looking across the water at the kite fliers I wondered what Lark might say about immortals whose eternal obligation was to waft in the vicinity listening for truculence.

I said, "Sol, do you like pancakes? What we need is some pancakes."

Her nod had an element of suspicion, as though my casual dismissal of death angels was the surest way to bring them hissing, but we lit the stove and took turns frying cakes that looked like tigers or plump sparrows or full-maned lions or lynxes with tufted ears. Sol loved the predacious cats. We had neither syrup nor honey but the cakes were excellent rolled up plain and eaten in the sun. We ate until all we could do was yawn and blink. There was no more talk of death angels or any other kind. I felt better. A rising breeze wrinkled the water.

"Let's go over there," she said, nodding at the kids. In the bright morning, the whole kite arrangement was easy to see. The line glowed as if wet. The kite was patched and stitched in many places, and light shone through tiny holes that had no patches yet. It had a short, fraying cloth tail wagging this way and that. It might have been the tattiest kite ever to fly the Michigan shore.

"It's pretty. I bet they'd let me try," Sol said.

Now that it was a kite and not a malignant apparition she was determined to get the string in her hands. I had to smile. She asked if I'd ever done it—flown a kite.

"A hundred times." There was an old man when I was a kid who always had one in the air. He flew on the shore in treacherous weather—adults feared him, roaring out poetry in his gruff voice, but I thought him a champion from early in the world.

"What's it like?" Sol asked.

"Like catching a big smart fish in the sky."

"I want to try."

"We'll build one later," I said. The canal was coming awake. Birds whistled, a dog was upset somewhere.

After some teasing the outboard started and idled uneasily. Sol went below while I pulled the anchor in a plume of murk off the soft bottom.

When I looked up a clutch of boys was coming along the near shore. Ten at the oldest, five or six of them, big grins and black teeth, jostling and poking and whacking each other as they came. A couple had plinky little air rifles slung soldier-style across their backs; another carried a length of PVC pipe. The smallest among them struggled with a bucket of pale lumps that turned out to be rutabagas. This crew looked so happy and dirty and free and good-natured it kind of lit me up. I waved and they waved back, hollering something I couldn't hear over the outboard. Then one of these innocents unslung his air rifle, knelt in the weeds, and pointed it at me. Well, we were all of us laughing. I held up my arms in mock surrender.

His gun barrel jumped with a visible puff, and something hit my chest like a wasp.

"Hey!" I roared, and a few other things I do not remember, and boy did *that* please the next generation. In half a second I was looking down two more gun barrels, and wasps were hitting my arms and cheeks and a place just above my left eyebrow that hurt all out of proportion. I stepped behind the mast to hide at least part of myself. When I peeked out the tall kid with the PVC was sloshing fuel from a gas bottle into the base of the pipe while the infant crammed a rutabaga down its wide mouth.

All this time we drifted slowly closer to shore. The air guns weren't lethal but they stung hard and these joyful little bastards were crack shots. I was preparing to cover my face and get to the outboard when the PVC pipe made a deep hollow *foom*. A rousing cheer broke out as a root vegetable whistled past my head. Who knows the physics of rutabaga velocity but it landed at least fifty yards out.

Then the onslaught suddenly stopped. They saw Sol before I did. The hatch slid open and up she stepped in shabby long cotton, sleeves rolled up, feet bare on the planks and the wind knocking her curly hair around. Maybe what quelled the monkey brigade was the glinting three-pronged spear in her hand. Maybe it was just how she stood there silent in full view like something from an ancient story none of them knew yet each somehow remembered. Their paralysis or confusion held for long moments until one of the marksmen raised his weapon and took faltering aim at her. Instantly the tall one reached over and slapped the air rifle out of his hands. Busy with embarrassment they gathered their gear and went trotting along toward the canal entrance.

Before they could reconsider I hunched over the outboard and got us moving. The canal narrowed and the wind came up. It was nice to motor along not bothering with sails. My clothes and blankets had finally dried. Sol vanished below and returned wearing everything she owned. Looking behind us her face hardened. Those boys with their primitive ordnance had stopped opposite the kitefliers and were firing rutabagas at the big wing as it trembled in the sky. From her chin it was plain Sol wished to turn back and enlist me in combat against those piranhas, but I and not she had the tiller, to say nothing of eight or ten stings still bright from the earlier skirmish. I held course. The motor hummed. The war faded behind us. There began to be farms and smallholdings, woodlots, orchards, and orchard remnants. A jouncing car on an invisible road. The world got smaller and more peaceful. Burrowing inland we smelled dirt, oil, plants, impromptu septic arrangements, and dark wet smoke tumbling from chimneys on the mainland side. It was Sol who pointed out how few chimneys on the island side smoked at all, and these emitted no bold plumes but instead frail white spirits scattering in the gusts.

Noting such disparities became a dismal game as we pushed farther into the canal. Mainland houses wore proud paint and shingled roofs; island homes went to bare weather and windows tilting in their frames and rafters showing themselves. On the island, dogs were rangy coyotes running loose with heads held low. The few cars we saw were covered with muck and squatted randomly at angles of disuse. The island even had lousier weather—so many of its trees were cut down or broken off that winds had undisputed fetch across the landscape.

It was easy at first to crack wise at the expense of unlucky islanders but this soon wore us into silence. Nothing sinks your spirit like your own cruelty. Sure the canal was pretty, just as Folsum said. Sure the sumac was a *scarlet cloak spreading over the hillsides*, the water *unspooled before us like a glimmering ribbon* and so forth. It also resembled the frontier of an intermittent war in which one side endured continuous defeat.

I was looking for a gas station. There'd been plenty on the canal in Folsum's day, and I wanted to be sure we could attain the lower entrance.

Besides fuel we needed facts. Every mile the specter of the lift bridge troubled me more. The Mighty Huffin. Many times I'd seen the similar bridge in Duluth majestically hoist its slab of roadway into the sky, ships of all sizes passing easily beneath, but how much major engineering from the early twentieth was still in operation? I did not want to navigate half the canal only to be turned back by a stuck bridge. Meeting even one large vessel coming from the lower entrance would've been reassuring, but the few boats we saw were small—a motorized canoe hugging the mainland, a paddleboard poled along by a woman, her small patient dog balanced up front.

Then, as we eased round a tallgrass promontory, Sol aimed her finger at a shoreline fuel station on the island. Once-bright stucco gone yellow as teeth. Part of the roof looked to have lifted off then settled back askew as if from a bomb or tornado, and a boxy addition had detached and leaned away. It didn't look open, but at least there was a person there—a tall man in colorless clothing, shading his eyes with his hand and looking our direction.

I adjusted course but maintained a cautious pace. In her excitement Sol waved, but the man did not wave back. The closer we got the more woeful he appeared. Short thick legs, sloping shoulders. I expected him to brandish something. A cudgel would not have been a surprise. Still he didn't move. Twice Sol hailed him which he ignored. Everything about this reticent brute set me on edge. His candid glower, his crude posture. Eyes set back in his head as if with a ramrod. Could a stranger just once be friendly? We got within thirty yards before Sol startled me with a barking laugh.

"Not real!" she shrieked. "Rainy, look! He's a picture."

I cut the engine, bumped up to a creaky dock, and out Sol leapt twirling a line. Sure enough the gas station man shed bulk and threat as we walked ashore. At forty feet he flattened into a competent painting. At ten it was clear his proportions were dicey and the artist had trouble with hands. I felt stupid to have bristled at this amateur likeness, which from its faded pigments had been there for some time. Meanwhile the building was locked and the gas pumps shut off. We cupped our hands, peering through glass at bare shelves.

There was nothing for us in that place. We scouted around a little. Behind the building was a bulk propane tank, empty. A brown dumpster had been tipped over and lived in. Over the back door hung a shredded awning and the door itself was damaged, secured with padlock and hasp. Sol urged me to put my shoulder to it but I saw no upside to this. The sky had earlier gone a bashful pink but now cold gloom returned. We boarded *Flower* and cast off. As we backed into the canal the painted man reacquired depth. His dour spirit revived. I kept having to look back. His eyes appeared to glitter in their holes.

At this point, I nearly decided to reverse course and head out the way we'd come. The canal was lonely and depressing and I was spooked by the painted observer and hostile children. We weren't many miles from the entrance and still had fuel enough to regain the open sea. So what if it took longer to reach Redfield and Griff? I was in no hurry. Nor was Sol it appeared.

We needed provisions, though. With two people it was shocking how quickly the food disappeared. Also it had begun to rain. The wind came slicing out of the northwest, which decided it. I didn't want that gale in my face.

Rubicons get crossed for all kinds of petty reasons.

Forward then past farms and orchards and fallow plots, scudding along through sudden gusts that whitened my hands on the tiller and drove Sol below to paw through our diminishing supplies. She found our last two apples and ate them both. She lit the chilly little alcohol burner and brewed coffee and brought me a cup that steamed and dimpled in the rain. When the weather began to lift I saw a woman on the island side, watching us from an upstairs window. I raised my cup to her in greeting.

"Don't bother," Sol said, hugging her elbows. "She's a painting too."

"Really?" But I could see it now and another static figure on a house a hundred yards along. "What about that one?"

"They're everywhere," was her observation. Clearly some artwork had slipped past me in the rain, but once I started seeing them I couldn't stop. There knelt a man working on an upturned bicycle, farther along a grandmother with trowel in one hand and seedling in the other. An old man stood tall beside an empty wheelchair. A tiny girl held a basketball at her side watching a young woman ascend into the sky on fierce black wings sprouting from her shoulders. What really stood out wasn't even her wings but her laughing expression as she glanced back toward the canal—surprised, beaming at the enchantment of flight, and thrilled to be getting out. All these figures were depicted in muted colors and all adorned buildings leaning or abandoned. Mostly houses but also barns and bait shops and long low broken-windowed poultry sheds from better days. Through a veil of rain they were both unsettling and spellbinding. A few were emphatically sinister and hinted at retribution. It was impossible not to see these as memorials to the dead who from all appearances outnumbered the living.

I was so taken with this silent rainy ghost parade I didn't hear Sol trying to get my attention. It took her actually tugging my elbow, or I'd have gone right past what we were looking for—the open fuel station on the mainland, with a pump at the T-shaped dock and what looked like a small grocery on the shoreline. The grocery had a flagpole and was flying a double banner that flopped around heavily like trousers. Beside it a mesh corncrib contained a bucket and a heap of fur. A plank sign said ONE DOLLAR FEED THE BEAR. Coasting up to a pier of warped pine, I cut the motor and Sol hopped out to secure the boat. How did it not seem strange that her dock line fluency surpassed my own?

The proprietor sat outside his shop in a motorized chair creaking back and forth as he lifted blocks of ice from a wagon into an upright freezer. When the wagon was empty he closed the freezer, locked it, and spun the chair around. He was gray-faced and broad with a big green slicker on and a dappled cotton scarf wrapped five or six times around his neck. One leg stopped at the knee and the other had wilted from disuse. His voice was beseeching and high-pitched and gave even neutral statements a tone of complaint.

"Fuel shipment's way behind," he announced, seeing the empty jerrican in my hand. "So there's your disappointment for the day."

I asked when the shipment was due.

"Yesterday. They used to catch me on their way to Blinker, but they keep changing routes. It's potholes and pirates and God knows what all. It won't be this afternoon, and maybe not tomorrow."

"Would I find gas in Blinker?"

"Probably. Right now your best shot would be Ray's. Two miles past the bridge, you'll know it when you see it. Anything else I got you covered. I'm Douglas, by the way." To Sol he added, "Did you see my bear? How would you like to feed him? I bet you never fed a wild bear before."

She glanced at the corncrib with its dark hump sleeping beside a bowl of dirty water. It may have been dead. A small sheaf of coarse fur lifted and settled in the breeze. She said, "That's no bear. That's a bulldog."

Her disrespect was a blunt object but Douglas was unbothered and in fact seemed happy to engage.

"Nope, sweetie, that animal is a bear. On the small side I admit! But a bear he is. Normally I charge a dollar to feed him"—Douglas reached under his chair and produced a crust of bread—"but I like a skeptic. Good for you! Iron sharpens iron! Here now, keep track of your fingers. He's not a pet."

Sol reached for the bread, but he pulled it away. "And what is this creature you're about to feed?"

"A bulldog."

"Ope, no, we haven't got any bulldogs here," said Douglas. "Tell you what. You call him what he is, and then I'll let you feed him."

Sol's eyes went behind a cloud.

Douglas hesitated, then swelled with generosity. "You know what? It doesn't even matter what he is. Wah hey! You say bulldog. I say bear. People of goodwill can disagree!" And he held out the bread to her again.

"He isn't hungry," was her curt reply before I hastily asked Douglas what he had by way of fresh produce, and he led us into his shop. Before the door swung shut, the furry hump sighed and lifted its head. Pushed-in nose, red-rimmed saggy eyes, a single broken fang—a forlorn old English bulldog, thinning on out of this earthly life and meantime bored off his nut.

The shop itself was a dim stew of batteries and bruised light bulbs and ferruled graphite fishing rods alongside chisels and breakfast cereals and local spirits in glass jars, squalid stacks of magazines, bits of verdigris copper ore, a clumsily taxidermized sturgeon, a *Rand McNally Road Atlas* propped open like a fantasy of painless travel. A chalkboard listed items for which Douglas would barter. I had several of these on the boat, including standard open end wrenches (*no metric* specified in red) so I went up and down the few short aisles collecting what we needed in a cloth sack. Sol went out the door I assumed to see the dog. Douglas rolled along in my wake. He was lonely and eager to please. His high voice was disarming and for a fact it never stopped. Above all else he was a narrator.

"Your girl's a sparkler! *That's no bear!* I got a niece like her. Keeps my sister alert I can tell you."

I picked up a cabbage, asked about the Huffin Bridge. Did it still operate?

"Does it *operate*? Like an army surgeon! I was on the committee eight years. We were the ones made it a free market bridge. Alistair himself appointed me," he said, swelling a bit.

"Who's Alistair?"

"The bridgemaster. You'll meet him. He's credentialed as hell. Wide discretionary powers. His first move was raising the tariff for islanders coming across."

"How did the islanders feel about that?"

Douglas was amused. "You're imagining that matters. Have you been to the other side? Had dealings with islanders?"

I lifted some potatoes into the sack, two cans of chili, coffee. "Haven't seen anyone except some kids flying a kite."

He said it was just as well. There were no guarantees, over on the island. He said Blinker and Brighton used to be like one city. People moved easily between them. Kids flirted and dove off the bridge with each other. Now the islanders hated their mainland neighbors. "We got to defend ourselves," Douglas said. "They've gone full evil, over there. You wouldn't believe it, how they hate us."

"Maybe the bridge tariff seems unfair," I suggested.

"That's not it," said Douglas. He said it was because mainlanders were happy and took care of their houses and had good jobs and compliant women. The islanders were filled up to here with the sin of envy. They refused to be grateful and chose to be insolent. They also left. Their hardware closed, their pharmacy. Teachers disappeared, then city staff. Postal clerks and orchard hands and wind-turbine crews and ministers of the gospel followed. Those who remained forged a cult of rage. When someone died they were cremated in open bonfires and their likeness painted on derelict walls. The painter knew sly incantations from the voodoo latitudes and after dark his images peeled themselves off the ruins and drifted across to moan at Blinkerites. Douglas had seen them shimmering past windows, sliding under locked doors. To fight this devilry he joined a sacred brotherhood that crossed the bridge once a month to evangelize the man burners and druids and wicked poets and ordinary perverts, a daunting enterprise with pagans prancing up out of the shadows to pitch rocks. "We go the last Friday night of the month," he said. "That's tomorrow. You could join us, if you like."

"We have other plans."

Besides groceries, I'd picked up a rolled sheet of silicone and rubber cement. Douglas rolled up behind the cash register where I stood calculating what I had to barter. I hadn't seen Sol reenter the shop, but there she was at my side.

"Cash or trade," said Douglas in his high voice.

While opening my mouth to offer sockets and box-end American wrenches, I heard Sol answer, "Cash."

I looked down. She held in her hand a large tan envelope. It was tattered and resembled a folded roadmap with its history of stains. The envelope was tilted wide open and in fact was stuffed with green money.

"Sol?" I asked in confusion.

The envelope got the attention of Douglas, who quickly tallied up our purchases and asked what else he could do to help us on our way. He had a beautiful small generator but no fuel to run it. He had a blued Ruger precentury handgun and as many rounds as we wanted. There was also a wall of spooled rope in diverse materials. We said no to the generator and sidearm but yes to two hundred feet of nonstretch polycore in startling azure. He measured out the rope and cauterized the ends. Expensive, but Sol had the cash. Erik used to say only mountaineers and boat people know what rope is worth.

"Listen," Douglas said as we departed. "Alistair is on nights at the bridge office. He's a legend! Wide discretionary powers! You greet him for me. Yes? All right? Tell him Douglas says hello."

~

We set off in a bright blistery chop. I was glad to leave Douglas behind. He made me tense, with his constant narration and his redefined bulldog. You try to occupy this actual world but man there is always a Douglas, always someone ready to fly his pants and call them a flag. Looking back the sun caught the undersides of his curling shingles. The corncrib roof glinted and the flagpole shook and the strange forked banner leveled out straight in the wind.

"Hey, Sol," I said. Something was different—something was gone.

"What."

"Where's the bulldog?"

The corncrib was, as the song goes, empty as a pocket.

"I turned him loose."

"Okay." And then, though I didn't want to bring it up, I said, "You need to tell me where you got that money."

Death right down to the cheekbones

SHE ADMITTED with pride that she took it from Richard. Besides spooking him generally, she knew of seven or eight money caches in his basement, his attic, the rafters of his retail establishment. He hid it mostly in plain green ammo boxes tucked under floorboards and not even locked. She was cautious at first and took only a few dollars with which to buy snacks and the goodwill of urchins.

"But this time I cleaned him out," Sol said, adding it was too bad we didn't get to "hit" the store, King Richard's, since he had at least this much more money over there, plus several cases of bagged caramels we could be eating at this moment. "And what's the matter with *you* now," she finished. No doubt I was gnawing the inside of my mouth.

"He's probably already after us. Wouldn't you be if somebody robbed you blind?"

If I sounded anxious I was. Flagrant theft seemed a rash move for someone who believed in death angels. Hadn't I given my bass guitar to extract Sol from Richard without pursuit? Now pursuit seemed all but certain. As for retracing our route to open water, that notion now ran face-first into a picture of Richard in a speedboat, spotting us easily and roaring alongside in vengeful grandeur, flourishing six or eight high-powered weapons like verbs in his favorite language.

"Don't be so worried," she said. "Richard can't count higher than twenty! He won't know the difference!"

"Sol," I said, as quietly as possible. "Does Richard have a boat?"

Abruptly her face reddened. Her eyes got small and narrow and wouldn't look my way.

I said, "What kind?"

She blinked, swallowed a hiccup of wrath, then loosed a vivid torrent at old Richard, calling him *suckweed*, *fartblister*, and many similar jeweled idioms I do not remember, and all I could do was nod along. Eventually, she did get around to Richard's boat. It was a sturdy old diesel-powered tug that feared no weather but moved at a waddling pace and was named, in fact, *Relax*. Well, I'd feared Richard would own some vessel of devastating speed, something suitable for smuggling or piracy or just inspiring dread. My nod of relief at this *Relax* freed Sol to return to her catalogue of juvie epithets.

"He is all those things," I agreed.

"And you barely met him," she spat.

"I know it."

"You met him twice. That's nothing."

"I know it."

"You didn't have to smell him all the time." This brought back in full the eye-watering air inside Richard's house, the stink of infections past help. I fell silent then, and Sol sulked and wouldn't look at me, because at the age of nine, with years of abuse already behind her, she had the flair and velocity to steal more of Richard's money than Richard could apparently count, and I didn't treat her like a hero for it, though she obviously was.

After a suitable interval I said, "How high can *you* count?"

Still looking away she said, "High as I need to."

"Fifty?" I said.

"A hundred!"

"All right then. Go get that envelope. Let's count Richard's money."

"*Our* money," she replied.

Looking back, that was one of our better afternoons—rolling along the waterway at a few miles per hour, watching the mainland turn busy and messy nearing Blinker and Brighton and the bridge in between. It did not hurt that the envelope contained four hundred twenty-two dollars, even after our splurge with the extortionate Douglas. After a bit Sol took the tiller while I cut a piece of silicone into new bellows for the leaking bilge pump and glued it in place. Sturdy as *Flower* was, water came in through so many cracks and rivets and iffy joints it was necessary to pump every two or three hours, otherwise you were apt to wake to a freezing inch sluicing across the cabin sole. While I repaired the pump Sol guided us down the waterway, pointing out strange herons alert in the rushes and warlike flags snapping over the mainland, also increasing numbers of painted islanders gazing from abandoned walls. Some were defaced and some had been repainted with deep black strokes and expressions of disdain. At one point she asked whether I believed they could really slide off their bricks or stucco and glide across to petrify mainlanders.

"What do you think?"

"Douglas thinks they can."

"Douglas thinks bulldogs are bears."

"Why do they do it, though? Paint those people on the walls?"

"To remember them, would be my guess. Like you remember your uncles lost to the water."

In time the canal narrowed and deepened. The sky deepened too as evening came and near the island we spotted a coracle no more than eight feet across tilting under the weight of a kneeling woman with her hair up in a blue bandanna and a cigarette dangling off her lower lip. She was raising something heavy on a rope. As we passed she lifted a shank of old meat from the water. It was black and writhing with leeches. The woman held up this gruesome spectacle and scraped the leeches off into a lidded bucket, where they landed with a squelching sound. Lowering the haunch back into the water she gazed at us dubiously. I waved a greeting she did not return. Her eyes were clear and farcical and I fell short in her assessment. The tip of her cigarette brightened.

Then we rounded a bend in the canal. There lay the lights of Blinker and the dark stretch of the Huffin Lift Bridge.

We tied *Flower* to a dock below the bridge office. Sol stayed on the boat while I went up to talk to Alistair.

He sat behind a glass window overlooking the water. He had a wide grave face like a lion's that swiveled with an expression of weariness at my approach.

"Your business on the canal?"

His voice was deep and his diction formal, matching his bored and regal face.

"Delivering a passenger to Redfield."

"Carrying goods to sell?"

"No."

"You've traversed the waterway before?"

"No."

"Do you plan to return by the same route?"

"No." I tried to establish eye contact, but Alistair kept looking over my shoulder. He asked the boat's value, and I threw out a number that he punched into a whirring machine. He asked about mast height and punched in forty feet. The machine made a satisfying sound like a small ratchet. It had old round numerical keys but looked well-oiled and capable. I trusted the machine more than I trusted Alistair, whose decorum and unwillingness to meet my eyes suggested imminent robbery. I said, "Douglas sends his best."

"Does he."

"Sold us some groceries this morning. Called you a longtime friend and a man of fair play."

"Right. Douglas. I've known him since he was Doug." This diffident remark was hard to read, especially since Alistair kept his face angled away, as though I were barely perceptible and best viewed slant. He said, "Nothing to declare then?"

"No."

"Three hundred seventy dollars."

At my silence he glanced off to my left. "You seem surprised."

"Three hundred seventy. What cargo do you think I am carrying?"

Alistair's voice turned soft. "Does the fee seem exorbitant to you?"

I said nothing.

"Because you are a first-timer I will explain that maximum outlays are a fact of operating this bridge. Do you know what a yard of high-tensile cable costs? Do you know where it has to come from?"

I did not.

"Do you know how many of these bridges are still in operation?"

I didn't.

"Most shut down long ago. This one has not. It will not as long as I am here. Three hundred seventy."

When I still hesitated he said, "If you're not in a hurry, you may wait until another vessel arrives and negotiate to share the fee with them."

"When will another vessel arrive?"

"None are scheduled. Could be a few days. A week." Alistair moved his face slowly until his eyes settled over my right shoulder. "There are worse places to wait. Blinker has eating establishments, blackjack rooms, retail shops. We are proud of our many churches. It might not hurt you to visit one of them. Of course you also have the option of returning to the upper entrance and taking the long way around."

"Or I could drop the mast and motor underneath without paying a dime."

"You would be in violation of the bridge charter. Any craft longer than twenty feet is subject to a passage fee whether or not the bridge goes up."

"What's the fee?"

"Three seventy."

At this came a slight pressure at my waist, which was Sol pushing the envelope of money at me.

I pulled her aside. "Are you sure about this?"

She nodded.

"You think Richard's coming?"

"Yes." She thrust the envelope into my hand.

It entered my mind that in addition to fleeing Richard, Sol was also hedging her bets. If he actually did catch us in his dawdly tugboat, she wanted to make sure all his money was gone.

I counted out the cash by ragged tens and twenties while Alistair typed numbers and pulled a long lever producing an embossed document like a passport or notarized permission. This he handed over like the precious paper it evidently was, along with a dated receipt.

"Here you go. Return in the morning and present that permit, and we'll get you on your way."

"In the morning."

"Correct. We're currently on an emergency curfew schedule." He lifted his chin, spoke to the air above my head. "We've intercepted some chatter from the other side, a threat to the bridge. Our directive calls for an abundance of caution. You may stay at the dock tonight for ten dollars or anchor out for free. Show that permit to the morning operator and he will raise the bridge. You *be* here," he then admonished, as though we might lose ourselves in the delights of Blinker—its blackjack, its profusion of churches—and forget to show up.

We remained at the dock until a city worker started down to collect the ten, then backed out and found a clearing in the tall rushes and set the anchor. A strange fraught too-warm evening under clouds. In the near distance a man screamed twice, the second cut short followed by a swelling silence until the insects started up again. Later came periodic gunfire, a euphoric rise and fall like babbling talk, a clanging bell, the metallic *bloop* of marsh herons. A rooftop bar on the shoreline had a live band—good pianist, capable rhythm guitar. The bass stayed mostly inaudible. There were vocals too. Not everyone can sing though many try.

Eventually I sent Sol down to her bunk, but after a bit she scrambled back up. The night had cooled, the band had finished, and the lights of Blinker had extinguished except for the bridge office where Alistair remained in stale florescence behind his square window. He didn't move but sat inert like a machine turned off. I was falling asleep when Sol asked was it true the world would end in fire like King Richard said. I said Of course not. Ice? she inquired. No again. She then asked would there be a Rupture of the Saints. I said I didn't think so. She was quiet twenty seconds then said, "I miss your low guitar."

I missed it too.

"If you played your low guitar I could go to sleep."

"Not a thing I can do about it."

"You could sing."

"We'd both be sorry."

"You could hum."

"I'm going to stop answering you."

"You have so many books," she said, meaning my library of seven, the most she'd ever seen in one place. "King Richard has four, counting two Bibles. He never reads. He says he can but chooses not to. You could read me something."

I reached for the *Folsum*. It was right there.

"Not that one. No. I hate that guy with his timothy grass."

"Pick another one, then."

Down the hatch she popped and of course came back with Molly Thorn. How could she not? All the others were field guides to clouds and shorelines and animal tracks, whereas Molly's book had a drawing on the cover of a small girl peeking through her fingers at the reader.

Five years old and fed up to here I rolled a sleeve of saltines, a Nesbitt's Orange, and two of my brother's crumbly cigarettes into a woolen blanket and waited for my chance to slip out.

That's the first sentence of her opening chapter, entitled *I Run Away*. I'd attempted the book several times before, but in those silent readings the words arrived in Lark's voice and swamped me with grief. It was different reading aloud to a tiny rapt human. Molly told her life as if she were that moment dreaming it into existence and stamping her feet to see where it would go.

Earlier that day I'd asked my valiant dad about Death, which in pictures was a robed wanderer with carven cheeks and skeleton feet. So fearsome! And on this topic he was not reassuring, but then Dad himself had mysteries by the handful. Didn't he calm the wild dog who raged and snapped at others? Didn't he survive the tornado that sucked him into the sky with tree limbs and street signs? And so while I had no doubt Death was real, neither did I doubt that Dad, who often chuckled in his sleep, had in his possession a way to get around it.

"Right," Sol said in a skeptical tone. "A way to get around Death."

"Well, she was five," I pointed out. "She didn't have your advanced years. Maybe we give her the benefit of the doubt."

She made no reply, so I kept reading. Off trots Molly to a narrow green river where she spots an ancient stone arrowhead on the bank. She wants the arrowhead, but a few yards from it stands a stranger, looking out over the water. When he turns she sees the stranger is Death. With a tailed black coat in place of a robe and soft-soled boots instead of skeleton feet, but otherwise Death right down to the cheekbones. That sat Sol up! There follows a page or so of genuine suspense, Death easing closer to Molly line by line, until she thwarts him by demanding he answer a perplexing riddle taught to her by her atypical father.

"Wait," Sol said. "That wouldn't work."

"What?"

"A riddle. Come on! What riddle's going to keep Death away?"

"You didn't like it?" It was a silly, irreverent riddle I thought Sol would enjoy. It was all about fingers and nostrils.

"I just don't think Death cares if you're funny," she added, because I kept laughing at the riddle.

"Well maybe he used to care," I said. "It's an old story."

"If Death cared about riddles there'd be more smart people around. No, he takes the clever ones first. That's what I think," she asserted, adding darkly, "It's the stupids who live forever."

I set the book aside. "We'll put the story away, then, since you know so much about it."

Straightaway Sol's mouth crimped, her eyes shone wide then narrowed into belligerence. Weary as I was, nothing would do except another chapter, which thankfully contained no immediate peril. In fact a massive brindle-colored dog entered the story, a sinewy animal with a deep chest and eyes of ruinous kindness. As I read, Sol eased and settled, even laughed a little. The lamplight wavered and shifted. That dog was the exact creature anyone would want by their side in a crisis, especially if Death were only recently outwitted and might still lurk nearby.

~

Having no clock we were early to the bridge office and waited in a chill wind containing bits of ice. Only last night it had been warm enough to raise gnats off the water. I was anxious to get going. The morning operator appeared in the office. He had glossy short hair like a seal's and rimless glasses behind which he blinked constantly. He slid open his window and I handed across the certificate.

"This is from yesterday," he observed.

"Right, we paid yesterday. The operator, Alistair, specified we come back this morning. He said you'd stamp the pass and lift the bridge. Now we're here. We'd like to go under."

He held my paper up to the light. "The problem, my friend, is that this is yesterday's pass." He slid it back to me.

I pointed to the stamped announcement: PAID IN FULL.

In reply he pointed to the date. "Appears to me you came through from the lower entrance, transacted your business over here, and are now looking to return. You will have to pay again."

"I have never been on the other side of this bridge. Talk to Alistair. I came in yesterday from the upper entrance. Talk to Douglas. I purchased this document last night. Alistair said he was unable to lift the bridge because the night curfew was in place."

"Pardon?"

"Night curfew. Alistair said there was chatter about a threat to the bridge. He said to come back this morning because of night curfew."

"No such designation exists. Bridge operators lift and lower at all times of day." He said, "A suspicious man might think you were trying to game the system."

"Where is Alistair," I said.

"He is not here."

"Call him."

"Alistair is off duty."

"Alistair charged us three seventy. This is the receipt. He said the bridge would lift for us this morning. It should be going up right now. Talk to Alistair and he will confirm what I have said."

I felt anger building and this operator no doubt saw it. Behind him a door opened and a man stepped out. His brown uniform had aggressive scarlet highlights and scarlet threads ran through it. He had a square pleasant face and a holstered pistol on his belt. He said, "Everything easy out here, Ricky?"

Ricky looked at me. "Sir?" he said. "You easy?"

"I will be easy when you lift the bridge."

"Then we'll need to reach an agreement," he said.

"We haven't got the money."

"Many travelers find themselves at a cash deficit. We are open to barter." Ricky squinted past my shoulder. "I see an outboard motor on your transom. How would you describe its condition?"

Behind him, the uniformed man picked up a pair of binoculars and peered through them at my boat.

I said, "You people are running a con. We paid for the lift and now you deny us passage. Lift the bridge or return the three seventy."

The officer said, "Ricky, that vessel doesn't have a current sticker. If it does, it is not properly displayed."

Ricky eased up a few inches off his chair to look past me at the boat. "Sir, when was your boat last inspected?"

Of course I had seen boats with bureaucratic decals or stickers, but this was years ago. No one in Icebridge ever asked. Lark entered my head advising caution. I said, "Ricky, I only want what I paid for yesterday. You know what I'm saying is true. I am asking you to treat a fellow citizen according to your native honesty and goodwill."

Ricky's face looked moist and soft. His left eye blinked as if expunging a speck of conscience. Watching him struggle I suddenly remembered my access to what Werryck had called an almost infinite bank balance. I might, with a Willow or two, buy passage and be off.

At this my own conscience fluttered away.

"What about," I began, in a casual tone, "if I were to offer—" but then behind Ricky I noticed the uniformed man eyeing me closely. What stopped me was no fit of integrity but rather the likelihood that such a proposition would launch these public servants into a full search of the boat. A few doses of Willow might be seen as almost legitimate currency—a few thousand, probably not.

Ricky said, "You were about to suggest a trade."

I said, "I need to go down to the boat and look over my inventory."

"Fair enough."

I nodded and left him there. But I didn't rejoin Sol on *Flower*. Instead I walked into Blinker to knock at the door of the first house I saw and ask where Alistair lived. It wasn't subtle but who had time to be delicate? The woman at the door closed it in reply so I went to the next. Where is Alistair? Nobody said, but no one played dumb either. No one said, *Alistair who?* Eventually the door of a rundown rambler opened and there stood a young man wearing pinstripe pajamas and a cheated expression.

He said, "You mean the bridge troll?"

"Yes."

"You a friend of his?"

"No."

He seemed pleased to give me directions.

Alistair lived in a three-story pile of powdery red brick. According to the lawn plaque, it had been built by a copper tycoon in the 1890s, then owned in succession by a timber baron, a hotelier, and the Roman Catholic Church. And now Alistair, who answered the door at my fourth ring. You would think in the context of a grand house he might seem a bit reduced, but no. In fact he seemed taller, dressed even now in somber darks, his eyes drifting as before to some spot over my shoulder. He did not seem annoyed to be interrupted at home and asked my name and business.

I reminded him of our transaction and showed him the receipt and the paperwork signed by himself.

"This is from yesterday," he said.

I explained again and he said, "The bridge is raised and fees collected at the discretion of the operator on duty. Ricky is on duty. If you want to pass, you must come to an agreement with Ricky."

"But you remember me. I can see that you do. I am only asking not to be robbed a second time."

He stepped back. I thought he was inviting me in but he was only reaching for his huge rimmed glasses. Behind him an old woman entered the room. She wore colorful silks and her hair was awry. Something bad had been smeared on the walls. The place smelled faintly like Richard's. Alistair put on the glasses and looked me up and down.

I put a smile in my voice and said, "We meet again."

"Go away from my house," he said.

"Pardon?"

"I never saw you. You may negotiate with Ricky for passage or with me when I come on shift. If you come to my house again I will put my hands on you."

"Alistair," came the woman's wispy voice. "Alistair, there's a right way. Do it the right way. Have him arrested."

He turned and stared the old woman out of the room, then closed the door as though I were not there.

~

We motored a quarter mile back, rounded a bend and anchored next to bullrushes on the island side. Sol stayed quiet and clear of my steam. No doubt I stamped around. No doubt I had some things to say about Ricky and Alistair and Douglas and people raising their kids to shoot at strangers for sport. Nothing brings rage like humiliation. I had been taken by donkeys, and here we still sat on the wrong side of the Huffin Bridge.

"Hey, sailboat," said a woman's voice close by.

I turned. It was the woman we'd passed yesterday scraping leeches off a shank. Not kneeling today but standing upright poling along in her little coracle, no easy feat. She was tall and narrow and ageless. Minus yesterday's bandanna, her hair was gray with glowing red strands.

She said, "You two should buy some bait."

Sure enough, there was her lidded bucket and beside it a dirty foam cooler.

"No thanks."

"Best leeches on the North Coast." She was a solemn totem pole until her eyes gave her away. "These are in high demand. Spotted Ornamentals, Midnight Flatworms. Nimble Swifties. No lake trout refuses a Nimble Swifty! You also can't go wrong with the classic Hirudo Medicinals."

I shook my head, but Sol dissented immediately, *Come on Rainy, we'll catch fish, I'll clean them myself*, etc. As if there were still clean lake trout waiting to be caught! As if it weren't all carp and nauseating lampreys! Next moment she was leaning over the gunwale as the woman, name of Essie, reached into her cooler to display one twisty variety after another. Her monotone delivery accentuated her unexpected word choice. These bloodsuckers were *acrobatic* and *succulent*; they were *hypnotic* and *spicy*.

Sol was electrified. "You know everything about leeches!"

"Oh, I'm a connoisseur," said deadpan Essie.

We bought a dozen Nimble Swifties in a half-pint container. I peeled back the lid for a look. The leeches were gathered in a writhing Medusa knot.

Essie said, "I take it they won't lift the bridge."

I looked at her. "Wide discretionary powers."

She was a lifelong islander with a sighing contempt for the mainland. She told us after the bridge went free market, resourceful shippers improvised low barges designed to carry goods in a single flat layer, avoiding the lift fee. Thereafter the Bridge Committee gave itself authority to stop and board all vessels and charge not only for passage but also for "any other fees deemed necessary and reasonable."

"What you ought to do," Essie said, "is motor back out the way you came."

But Richard and pursuit were on my mind.

"Not optimal," I said.

Essie stood there in her coracle. Thin shirt thin pants yet she didn't freeze or even shiver. She removed from her pocket a small King James with leatherette cover, tore a page out, and rolled a cigarette using an herb I could not identify. Its dark wet smoke smelled of loam and drifted sideways through the rushes. Essie herself resembled a bullrush wand, swaying atop the water, brown and reedy, at ease with silence. With slow grace she placed a bare foot on the rim of the coracle. The foot was slender and flared at the toes.

"It's possible," Essie mused, in a low voice, "if you're careful, to pass under the bridge without payment."

"How?"

"Are you serious about this conversation?"

I was.

"Do you have coffee?"

"We can brew some."

"Brew it then," said Essie. "Also, you'll need to buy"—she leaned over her bait box—"three dozen Midnight Flatworms. Then I think we can talk."

the bitter ends in their teeth

BY DARK it was frosty and my limbs were brittle with cold. No one can make a sailboat invisible but we spent the afternoon trying. According to Essie's crisp directions we stripped all canvas, the bow and stern pulpits, and lowered the mast and tied it along the coach roof, then I went over the side with a bucket and brought up gallons of muck from the bottom to smear over deck, topsides, and spars—every surface apt to reflect light. All this we managed in a slurry backwater on the island side, behind the hulk of a small grounded freighter we'd passed the previous day. Every time I came out of the water Sol had a big laugh at the snotty black leeches clinging to my legs and back. Did Essie talk me into the family business? Were they scrumptious acrobats? Was I a connoisseur?

"Remind me how I survived without you, Sol." The words came out in clouds it was so cold.

Some hours earlier I'd left her aboard eating crackers and followed Essie's zigzag map up the streets of Brighton, a strange walk haunted by dozens of dead citizens watching from the walls. Most homes were empty but I glimpsed a few live kids in attic windows and two or three surly grannies standing on front porches. Some sidewalks were swept clean, elsewhere gutters glittered with shards of glass, and rubbish smoked along the boulevards. Fire seemed a common hazard in Brighton—at least one house per block was charred and slumping into its own basement.

Essie lived in a low rambler with a concrete shrine out front. This grotto was stuffed with doused candles and plastic flowers and framed photos of a dark-haired young man of unguessable tragedy. Essie opened the front door and led me through into an attached shed where a wooden dinghy was tucked in the rafters. The boat was short and wide, its planks bent into a lively sheer. She called it a nutshell. Her son built it before he left the island never to return.

I said, "Maybe he'll be back. Home is a powerful draw."

"Not that powerful." She told me her son, unemployed at thirty, had been accepted into a test-patient program on one of the medicine ships. He underwent a series of behavior-renovation treatments designed to increase productivity and workplace obedience. Six years later he returned, aphasic and unable to brush his own teeth and somehow deeply in debt.

She ran a hand over the beautiful gunwales of the nutshell. I saw she was reconsidering her offer.

"Are you sure about this?" I asked.

The truth is our plan felt iffier by the minute, hinging as it did on Alistair's bad eyes and *Flower*'s intrepid bowsprit.

She said, "Of course not. I still recommend turning around and going back the way you came."

"We are pursued and need to move forward."

"Then your decision is made. I only ask that you return the dinghy afterward—it's all I have of him."

"I will if I am not arrested."

"Arrest is not what I'd worry about," she said. I will always remember her arid tone, the forward curve of her tough slim shoulders.

As twilight neared we eased the boat forward into a stand of rushes a hundred yards from the bridge. Again the mainland lit itself up against the night with sound and nervous energy while the island grew haunted and dark. I pulled *Flower*, her mast down and her beauty hidden, by a rope tied to the stern of Essie's nutshell. It was slow rowing. The weeds were heavy and taller than me. They made a calm shy sound as we moved through. Reaching a place that offered views of the bridge and bridge office, I climbed back on *Flower* and we waited. Full dark arrived. There sat Alistair in his lit booth. I watched him through binoculars, his proud old face and mane. A flotilla of ducks landed just outside our screen of rushes—they muttered quietly and paid us no mind. A pair of boats cruised past, each with short waterlines to escape the passage fee. The first, powered by a small electric, hummed without challenge beneath the bridge; the second with its throaty outboard caught Alistair's attention and was abruptly struck with a beam of light so intense it had sharp edges. Essie had warned of this. The spotlight used to go on automatically at night, aimed across the canal as a deterrent, but in recent years power was unreliable and the LED bulbs difficult to find, so the bridge operator employed it as needed. The boat's engine went quiet and its owner stood up. Pinned in place by the light. Through a bullhorn Alistair asked the owner's name, the boat's cargo and length at the waterline. The man had no amplification and had to shout his replies. Eventually Alistair let him proceed and switched off the light. I heard the outboard restart. He puttered under the bridge and faded down the canal.

My throat was dry and my palms wet.

I didn't notice Sol next to me until she whispered, "When?"

"Not yet."

"Are you chickening out?"

I pointed along the mainland shore. Men were gathering, men and boys. Some carried flashlights or lanterns, some had what looked like sticks or truncheons. Most wore holsters that flapped against their hips as they trotted out of the shadows.

Sol asked what was going on. She hadn't been in the room when Douglas described his group's selfless mission to sway tenacious pagans. In fact as I filled her in Douglas himself appeared in his motorized chair at the foot of the bridge. At that distance we could hear his high fervent voice. He shook some hands on the edge of a knot of men who seemed to be taking a headcount and were glancing peevishly across the canal as if sniffing for debauchery. Over in his booth Alistair had swiveled to watch the group form. Call it sixty men. Plus the boys—at least a dozen, some no more than belt-high. The gathering compressed at the bridge entrance where a voice was raised. Grave and ardent, indistinct, with the cadence of public prayer.

"What are they doing?" Sol hissed.

After benediction the men formed loose ranks. A jostly rickrack of flashlight beams, nervous laughter. They seemed to wait on a signal and as I turned the binoculars to Alistair he gave it. A swift flat motion of his hand. They set off across the bridge at a walk or slow march. Some took a stab at singing that petered out fast. Then Douglas appeared in front, his chair accelerating, himself leaning forward, light bouncing, and behind him all surged ahead, a river of roaring men and whooping boys. Douglas was overtaken and the bridge rumbled and shivered. In a minute they were all across and scattering in twos and threes up into the streets of Brighton.

Now came minutes of taut peace. Peace for us not Brighton. A zealot always finds the lost and soon enough came a whistle and shouts and running feet. Against the dark sky the facade of an empty bank building became visible like a tea-colored shade of itself, which confused me until Sol said the word "smoke," and I understood the bank was reflecting a fire lit downtown. Quickly more fires broke out so that Brighton became an underworld of hollows and shifting flame, with shouts and sometimes gunfire. Sol later said nineteen shots. I didn't count.

All this time Alistair sat in his booth looking out over the water.

"Now," said Sol.

"Not yet."

I could see she did think I was chickening out and indeed I felt chickeny right then, but it was good we kept still and kept quiet because there came a bustle of little yips and shouts and down out of Brighton marched our torchlit missionaries. They'd regrouped and were jubilant. The smaller boys tumbled and danced and hand-sprung around a bedraggled clot of detained pagans. Two men and a woman—for a moment I thought she might be Essie, but no. The three were pushed along with their hands tied behind them and the larger man stumbled and went to his knees. At this two boys darted in close and kicked him in his back and sides and another boy whipped off the belt he was wearing and lashed the man in the face before he was yanked back to his feet. The group marched to the center of the bridge where immediately three boys were sent up like nimble apes into the cabled rigging where some manner of blocks or pulleys were arranged. They trailed long ropes behind them as they clambered and fed them through the blocks and climbed back down with the bitter ends in their teeth.

"Go below," I said and Sol said she would not.

While that mob was pouring onto the bridge they'd been shouting and whistling, but now they were silent. Of the three pagans only the woman had things to say and she managed to call out the names of several mainland accusers, demanding to know what charge had been laid against her. No answer came that I could hear. Instead a large man stepped behind her and pulled a twist of cloth into her mouth, knotting the ends viciously. A kind of show now commenced where a man in white sleeves stood forth to condemn what he called the prisoners, though clearly they had not been imprisoned nor tried nor formally indicted and now faced definitive judgment. The white-sleeved man had a clarion voice full of controlled fury. He said the crimes of these pagans were longstanding and known to all and included blasphemy and indecency and foul expression among too many others to list. He said he was especially pleased, because tonight the Lord of Hosts had delivered into their hands the foremost painter of dead islanders. No more would his images appear at mainland windows, nor haunt the bedsides of the righteous. At this a cheer went up and a tiny boy zipped in with what looked like a baseball bat and cracked the tall man across the shins.

It appeared they would hang the three without further ceremony but someone cried out Alistair, Alistair, and the name became a chant. I watched through binoculars as he made his way out onto the bridge. He moved slowly, using the handrail and nodding at the sound of his name. An old black lion still heavy in the shoulders. As he neared, two of the smaller boys ran and took his arms to lead him the rest of the way, and he felt for their heads and patted them like a blessing. When he reached the condemned, all knots were affixed and the assembled stood quiet. Alistair said nothing but instead held out both hands. Someone placed the loose end of a rope across his palms. Without hesitation he took up the slack and with sudden force hauled down and jerked the littlest pagan into the air. While he thrashed, a few other men took the rope from Alistair and hauled him up farther and tied off the rope. The pagan spun kicking and managed to hook a bridge spar with his knees but soon lost strength and finally swung twisting with his feet a few yards above the roadway. Again Alistair was given a rope, the woman's. Again the swift rough pull. Up she went and such was her will she denied them the spectacle of struggle. Last came the tall man, the painter apparently. He tried to speak but was struck on the mouth and sagged until Alistair and others hauled him up. But his knot was badly tied and came loose as he struggled. Down he dropped into the water, where he surfaced and kicked haphazardly for shore. This brought gasps and hoots, and two or three boys no older than Sol leaned out from the bridge and started taking shots at him with short-barreled handguns. Bullets striking water *pop pop pop* like flat stones. There followed a silence with people craning over the rail. Pointing at the spot where he had vanished. *Diddy sink? Izzit him?* There was frantic speculation lest he swim underwater to freedom. The kids sighted down their firearms in case he reappeared, but he never did.

Over the next quarter hour the gathering broke up and vanished.

Sol looked at me and I saw her question.

Now.

I raised the anchor out of the weeds and bundled the rope and tied it down. Essie's nutshell lay alongside, the blades of its oars wrapped in flannel as she had recommended for silence. Sol was at *Flower*'s helm to point her true as I descended into the nutshell and quietly towed her out of the rushes toward the bridge. I stayed as near the island as possible. The fires had died down or been extinguished and no lights shone, while on the mainland at least two bands were playing and electricity danced in the windows. I would put *Flower*'s weight at four tons but she slid along smoothly behind the nutshell.

Alistair remained static in his chair as we approached the bridge. Seventy yards, fifty, thirty. I concentrated on long slow sweeps and refused to look either at Alistair or at the center of the bridge where the two pagans still dangled among the beams and cables. It was only when I entered the full shadow of the span itself that a terrible fact became clear: *Flower*, now coasting up slowly to the bridgeway, was not going to fit beneath.

I stowed the oars, grasped the underside of the bridge, and caught *Flower*'s bowsprit before it touched. I'd stripped off the bow pulpit and all hardware, but the proud little sprit was inches too high.

There we sat. And across the water, there sat Alistair in his lit window. Knobby fingers scratching at his massive old head. He appeared to be gazing straight at us but raised no alarm and shone no spotlight.

I rapped lightly on *Flower*'s hull. In a few seconds Sol appeared at the bow. I explained in a stressed hush what she could clearly see for herself.

There were few options. We tried getting all possible weight onto the bow, but even when I hung onto it from below, it remained too tall to pass.

"We could still turn around," I said.

Sol replied, "No. We got to sink the boat."

Some solutions are too plain to see. In fact nothing's simpler than letting water into your boat. There's a hose to loosen, a lever to twist. It's not a lesson I ever imagined having to teach someone, let alone in whispers under the blind gaze of a bridge troll, but as they say: a child could do it.

She slithered below and soon I heard water rushing into the bilge. Immediately *Flower* began to settle herself like a hen for the night. Standing in the nutshell I reached for the sprit. Already it was level with the bridge. Moments later we had a half inch to spare.

Alistair was moving. I'd slung my binoculars round my neck and watched. He had his big glasses on, and his eyes filled the lenses as he leaned forward. His right hand reached for something out of view.

I tapped the hull, heard the squeak as Sol twisted the sea cock shut.

And the spotlight came on with a whack—the light so hard we couldn't move, Sol frozen emerging from below and me at the bow. Two flies on the sun.

Something crackled across the water and Alistair drew an amplified breath. I braced for his voice ordering us to declare ourselves.

Immobilized as I felt, I'd certainly have done so.

But Alistair did not speak.

He only cleared his throat, a rough sound roughly aborted. Essie was right. The man was nearly blind. *Flower*—covered with dried mud—was the color of the riverbank. Spotlight or no, Alistair wasn't sure we were there.

In the pitiless light we stayed in place. *Flower* lifted on an infinitesimal swell. She seemed to breathe. I became conscious of the two pagans still hanging in the steel latticework above us. The woman's loose sleeve rippling in the breeze.

At the squeal of an opening door I shielded my eyes and looked toward the bridge office.

Alistair was coming out.

He left the spotlight burning and he had besides a long flashlight in his hand. Just as before, he came feeling his way onto the bridge. A prodigious old brute of gravitas and cataracts.

When the walkway hid him from view I sat down in the nutshell and lifted the oars. The blades dead quiet in their flannel jackets. I pulled hard and *Flower* moved under the bridge. The bowsprit did not scrape, although later I would find it tipped with green moss where it had slid along the bottom of the span. We crept at the rate of agony into the shade and out of the damned spotlight, emerging years later on the far side, where I leaned into the oars and swept us away even as Alistair followed his flashlight along the bridge. Reaching the pagans he shone it briefly up into their ruined faces, then bent over the rail and looked down into the water exactly where we had been.

I focused on rowing and do not trust my memory of these next minutes. I imagine the sweat of fear at my neck. Sol standing at the tiller. *Flower* riding low with her bilges full and her decks besmirched, brave and at her finest.

I wonder still how Essie fared in that night's cruelty—how she and all of Brighton could endure it. I couldn't shake that spark in her gray hair; she seemed about to catch and burn. Down the canal we went a quarter mile, then found a quiet weedy dock where we could tie up briefly. It made me nervous to leave Sol there alone but this was the bargain I'd made with Essie—the return of her nutshell—so I set it on my shoulders and worked up into Brighton by back lanes and alleys. No easy trip. The streets had fallen silent, but some were rubbled and holed, with burst windows and torn canopies and paint sprayed on storefronts. Fires smoldered on the boulevards, and once I fell into a great sink in the pavement—down I went and the nutshell with me, but we were both undamaged. In the end I found Essie's place and eased into the shed which she'd left unlocked. I tucked the boat into the rafters nesting on its flanneled oars. Her windows were dark and I left in silence. By then she must've known of the hangings. I still imagine her simmering anger. I didn't know what to hope for and still don't. When I complained to Lark about the last pages of *Quixote* she defended its author. Sometimes no right ending can be found.

It was a thick ten minutes getting back to *Flower* where she lay at the dock dismasted among the living weeds.

The wind rose.

A strange new glow came from the mainland, and I saw the base of the bridge was burning—not a conflagration but still a considerable flame slapping against the stone piling on which the bridgehead lay. It threw enough light to show on the water, enough to show the stretching forms of those poor suspended pagans. A man whacked at the fire with a blanket, doing little good. Climbing aboard *Flower* I called Sol's name. No answer.

Where *was* she?

Where were you, Sol?

Did you even begin to wonder what I'd think, when I came slinking back and you were nowhere to be found? And yes I hissed your name, and yes I risked a shout, and yes I lost most of my temper, glassing shorelines up and down.

How did you know I wouldn't leave?

It was moonless with little light except that thrown by the bridge fire. How did you think I'd ever find you in those binoculars, standing on the mainland, waving your bony arms?

the djinn

IT WAS SHORT WORK crossing to the rocks where Sol waited. Climbing aboard on shrunken white feet, drenched from her swim across the channel, she shook too hard to speak. I wanted an explanation but first things first: every dry blanket we had. And coffee. She craved her bunk but was hypothermic and I needed her awake and in sight. Wrapped in wool and coffee steam, she watched me steer or watched the passing shorelines and barely spoke as miles murmured past. I struggled to speak myself. I never was anyone's parent, so this rapid expansion of love and terror confounded me. Both things occupying the same space. Lark would've recognized it, known what it was. All I could do was steer the boat and keep Sol alert and watch the sky hinting at dawn. She groaned when I made her move her limbs, but Harry the drummer wandered off in a blizzard once and a doctor said only his refusal to be still had saved his life. Eventually I sang badly and roared out jokes and told stories of knights and maroons. We made it farther than I expected before the gas ran out. When the outboard sputtered it was nearly sunup, and I guided *Flower* into a patch of still water on the mainland side.

I had to carry Sol below. By now she wasn't just warm but feverish, not just conscious but talking fast nonsense. Eventually scattered fragments began cohering. A tale emerged of the old brute Alistair at ease in his booth when he detected smoke near at hand. Up he leapt or let's say creaked and hurried out with his sidearm and a jacket to beat out the flames. He couldn't have seen Sol flitting in the shadows like a djinn from *Arabian Nights*, but that's how it must have been. Himself sweating and woofing for help and flailing pathetically at the flames until his glasses slid clean off his face while Sol, the djinn, dodged into the firelight to scoop them away from his frantic old fingers. I'd have thought she embellished if she hadn't produced two items from inside her cocoon. First was my waterproof gas match, which she'd strapped to her leg like one of Stevenson's pirates before swimming across the waterway. Second—and more impressive—were Alistair's massive specs, which she dropped clattering into my palm like a gigantic repulsive dead insect. God they were heavy. May all hanging judges be judged themselves at last. The pride I felt was unmistakable, though to be clear it's rarely smart to burn a bridge.

Late in the morning Sol's fever broke, and she slept while I put *Flower* in shape—pumped the bilge and cleaned her up, bolted hardware in place, set shoulder to spar and heaved it upright so we became a masted vessel again with all the world before us. In a soft southeasterly I lifted sail and we were off—Sol still asleep—the canal's last miles smelling less like land and more like open sea.

~

At the lower entrance we tied up to a seawall, which in Folsum's day was topped with flagstones *for frolicsome picnics* but now was a shoulder of cement rotting back to sand. I was eager to head upcoast to Redfield, but Sol was still fragile—unable to keep food down, sporadically feverish, thinning by the hour. A store nearby had rice, beans, and even a bunch of bananas, bright green when I bought them but soft and brown within hours as if catching my unease. Light hurt Sol's eyes. At night she dozed, waking often to drink boiled broth and to demand stories. I never knew anyone so hungry for stories. This is what happens when you reach the age of nine without any. I told her what I could of the mythologies and planetary operas and Ratty and Mole and Robin Hood and all the Dickens and McMurtrys I remembered, but these retellings were superficial and I misplaced characters and got lost in thickets of detail while inventing new substandard endings to supplant what I'd forgot. Growing cranky with me, she asked for Molly Thorn, and I read a bit where Molly age six plants a garden in her yard. A salesman comes by peddling seeds—flowers, cucumbers, beans, melons—but what transfixes Molly is what the salesman calls the *mystery packet*, a diversity of kernels and pips all thrown together. Though her skeptical brother calls this 'what got swept off the floor,' Molly yearns for the mystery packet, and on his way out the salesman tosses her two of the plain yellow envelopes, completing, it seems, her world.

> *I couldn't imagine wanting to know what the seeds were. Shouldn't it always be a surprise? Shouldn't you step out one morning to find your yard overwhelmed by blossoms whose names you don't know and pumpkins of lunar immensity and peas so ripe they burst when you look at them? Plus I'd overheard Eloise at the bakery tell a customer she had "picked" two dozen cream horns for his event, which signified to me that these dazzling pastries were not*

made in kitchens but grew out of the Earth, no doubt on curling and beautiful vines, so surely the Mystery Packet would yield some cream horns or at least long johns as well as more conventional produce.

It struck me that while the stories I recounted were hit-and-miss, Molly never failed to connect with Sol. When Molly fought, Sol wrung her hands. When Molly imagined her outlaw self, Sol trembled. When Molly raked up a bit of yard and planted her ultimately dismaying mystery seeds, Sol sank into contentment and slept. Not only did she like being read to, Sol also seemed enthralled by the physicality of a book—she ran her fingers over Molly Thorn's blue cover, riffled the pages for their comforting sound. Lark would've made a reader of this girl in about eight minutes.

I said, "Sol, do you know the letters?"

She shook her head no.

It was a clear night and dew had begun to form on the decking. I reached out and wrote with a fingertip in the moisture, tracing out the letters S, O, L. "See, that's your name," I said. She frowned and squirmed and said to do it again.

I wrote her name again below the first, with more intention, even a little elegance, and dew gathered at the edges of the letters. She looked at me as though I had performed something either godlike or unspeakably wicked.

"All right, listen, hang on," I said, and I went below and found an old tool apron of Erik's that was still rolled up in a storage nook above the folding table. Inside the apron's pocket was a carpenter's pencil, the wide kind you sharpen with a knife. I grabbed it and also the *Field Guide to Animal Tracks* by Olaus Murie and returned to the cockpit.

"Look here," I said, flipping to the back of the field guide where there were a few blank pages. I rubbed the tip of the carpenter's pencil with my fingertips so a little graphite came off, then flattened the open book against my knee and wrote *Sol* at the top of a page. "See, S, like a winding stream. O, like somebody's head. L is just a straight line, north to south. There it is. Sol! What a good name you have. Now you try."

I held out the pencil, but she shrank away as if I'd offered her a snake. She said, "You do it some more."

So I wrote a few words, deliberately—*boat*, *bird*, *Rainy*, and so on—saying the letters aloud as they appeared.

Still she wouldn't take the pencil. At one point she touched it only to yank her hand away. It was plain she felt some shifty wizardry was at work. Her face turned small and distant and she said, "It isn't for me."

Well, I wasn't going to be weird about it. I just thought she'd be interested—someone who sparked and flared the way she did.

"It's okay." I closed the book. It had a faded paper jacket with a deer looking over its shoulder at the reader. Something about the deer caught me—maybe its curious expression. I said, "This was written by a man named Olaus, see?" I pointed out the author's name. "Before it could be a book, Olaus had to write down all these words. Probably used a pencil, like this one. Wrote one word at a time, about the tracks of raccoons and bears and wolves and big cats. He even wrote about the tracks a maple leaf makes when it blows across fresh snow. And now this book"—I tapped its cover—"is Olaus's track. Because of it, we know this guy Olaus was here before us, and he loved animals and knew all about them."

"And maple leaves."

"Right."

She was quiet.

"Words are one way we leave tracks in the world, Sol. Maybe one day you will write a book, like Olaus did, or Molly Thorn. And people will read it, like I've been reading to you. And they will know that you were here, and a little about what you were like."

Sol's face remained far away. Her cheeks were white and hollow, but her eyes shone a bit, I was fairly sure.

the phantom gramps

OUR THIRD MORNING on the seawall Sol climbed on deck for breakfast. An improvement, yet the sight of her was troubling. Unstable on her feet, eyes too shiny in their sockets—it felt to me as though a second child lived behind those eyes, a wartime girl or daughter of famine. To keep that waiting child at bay, I heaped her plate with eggs and potatoes. She ate some but not enough. I thought we would stay longer in that place, but later that morning an official-looking vessel came trolling down the waterway and tied up behind us. It was plastered with state and federal insignias and flew a coast guard pennant, and when the pilot strolled past us in his brown uniform he looked with weathered boredom at our transom, which was bare of all credentials. He paused, peered at the watch on his wrist, continued down the seawall.

I suggested to Sol we throw off lines and sail up the peninsula and find the splendid Griff.

She paled and nodded.

The breeze was dead perfect and I'd refilled our jerrican with dubious gas from a mainland entrepreneur and strapped it to a stanchion out of the way. I'd also scrubbed *Flower*'s deck and topsides, rinsing with buckets of lake so she was close to spotless. We cleared the breakwater and in minutes were under full sail, heeling under a flattened main and the entrance falling away.

~

We looked for Griff the next handful of days. Though Sol had sworn he lived in Redfield, she now got vague on his whereabouts. She said he traveled for work as a machine mechanic and vendor and part-time stage actor. He was sought after for musicals about dishonest salesmen. His wit and good looks made him hard to keep track of. When I set the map out for clarity, she obfuscated. He lived in or near a small town within sight of the water, and that was as far as she went.

"Sol," I said, the idea seeming more and more true, "did you invent this Griff to get away from Richard?"

She was affronted.

"If you did, it's all right. I am not angry."

Sol seemed to consider this. We were on a splendid broad reach moving up the coast, and for a moment I was sure she would surrender and cop to what now seemed an obvious fabrication, but in the end she stuck to the grandfather story and said he might even be in the town we would soon pass, called Ghent, whose water tower rose in silhouette over the conifer coast.

"Ghent sounds right," she declared. "I think he's in Ghent."

I was annoyed. It was lovely to be on open water on the rarest kind of benign Superior day. But she set her face for Ghent, so I altered course.

But we did not find Griff in that town, since in fact there was no town, no business block, no residential streets. What Ghent did have was a few brick chimneys, a blind raccoon, and a breakwater gone fragile from a million waves per year.

We also didn't find him in Baglow, a few hours along, home of two long Quonset huts that had once housed turkeys and another complex of personal storage units, some of which had been broken open and lived in for a while. There was an open cafe that smelled appealing against all odds and a lonely wind generator in such need of maintenance that every turn of the blades made a groan you could hear for miles.

Nor was Griff anywhere in our original target of Redfield, a town I liked very much, with clean boulevards and a school that had moved into the main street theater and changed its marquee to say: NOW SHOWING: REDFIELD K–6! But though we asked up and down, no one knew of any Griff.

It seemed plain to me now there was no such individual—that Sol had made the liar's classic error of overstatement followed by insistence. It made me feel gentle toward her. Clearly, she had constructed from the ground up what seemed the ideal protector, a canny and handsome adult who would defend her from the wicked and whose travel gave him access to mysterious secrets.

So I played along. The days were pleasant. After the stifling long canal it was good to sail at a relaxed pace beside a pretty shoreline. Days we sought the phantom gramps; evenings we anchored close to shore and I read aloud from Molly Thorn while Sol tried catching fish with Essie's leeches. We didn't have a pole, so she wrapped the line around a cleat and lowered a baited hook over the side. These nights were also raven's-eye clear and so still that sky and water both were full of stars. I brought up the German binoculars and she swept the heavens with them, the sliver of moon bright through the glass, so it seemed a coincidence worthy of Quixote himself when Molly, in the essay I was reading by lantern light, took a turn into astronomy:

Many have forgotten the Great Comet of 1965. In North Dakota we were surprised at breakfast to see this pink-tailed apparition just below the sun. It was breathtaking, and because of it I was to learn one of the prettiest words in the language, "perihelion," which is the point at which a comet, or any orbiting body, is nearest to the sun. But this was a Saturday and next morning at church the pastor said our beautiful visitor meant war was coming. Not some piddling war—no, comets like this had portended Napoleon's campaigns and Julius Caesar's and they foretold the hard riders of Genghis Khan and also the arrival of the Great Heathen Army in England, an event Pastor Leake seemed to regard as a personal insult. At twelve I was unsure what to make of his sweltering interpretation but noticed a strain of quiet annoyance in my stepmom's demeanor driving home. When I asked about the promised war and how we ought to get ready, she pulled the car over and looked in my eyes. Her kindness was like water over smooth stones. She said Pastor Leake was a decent man who often mistook his worldview for the world, a common churchman's error. She said the church was a broken compass. That our job always and forever was to refuse Apocalypse in all its forms and work cheerfully against it. She asked what I would think about attending church no more? I agreed instantly and became deeply excited. By Tuesday however she remembered having promised a hot dish for next week's potluck, so my life as a normal person was once again postponed.

Of course this pastor of Molly's reminded me of Labrino and his dread of the Tashi Comet. I laughed so I wouldn't cry, but then something bit Sol's hook and she pulled up the line until a fish with white eyes and long barbels lay on the surface. The fish was large with scales like guitar picks and bulbous asymmetrical deformations on its sides. It had no fight in it until I reached over the side to try to snag its gills—then it thrashed and threw the hook and vanished.

"What was that?" Sol asked.

"You tell me. You're the fisher."

"I think it was sick," she said.

I thought so too. After its escape a smell lingered over the water that made us quit for the night. It was a disturbing fish, and the first of several like it she was to catch in that short stretch of days.

At the peninsula's northern tip was a town called Port Mineral. As we approached I began working out what to do about Sol, now that Griff appeared imaginary. I couldn't shake the memory of the small community of Jolie, where the bereft doctor and his gardening Evelyn bore up bravely and dealt with all neighbors in civil fashion. They seemed the rare people not waging war of one kind or another. The chart book revealed that from Port Mineral to Evelyn's overgrown veranda was only a lucky day's passage. And yes, such calculations invite disaster, but I couldn't help thinking Sol might find at least the beginnings of a future there, among adults who were not insane, with plenty of food, under a roof of tranquility. That's what I was thinking as we sighted the Port Mineral lighthouse and crossed the last few miles into its harbor as twilight turned to starlight.

We slipped behind the seawall and dropped the sails, easing up to the pier where a rope dangled off a cleat. There's no relief like that of docking after days afloat, and we put *Flower* to rights, pumped water from the bilge, wiped down surfaces and restacked groceries where they'd scattered in the lockers. I suggested we walk up into the town. Sol didn't want to—she seemed to distrust Port Mineral—so I left her aboard and went for a quick recon. It was uneventful. There was haze drifting and a hint of dread as of distant fighting. The streets were quiet with a few lit windows.

When I got back to the boat, Sol had Essie's last leech on a hook and was lowering it over the side. She was so pensive I again suspected she might admit conjuring Griff, but she only asked what came next. She later confessed her belief that I would eventually abandon her in one port or another. That was her expectation. Instead I pitched the idea that we take the westerly shaping up for tomorrow and cross over to Canada, to the promising village of Jolie. I painted the place in sunny colors, as much for me as for her.

"All right," she said, then her line tightened and she pulled from the water no pallid grotesque but an honest-to-God lake trout. It was tiny, no longer than Sol's own foot, but it flashed with color and twisted in the air, throwing off water like sparks.

In the morning, we paid for dockage, topped off with fuel, and were permitted three gallons of clean drinking water from the municipal tap a block inland. The sky was clear and the sun cool; the wind fell calm then freshened again from the west. Sol seemed distracted but also game. I primed the outboard and gave it three or four pulls, but silence. In deference to Erik I praised the little engine: *My sturdy friend, my right hand against the storm*. It caught but died again.

Sol stood on the dock, ready to cast off lines, and that is when a crisp deep voice, incredulous and very close, said, "Sol? I don't believe it. Is that you?"

I let go the cord.

A slender man with hard lines and blue-black hair stood holding an overnight bag on the dock.

Sol's expression was convoluted. Joy was in there and also relief, but I would say resignation had the upper hand as she walked tentatively toward this familiar person I already didn't trust.

"Papa Griff?"

"My God, Sol, what are you doing here?" The man sounded honestly shocked by this turn of events, but he was already regarding me and not the slight girl who now picked up her pace and embraced him where he stood.

"We found you," Sol said uncertainly.

What choice did I have but to climb onto the dock and meet the phantom gramps? As I watched, Sol's diffidence receded and she turned shiny and pink. "Rainy," she said, "here's my Papa Griff."

"Ho ho," said the man. "What about that!"

Reunions must shoulder their joyful freight, and I resigned myself to a morning of adjustments during which I kept a close eye on Griff for signs of shade. He stepped down into the boat very exclamatory about its charms, its timeless lines, its springy sheer, etc., throwing out such lingo as a person acquires who wants to look salty. I did the same myself in early days. He held himself upright and pulled in his gut and asked about our story, looking alarmed when Sol mentioned we'd stopped in Redfield and Baglow and Ghent. "Mmm," said Griff. "Fine people indeed, I like them very well," and so forth, all of which she accepted with a kind of breathless rush. As for his appearance in Port Mineral, he said he was there "looking for transit," no doubt the occasional ferry that still operated on mysterious timetables to Blinker and Marquette. He no longer had the home she remembered—or any home at all. "I let people take advantage," he said mournfully. "It's my fatal flaw. Conflict is too hard on me, and life's too short, my friend." While he spoke Sol slid closer to him at the dropdown table, and as for Griff he seemed ever more at ease, not only with his dear long-lost but on the boat itself. He began to look around and take notice of its more graceful accoutrements, the paraffin lantern, the fiddled bookshelf, the tiny oven shifting back and forward on its gimbles.

Three things by then were plain to me. First, Sol was glad to see him. Second, he was looking to escape some debt that might be close behind—it was hard not to notice his physical relief when we stepped down to the private confines of the cabin. And third, whatever he was, and whatever that meant, the Canadian shore was still just one day's sail away, and so it didn't feel like taking on a problem that would last beyond that time. Therefore when Sol piped up asking whether he could make the passage, too—to Canada, to start something new in wonderful Jolie—it didn't seem unreasonable. Sure he was looking to get out, but who wasn't? Who didn't have some insolent bastard on his tail, and who was I to deny a lift to another who'd lost home and people and was making his way by any means to an unknown destination?

I did question him, after a fashion, wanting to know where on the boat he might be useful—could he keep watch, could he operate the winches—and he said he hadn't much experience except as "driver." In other words he could steer. That was as much as he'd done on a boat, but he was, he assured me, excellent at steering, had done a lot of it, steering was right there among his top skills. Moreover he agreed, in docile fashion, to acknowledge that he was only a "hand" on this trip, in other words, not in charge. If I ordered him below—for example, in a storm—he would go there and stay until I called him up. In this way I did the thing most uncomfortable to me, which was to set myself in authority over another, but given his manner it seemed likely we would need this understanding if all were to be well.

As we cast off I did see Griff scan the shoreline and the near streets, and I thought his eyes exulted at finding no one there he recognized. But again: we were off, with a fair wind, a finite objective, and Sol smiling, her reservations overcome. The sails filled, *Flower* leapt forward, and we set a course for Jolie. The sun was warm on all our skins.

~ *lines of poison longitude*

WE DID what outbound sailors do—made coffee and jokes and watched the sky. I remember Sol's excitement and how she tried to be useful, to impress her gramps by constantly bringing out food. And Griff was impressed. From the look of him, he didn't eat often, and he settled into a spot in the cockpit and began to fill his stomach and rebuild his world. He said he'd always loved to sail, so much he nearly had an anchor tattooed on his shoulder. It had long been his dream to sail not just this paltry lake but across the By God North Atlantic. He said the astronauts had boats a thousand feet or more, private vessels with crews of fifty and tennis courts and women on the decks. He worked once for an astronaut, a rainmaker, whose ship grew beefsteaks in its lab that would fool a Montana rancher and who had them prepared daily by a Michelin chef he'd bought off a friend in Marseilles. After an hour Griff wore a glow of inevitable triumph; after two, he declared his desire to take the helm.

"I'm good at steering, come on, let me have a go," he said.

I put him off, but soon he asked again and I thought, well, we have a friendly wind, we have sun, there will not be a better time. So I placed Kellan's pocket compass where he could see it and handed

Griff the tiller. "Odd damn," said he, "it does feel fine to steer again! To do the thing I'm born to!"

Almost immediately we began to fall off the wind, to stray from north, so I said, "Griff, steer us a bit to port now if you would."

"Say again?" he said.

"Left."

"Very good, sir," Griff said in a jocular tone, and he immediately put the tiller hard left, so that we went to the right and lost speed and rocked in the troughs so that things which had adjusted to our steady heel were suddenly released and banged around in their lockers, and the only serenity left on the boat resided in the face of Griff, who noticed no clamor but kept us on this new course of east-northeast, which was the wrong direction.

Staying calm I said, "Well now, you're going to have to bring us back to wind a bit."

"Which way?"

"We need to bear left," I said, this time pointing helpfully.

"Aye aye," said Griff—and again he steered us right, and again we were utterly disrupted, with sails flapping and pots flying out of cupboards and tinned fish skittering across the saloon like resurrection day. And still Griff showed no understanding we were now ninety degrees off course.

Not wishing to raise a scene I called to Sol and said, "Maybe show your gramps how to handle this broad reach."

And I was proud of how she did it—taking the arched tiller while I tended the sails and we swiftly corrected, once more heading easily for Jolie now some seventy miles distant. But this was clear: though she gave Griff the truth in twenty gentle ways, he could not tell left from right. Which in itself was not the problem. The problem was that when he turned, and the world turned round him, he could not adjust. The evidence was not enough. He had no compass of his own, yet wouldn't follow the one before him, its trembling needle pointing out directions for anyone with eyes.

Still, we now bounded forward on the proper course. The long reach was a swift slow-motion gallop, each wave lifting then easing us down in foam to lift again. This on a sailboat is when the gods are smiling. Only a fool expects they'll still smile in an hour, and yet that hour passed and then another. It was early afternoon when Griff, talking of weather, began to share his own expertise as an amateur forecaster. Once, annoyed with the Old Farmers for their inexact predictions ("It was all speculation!") he wrote his own prophetic almanac, with precise highs and lows laid out for not twelve but eighteen months ("eighteen moons," he repeated sagely) with storms, floods, and droughts specified as well as auspicious planting dates across the Upper Midwest. When I remarked that it sounded like a lot of work, he allowed this was so, but then hard work and study never frightened him. The sciences, he said, were like languages; once you had a handle on one, you could slip into eight or nine others easy as changing shirts. He'd rarely encountered a science that flummoxed him. He had an innate understanding of the world, including biology, chemistry, and economics; he understood success and how to achieve it better than an astronaut did. No one ever gave Griff a thin dime, but he didn't mind—he held the upper hand by default because there was something in his constitution that made it impossible to be afraid. It had simply never happened. He took no credit for it, didn't think he was exceptionally brave. He just lacked the genetic makeup for fear—in times of stress, other men looked at him in wonder. "I won't say awe," he modestly declared. The longer he spoke, the older and more creased he became, and the more Sol began to look anywhere except at him. As the afternoon wore on even the wind tired of Griff, because it rose to drown him out. This wasn't a storm—no—only a breeze that gradually increased, moving from west to northwest. As it crept round, we pinched up closer to weather in order to keep the course. And as it rose, so did the waves bit by bit until Griff began to look a little off. He got quiet and eerie and dry around the eyes. Then for sure the wind rose crackling, and Sol brought out the flotations, which Griff said were useless. Though he was right I pulled rank and said put one on or go below—so down he went, moonish and scowling, calling me Captain Bitter and so forth, and the wind kept shifting and clouds kept boiling in. Before it got worse I went forward and set the tiny storm sail, then heard pounding and bleating and through the hatch saw Griff sprawled on the cabin sole with water flooding up beneath him. Sol later explained that Griff had opened a port and taken a little spray and thought the boat was sinking. He began shrieking for a bilge pump and, seeing a section of floor with a ring in it, he ripped it aside and fumbled with the plumbing he saw down there, opening the water intake and liberating a geyser that would've sunk us in fifteen had Sol not closed the valve. What could I do except haul him back outside? But while my hands were full of Griff an enormous wind shift rocked *Flower*—the boom went crashing across and the mainsail ripped into three pieces snapping straight out like the flags of hell.

Then *Flower* turned herself into the wind, which let me get the canvas down, all but the scrappy storm sail which held us steady as we bore away from north, away and away, and Jolie packed up its clean horizon and vanished from our future.

On then through the night: the wind leveled and *Flower* sighed along in the troughs and surged atop the crests. The cabin was quiet. At length, I heard Sol clanking in the galley making coffee—and what timing, for I was nodding at the tiller. She slid the hatch open and appeared as a pale blur with hands of steam. Griff was unconscious.

He'd raved a while, spoke in anger tongues, cried a little, then rolled up his eyes and fell like something slaughtered onto the forward bunk.

Sol's remorse at Griff was palpable. I reminded her he was not her fault and later understood she wasn't claiming blame, only burden, and she bore it bravely. The night passed with a sense of black turning blue, a slowing rise and fall. The mist on my face had a fish-scale tang. I straightened my knees which audibly complained.

Ahead lay a shape on the water like a sleeping animal, its nose at rest on the horizon. I reached for the chart book which was swollen with damp. The shape was an island, a big one. It could only be Michipicoten, some twelve miles across as measured by my thumb against the chart. The prospect of shelter made me weepy. A slice of moon showed pines like fur along the island's spine.

We rounded the island's tip at the sky's first color. I remember my surprise at the debris dotting its stony shore, bits of plastic and netting and bottles and paper waving and drying. I registered the trash but was too tired to wonder where it came from. It was only trash.

The hatch slid open. I knelt on the foredeck tying down the storm sail, and Sol stepped up into the morning. Turning to face me she began to speak but stopped. Then, "Rainy?" she said, her eyes looking past me toward the dawn.

I turned.

Anchored not half a mile distant was the silent dark cruiser whose angles and ugliness I remembered from the Slate Islands. It seemed to have been waiting for me there, and I felt a weary chill, for here, too, it seemed to anticipate my arrival.

And this was not the worst. A massive ship was moored beyond the cruiser. Its topsides painted red and streaked with black corrosion to the waterline. Its wheelhouse rose up off the aft deck, five stories of steel and filthy glass. It flew no flag of nation or purpose. No sound came, though there were people aboard—smoke rose from chimneys fore and aft, and a third chimney sputtered and began to smoke even as we watched. Tied alongside were two open boats held off with fenders and bobbing at their lashings.

Already we were seen.

Already a man on the ship climbed down a glinting ladder to a tied power skiff. The skiff's engine rumbled; exhaust rolled over the water. Two more men descended the ladder. They didn't hurry and why would they? They had time to spare, to joke, to have a longish breakfast if they wanted. That antique sailboat with the lead keel wasn't going anywhere.

And I had time, too—time to pivot toward the long view if I could. The next thing was happening and I was not prepared. In Sol's face I saw gears shifting to ride out this bad luck. I wanted to shift, too, but it was hard. Because I didn't feel unlucky. I felt betrayed. Again and again I'd fled to the lake for refuge, and the lake had not refused me. I'd given myself to storms, and it had kept me safe. I'd been swept overboard at midnight and even then it spared me. I felt, in fact, set up. The damn lake had carried me all this way only to turn on me now—sleep starved and responsible for two lives not my own—and deliver me so precisely to my enemies they barely had to move.

The skiff approached and slowed, surfing forward on its wake. Its driver was a man with a pleasant square face who could not disguise his admiration for *Flower*. Behind him stood a second man whose features I don't remember but whose wide-bore rifle I do.

The third man I had seen before: in the alleyway the night of Lark's birthday, quietly insolent behind his cigarette, and then again in the doorway of my violated house the night I fled to sea.

His name I would later learn was Tom Skint. He was missing two fingers from his right hand, and the hatred on his face looked specific and personal, as though I myself had cut them off. Skint it was who ordered us off our boat and onto theirs; Skint again who cut our anchor rope and tied *Flower* to a cleat to be towed; and it was Skint to whom Griff made a personal appeal, mouthing approximately what a protective grandfather might say, even as the skiff moved at a leisurely rate toward and then into the ship's black shadow.

Details crisped as we neared. The frozen blisters of rust and chemicals striping the hull like lines of poison longitude. The ruined mizzens and rusty cranes. A brown oily liquid pouring in thick streams from pipes and spreading on the water. The picture of a failed colossus dying in its filth.

the medicine ship

THEY PUT ME in a low cell in the middle of the ship, down a long khaki hall with endless pipes running along the ceiling. Thin stripes of faded paint followed the corridor waist-high, green and blue and orange, sometimes angling into dim passageways and reappearing farther on. Water dripped and gathered. A fungal reek pricked my eyes. We walked and turned, walked and turned. Oh for a ball of twine. We stopped at a narrow door my escort opened with a key. I ducked inside and was alone.

A yellow caged bulb over a canvas cot. In one corner a metal sink with a cold-water tap and a bar of brown soap, in another a lidded bucket and a pail of lime. I touched both sides at once, placed my hands flat against the ceiling. The door had a narrow slot at shoulder height, which showed a letterbox view of the tan passageway like a movie about tedium. Through the slot came the distant hum of generators and a listless, stagnant dripping.

Hours passed, who knows how many. Day and night were the same barren yellow in that moldering box. The more time stacked up the deeper grew my bitter apprehension. Where was Sol? What would be done with her? She had only just stabilized when we were taken, had only begun to show color and appear in three dimensions.

This panic over a child I'd known less than three weeks bewildered me. My chest was knotted up. I neither had nor particularly wanted any hold on her—Sol was no blood of mine, and in fact the man she called her family was on board. I tried to take comfort in that, tried to think of Griff as Lark might have done. Heedless as he seemed, maybe Griff could rise to the occasion. Be some kind of safeguard for the girl.

It was hard to imagine, though.

Eventually I got thirsty enough to drink from the greasy tap, even though the water was brown and streaky with tiny pale motes that swam away frantically when I poked my finger at them. Eventually I heard steps, which slowed and stopped. A set of eyes peered through the slot in the door. A man's eyes, blinking. When they saw me looking back they disappeared and a piece of bread came working through the slot. The bread was dry and cupped. It made a scraping sound on the way through. It dropped to the floor and broke in three pieces.

"Hello," I said. No answer. I went over and knelt and picked up the bits, then stood and peered out the slot. I saw no one but heard a person breathing just out of view. "Thank you," I said.

No reply.

"The girl who arrived with me. Where is she?"

The breathing caught and held.

"I just want to know," I added, trying for a reasonable voice.

But the man would not engage. He headed down the corridor, steps fading.

I hoped that Sol and Griff were in quarters higher than my own. Someplace with a window. With cleaner water. It was a torment that they were here because of me. By now *Flower* would've been searched, the canister found. But Sol and Griff knew nothing of that. I could only hope their ignorance would shield them. Maybe they would simply be taken to the mainland and released, not much worse off than before I stumbled through their lives.

I lay on the cot. Beneath it was a short stack of printed material: a 3D photo novel about foreigners come to topple our republic. A recruiting magazine full of soldiers in sunglasses doing calisthenics on a football field, one large exclamatory on each page: WOW! RIPPED! AGGRO! BEST! And finally a wordless line-drawn tract in which Jesus finally returns—looking fantastic, it must be said, a boardroom god in robe and power beard, swinging those deals, maximizing profits. Late in the proceedings there's a page where a horde of naked beggars shows up, beseeching as usual. There's no dialogue, but these scroungers are absolutely after something: food, medicine, pants. Jesus is having none of it. His brow is a storm, his strong teeth are lightning. He points the beggars toward a burning lake.

By the time another crust showed up I had drunk more ropy tap water and got sicker than I like to admit. My legs were weak, and it wasn't easy to sit up on the cot let alone stand. When the bread came through the slot and broke on the floor I didn't make a dash for the pieces. I did say thank you and ask for water.

A man's reluctant voice said, "You have water at the tap."

"I had some, it won't stay down. I'm afraid of it."

His steps retreated. I eased off the cot and crawled over and picked up the bread, let each piece soften in my mouth a long time before swallowing. When I had finished, the man returned and spoke into the slot.

"I have water for you. I am opening the door now."

But he didn't come in.

He said, "I am entering now, stand back, I am armed."

"All right."

The door opened. He was a short broad man with hair black as rubber and skin that twitched like horsehide. He didn't meet my eyes and carried himself braced for violence. Despite his claim I saw no weapon on him. He carried a large jar of water, maybe half a gallon. The water looked clear. He'd also brought another piece of bread. I remained seated on the cot as he handed me the jar. I unscrewed the cap and drank while he stood there. The water was fresh and almost too cold.

"Save some," he advised. I nodded and lowered the jar and held it between my knees, then dipped a piece of bread in it and put it in my mouth.

The man made to leave, backing away from me to the door. When he turned I saw he did have a short bludgeon or billy club dangling from his belt.

I said, "Thank you for the water. I am Rainy."

"I know that."

"There's a girl, a little girl, a kid. Her name is Sol," I said, but he let himself out and locked the door.

I drank more of the water, felt it working calmly through my veins. I stretched out and tried to breathe to the bottom of my lungs. To think of time as neutral and not for sure my enemy.

This was not my first incarceration.

There was a time early when things went wrong for me. I took a ride with a friend who got pulled over. He had substances in the car that were also in his bloodstream. Also in mine. He also had no driver's license or registration for the car, which it turned out wasn't his. During these proceedings I said something to the officer, something ignorant. I have no excuse. It is also true I got hold of him. I remember his squawking voice, his fragile upper arms, but I failed to register he had a partner, so memory drops away here for a while. Later, my friend said officer and partner took turns dancing on my face. Some departments have banned cowboy boots for exactly this reason.

I guess I slept. Slept in the glow of the permanent bulb. At one point, electricity failed and the darkness was entire. A far-off pounding commenced in the plumbing and did not stop until the light came on.

Some hours later, voices came down the hall. I couldn't tell what they said. They stopped at my door.

The latch clicked and Werryck stepped in. Leaning and gaunt with his sober long jaw and pocked scalp.

It was no surprise to see him. I thought he'd come eventually, to smirk, but instead he seemed civil and at ease. The same man who'd walked into the bookshop like one of Lark's wayfaring readers.

In fact, the very nonthreatening nature of him set me on edge. For months the thought of Werryck had provoked both dread and a scraping interior pain I came to recognize as rage. Now he stood in front of me—fairly tall but pale, thin limbed. Frankly delicate. It seemed unimaginable that I had fled when he appeared that night at the Lantern.

Rising slowly from the cot, I became aware of being strong. Too thin now to be a bear, I still threw a menacing great shadow standing up in that poor light. My shadow covered him entirely. His fingernails were dark and he looked parched and yellow.

I tell you I was six of him.

Then as I crossed the short distance between us he looked into my face. That's all he did: he looked. There was no gathering of will or straightening of shoulders. He only turned his ancient dismal crosshatched face in my direction.

I stopped where I was. My words went missing. My boldness was extinguished. I wanted to vanish—to fade from his sight and if possible from his memory. Lark said the word *apocalypse* originally had nothing to do with nukes or climate but came from a Greek term meaning to uncover. To reveal. Maybe Werryck for a second took the cover off. Some holes you can't see bottom.

In a quiet tone, he said, "Rainy, we are going to do this respectfully. Don't speak until I say you can. Do you understand?"

I did.

"Most immediately, we have the stolen property. The pharmaceutical, which we did locate on your little craft. Nearly ten thousand dissolves. I now believe you were being honest with me. That you didn't know they were there. Confirm this."

I said Kellan must have stashed the cylinder aboard without my knowledge.

"Knowingly or not, you had possession. You fled authorities. Pursuit is expensive. Before that, you harbored a fugitive. You knew what he was yet you sheltered him. None of this is speculation."

Werryck paused to let me adjust and to emphasize what came next. "I am here to inform you of your conviction on charges under the Expedited Judicial Fairness Protocol. Confirm if you understand how things are."

"I don't understand. No."

"What do you need clarified?"

I said, "Conviction requires a trial, or at least a guilty plea."

"There was a trial," he said.

"Was there? Where was I?"

"You were spared the agony and discouragement of a yearslong wait for jurisdictive attention. The Protocol allows court decisions to be made efficiently and carried out swiftly. Better for everyone. You know the proverb."

I knew it bitterly well. "You spared me delayed and went straight to denied."

He seemed pleased at my comprehension. "Some cases are more straightforward than others."

"Then I appeal," I said, in desperation reaching for an elegant old idea we both knew was obsolete.

"Appeal is not available under the Protocol."

Again the thought crept in: I was large, and he was rickety. Yet I stood still, unwilling to meet his eyes. He waited comfortably for me to realign.

"What is my sentence?"

"It will depend on my recommendation."

"What will you recommend?"

"I recommend you stay quiet. I recommend you show respect," he said. He went on to tell me the ship, *Posterity*, in addition to its roles as laboratory and pharmaceutical manufactory, was an accredited facility of Civil Corrections. He said I was extremely lucky. The mainland facilities were more crowded, with worse food and meaner security.

While he spoke I kept my eyes down.

"There is one more thing," he said, and his voice turned less official, a note entering that made me remember him as the displaced academic I'd taken him for, back on that first day. He rapped at the cell door, which opened immediately, stepped into the corridor, and straightaway returned.

In one hand he held a small tufted amplifier and a coiled black cord, and in the other—well, in the other hand was my bass guitar. My Fender Jazz, my lost and gone. Last seen among shedding animal skins on Richard's flyspeck countertop.

"How long you'll be with us has not been determined," Werryck said. "But it seems proper you should have this back for now."

His voice had almost fully changed—had taken on an affable lilt, the tone of a man pleased to deliver an upbeat small surprise. He said, "I hope you'll play. Take a little time, Rainy. Get your hands back, as they say. The amplifier has fresh batteries. Let me know if you need more."

I accepted the instrument. Looking cautiously at Werryck I saw a slight smile, deep lines, pouchy eyes with sallow whites. For a moment he resembled any old man again, and not the end of everything. I said, "The girl who arrived with me—I need to know she's all right."

His eyes hardened. "Her with the reckless uncle."

"Grandfather. He is not her fault."

"Well, he somebody's fault," Werryck said. "In any case, they're fine. Cheer up, Rainy! This ship is in the medicine business. What safer place could there be?"

~ *stubby golems on the fretboard*

YOU'D THINK I'd sit straight down and play for hours. And I wanted to at first—just the sight of Mr. Fender was enough to pull me off the bottom. The heavy old bass was in fine trim, considering where I'd left it. It set itself easily in my hands. There was the smooth maple where my thumb had worn the finish off the neck, there the familiar scrapes and dings from the carelessness and belt buckles of previous owners.

I strapped on, plugged in, tuned by ear. Ran some scales: major, minor, pentatonic. My ears remembered everything, my fingers knew the way.

What I didn't count on were the pictures playing would dredge up. Pleasant to begin with—early tryouts with local groups, the triumph of the invisible groove, the first time Lark came to hear me play. But Mr. Fender also recalled a thousand glooms we failed to lift, with drunks and inept fights, poor lovelorn Harry weeping as he played, Labrino's melancholy confusions and his finale in the living room with torrents overhead. And finally a tide of images from Lark's last birthday: Maudie and the neighbors dancing in the lake fog, dogs and babies darting at their feet—so far so good—my darling in her glimmering scarf laughing with our friends. Her laugh started low and cascaded upward—wherever it landed it caught and spread. That's how I learned Werryck had arrived that night. He stood in his tweed jacket at the edge of the yard, laughing because Lark had laughed and he couldn't help himself. Holding the two of them in my memory at once became so painful I said Enough. Switched off, unplugged. Leaned my old companion in a corner of the cell.

Another fragment of bread slid in. Another night passed.

More steps in the corridor, and again Werryck entered. He gave a single quiet cough and stood politely with his hands clasped at his waist. A trim professor.

"The girl is a massive headache," he said in a pleased tone.

"She doesn't thrive in captivity."

"Who said she was a captive? She's a guest, for now, along with Uncle Showbiz."

I said, "They were never aware of the canister, you know. You really have no use for them."

"Don't I?"

"You need to let me see her," I said.

Something in my voice darkened his face, but only for a moment. "Doubtful," he said. He had some spring in him, some light I didn't understand. He batted aside my questions about where they were on the ship, how long they might remain, saying only that he'd spoken with Sol and was intrigued by her pugnacity.

"She trusts you," he said. "It's impressive. If she understood the notion of parents, she'd imagine you as hers."

I again suggested he simply free the two of them. He'd retrieved the stolen product. I was tried, convicted, locked away. Sol and Griff represented only expense. But he brushed this off. He used the word *accessories*. The Protocol demanded facts be found. Then abruptly he nodded at the bass leaning in its corner.

"You have not been playing."

"Not much, no."

"Play, Rainy. Stop pouting. You hate me and who wouldn't in your shoes? But I didn't take your instrument from that clod Richard just so you could ignore it."

This was unexpected. I asked what difference it made if I played or not but by *difference* he was out the door.

So I did play. Of course I played. You spend three or four or seven days in a claggy dripping cell you can touch both sides at once and no window to peek out and nothing to read but RIPPED, AGGRO, and I promise you will play the instrument you're given, bass or bagpipes or comb and paper. And while it called up painful times, it also began to work in me: the scales and runs, the simple math, the amplifier hum. I kept the volume low since the acoustics in that box were fairly hostile, but I played each morning and stretched my limbs and jogged in place and played again each night. Nearly every day Werryck appeared, ostensibly to deliver some piece of news. Sol was eating well, Griff had spoken up boldly about his flair for management, two test-patients had attempted and failed to leave the ship. But he always took note of the bass and amp and made sure that I was playing.

One evening the door opened. This time the man carried neither bread nor water. He said his name was Ivar and he was the ship's steward. He said to come with him.

My first trip outside the cell.

Again the labyrinth of halls and dripping pipes. I asked where we were going and why. I had hopes of seeing Sol, seeing strangers, seeing sky. My legs shook from disuse and malnutrition. Ivar was not talkative. I brought up Sol again and he told me to leave it be.

He walked fast and it was hard to keep up. He would only say he was acting on Werryck's order. That was his sentence: "Mr. Werryck said." His tone was so neutral I couldn't tell if better or worse were coming.

Some fifty paces down the hall we stopped at an oval door. Ivar nodded me inside. It was the cleanest place I'd seen aboard, tile floor, flush toilet, private shower. The steward pointed at a shelf with folded gray clothing made of heavy paper. There were towels and soap. He left me alone. A small square mirror was mounted on the wall where I glimpsed Primitive Man and fled from him into the shower. Let me tell you I wasted a great deal of hot water standing under that forceful stream. Last time I was both warm and clean was in Jolie at the home of the Great Girard. There was a momentary urge to laugh but I don't think I did.

Ivar led me back to the cell. To my surprise it had been thoroughly cleaned. A small table had been set with a single chair and a covered plate. I lifted the cover. Meaty steam plumed up from a dish of braised beef and onions. Potatoes with gravy. God my witness fresh green beans. Begrudgingly Ivar told me such meals were normally the domain of the guard units. No one else ate like that. The gravy alone was envied to the reach of its aroma. Again I asked why this treatment and again he said Werryck. Red wine arrived in a small carafe. To this good hour I can taste it all. Ivar looked at his watch, said, "Get on with it," and left me there to do so.

Ivar returned when I was done. He picked up the amplifier and reached for the bass, but I preferred to carry that myself. This time we followed the corridor to a lift that opened at his request. The elevator lurched and paused. Eventually the doors opened and Ivar led me down a short, windowed hall. My first look at the sky in days. I could've wept and might've. The clean hot water, the feast, the wine, now the blue night sky, saturated and shivering with stars.

The corridor ended at a painted steel door lit by a sconce. Ivar knocked and entered, and that is how I first arrived at Werryck's quarters.

Whatever I expected was not this.

The apartment was small with a damp odor and little evidence of the man who occupied it. The walls had many coats of enamel now chipping away. The browns and yellows of foregone decades. Three modest windows looked out on the night, each clean in the center and caked with dust at the edges. Not the lodgings of an apex human. Only two items seemed like luxuries: Werryck's floor rug, heavy and warm with dense burgundies and golds, and the tidy hardwood bookshelves attached to one wall. The shelves were fiddled like my own on *Flower*. The editions all looked twentieth century and included one I recognized—*I Cheerfully Refuse*, Lark's own copy with the torn spine, which Sol and I had been reading just days ago. It occurred to me that Kellan may have stolen it from this very spot. Werryck sat upright in the middle of the room beside a small table like the one set for me in my cell. His dinner steamed in front of him. At this I remembered manners and thanked him for my meal and hot water and scrubbed cell. He nodded in a distracted way and waved at a corner stool.

"Sit and play," he said.

I asked what he wished to hear and he ignored the question. A bigger surprise than his modest rooms was Werryck himself. Tonight he seemed neither lettered eccentric nor prodigious bloodhound nor skin-covered howling void. He leaned in his chair, face drawn. Ill at ease or simply ill. He was gray and the lump on his neck was dark and puffy, not just a thumb now but one struck with a hammer. He also couldn't remain still and constantly adjusted his arms and legs and rose from the table and listed around while his beef stopped steaming and began to congeal. Silence seemed to magnify his discomfort. I bent over the bass and touched the bottom string.

Since he offered no guidance I played what seemed best. Jack Labrino loved slow movements in minor keys that hinted at paradise lost, but these attempts didn't take for Werryck, who frowned in agitation. Thinking of Tonio, I produced a livelier and more melodic line evoking rhymes and easy favorites, but at this Werryck turned plum and his wrinkles deepened. I asked again was there anything he'd like to hear, but he only turned away. It was as if there were no songs in his memory to name.

At length he said, "Is this the best you can do?"

It's true I was flailing. It's one thing to play for your own enjoyment or momentary trance and another to have your actual jailer six feet away expecting something you can't give and he will not describe. My rhythm was shot, I had no ear. My fingers thudded around like stubby golems on the fretboard.

In a tone both musing and threatening, he said, "How about this, Rainy? How about if I just order you to play better?"

I said, "Well sure, that never worked in the history of the world but go ahead."

His gaze burned. You see I'd got frustrated enough and spooked enough I forgot he was a walking Armageddon and said a smartass thing in front of his face. Too late now to head off the worst, but all he did was grab the nearest thing—a book from his shelf—and throw it at my head. I reached up with one hand and caught it. A nice hardcover edition with a title I don't remember by author Will Saroyan. I set it on the floor.

Remembering Kellan's description of the man I said, "Is it true you haven't slept in seventeen years?"

He didn't reply. He seemed about to but then received some cranky-sounding alert from his phone and got up and spoke into it. The alert made him terse, and he put the cell in his pocket and pressed a button like a doorbell on his wall. Turning back to me he said, "Tell me what you need, Rainy. In order to play the way I know you can."

"Let me talk to Sol."

"She is safe and fed. There is nothing you can do for her."

"You asked what I needed. That's my answer."

"She is under the care of medical!" Werryck's shoulders trembled in what looked like a small neural convulsion. He said, "She is not your obligation. You may not see her. Ask for something else."

My eye landed on his shelf. "I'd like that book back," I said, indicating Molly.

"Why that one?"

I could hardly answer without mentioning Lark yet found I could not say her name to him. Still, she helped me because I remembered the way she talked about her favorites. I said, "I like its voice."

"That book was stolen when your wife acquired it. When I saw it in her shop, that is how I knew I was close. You cannot have it."

"Maybe it's best I do not play for you."

He said, "That's up to you. But I'm taking back the bass guitar. Maybe I'll hang it on the wall. What a disappointment you are, Rainy. If you decide not to play, you'll experience the ship as an ordinary inmate. I doubt you'll like it much."

I saw I'd overplayed my hand. No. I saw I had no hand. For reasons of his own Werryck wanted bass lines. Maybe the reasons were simple. Maybe like Labrino he was settled by deep tones.

And, selfishly: fraught as it was to be Werryck's prize inmate, at least I got to play. I had no wish to be the ordinary kind.

I said I would keep playing. I would do better. Cautiously, I suggested it might help me to move around during the day. "On the way here I saw a paint crew in the corridor. I'm good at painting. Let me do some work."

"And this," he sighed, "will improve your playing."

I said I thought it would.

"Start tomorrow, then."

"Thank you."

Ivar came in and lifted the amp. I took the bass and followed him out, Werryck's eyes on me all the time.

~ *Kellan had drawn his face*

NEXT MORNING I was rousted early and taken to an upper level where the paint crew was assembled. This was the commissary or lunchroom used by the ship's medical staff—the doctors and attendants—also its team of mechanics and engineers, its officers and wardens. A few of these were finishing breakfast and their low laughter rose echoing to the ceiling.

The crew amounted to five of us, informally led by a miniature woman named Beezie of relentless private motivations. I came to think of Beezie as our drummer, a maintainer of momentum and order. She greeted me skeptically and why not? Any group develops its own balance. Still, I'd done enough painting to see no one wanted the tiresome job of scraping the commissary walls, which were in awful shape below knee-level, so I helped myself to a blade and wire brush and went to work. The others were Verlyn, a boy in his teens with lambent alopecia, who coasted around silently with step stools and folded drop cloths in his arms; an arthritic older man who went by Didier and had a spray of emblematic scars across his forehead; and Harriet, a woman whose round face and white hair belied her innate ferocity and who feared no heights and was our ladder boss.

In my weeks on the crew I would learn Harriet was a stoic practitioner who believed that everything you produced, from a painted railing to a careless phrase, went into the world with intention. No statement would be denied its effect. Your very gaze had a resonance that rang in bodies and souls and inanimate objects long after you left the scene. "Nothing is wasted," Harriet said darkly when I had known her thirty seconds, which won my heart forever.

The crew was also sometimes accompanied by a guard named Burke, who wore a long sidearm and was not cruel. This was the open-faced man who drove the power skiff that brought us in. He had other duties, too, and came and went and was mostly on hand when we were assigned to the depths of the ship where it was thought we might do mischief unobserved. Two things stuck out about Burke—first, his brawny good health. He wore his weight like five years' extra life. His cheeks were pink and his trunk was a tree and I once saw him lift a two-hundred-pound anchor and hold it straight out on a bet. The other thing Burke had was curiosity about our lost or negated or worthless lives. He liked us, you could tell. Sometimes this got in the way of our jobs, as when he asked Verlyn a question about his boyhood in a commune dedicated to "metamorphia," and Verlyn in the cadence of Holy Scripture described a man turning into a massive dog right before his eyes. The cramps and sudden hair growth! The horn-rimmed glasses falling to the floor! The panicked, *No, wait, wuff!* The scene was exciting vindication for the commune, but then the dog, a Newfie or Pyrenees, got freaked out by his own big paws and ran out in the road and got mashed by a truck hauling liquid propane. This was outside Erie PA. None of us would've heard Verlyn's story if Burke hadn't weaseled it out of him, but of course then we all had questions, and Verlyn to my surprise held forth with gradually increasing horsepower until Beezie said it was high time he got back to painting. She was grumpy for hours after this derailment. Even though he was a guard I was glad Burke was there—not just because he was snoopy and talkative but because it was Burke who introduced me to Marcel, my very first day on the crew.

I was scraping paint, chips falling like weather. My back and knees ached but still how nice to move about in a large space with other people, our sighs of complaint and snatches of talk fading into the hollow, boomy hum of the ship. The big topic was a mass escape that happened a day or two before I came aboard. A dozen squelettes—including three on pump duty and two more detained in what they called the Shambles—had contrived to slip out in the night. Most escapees either drowned fast or made it to nearby Michipicoten Island and were swiftly retrieved, but this group had found a maintenance raft tied alongside and by morning were long gone. The absconders were spoken of with disdain above decks and reverence below. Harriet called them *the twelve*, which rang like a myth and came into my head when I laid down at night. Every day that passed without the twelve's return was a good one, and I was listening to quiet speculation on this subject when Verlyn came along, washing down the scraped walls with a quick-dry solution. "Verlyn, not now," said Didier. At first it just smelled clean, but in minutes an astringent cloud developed that watered all our eyes. We needed ventilation, but Burke was under orders to keep the ports and bulkheads sealed, so all we had was a big fan moving poisonous air in weary circles. The stink put us on edge. Harriet began making escalatory remarks. I was starting to panic-sweat through the paper jumpsuit when a door banged somewhere and a cool sweet breeze came through. Straightening up to enjoy it, I saw a young man pushing a large square bin on casters. That same rolling clatter had gone up and down my corridor several times daily, and when I saw him I had a feeling of familiarity or even kinship. He was tall and slender and wore the same jumpsuit as us all, but he actually *wore* it, walking as if that's what he would've picked from any closet on Earth. He had a wide kind brow and a beginner's mustache and skin like a penny with the shine worn off. Right away I had the sense this youngster was in a story of his own. A big story. I didn't know what kind. Things freshened around him. When Burke ordered him to go back and shut the door, he instead stepped up to the guard and spoke in a smiling voice. Burke replied in a tone of indulgence, and this young janitor nodded and pushed his bin toward the kitchen. The door stayed open; the breeze washed through. Disappearing into the kitchen, he was greeted by shouts from the cooks.

I don't want to make too much of this, but it felt bad to lose sight of him. The paint crew was suddenly desolate. Beezie herself seemed to yearn after the janitor who had brought the cool wind. Even Burke frowned and looked toward the kitchen.

Didier was next to me stirring a five-gallon pail of gray primer. He said, "Look at us, man. Marcel walks through and we all wish we had a daughter to throw his way."

Marcel. That's why I knew him—Kellan had mentioned the name. Kellan had drawn his face, three-quarter view, looking out knowingly from the paper.

Next few minutes Marcel's glad baritone went to and fro in the kitchen alongside enticing laughter, and I was treated to the paint crew's vivid speculation about him. Harriet said he was the son of an exiled filmmaker and union organizer. It was only a rumor, but it fit with his mojo. Didier said he was tight with a cook named Tove. In fact it was Tove we could hear laughing behind the kitchen door. Lark liked the noun *coquette* and Tove's laugh had a bit of that. But then Verlyn said he'd spotted Marcel emerging from the wheelhouse apartment of a young woman, Luca, who wore a long gray lab coat and worked in the manufactory. Inevitably she was known as Pharma Luca, and Harriet said she'd seen the two of them together more than once. Was a love triangle in progress? Even convicts want spicy gossip. Then Marcel emerged from the kitchen and came trundling toward us again. He pushed the bin with one hand, balancing a tray on the other. What was on that tray? Nearing us he caught Burke's eye. The guard nodded, and Marcel let the bin coast to a halt.

He carried the tray over as if its cargo were no big deal.

Picture rows of pastries with brown-sugar caramel and toasted pecans and cinnamon twists and raised glazed etcetera. Picture this after you've been locked up eating bread so dry it's warped. We could only laugh. Beezie forgot efficiency; Burke forgot he was a guard. There we all stood eating rolls baked for doctors and chemical engineers. We licked our fingers, picked at stray pecans. We ate until we were full. Marcel had a word or question for everyone. To Didier he promised some unspecified delivery; to Harriet he whispered something that turned her soft and inward for a moment. Verlyn had taken a pastry and sat with his back to the wall. Marcel bent down and put his hand on the boy's shoulder, keeping it there until Verlyn got embarrassed and pushed him away, only to call him back and press a tiny carving into his palm. It looked like a seahorse. Marcel took hold of the bin again and was on his way out, then paused to point at me and say to Burke: "Is this the bass player?"

Burke waved me over.

Marcel said, "We don't get much music here. I go past your door. It's nice to hear you play."

I thanked him and he said, "How'd the other thing go?"

"What's that?"

"The private audience."

Somehow no surprise he knew. I told him it went badly. He seemed to know that too. I asked was it true the old man was seventeen years past sleep. Marcel knew the legend but couldn't vouch. He did say Werryck appeared without warning at random times and places. In the lab wing, startling chemists; in the cells of inmates and lab rats at three in the morning. It was commonly believed he could be in several places at once. I asked were this true and he said maybe not. He laid a hand on his bin. He'd stayed longer than he meant to. He was on his way down to the engine room to incinerate the trash.

Before he could leave I said, "Have you seen a nine year-old girl named Sol?"

"No. Who is she?"

I gave him the short version. He said he'd keep an eye. Somehow I believed him.

He said, "Is there something else?"

"What should I play when Werryck sends for me again?"

"Whatever he likes, I guess," said Marcel. I was momentarily stunned by this dismissive reply. Maybe his earlier miracles—the fresh air when we needed it, the pastry feast from nowhere—made me think he might also know a magic spell for Werryck.

"I don't know what he likes, and he won't tell me."

Marcel looked at me patiently. God he was young. Kellan had got him just right—looking at me now from the corner of his eye.

He said, "Werryck has a lot on his mind. He's old and stuck out here with all of us. And now he's afraid of never getting them back. The twelve. That would be bad for him I think. What do you usually play, for a worried old man like that?"

"I don't know. Blues, maybe."

"All right," said Marcel, and he walked off pushing his clattery bin.

~

I'd barely got back to my cell when the steward came for me. No special dinner this time, we just hauled my gear up the lift to

Werryck's door. Werryck opened it saying dryly, "The workingman arrives."

I took the stool, plugged in, warmed up with some scales. Werryck seemed in better form. He moved stiffly but without agitation. He lowered himself into a heavy armchair of ornate and threadbare pattern. His color was normal and he wore a long wool scarf around his neck, which made him the fastidious scholar once again.

I tapped four and eased into a blues shuffle in E.

Werryck instantly relaxed.

I concentrated on the strings, the rhythm. Sixty per minute. A healthy heartbeat.

When I glanced up he'd thrown a leg over an arm of the chair.

For the next hour I played, and Werryck seemed at home. Sometimes he got up and walked the floor but not in his lurching, unnerving style. He moved slowly and easily, at one point sliding a portlight open and scanning the dark horizon. He poured a brandy and made it last; he had a snack of hard cheese and dried fruit. He said, "I saw your girl Sol today—no, keep playing."

I resumed and asked was she healthy, did she look all right.

Werryck smiled and said, "The kitchen staff is doing well by her. And she by them."

I took this to mean Sol was at least holding her own and no longer wasting into the hollow wartime child I'd glimpsed back on *Flower*.

"Real progress for her, you'll be glad to know," he went on. "The girl is gaining."

He was to make this same remark several times in the coming days. "The girl is gaining." I was happy and didn't take anything bad from it.

I asked again to see her.

"No. Her legal guardian has the right to decide whom she sees. You are not on the list. In fact, you are specifically denied."

"Her legal guardian. You mean Griff."

"Yes, Griff. She did not win that particular lottery," Werryck observed. "The man's an ordeal. He's a bludgeon of talk. I keep him around to irritate Skint."

There came four swift whacks at the door, march tempo. Werryck got to his feet. He said, "Keep playing, Rainy."

He opened the door. As if summoned by the mention of his name, Tom Skint stood in the corridor. To me he looked enraged, but then rage was his default, his face the lurid purple of perpetual offense.

I kept playing but not because the old man said to. I played to keep my pulse in check.

Skint's voice was urgent but he kept it low. He seemed to request some special authority. No doubt something needed quelling. Even as he spoke to Werryck his eyes remained on me. Dumb wrath is what I saw there and no doubt what he saw in mine.

Werryck nodded, released Skint to his errand, shut the door.

When Werryck sat, I said, "I know he is the man."

Werryck regarded me.

"I know he murdered Lark," I said. It was a guess but not really.

Werryck took a moment to consider his response. "Skint has paid. He went against my orders. There's a price for doing so, which he didn't expect me to enforce. But I did, and he has paid it."

"He took her life. You took two fingers from his hand. Show me any parity in that."

He creaked up out of his chair and came over and squatted before me. I smelled decay and turned my head from his gaze. My fingers fell still and we had silence.

Werryck said, "Listen to me, Rainy. No, you don't have to look. Are you listening?"

I was.

"I met your Lark, remember? And liked her. Truly. I liked her rogue bookshop, her smoky voice. Her birthmark like war paint. Who could resist that alluring little world? So yes, I liked her. For that matter I like you. At least I like to hear you play. It calms me. So pay attention now— Rainy, have I got your attention? Because here is what happened. You had a boat, and you owned it. Now you're on another boat, and it owns you. You're a possession. That is your status. So while you're on this boat you don't negotiate with me. You play the notes I want to hear. You speak softly or not at all. And if you utter that word *parity* again then things will fall apart. I promise you they will. First for Sol, and then for you."

The wind rose knocking and the vessel shifted against it. He returned to his armchair and sank down in. Abruptly he became jovial again and loose-jointed and glad to be who he was. "Come on, play that backbeat thing a little more. I like that one. Relax, Rainy. Hackles down, yes? Do you think you're the first one on this boat to make a fist?"

forty-two years

AFTER THAT, I went to Werryck's almost nightly.

Sometimes he was agitated, muttering about the twelve, tilting on his old man's feet with violence buzzing at his shoulders. Other times he wanted nothing but peace, a moonlit soundtrack to whatever flickered in his head. One night it was three straight hours of the same blues pattern—the first the fourth the first again, the fifth and turn around. Yes it was tedious. Yes my fingers turned to knots as he rose to boil water and make tea and smoke a fragrant cigarette. Well into hour three, having uttered not a word, Werryck said, "Forty-two years."

It took a second to realize he meant not sleeping. Not seventeen but forty-two! The rare understated rumor! He was in his twenties when he lost his sleep and ever since missed dreaming. "You barely remember them anyhow, but then they're gone entirely."

I asked how it happened—the end of sleep for him. He said only that he had traded it away.

"For what?"

"What do you think? The usual. Revenge, dollars, influence. In my case," he said, thinking it over, "mostly revenge."

I asked did he get it, the revenge, and was it a good trade.

"Of course. Revenge is nourishing. It is for me, anyway." He paused and continued. "Obviously once you've accepted terms of this kind, it's self-enforcing. Once you choose, you've chosen."

I remembered Lark and her campaign for leniency in the trial of Large Beef, who tried to firebomb her shop. She continued to think that Large, whom she called William, could be different if he wanted to be, even years later.

Werryck said, "I must look simple to you."

He didn't. In fact it was the opposite. I felt too simple to understand him. All I could manage was to look down at the strings and ease into a little walking sequence, a reflex, one of the first bass lines I ever heard. I play it often just to get from here to there.

He heard this shift and laughed. "Yes, stick with that, Rainy. It's minimal. Familiar. Stick with what you're good at."

He sounded like a man talking to a dog he'd gotten fond of. Then he was off describing one of the few dreams he remembered having, before he bartered sleep. There was a fast car in it, a winding mountain road. In the dream he drove right off the mountainside, sailing in vivid sunlight over a valley of pines. "And I never hit bottom!" Talking about it made him excited. With no new ones in four decades, Werryck spoke of dreams as if they were elephants—amusing giants that no longer exist, bellowing and shaking their ears in a place we'll never reach.

That night in my cell, I welcomed sleep gratefully. Can you imagine losing it? Sure, I'd miss the dreams it brings, but even more the sense of buoyancy. Of a body adrift at medium depth. For the few seconds you notice that sleep has found you—on your way down to it, or on your way up—that's when the world can almost fit. Chaos, horror, the great unspooling—all suspended. How long could anyone last without such rest? In the moments before I dropped away I felt the last thing I expected, a weight of sadness for Werryck. Then thought of my old friend Erik and his joke about the pragmatist who died and went to hell—a bad surprise, but a couple months in he started to like it.

~

When Beezie said we'd been assigned to reseal the Shambles, a generalized moan went up. I asked Didier why and he said, "Cold and wet and dark and loud." Verlyn looked afraid. Harriet, hard as granite, put her arm around his shoulders and pulled him in.

A word here about the ship, which I was getting to know. The wheelhouse stack—where Ivar took me to play for Werryck—housed security officers, medical researchers, genome wranglers, and, Didier claimed, visiting politicians.

Sprawling like a covered warren over the main deck was the pharmaceutical manufactory, where tablets and capsules and silicon dissolves were produced. I never did get beyond the massive stainless doors that sealed it off, though I did see workers coming and going in their long gray lab coats resembling vestments.

My paint-crew colleagues and I lived one level down, on what was called the Medical Deck. I've described already the dirty light, the relentless dripping, the festering tap water and diet of rusks.

The best part of residing on Medical was this: we did not live in the Shambles.

The Shambles was under us and in fact below the waterline. Detention cells, a labyrinth of an engine room, a series of overworked bilge pumps that never stopped complaining. I assumed its name meant messy until Didier told me *shambles* was old British slang. Slaughterhouse is what it meant.

We suited up and went down in. We were given respirators for this job because instead of paint we used hot tar, but the respirators were bulky and hell to breathe through. The tar was heated to a molten stink in a tank of carbon steel. Though daytime it was night in the Shambles. The few lights mounted in the main corridor and the large compartments didn't carry but seemed to remain always at a distance like lanterns in a photograph. I didn't even realize we were passing cells until the metal bucket I carried banged against a set of bars and someone drew back snarling.

Reaching the work area Beezie switched on a set of floodlights and the reason for the job came clear.

The hull was of sheet steel half an inch thick and a century old. The metal was pitted and lunar and these craters were fusty with corrosion. Some seeped water, and though Beezie assured us it was "only condensation" we were pretty sure the spreading capillaries were scouts of the sea finding entrance at last after a hundred years of trying. We filled our buckets with tar and dipped our fat brushes and went after it. Heavy, sloppy work. The tar steamed on our brushes and steam billowed off the steel where we spread it. It was cold in the Shambles. Water stood in freezing puddles. Across the ship a mighty clanging began and we couldn't hear ourselves or each other above it. Seeing my confusion Didier pointed at a pair of men walking in no hurry toward a humpy steel cowl mounted to the floor. One man rolled a toolbox. They opened the cowl, revealing a spinning flywheel and shut it down. Sudden quiet. This was one of the ship's many bilge pumps, a far cry from the little manual unit I'd repaired several times on *Flower*. In the absence of machine noise came the sound of water. Water dripping, water flowing from all directions into what sounded like a deep basement mostly full already. Verlyn motioned me over to what resembled a manhole cover. He lifted it so I could stare down into the bilge. It didn't look like water. It looked like sewage cut with diesel fuel. The mechanics talked in low voices. I was ready to leave the Shambles.

The floodlights also illuminated the long row of barred cells we had passed. Not all were occupied. I think there were eighteen inmates at the time, mostly squelettes serving the mandatory three months for attempted escape. A few were waiting for their medical-testing applications to be approved—Didier told me that those who were healthy enough could shorten their time by volunteering to test the new generation of compliance therapies. The light didn't reach to the end of the corridor so the impression was of prison cells without end stretching into the night.

At the farthest reach of light, a man sat beside a cell. Cross-legged on the floor reaching in through the bars. Beezie was surveying another section of hull so I walked down the corridor. The sitting man was Marcel. He hummed some tune I didn't know. In the cell was a woman. She was old or looked old and wore clothes of damp paper and a shroud-like cloth around her neck and shoulders. Marcel held her hand. Her eyes were closed but her head high. She sat on a pallet listening to him hum. I don't know how long he had been there. He said, "Rainy, come here."

I approached. I was surprised to see him there and said so.

He laughed softly. "Is someone else gonna clean up the spills? Change the lights, collect the trash? A janitor goes everywhere, Rainy." And to the woman he said, "Maggie, here is the man you asked about."

She looked up, a faint light in her pupils. Marcel introduced us. Maggie had been hearing music in her cell. It came at odd times and was low and rhythmic. It arrived in the plumbing pipes that ran above her head.

"Rainy lives just above you," Marcel told her, pointing at the ceiling. "He plays music. That's him you're hearing."

I told Maggie I hoped the noise had not disturbed her.

She gave a wheezy chuckle. "Disturb, no. I like to hear it. If I stand up and put my hands against the pipes, the sound comes into my fingers."

I found myself unable to speak.

She said, "Your name is Rainy?"

I nodded.

"Thank you, Rainy."

Back up the corridor Beezie was striding forth again.

"I better go. I'm glad to meet you, Maggie. Is there anything I can play for you later?"

"Anything is good," she said, adding shyly, "you could turn it up a little, if you want to."

Walking away I heard her tell Marcel, "I love Rainy."

He laughed softly.

Maggie said, "I love you, Marcel."

That was a long day, and just when I thought it was over Ivar appeared to drag me up to Werryck's. I was so weary I asked if there was any way to beg off, just for a night.

"How did you like the Shambles?" said Ivar.

"This is better."

"I'm glad you think so."

I expected him to pick up the amp as usual. Instead he looked behind himself into the passageway, shut the door, and pulled a slip of paper from his pocket.

More than anything I wanted to reach for that paper.

He said, "You can't keep this. I will let you look, but then you have to destroy it. Swallow it or let me dispose of it."

"All right."

"You cannot ask where it came from."

"All right."

He handed it over—a ripped corner of cheap paper, folded in half. I opened it.

It contained a single handwritten word, untidy and awkward—a beginner's attempt—but also dark and heavy lined, as if the writer, her decision final, meant to make an impression.

It said, in full: *Sol.*

The paper seemed to contain a living charge. She was still herself; she had braved the letters and written her name. Ivar had never heard me laugh before. It unnerved him, and he grabbed the amp and hustled us out of there.

Werryck was distracted that night. He seemed quite mortal—in other words not fearsome—and wanted nothing from me but a tranquil coda. I shut my eyes and played. I don't remember what.

When I opened them, Werryck was sound asleep.

It was his mouth that gave him away, gaping raggedly open, as though it belonged to any old senior citizen.

I was stunned and yet not really. He had seemed for several nights to be working up to it—working toward the edge and peeking over.

I kept the rhythm moving, slowing by degrees, then dialed the volume down until all you could hear was my fingertips touching the coiled strings.

I played this way a minute, then stopped.

Immediately Werryck opened his eyes and closed his mouth.

He blinked and smacked.

He said, "Well now."

"Well," I replied.

“Go on then, Rainy, play some more,” he murmured and, adjusting his scarf for maximum snug, tried to get back to wherever he was a minute or two before.

It didn’t work, though. You know how it is. You might be a monster or undead genius or a screaming black vortex under regular skin—once you blink and smack, once you’re awake enough to say *well now*, you might as well get up and read.

⁓ *skeletons climbing stairs in the rain*

I WON'T EXHAUST YOU with another day in the Shambles, which anyway was like the first. Hot tar hissing on corroded steel, caustic steam, an even greater racket from a pair of bilge pumps whacking toward obsolescence. We shifted the floodlights to illuminate a forward section of the hull. In result the row of cells behind us looked even longer than before, and still the corridor narrowed down to darkness. If someone had asked me then how far light travels I'd have said four hundred feet.

But I learned something new that second day, when Marcel waved me over to the engine room. He was working the incinerator—his shoulders hunched, his young face glazed with dirt. He looked, for a change, like bad news. I thought of the twelve. Instead, backlit by the burning glow, he said, "Sol says hello."

Sol again! I wanted to grab Marcel or shake his hand, but he was on edge. I said, "Where are they keeping her?"

"Wheelhouse stack. With some other kids her age. That's not important. Rainy, listen. They're putting the lot of them in trials."

"What—"

"Trials. Testing. Compliance therapeutics."

"Wait." I knew the phrase. Kellan had been part of this program. Had fled the ship rather than remain in it. I thought of Essie, back in Brighton—of her ruined and rewired boatbuilder son. Of course both those men had signed up for it.

I said, "Marcel, she's nine."

Marcel laid a hand on my shoulder. Calm except his simmering eyes. He told me about seeing Sol and Griff in a Research conference room. He was emptying trash; they were waiting for a man in a lab coat who was talking in the hallway.

"It's legal," Marcel told me, "if the child's guardian gives permission."

It was too easy to imagine Griff being presented with this proposition. Venal, petulant, idiot Griff—did he hold out five minutes before bargaining her off?

I asked what the "therapeutic" was. Apparently a new entry in the crowded field of child correctives. Marcel said it was aimed at noncompliant minors rated "five or higher" on the Feral Comportment Continuum.

"When is this happening?"

He didn't know. The rosters were complete. Days not weeks he said.

"I'll talk to Werryck," I said in desperation.

"What for?"

"He could maybe do something."

"Why? Why would he? Does Werryck owe you anything?"

I looked away.

"But you play for him, right? You're *his* therapeutic."

"More or less."

Marcel was silent. The engine room door opened and a woman stepped in. She froze at the sight of me. Marcel clearly wasn't expecting her. She was young with long straight pulled-back hair. She wore a gray lab coat and looked at Marcel with undefined urgency.

He said, "Luca, here is my friend Rainy."

The famed Pharma Luca. I nodded and she looked away.

As I left Marcel touched my sleeve. I couldn't tell if this was meant to reassure me or ask for my discretion. Heat glimmered at the ill-fitting incinerator door.

I expected to be summoned that night, but it didn't happen—not at the usual time, anyway. I stretched out on the cot and was way down deep when the steward arrived and stood tapping his foot, twitching his horsey skin.

It later came clear Werryck delayed for a reason. A moment was coming he wanted me to witness.

When I reached his quarters he was dressed for weather. Heavy felt boots on his feet, big wool sweater with a knitted cowl covering his gristly neck. He brimmed with expectation and remained distracted even as I played, leaping up to pace or stand squinting out his trio of portlights over the incoming waves. A tough easterly blew rain against the glass, *tink tink tink*, dirty weather as they say. Werryck could not settle.

"Mr. Werryck," I said over a twelve-bar shuffle.

I felt his eyes on me and avoided them. He said, "Oh, don't be tiresome. Are you going to *petition* me about something?"

I told him I'd heard Sol was soon to enter a medical trial.

"Where did you hear this?" was his weary question.

"She's nine years old," I said.

"The medical people are their own universe. It's not my zone of interest."

"But you know her situation—you know *her*, a little. You've told me several times she was doing well. Recovering her health. You liked her pugnacity, if I remember."

"And you want what from me, Rainy?"

I took a little time with this, my fingers working the roots of an old blues hymn in which despair is upended by a stream of back-door sunlight. Finally I said, "I've no standing to ask for anything from you. I only know you're the authority on this ship. You're the one who makes decisions. It's up to you who's spared and who's condemned."

In fact, I didn't know the extent of Werryck's dominion. Maybe he was nothing but a warden and a watcher and a bully truncheon. But my tone of subjugation pleased him. He listened to what I was saying, and I seemed to feel his eyes leave me and drift around the room. At length he took the sort of breath one takes before making some pronouncement.

Then his phone chirped. He held it to his ear, barked an affirmation, slid it in his pocket.

"Come on," he said, suddenly crackling. "Come on, come on, let's not keep our heroes waiting."

Following him out, I cast a look back and saw through his ports the jagged black cruiser, angling in, running lights ablaze, engines now audible as it approached.

We made our way to a small outside platform over the main deck. The rain still came and was starting to freeze as the cruiser tied up alongside. Werryck, fully animated, face lively as I'd ever seen it, described in ruptured clichés the capture of the twelve: abandoned cabin, neighbor saw lights, inevitable outcome and so on. What really lit him up was that they were so sick and cold and hungry—starving in fact—that they came piling out of the cabin and threw themselves on the ground, begging to return to the ship.

An aluminum staircase was swung into place from deck to cruiser. A hard white floodlight burned. "Ah," Werryck said. "Here they come. Let's see how they look."

Spectral and wavering, that's how they looked. Heads-down skeletons climbing stairs in the rain is how they looked; shredded and soaked and past all hope is the way I would say they looked. Still they managed the climb under their own steam, except the last in line who crumpled halfway up the steps and was caught by the guard behind him.

Werryck watched them closely, turning to gauge my reaction. "Anything catch your eye?"

It still took me a minute, these gauntlings so tattered and unresponsive they all seemed copies of the same misery. Young from old, man from woman, who could tell?

One swung an arm up to scratch his head. His hand a shiny burnt claw.

Kellan.

"Little bastard has spine," Werryck said at my expression. "We only got him back two weeks ago, and he didn't stay twenty-four hours. Slipped out with these others."

Once I knew it was him it looked like him. The concave limbs, the kid-brother frailty in his face. The rooster comb still there but flattened to his scalp.

They stood on deck in the falling sleet while Tom Skint talked and pointed here and there as if directing a film. Once, Kellan looked up at Werryck, and his glance deflected to me. I saw no recognition and will confess to some relief at this.

"What's next for them?"

Werryck said, "I'm thinking it over. So many resources spent on recovery. So much undeserved support belowdecks. The twelve, the twelve, it's all they talk about. Comeuppance must be public I'm afraid." He gazed at them with gratitude or fondness, a worried man no more. "As for your friend, it's his second unapproved leave. Plus there's his original theft to be dealt with. He's made things serious for himself. It's freezing, let's go in."

All this time we'd been standing out there—Werryck with his big coat on, his felt boots, me beside him in my paper wardrobe sodden and stiff with ice. How did the twelve still live? I was out in that weather maybe ten minutes. Stepping back in I began to shake and didn't stop for two days.

the twelve

THEY PUT THE TWELVE in the Shambles.

I wanted to talk to Kellan, but I was sick—I'd got so cold my mind slowed down. I couldn't stand or hold a brush and instead lay sweating on my cot. When Ivar came in with an armful of blankets and mug of hot tea, he looked like my oldest friend.

He covered me with blankets. For forty-eight hours Ivar's was the only face I saw.

On the third day I descended and took my place, the paint crew now nearly finished with the tar. They were very subdued about the twelve but roused themselves to give me grief for missing work, which made me feel better and a part of things. When we broke for a standup lunch of hard bread I went down the hall in search of Kellan. All twelve were in consecutive cells, draped on cots or sitting in the damp. Someone had cruelly set up standing shop lights in front of each, and it was impossible to miss that every squelette bore some combination of open sores and ragged scars. None could bear to open their eyes to that malicious light. Pinned by radiance they looked like fresh exhibits in a museum of distress.

Kellan occupied the last cell on the corridor. He sat up hearing my footsteps. This time he knew my face. His own crumpled at the sight of my paper jumpsuit.

"I got you in trouble—I'm sorry, Rainy." He wasn't crying but almost. "You shouldn't be here. I can't stand it that you're here." Getting hold of himself he said, "Is Lark here too?"

"No," I said. You see what a boy he still was?

"Well, that's something, anyway," Kellan said.

I didn't want to tell him—didn't want to say it or make him hear it. Instead I let him talk, which he was glad to do. He'd made it to the fabled Oregon farm, stayed one night with the uncle, an orchard keeper, stole some gas from the old man's bulk tank and shoved off. The needle on Full gave him confidence, and he turned west toward a place in the deep toolies he'd heard about for years, a refuge for nonplayers and unluckies like himself. Maybe the place was still there. Maybe it still is. He never found it. He ran out of gas and walked two days through mossy-fog forests of tilting pine until a woman resembling Mrs. Claus pulled over in a creaking hybrid. She dropped him off in the next hamlet with a few bills for a sandwich. The cafe was a trailer house with a picture of a steaming cup in the window. A bruised girl inside gave him extra baloney, then risked a beating by slipping him half a jar of peanut butter on his way out. Supper and breakfast and supper again.

"How'd they find you?" I asked.

He still wasn't sure. He got work with a man digging for ammolite on a public lease, but pay was contingent on actually finding ammolite, a stone in scant supply. After a week Kellan began to think of moving along, then arrived at the dig one morning to find his beardy employer sharing a thermos of coffee with Tom Skint.

"I hate that unkind bastard," Kellan said.

I said I had to go; the crew was shuttling gear to the final section of hull.

"Rainy, you got to stay away from Werryck." He waved his claw.

I said, "He did that to you, didn't he?"

Shame flooded Kellan's face. He said in his lab-rat days he underwent a compliance therapy similar to that used to keep peace in prisons. This version was demanded by employers weary of underling grievance. It was tasteless, odorless. The effect took hold in a day or two, after which Kellan became convinced the researchers had his best interests in mind.

"If it worked so well, why did he burn your hand?"

"He didn't. I burned it myself because he asked me to. He brought the torch and set it up on a stand and handed me the lighter. Said I didn't have to if I didn't want to."

"Then why do it?"

"He said he wanted the best for me. I'd have burned them both if he asked."

Down the hall, Beezie shouted my name.

"I have to go."

"Where's Lark, though?" he asked mournfully.

So I told him. He didn't say anything, just retreated to the back of the cell. Put his hands over his eyes, rocked against the bars. I said his name twice but he did not respond. I went back to the crew.

By the time Werryck decided what to do with the twelve, a storm was coming. If a storm had not been coming, he'd have thought of something else—but a storm was definitely on the way, a colossal nor'easter packing snow. My bones knew it. The sky was bruised and funky.

On the main deck a team of welders was constructing a cage.

You wouldn't think it could hold twelve people—or that anyone could stand inside. It did and they couldn't. The welders were swift, and under flying sparks the bars took shape, the small square door, the crisscross ceiling four feet high. When the cage was finished it was lowered overboard onto a maintenance raft like the one they'd stolen to make their escape. Ten feet by ten would be my guess. The cage was bolted in place.

While the work went on the deck filled up. We weren't required to be on hand, but Ivar went round unlocking cells and when your door is open what do you do? You head for the action, and that was on deck. Here then were my paint-crew friends, there a cluster of kitchen staff. I saw Pharma Luca standing with her tribe from the manufactory. At the rail Tom Skint gestured toward the floating cage, his voice a ratchet tightening in my chest. Some yards away Marcel stood with Tove from the kitchen. They didn't look like lovers now but rather comrades or subversives, his face calm and watchful, hers alive and savage. Even the twelve's fellow inmates had been let out of the Shambles and stood with each other peering over the side, where the welded cage bobbed on its raft. Search as I might I did not see Sol, nor Griff either. Maybe they watched from the wheelhouse stack.

And Werryck? He'd dressed up sharp in a trim white jacket with a black fur collar. His hair shook in the wind and his cheeks were red and his smile snowy. So much for my thoughts of his failing health. Sleep had restored him. He looked good for twenty more years.

When the twelve were paraded out in their paper shifts, Werryck checked his watch and I looked at the sky. Call it late afternoon. There was no ceremony. No one said any words or needed to. In the general hush the twelve were led single file to the swinging staircase, which was now attached to a long power skiff, itself lashed to the cage raft. One by one they descended and were bent over and pushed through the short door into the cage. The guard was Burke. You could see he didn't like doing it. Kellan was the second one in. He looked blank with fright and scooted over like a kid making room in a game of sardines. It took a few minutes to pack them all in. The cage was stuffed and none could stand and the twelve hugged their knees or laid limbs across each other. Burke padlocked the door. The skiff towed the raft twenty yards from the ship and anchored it there. Close enough for us to see their fearful expressions, to hear their cracked voices. Watchers lined the rail in silence. No one knew how long the punishment would last. It was cold already and wind coming. Dark in the east. The twelve didn't call out though we could hear them speaking among themselves. Sometimes they slapped their skins to circulate the blood. As the light declined, one moaned and then another. A chorus of moans arose, the substance of which was remorse. A refrain of apology. The sound of this was more than most could bear. People drifted away. Marcel's friend from the Shambles, Maggie, walked past weeping. No place to go except her cell.

Ivar brought me a baked potato. It was so hot it steamed when I opened it. There was also salt and butter, so that eating it felt privileged and heartless, not that this held me back. Ivar leaned against the door while I polished it off. He didn't say a word about the twelve. His skin twitched and lay still and twitched again. The moment I finished the potato, he picked up the amp.

I said, "You all right, Ivar?"

He nodded. He said I should be cautious tonight. I should not cross lines as I had in the past. I should play what Werryck wished and if possible not speak. Not be tempted into unwise discussion.

The elevator trembled and jolted even more than usual. Stepping into Werryck's windowed corridor, I looked east. At the edge of the ship's yellow light was the raft. Pitching against its anchor in the swell. It was raining lightly. I couldn't tell Kellan from anyone else. A pile of limbs in a heaving cage.

Werryck nodded me in and I went to my usual corner. Unlike his triumphant self of hours previous, he looked ruined. His neck skin hung loose and dark. He wore a wool sweater and did not come near filling it. One of his portlights was open and cold air entered and moved restlessly around the room.

Taking no chances I started with a hazy bayou blues, but Werryck said sharply, "None of that, no," leaving me orphaned and unsure what to try. I moved up the neck, searching for a rhythm. Nothing stuck, no place seemed safe. Eventually I came down on the bedrock of an old American hymn. An earnest chant from before my time, when the church was briefly other than an instrument of war. I liked it for its charity and yearning, its warm dawn of a chorus. Werryck breathed heavily through his nose.

I played and tried to keep my mind clear, but my fingers stumbled on the strings.

He said, "Go ahead then, say what you have to."

"I respectfully ask that you bring those people in."

It was as if he didn't hear.

"They're wearing paper gowns. They're unprotected and starving. You know they won't live through the storm."

He said, "Their circumstance is of their making. Not one of them is surprised. Nor do they blame me. Even in their trouble they would tell you. They knew the penalties and signed the contracts anyway."

"Right, the contracts." I lost the hymn a moment, forgot how it went, but got it back, or something close. "The paperwork is in your favor, but I'm appealing to your humanity."

"You use that word 'humanity' as though it represents your favorite set of virtues. It doesn't and it never did."

"They'll die of exposure."

"Then think of the incentive they'll provide toward good behavior."

It was hard to keep playing under this burdensome talk, and I remembered nervous Ivar's sensible advice. The hymn had a good solid structure so I stayed with it a while, exploring its rooms and transitions, the bridge between the sturdy towers of its melody. While I played the rain changed to snow. A plump seabird landed, exhausted, in the open port. It had a slightly offset beak, polished black eyes rimmed with white. I remember its bright yellow feet.

Soon both the bird and Werryck were asleep.

Maybe I slept too. Maybe I played several hours in my sleep, for when Werryck woke and spoke it was three in the morning, his longest rest in forty years it seemed, and my fingers still moved across the fretboard as if obeying orders. The wind still blew and the snow still came, a little drift of it on the rug beneath the open port. The seabird was gone.

"All right then, Rainy," the old man said. "You can go."

I pressed the button for Ivar who came in and took me out. In Werryck's corridor we stopped to see if the raft were visible, but the snow was heavy and the wind high. The twelve were on their own.

"Thank you, Ivar, good night," I said when we reached my cell.

He locked me in. Through the door I heard his tired cough.

I didn't sleep. It would be dawn soon enough. I thought of Kellan out there on the raft, how he'd first showed up with his books and his nitrous, his bundle of nerves. He'd brought hell with him, too, just as he feared. Right straight to our house hell followed that boy, and murdered Lark, and made me a fugitive and convict. Yet all I could see was him tucking his knees up into his chest. Shrinking himself inside of that cage. Maybe he and the others were alive out there, or maybe they were free as the snow. Nothing I could do but play, to coax what I could for as long as I could. For the twelve on the raft. For Lark and Sol. For those sleeping in the Shambles and those who might be fearfully awake, touching the pipes with their hands to catch the notes.

the day I remembered the future

FOOTSTEPS IN THE CORRIDOR, hustling up and down. I guess I did drift off at last, since that's what woke me up. Running feet, the walls and floor trembling, action in the architecture. My kingdom for a window. Then someone in the Shambles banged a pipe, with a spoon or just their knuckles, and someone else joined in, and this business caught on, so we had five or ten minutes of clanging I took to be a memorial or torrent of grief for the twelve. If it were dawn, as I imagined, their corpses would be visible.

A minute or so after this subsided, Ivar showed up with my morning rusk. I asked him what was going on.

"Some of them are alive," he said.

I didn't believe him. I wanted to see the twelve with my eyes, but instead the paint crew was taken to a seldom-used corridor on the west side of the ship and told to get to work. A stupid assignment—those walls were in great shape, the usual boring tan, barely chipped and free of mold.

Harriet with no fear of Burke went right up to his face. "This is a crock," she said. "We did this hallway a few months ago. Look at the paint! It's pristine! This is crockery. I won't do it." And she parked herself down on the floor—only to pop right back up. Like every other corridor, this one hosted pools and intermittent small rivers of cold water, and she had sat in one.

So Burke was spared confrontation, which he didn't like and wasn't good at, and we did get to work, and still the ship around us seemed to hum. Far down the corridor sunlight streamed in from ports we couldn't see, and we brushed and rolled and the paint fairly spread itself along the walls, and no one passed without delivering some headline of events. A limb at the top of the pile had moved! An elbow emerged, then a muffled cough. As the wind died, more limbs began to shift. We later learned that Tove, watching the raft from a kitchen port, had a set of binoculars and would shout, "Arm! Knee! There's a head moving!" And once when someone dared to yell out to the cage, in reply a hand shot up through the bars, not clenched in defiance but open toward the sun.

It was unthinkable any of them lived, and yet they did, through wind and rain and snow and rain again. It was Marcel—could it have been otherwise?—who brought us word they'd *all* survived, the weak and the weaker, in their paper shifts. He said a big brown pelican flew in with the sunrise and landed on the water beside the raft. It raised its wings and went on little explorations and also dove for fish but always returned to the twelve, scissoring its head around and shaking its gingery bill.

Then Verlyn said, "That's enough, I got to see," and set down his roller and walked up the corridor, all eyes on Burke who called after him: "No, don't do that, son." But Verlyn kept walking. We all knew Burke wouldn't shoot him. Right on his heels went Harriet, irritated she didn't go first, then Didier. Finally Burke caught up and the whole paint crew reached an agreement to stay together under his watch. Safer for all including Burke. He wanted to see the twelve, too. Burke led us to a sheltered alcove where we could see over the rail to the east.

Again, the deck was crowded. No one not locked up would miss it. There again were Tove and Marcel, there some manufactory priests, there a trio of lab techs mixing with kitchen staff.

And there at the rail, a hale surprise, was Sol. Not yet trapped in a testing cell and in fine insubordinate form. She'd slipped away from Griff—or whoever's duty she'd become. She looked taller and craftier than I remembered, her eyes flashing this way and that. I raised a hand to get her attention, but then she seemed to catch sight of someone she wished to avoid—she turned her shoulders slightly, and I lost her.

The cage rocked glinting in the newborn sun.

Deliberate motion out there on the raft.

Limbs and papered torsos in methodical adjustment.

It took a minute to see what they were up to, which was straightening—unfolding themselves, helping each other to stretch on out. They did this one limb at a time, difficult work after the cold dark hours, and some cried aloud as frozen joints yielded, but others also laughed, right there in front of us, laughter rising off the twelve as sunlight hit their skins. The sound made me uneasy. It crossed my mind they had died as expected but come back somehow and were about to drop some netherworld karma.

Werryck appeared on deck, grim lipped. He consulted with Skint who looked supremely red, his limbs red, ears red, forehead nearing scarlet, thick with resentment at the twelve who had the audacity to live and stretch their limbs and laugh.

When Werryck waved a signal to bring them in, Skint somehow grew still redder, so that I pictured a blood vessel ballooning deep in his brain, imagined the tiny muffled pop. Then the skiffmaster eased his craft out and towed the raft back to the ship. A guard bent to the cage and unlocked the little door, and the twelve crawled out one at a time and climbed the staircase, firm and mostly steady until the last was aboard, at which time three of them collapsed and were carried below.

The rest Werryck looked over closely. He leaned down, peering hard at their faces, Kellan's especially I thought. Trying to ascertain something. Squinting in as though looking for the source.

After that start any day might wilt, and yet this one did not.

I guess we finished painting the corridor and started another. I guess the lab rats accepted routine injections and dissolves. Upstairs, chemistry kept right on messing with biology. Downstairs, inmates dozed and machines clattered. Water came in and was expelled to try again, and black mold prospered in the bilges.

And yet the day was altered.

For me it passed in a kind of suspension. The twelve were still alive. Sol was still herself. A door had opened to what might be. That was the day I remembered the future, reimagined a path of years with books to read and bass lines to explore. The idea was so tempting I set it aside, but it kept returning, wider each time. Long walks might be out there down unknown roads. Days of work, weary muscles, sores and ointments, goodwill toward creatures, questions to ask, birds to hear, and stars to watch. For a moment I panicked: had I missed the Tashi Comet? Time gets lost in a place like this. But no—the comet was still coming. It was almost here. All day the future pulled at me, it scampered out front like a pup. I said nothing of it to anyone but noticed it everywhere: the paint crew looked resplendent to me, the bilge mechanics ebullient en route to another failing pump. Sent by Beezie to fetch more primer I passed the commissary, where cook staff were serving the night guards their usual preshift dinner. There was the rich tormenting smell of gravy, but my envy felt transitory—almost enjoyable. Even among the guards the mood seemed expansive. Marcel was in there with them, standing beside his rolling bin, making some joke that was clearly a hit. Through the service window I glimpsed Tove. She was eyeing Marcel, but then her attention shifted. She turned and caught me watching her. I remember her expression, both vigilant and reckless, like someone determined to catch the light while it shines. It was easy then to feel the future coming for us all, to imagine in some way all of us knew it.

~ *the twelve, again*

IVAR CAME FOR ME early—actually took me off the crew, which still had work to do. He warned me Werryck was under the cloud of a ferocious migraine. A medic had already given him an injection, but the pain continued. Ivar made me hurry.

"It's just a bass guitar," I said. "It can't cure migraines."

"Desperate times," said Ivar.

Werryck's quarters were dark. He'd ordered Ivar to cover the ports with heavy blankets. It was hard to breathe in there. Moreover, I'd forgotten the way a migraine smells, like cheese sweating in a warm room.

I couldn't even see Werryck at first—but there he was, crumpled in his chair like a couple of sweaters, a wet cloth draped over his eyes. This he removed and turned to the cool side every few minutes. Given his condition I asked quietly was there something he wanted to hear, but he only lifted a hand in the universal *get on with it* gesture.

So I got on with it.

And could do no wrong.

That's my interpretation, anyway. Normally Werryck got agitated when I played a line that bothered him. He'd shift and grump, he'd pace about. This time no. He wanted only darkness and slow stuff on the bottom strings. Adjusting to the dim room I noticed him looking over at me while turning the wet cloth. At these moments, his eyes were feverish but not insane. Maybe sparing the twelve had allowed the return of vestigial humanity. I accepted his silence with gratitude.

At some point he fell asleep.

When my friend Erik would fall asleep, near the end, he resembled a strange spotless child: his lines fell away, his skin appeared waxed. This sleep of Werryck's wasn't like that. He didn't look young or fresh or kind. He looked like a late-season gourd falling in on itself, an old man dead for days not yet discovered.

That is how he looked when footfalls came piling up the corridor and Tom Skint flew in like a storm.

"They're going, Werryck. They're leaving the ship! Come on!"

Well, that levitated the old brute out of his chair. He got his feet under him, got his shoulders aligned. From the resentful way he looked at Skint, you could see the migraine running the show.

Skint was out the door at full shove. Werryck slid into his coat and followed.

I went too.

Twice Werryck stumbled in the corridor, unable to keep up with his man. Both times I set him on his feet. Eventually we went through a door and onto a railed catwalk thirty feet above the deck. There stood Skint, breathing hard.

Given this burst of drama, I expected to see a throng in mid-revolt, but no. The lit deck was calm and orderly. Most of the paint crew were there, including Beezie, and some kitchen staff were paying diligent attention to a stacked pyramid of crated produce and canned goods. What was Skint talking about? A light rain fell, and nothing either bold or secret appeared to be underway. But the black cruiser was tied alongside, its engines were idling and its lights were lit, including the navigation column on the flybridge. A man I didn't know was leaning over it, his face lit by the glow.

Four security guards stood on the main deck looking at the cruiser. Burke was among them, looking perplexed. They wore their sidearms on their pants and rifles on their shoulders, but there seemed no threat. My confusion increased when Marcel stepped off the cruiser. He wore janitor clothes but moved with authority. Something was off. Reality was in retreat. Marcel rubbed his hands and nodded at Burke politely.

"Everyone to quarters," Skint shouted. His voice made me flinch, but down on deck no one paid attention.

The rain picked up intensity. Tove lifted a crate containing what looked like potted meat and carried it to the cruiser.

Two more security now arrived, and again there was a bit of pointing and consulting and looking skyward like umpires mulling a rain delay.

Skint tried again. "This is a lockdown!" But he was ignored. A single guard turned his face to squint up through the weather.

Marcel put a box of oranges on his shoulder.

"Don't, Marcel," Burke suggested. Burke never sounded all that commanding, but this was noncommittal, even for him.

Marcel loaded the oranges onto the cruiser, stepped back off, and took another box from the pyramid—grapefruit, ripe ones, a full crate of moons dripping rain.

"Burke! Take him now," Skint ordered, and Burke did not respond.

Marcel stopped where he was, holding the citrus. To the guards he said, "My friends, this isn't necessary. We had dinner together three hours ago. Do you remember?"

Burke said, "Marcel, put down the box."

"Mr. Burke, nothing is wrong. Nothing bad is happening.

Those who want to leave the ship are leaving. Stay if you like," Marcel said. "But you are also welcome to come with us. Imagine if you came along! We hope you will. There's room for all."

This seemed to throw the men into turmoil. They looked at each other while Marcel loaded the grapefruit onto the cruiser. Burke looked up at Werryck on the platform poor shrunken Werryck fighting off a migraine, and now whatever this was too.

Then Burke appeared to rally. "Marcel. Stop loading that boat. And shut off those engines! Nobody's leaving."

"We *are* leaving," Marcel replied in a steady voice the rain all but covered. "We have to. We always had to. Now is the time." As he said this, one end of a stacked box gave way. The rain had soaked everything through. A head of cabbage rolled out, and Marcel bent to pick it up. Wiping rainwater off his face he said, "Go ahead now, Mr. Burke, and lay that rifle down."

Burke hesitated.

Marcel said, "It's all right. It is. It was always going to be all right."

And Burke knelt down and lay his rifle on the deck.

Werryck covered his eyes. I didn't understand yet what was happening, but Werryck did. He saw the future coming more clearly than us all.

Skint shrieked an order, but he was beside the point. He was a dog barking. The remaining guards meekly disarmed. Rifles, sidearms. The pile of munitions they made slipped and clattered in the rain. They regrouped and stood like shriven monks, their slick hoods helping with that impression.

Then Skint lifted his sidearm and fired. I believe he was trying to shoot Burke, but that's a long shot for a handgun. The guard next to Burke tipped his head and fell.

He fired again and Marcel dropped to his knees. He wavered

a moment, tipped forward onto his face. The cabbage rolled away from his open hand.

Skint didn't shoot a third time. His feet came off the platform—that's my clearest memory—his hard pointy boots turning frantic. His arms wheeled for balance as I lifted him up. His gun dropped away and I took an elbow or something to the face, but that didn't matter, didn't stop what was happening or change by a millimeter where Skint was going. I don't remember making this decision—I've tried, but can't remember. Maybe I'd made it months before. Maybe that's why Skint weighed nothing to me—I was used to his stupid weight, having carried it so long. Up he went and over the rail. Harriet later described the appalling sound he made hitting the concrete deck *like something dead already.* I didn't hear it. All I heard was a sort of interior creaking noise, then my back started hurting pretty bad.

On deck Tove sprawled toward Marcel. A couple of guards, startled at the wrecked and misshapen pile of Skint, scrambled for the weapons they had shed, but Didier and Harriet and a dozen others broke over them like a wave. Werryck in his misery had left his quarters unarmed. I have since read about every kind of mutiny and rising and prison revolt and few matched ours for speed.

The elevator was busy, so I wound up escorting Werryck down the long metal stairwell to the Shambles. A slow descent. Werryck wore his migraine like sackcloth and barfed a few times on the stairs. Arriving in that bottom space Harriet was already there, unlocking cells, shooing out squelettes in brisk fashion, these pale skeletons ducking about in fear and disbelief while Harriet shoved the guards inside and locked them in. Again I wondered at their docility, their faces of bewilderment and stillness. Werryck had turned so white he was nearly blue. I thrust him into a cell just as Kellan was stepping out.

"What do I do now?" Kellan asked.

I said to Werryck, "Give him your coat."

It was a woolen peacoat like a naval officer's. Werryck didn't want to, but I offered to go in and help him remove it, so he unbuttoned it slowly and let it slide off his shoulders.

Kellan accepted the coat and put it on.

"Go on deck," I told him.

"What is happening?" Kellan asked. "Rainy, can you tell me what is happening?"

I was still figuring that out.

Details would emerge in time, but even then the shape of things was starting to come clear. Pharma Luca meeting Marcel in the engine room and elsewhere—to whisper, yes, but not to sigh. Who else could've supplied Marcel with all the best and latest? And only hours earlier I'd seen him with Tove in the kitchen, serving the guards their dinner. What could make Tove happier than stirring an order of absolute subservience into their beefy gravy?

Moments from that busy night I hoard against the dark.

The instant when Verlyn and I, sent to retrieve anyone still in the wheelhouse stack, stumbled into a little hive of joined rooms. The lock took some fiddling, and when it opened, there crouched Sol beside her roommates, looking ready to tear the face off whoever came in. Indeed a small boy with weasel teeth leapt up hissing. I held him away at the cost of deep forearm scratches while Sol said, "Cut it out, Ferdie. Stop that now." And to me, "Are we leaving, Rainy? Can we go? Can they come too? Can we take some food?" Ferdie quit clawing my arm at last, and I said yes to everything.

The moment when the Shambles inmates saw—with alarm or dawning joy—the shrinking spectacle of Werryck, descending the food chain *bump bump bump* to land at all their feet.

Or the scene back on deck with everyone gathered—everyone

but Werryck and his futile security force. The rain still fell, the cruiser rumbled and diesel smoke drifted through the cones of light thrown by sodium-vapor lamps across the deck. When Harriet came off the cruiser, she carried a folding ladder. This she opened and climbed in order to speak from a height. She said Marcel was alive and conscious. Being attended to by one of the ship's doctors. Pressed for details she had none, nor any promises. She said it was time to leave, and the cruiser would accept any who wished to go. Twenty were already aboard but there was room. She couldn't speak for Canada, but on the cruiser all were welcome. Marcel had said it firmly: whether you lived upstairs or down, none would be refused.

"Let's go," said Harriet, yet no one moved.

There was so much fear of leaving. I didn't see that coming. Everyone had to choose and many didn't want to. Freed from their cells, the squelettes were in confusion. Depart the ship for a crammed vessel tilting through night weather toward unspecified landfall? No slam dunk apparently. How many people could fit on that boat? If it didn't sink, what happened when they reached shore? Their reluctance made sense. Some had left that ship before only to be retaken and brutalized. Many cited dead examples of bravery. There was a belief verging on religious that Werryck could still triumph. Half the people on that deck believed he could be in three or four places at once. What if this were a test? What if they left and then he appeared among them on the cruiser, eyes like holes of wrath?

Harriet began to fray. She never wanted to inherit any kind of mantel from Marcel but here she was. She held out her hands. She described their liberation as a jubilee: all slaves freed, all debts forgiven. Like in the Bible! Though from what I've read, they talked big about slaves and debts but never followed through. Harriet exhorted, she moved her hands. Urgency swelled around her. Lightning glimmered on the northern rim.

Then Sol clutched my arm. Pointed at a little cohort moving toward the cruiser. They held their heads up. Some couldn't walk on their own and were assisted by those who could. Forward they went, steady on. They were the twelve. Two or three had blankets round their shoulders, and a few had jackets. Kellan had given Werryck's peacoat to an older woman, and he himself wore only a bit of poly tarp over the same paper clothing that saw him through the storm. None spoke. They only moved ahead. People parted before them and many were swept up in their wake. They boarded the cruiser via the silver staircase which glowed with rain.

Minutes later every squelette was aboard, every lab rat, every painter and menial and mechanic and drudge. I saw Didier making room for Verlyn at the rail, next to Beezie and Maggie from the Shambles.

This left behind the professionals. Doctors, researchers, assistants. The gray-coat pharma priesthood. It did not occur to me that any of these might throw in with the desperate.

Then Pharma Luca wrung her hands as though to shake off something bad and trotted toward the staircase. Several colleagues followed. A stooped woman of tremulous bearing said that as a physician she was bound to go, to attend those in poor health. Others in her orbit agreed. In this way the cruiser filled far past its safe capacity.

When all who wished had got aboard, a cry went up from those remaining. Their cell phones had been swiftly collected and bagged after two medical aides were interrupted trying to call the mainland for help. This led to a take-no-chances sweep for such devices, and such a pageant of plastic and glass and silicon terabytes flying over the rail I never imagined, the tools of transmission blinking out like so many lit screens tumbling end over end into the swallowing sea. Now that it was clear we meant to leave them without communications, outrage erupted. Harriet did not bargain. You should've seen her on that ladder, growing shoulders as we watched. An indignant researcher shouted *This is just my job* and Harriet said *You took the job.* She said that choice made this one certain. She said *This is what happens.*

In the end most of the professionals stayed. They had people on the mainland; they had careers. In their place I would've done the same. I can also tell you there were three technicians whose job it was to break the limbs, burn the skin, and pierce the flesh of compliance patients, and these to a man remained rather than share a crowded deck with those they had abused.

"Come on then," Harriet said to me.

The cruiser rested low in the water. You've seen similar images. You know how it looked: a common sight, a vessel pushed down and top-heavy, obscured by its cargo of souls.

And I was glad to go with them, glad to take my chances. Sol and I stood at the top of the stairwell when again she took my elbow.

"Rainy," she said, pointing across the deck.

She had to show me where to look. Peeking above the opposite rail was the top of a mast, its tiny wind indicator shifting on its axis, pointing north and east.

It was *Flower*'s mast. The ship was so tall all we could see was its top few feet, shining in the rain.

I asked Harriet for a minute.

It actually didn't take much more. A rope ladder already hung over the side and Sol and I both climbed down. There was an inch of water in the cabin. While I tried the bilge pump—which still worked—I heard Sol speaking, not to me. "You are ready for this, that's what I think," she said. "I never saw anyone more ready. And look at you. So shiny."

She was talking to the outboard.

It started on the fourth pull.

~

I had only two more things to do—no, three.

Leaving Sol on *Flower*, I trotted back across the freighter's deck to where Harriet waited. I told her our plans and asked for Kellan. Word was passed and he climbed to the flybridge and spoke to me over the rail.

I told him about *Flower* and offered him a place with us.

Right away it was plain he would turn me down. He was shy about it and glad to be asked, but Kellan liked where he was—yes, on a boatload of exiles, with people he trusted who trusted him back. For now, at least, Kellan was in the story he wanted. They'd been through the worst and could see the way out. They would do it together.

"Long live the twelve," I said.

"Oh God, don't now," he said.

I asked Harriet would Marcel be all right. She hugged me so hard I cracked. I don't remember what else we said. Then she boarded the cruiser, and I went fore and aft and threw off their lines. A shout went up as they drifted away and the big growling engines took hold.

From there I went down to the Shambles. I went to see Griff, who'd made his choice. He'd specifically asked to be lodged with Werryck, imagining his loyalty would be rewarded. I went to ask him to reconsider. Honestly I didn't want to, but he was Sol's only family. I said he could still come with us.

"You mean on the cruiser?"

I told him the cruiser had left. He could join us on *Flower*, though.

And Griff said no. He practically snorted. Said we would die on that tiny boat. Maybe he was auditioning to be the new Skint. I didn't like his chances.

Buried in his migraine, Werryck rolled his eyes.

Then a voice said, "What about me? Could I reconsider?"

Burke, speaking from the rear of the cell.

"I'd like to go," Burke said.

"The worse for you," Griff told him, "the second we get you back."

"Rainy?" Burke said, coming forward.

He sounded so hopeful I felt a little sick.

I said to Burke, "How long do you think you'll be this way?"

"What way?" said he.

He was so eager and ready to go I went ahead and let him out. Was it a risk? Maybe, but he looked so normal without rifle and sidearm. He looked like a man with promise.

As we left the Shambles, Burke said, "I might be of use to you, on that boat."

"Don't say it unless it's true."

"I had a boat much like it, in better days. Put me to work and I'll do my best."

When we reached the main deck I left Burke there. There was one more thing to do.

My bass guitar was up in Werryck's quarters. I took the stairs at a run. His door was ajar, the smell of his headache still in the air. I uncovered a port and looked over the water. The cruiser was visible heading north, into the swells, its railing clogged with people.

Lightning forked at a distance.

I picked up Mr. Fender and helped myself to a book from Werryck's shelf.

I Cheerfully Refuse.

a bold round face and a curving tail

WE COASTED AWAY in a moderate swell and only looked back rounding the eastern tip of the island. From a distance the ship appeared as it must've a century ago—like a thousand-foot city, its wheelhouse illuminated, rain whipping itself into haloes around the sodium lamps. Then, since *Flower*'s mainsail was still shredded and useless, we raised the jib, which filled with a strong northeasterly breeze, and *Posterity* lost its hold on us forever.

Two surprises I remember from that long reach.

First, we were not pursued. We'd left Werryck and the others locked below, but I assumed it wouldn't take long for someone to scramble up keys or commandeer a cutting torch. By now the old tyrant would be out and blazing for revenge. Of course, pursuing us would've made no sense. All the value was aboard the black cruiser, which had gone another direction. Also it was still dark, with rain and hard wind. Yet I couldn't stop looking back.

Second, Burke was an actual sailor. I asked him to steer when I went forward to free a stuck line, and he said not a word but his ease with the tiller was plain. We moved swiftly on a heading of three hundred degrees by Kellan's toy compass, a course to reach Jolie.

Sol vanished below, crawled into her bunk, and stayed there until it got light.

I won't describe the damp day and next night, the shifts at the tiller, the soaked and hungry passage of hours, except to say I began to approach warily the idea that we'd gotten away. The wind continued, there were mountainous clouds behind us but they never caught up. We were not overwhelmed. The second morning I caught the smell of land before dawn. I thought we'd gotten too close to shore, but later realized we'd slipped past the Slate Islands, another near miss in the dark.

Late in the morning we eased into Jolie.

The harbor was still. A maple-leaf flag hung slack from a yardarm; the town lay at rest on its hillside. We tied *Flower* at the dock and made our way to the Girards'.

Nobody home but the gate was open, so we sat in the garden to rest and get used to the feeling of earth. Sol kept trying to walk and then tipping over like a top out of spin. She was exaggerating but not much. My feet felt made of wood.

We were still wobbly when Evelyn came in through the gate. She was startled for a moment, then beelined for me and wrapped me in her arms.

You forget how it is to have someone be glad you are there.

I said, "Evelyn, here are Sol and Burke."

She shook their hands. I watched her eyes. Already she was busy with our welfare. She said, "Sleep, soap, or a meal, what would you all like first?"

~

For a while we all stayed with Girard and Evelyn, and if this made their big old house seem small, they never let on. I don't know how much or how long that dose of compliance affected Burke. Maybe he was always that guileless. But when after ten days he accepted passage in a van heading west, we were sorry to see him go—well, not Sol. Burke may have been on board with us, but she was never on board with Burke. It turned out she'd been watching when he forced the twelve onto that tortuous raft. So had I, of course. But I couldn't despise Burke; I could've *been* Burke. That's what I believe. Maybe I still could. What scares me is the notion we are all one rotten moment, one crushed hope or hollow stomach from stuffing someone blameless in a cage.

I soon picked up some work. Stevie at the welding shop, who had repaired *Flower*'s chainplates, was expanding her reach and needed what she called "a back and two arms" for deliveries. Hours were unpredictable but more days than not I drove her bouncy old hybrid east or west along the coastline.

One morning before I walked to the shop, Girard said, "Are you thinking of leaving us too?"

It had occurred to me to find a place of my own. I'd lived upstairs at their house for six weeks, which is way past guest no matter who you are.

Girard then offered me the loft above the garage. It had been used as an apartment decades earlier and was plumbed and electrified. He said it was mine if I cared to clean it up and fix the broken parts.

Sol remained in the house. She barely noticed when I moved out—partly because I only moved sixty feet away and partly because she liked the Girards. One day I went into their upstairs library to browse and Sol was there. She looked overwhelmed, and I recalled how she thought my shelf of seven books on *Flower* comprised a giant collection.

"Evelyn says there is a school in town, and maybe I should go to it," she said. "But I don't know."

Girard had begun to teach her a little math, and I'd been reading to her most evenings. Already she had favorite stories and would ask for repeat performances. I thought she would adjust to school, but my instinct was not to push. Sol is always apt to revolt or vanish from sight, impulses that have worked well for her.

She said, "I didn't hate the ship, at first."

I sat down. Sol hadn't talked much about the ship, so far. Neither of us had.

"The door was locked, but the room was big and we all had our own beds in there. And clean blankets. And a bathroom with hot water. And I never ate that much before in my life. Three squares a day the woman called it."

"That sounds all right."

"It was. This woman brought the meals on a big red tray. She had dark hair and seemed nice. The food was good. She'd hang around and watch us eat. She made marks in a book and then she'd take the plates and everything and go away."

"You must've liked her."

"Sure, but she didn't like us. She wouldn't say our names. Look, there was Lisha and Betts and there was Andre and Ferdie and me." She counted them off on her fingers. "Five of us, and we told her our names, but she never said them. Not a single time. She said we'd get new names when we started the program and they'd be better names and we would like them more. Well, that was fine for Lisha. She hated hers, anyway, couldn't wait to get a different one. But I was scared to forget my name. What if I they called me something dumb? But I remembered the letters."

"S like a stream," I said.

"Right! O like a face, L a straight line up and down. I made those marks with my finger on the counter. I breathed on the mirror and practiced. Once when the lady wasn't looking I stole her marker. That night I wrote my name real tiny on the wall by the bed, so I would see it every day."

"That was good thinking, Sol."

"Then a man came and said he knew you and asked if I wanted to send you a message."

"And I got it," I told her. "It came when I needed it. I was proud of you."

Sol looked around warily at the Girards' well-filled shelves. "I still might not write a book ever," she said. "They take a lot of letters."

"You've got time," I told her.

In early spring, Sol asked Evelyn whether she could "have a few garden seeds." I instantly forgot about it, but a few weeks ago—about the time the Tashi Comet swam into view—I began seeing familiar plants in places you would never expect, up and down Jolie. A melon vine crossing the threshold of the abandoned petrol station, a stand of leggy sunflowers growing like a riddle from the crumbling chimney of a boarded house. Sidewalk cracks populated with healthy vines, their string beans plumping by the day. I said to Sol, "Is that you, planting these seeds all over town?"

She was pleased I noticed. I was pleased too. It seemed like something Molly Thorn would do, or Lark herself—once in her sleep Lark said *The best futures are unforeseen* and this keeps being true.

It took weeks to hear what happened to the overstuffed cruiser. When the answer came, it was incomplete and via the excitable *Mosquito*, which showed up in Jolie on its usual mercurial schedule.

The *Mosquito* had a field day with what it insisted on calling the black-clad cutter, which arrived at an undisclosed location on the northern shore to unload dozens of refugees in various states of distress. Across several editions a reporter using the name Bart Kidneystone wrote transfixing descriptions of a "miraculous mass escape" led by a daring young revolutionary who "shrugged off bullet wounds as if they were beestings." This impervious figure came with a Magdalene who never left his side and a dozen ascetic disciples who required no dock but simply strolled to shore over the rolling waves. Embroideries aside, it was pretty great reading. At least they hadn't sunk in the gale that night, and Marcel had survived. For the first time, I was grateful for the *Mosquito*. It was improving, just as Lark hoped. No more copy given to space aliens, fewer pictures of dogs wearing headphones. The masthead now read AFFLICTING THE COMFORTABLE—still pompous, but with clean spelling. I even forgave the slapstick bylines and began enjoying them for their own sake. How do you root against someone whose nom de plume is Harpy LaFierce, or Inside Pants, or my favorite, Frijole Regret?

As for the comet it arrived as predicted. It seemed like nothing at first. I'd heard it would start to be visible to the north in the small hours, so I began to wake myself and walk up through town to a height of land where neither trees nor buildings lived. I carried the binoculars and swept upward from the horizon in a crisscross pattern. That's worth doing, by the way, whether or not you are hunting a comet—the planets and star clusters and winking satellites predestined for silence and the wonder of rare jetliners would make anyone a happy insomniac. And then one morning it seemed a particular star was growing brighter. Day by day it gained weight, followed by a shadow of light, and then I moved a chair into the yard. Every clear night I sat in the shine of that space rock for two or three hours—depending on the atmosphere it looked like the mark an eraser leaves or else like the silvery wing feather Sol found on one of her gardening jaunts. It had a bold round face and a curving tail whose edges might look downy and shy or other times crisp as a blade.

One evening, just before dark, Harriet walked into the garden.

I was harvesting early carrots. I knew Harriet instantly by her vivid white hair—in a strong wind she'd have resembled a comet herself.

"They told me you were here," she said. She'd stopped in the nearby town of Marathon the previous night, took a room above a tavern where the Indolent Vagrants were playing. By now I'd sat in with them once or twice.

She was on her way across country to stay with her sister in Vancouver. She didn't have all the news, but she had more than the *Mosquito*.

The cruiser had landed at the dwindling town of Walda which still had a strong seawall and quiet harbor. Though the vessel was equipped with top navigation, either a solar flare or a rogue organization had disabled key satellites, and they ended up crawling along the shoreline for hours with the sky in a thundery mood, finally spotting the lights of Walda and entering the harbor to the consternation of locals who had seen squelettes before and didn't wish to antagonize the astronaut or his damned ship. In the end Harriet offered them the cruiser itself as payment for permission to land. This they accepted and hauled it out on a motorized lift into a massive shed.

I asked the immediate questions. Where did everybody go? What happened to Kellan and the rest of the twelve? Did Marcel really shake off that bullet so easily?

What a lovely stoic Harriet was. She fixed me with a stare of reproach, mockery, and wry confirmation at once. "You know that paper is written by simpletons."

"They mean well," I ventured.

"Never change, Rainy," she said and filled me in as best she could. The squelettes stayed a few days in Walda, where volunteers made up cots in the grade school and rounded up food and clothing. From there, residents drove them by threes or fours into neighboring towns. There was a network, Harriet said. An alliance of kindness. Some might still be taken for the small skanky bounties attached to their heads but not all. Not even most. The twelve also scattered in this way. Kellan went east, and that was all Harriet knew about him—except on the boat, when the waves got tall and wrathful, and the cruiser wallowed in the troughs, then people sought out Kellan to rub his roostery hair. "For luck," said Harriet, rolling her eyes.

"Did you rub it too?" I asked.

She wouldn't answer.

It seemed like maybe it worked.

Marcel was carried off the cruiser and spent time in two hospitals Harriet knew of, fighting a string of infections and fleeing both times when agents of the astronaut showed up wearing visitor tags. He and Tove were in Montreal, last Harriet heard, shopping for new histories and greedy for the dullest lives a human could invent.

Harriet lost track of Beezie—Verlyn too.

"Didier?" I said.

"Working for a beekeeper in the Maritimes. He seems happy. Wears netting over his face but no gloves. His hands get stung every day. It helps his arthritis."

It surprised me to hear nothing of Werryck or Griff. I'd assumed by now they would've made serious trouble for at least a few of us.

"You don't know," Harriet said.

I leaned forward.

"*Posterity* sank," she said. "It went to the bottom. Werryck went too. And the girl's uncle, or grandpa, whatever he was. And the guards. How did you not hear?"

"How would I hear?"

That's the trouble with the *Mosquito* being your primary news source. They didn't report any such thing—only that the medicine ship *Posterity* was gone from its anchorage of nearly a decade. A ship can go a lot of places besides the seafloor.

"Nope. Sank," said Harriet. She wore a cloud of guilt and silver lining of relief.

"The bilge pumps," I said.

"Every mechanic came with us on the cruiser," she said.

The pumps had given out within hours. As stinking water breached the Shambles, there was an immediate outcry. The upstairs professionals, the medics and aides and researchers, swarmed over the ship looking for the keys to let Werryck and the guards out. These keys, by the way, were neither digital nor skeleton but resembled any old deadbolt key to any house in the country. I know because I used them to open the door at the bottom of the stairwell on my way to invite Griff along. When I went to Werryck's quarters to retrieve Mr. Fender, I tossed the key ring onto his couch. I remember its jangly sound.

I suppose those keys slid down between the cushions.

Harriet was quiet a minute, during which I imagined in nightmare hues the panic of caged men in rising water, the wrenching at the bars, the futility and exalted rage at their looming, unkind finish. I think of those men more often than I'd like—two hundred feet down, rotating slowly in the currents of the Shambles. The drowned of Superior keep returning—not these fellows, though.

"What about everybody else, the staffers, the medical people?"

And that was the good news. Someone remembered the power skiff, which fully packed could accommodate fifteen or twenty at a time. By the time water filled the Shambles and started covering the next floor up, everyone had been ferried to safety to nearby Michipicoten. When the sun rose, *Posterity* had vanished, but a former coast guard cutter—owned by the astronaut and piloted by state police—was just arriving.

Harriet and I talked for hours; the night was cool and clear. I said, "Have you been watching the comet?"

"What comet is that?"

We walked down to the dock with its clear view of the sky. I couldn't imagine how Harriet had missed it—if you were outside after dark the Tashi was practically a banner. But when I handed her the binoculars she said, "Oh yes, there it is," while looking in an absolutely wrong direction. That's when I realized her eyes were bad. I asked about it, and she confessed her sight had been diminishing for years. Since long before her time aboard *Posterity*. Her parents had both suffered from macular degeneration and took medications no longer available. Days she could navigate but nights were darker all the time. She could make out the moon if it were full and if someone aimed her properly.

"I'm sorry, Harriet."

"Maybe you'd describe it to me, though. The comet."

I told her it was like a chalkboard smear ten fingers off the horizon.

"Is it gorgeous, Rainy? Tell the truth."

I said it was long white hair blown back in the wind, or a lit road climbing a distant mountain.

She said, "Comets used to predict terrible things. That's what people thought. Wars and epidemics, draught, famine. Locusts."

I said, "This one feels different to me."

"Me too," said Harriet.

I never had a sister, but she felt like one then. Heading back up the pier she was a little unsteady. I gave her my arm and she hung on to it until we reached Girards'.

Next morning, once it was good and light, she drove west out of town.

~ *perihelion*

SOL TOOK IT HARD, about Papa Griff.

She didn't cry or pretend Griff was better than he was, just stayed small behind her eyes until whispering that she would hate the lake forever. It had swallowed two uncles that she knew of and now Griff too. The lake was her enemy past forgiveness. The lake had better look out.

Listening to Sol made Girard weep silently where he sat, but Evelyn was distracted and got up and went to the kitchen. An hour later, the four of us carried a basket of sandwiches up out of town to an opening in the northern forest. A trail had been mowed leading to a wide clearing surrounded by cedars. The clearing was fragrant and the grass tall enough I did not at first notice the waist-high stone markers lined up in neat rows. They were shaped like obelisks and cut from native bluestone. None were inscribed with names or dates, and sunlight and birdsong washed over them.

Evelyn said, "It's all the uncles, Sol. The uncles and aunts and cousins. Yours and other people's. Here they are."

Then Girard explained that years ago a landowner of Jolie had died without heirs, bequeathing to the city this acreage and funds to bury the dead of Superior. Her husband, a freight captain of many years, had gone down with a load of Dakota wheat at the end of a violent season. The endowment even covered rail shipping—so Jolie began, every few weeks at first but now every couple of days, to receive those who surfaced, the officers and mates, the ordinary seamen, the navigators, stewards and cooks, aboriginals and voyageurs and black-robed priests, and all who rose and went unclaimed. The benefactor had a single request—that she be buried here, too, in a nameless grave, so that when her husband came ashore they would be close again.

We chose a spot with shade for a picnic. It was a warm day and I felt lucky to be there, though Sol short-circuited any hopes for resolution by saying, after finishing a cheese sandwich of frankly heroic girth, "I still hate the lake, though. None of you can ever go out there again."

In this I was to disappoint her immediately.

I had decided to spend the week of perihelion, when the Tashi was at its brightest, in the Slate Islands.

It was tempting to wait and go later, because Jolie was throwing itself a little midweek party. They'd built a stage on the street, and the Vagrants would play, and everyone would eat and drink and dance until midnight, then shut off all the lights in town and look up for a while. I didn't want to miss it, but any quixote would see the sense of this: if you're heading out to sea to find the spirit of your beloved, then go while something rare and infinitely lucky is hanging in the sky.

I left in cool sun with a light southeasterly.

Flower was in beautiful shape. I'd got hold of a mainsail that was easily altered to fit her rigging and borrowed a little rowing tender tracking straight on its painter. I'd also repaired nearly everything that wanted it. Well, not the diesel, but that still made excellent ballast. I told it so several times.

The Slates were as heartbreaking as I remembered, but livelier. I entered the islands from the northwest, and even as I set the anchor a family of caribou came down to see what was happening, just as before. A hard squawk went up between two peevish geese. An otter swam past at close range—Lark would've said *insouciant*—and just after sundown a great fish became visible, hovering like a shadow over the sandy floor.

I had enough ice and rice and tins to stay a week, longer if I wanted. Evelyn sent along a sack full of peppers and cabbage and broccoli; her vintner neighbor sent a bottle of wine, and their friend LaNona had tucked into this bounty a jar of preserves the color of sunsets. Besides the groceries, I had Mr. Fender along and also an armful of books. Girard gave me free rein with his personal library, but then, as book people will, kept pulling his own darlings off the shelf and stuffing them into my hands.

That first night was warm and cloudy, so no Tashi Comet for me. I didn't read and didn't play but instead sat on the deck with my back to the mast while night birds whistled and large mammals banged around in the underbrush.

At dawn I rowed ashore and walked the beach, putting my own prints alongside caribou tracks and the paw marks of a black bear. I climbed the largest Slate and looked in all directions.

The lake was so gentle it resembled someone else's.

Next night the clouds remained. In fact a storm rolled in. Total darkness, an atmospheric inhale, and then, minutes before the lightning, the scents of cedar and foxtail and trillium poured from the islands as if spilling out to meet the rain halfway. There was an eruption of frog song, the horsehair smell of reindeer. When the first nickel-size spots hit the deck, I went below. I made a stew of tinned chicken and peppers and broccoli. I drank the neighbor's wine. And though I had no bread, I opened the preserves. Besides sweetness, the jam had a surprising heat and the slightest bitterness that made me dip into it again. My eyes watered, my jaw hinge thrummed like a nerve.

In minutes I finished the jar.

All night rain drummed above my head. Morning came and it continued. I lit the paraffin and tried a few of the books Girard had sent, but Girard leaned heavily toward spies and wisecracking detectives. Much as I love all that business, I didn't feel like reading about courage and violence and bravado and sacrifice. It made me feel tired and dull. I played a few bass lines to pass the time, but the rain came ever harder on the coach roof and my low tones were overwhelmed. Time to time I took a cloth and wiped condensation off the ports, checked the channel where I'd come in, opened the hatches and watched for masts. None appeared. In that downpour the caribou retreated upland. No birds or other creatures showed themselves; even the otters stayed out of sight.

I had the Slates to myself.

That night in the bunk, I half slept. I didn't dream, or did and don't remember. In the dark, I surfaced on my side with the feeling I was home. It was confusing and awfully pleasant—I knew I was on *Flower* and not back in Icebridge, but in fact it seemed like both places—the crooked old three-story and the rain-swaddled sailboat drowsing in the Slates. Slowly I became conscious of a slight warm weight against my back, a pressure like a palm between my shoulder blades. I wanted it to stay but didn't try to keep it. The warmth remained as dawn filtered through the hatches, and then, as though catching a ride on the light, a series of pictures came fully imagined. Not like dreams, like memories yet to come. There was Sol a decade on, laughing with friends at a crowded park. And Kellan with a slender paintbrush, teaching a class the human face. And here was Burke of all people, hefty and good, carrying a crinkly old man to a table set for dinner. Evelyn and Girard, Stevie the welder, and Harry the drummer—here they came and all were older and changed by time. All but Molly Thorn, who sailed into this figment in her storybook vessel and dropped her anchor nearby. Molly looked almost exactly the same—a little frizzier, a little younger, if anything a bit more amused.

By full light the rain had stopped. I lifted the anchor and set a homeward course.

~

I heard the music still miles off—things start early in Jolie, and generally go late.

The Vagrants had gone and found themselves a permanent bassist, a girl of sixteen named Rachel. The band could not believe their luck. I had a pang of melancholy, learning this, but then heard Rachel play.

Even now, I can only laugh.

I used to feel quite pleased by my simple bass lines, my minimal approach. Mostly I think I did no harm. But Rachel's something new to me—where I might play two notes or four, Rachel spins kaleidoscopes. How hands that young know that terrain eludes me, but her lines are plate tectonics and her riffs are thrown confetti drifting down across your shoulders. All this she does while vanishing. When she plays, I have seen people laugh or weep and never know quite why.

That's what reached me first, miles out from harbor—a song I didn't know, its melody like liquid and its architecture strong.

The wind faded and *Flower* ghosted forward into nightfall. Lights appeared—streetlamps, pit fires, dim solar lanterns under which the band now shifted to a higher gear.

Above and to the right, the comet.

I am always last to see the beauty I inhabit.

The street was hazy and magnified, close to the sky. People moved on the sidewalks, swayed in the street. Ancient or ageless, that's how it looked, but also vital and recent. A new release, a first-hand world. I steered for home. Maybe I would dance.

Acknowledgments

It's my great luck and privilege to publish with Grove Atlantic. Thank you to Morgan Entrekin, for holding fast; Judy Hottenson, for fluency in midwestern English and boreal Raven; Deb Seager for remembering when I forget; and Elisabeth Schmitz, my clear-eyed editor all these years—no one sees more quickly to the nub, or coaxes a book more lovingly into shape.

I am dazzled by Kelly Winton's magnificent cover art.

Enormous gratitude to Marin Takikawa and Lucy Carson at the Friedrich Agency, and especially Molly Friedrich herself, whose concision, wit, and faith in good stories make her the advocate every writer wants.

Thanks to Liz for Kellan's octopus and Mike for the eternal law of electric bass, Lee for being Odysseus and Lin for being Homer. John built my mahogany writing desk above which hangs Reed's painting of the North Wind; and thanks again to Robin, firelit reader, always first to spot when a character goes wrong.